THE
TEMP

Center Point
Large Print

Also by Michelle Frances and available from
Center Point Large Print:

The Girlfriend

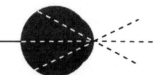

**This Large Print Book carries the
Seal of Approval of N.A.V.H.**

THE
TEMP

Michelle Frances

CENTER POINT LARGE PRINT
THORNDIKE, MAINE

This Center Point Large Print edition
is published in the year 2019 by arrangement with
Kensington Publishing Corp..

The text of this Large Print edition is unabridged.
In other aspects, this book may vary
from the original edition.
Printed in the United States of America
on permanent paper.
Set in 16-point Times New Roman type.

ISBN: 978-1-64358-145-3

Library of Congress Cataloging-in-Publication Data

Library of Congress Cataloging in Publication
Control Number: 2019002327

THE
TEMP

PART ONE

Carrie

1

"Eight's your lucky number," murmured Carrie in Adrian's ear, making sure her lips were hidden from the TV camera that was pointing at them. She kept her expression humble and nonchalant while she gazed up at the screens showing clips from the shows nominated for Best Screenplay. This was a live broadcast and you never knew when the director might cut to your face.

Adrian replied without looking at her. "And?"

"We're in the eighth row."

He glanced down at the seating in front of them, rows of the cream of the British television industry in the Royal Albert Hall. Carrie saw him mentally count and followed suit. They both automatically looked at the people sitting in front of them—on *their* seats! The A-list writer of a very successful crime show and, next to him, his leading man, who played a ruthless yet charming killer.

Suddenly the screen flicked back to the British Academy Film Awards logo and onstage the actress presenting the award stepped forward.

"And the winner is . . ." said the actress in a candy-colored, figure-hugging dress (Roland Mouret, the online newsfeed had declared the second she put a foot on the red carpet), "Adrian Hill for episode one of *Generation Rebel*!"

Carrie turned and flung her arms around him as he stood, looking dazed and smiling. She couldn't take her eyes off him as he made his way to the stage.

He's done it.

He took the golden mask from the actress, accepting a kiss on each cheek as he did so. The applause subsided.

"Er . . . well, that was unexpected," started Adrian, then made a joke of having to adjust the microphone lower so it fitted his small stature. The audience laughed. He ran his free hand through his tufty hair, and the familiarity of this gesture warmed Carrie further. "Seriously, I'd just realized I wasn't sitting in my lucky seat and was about to oust the most infamous murderer of all time when I realized it might not be in my best interests . . ." He paused while the titters rippled across the auditorium and the cameras cut to the killer leading man, who was doing his best to look amused and not seriously pissed off that his show had just lost.

"Thank you to BAFTA, the cast and crew, my excellent producer, Elaine Marsh, and most of all to my beautiful, clever wife, Carrie."

She quickly quashed the embarrassment and smiled as he looked down at her, shielding his eyes from the lights.

She watched as he was led off the stage to the obligatory photo session. *He won. He won, he won, he won!* Her delight was genuine. But deep in the pit of her stomach fluttered the nerves that had been growing there the last few days. There was something she needed to tell him. Perhaps his win might make it easier for him to hear.

Carrie milled through the after-party crowd, knowing that many a conversation would be the start of a new project, a deal struck, a negotiation finalized. She had lost Adrian a full twenty minutes ago, his ear "borrowed" by several people who wanted to congratulate him, attempt to lure him with the next brilliant drama idea, or just bask in the force field of his winning power, perhaps in the hope that some of it might rub off on them.

She spotted him finishing a conversation and made a beeline, carrying a fresh drink.

"A friendly face amongst the sharks," he said as she handed the glass over, then immediately poured a good third down his throat. She didn't touch her own.

"Better get used to it now you're a BAFTA-winning writer," she said. "Although, I hope you're not fraternizing with the enemy."

"Not allowed. Not now you've shackled me to your exceptional producing talent for the next three years."

"You make it sound like you're a man in chains."

"I am. Solid gold ones." He grinned and kissed her. "Seriously, though, I can't wait. Working exclusively with you as well as being married to you. I'm the luckiest man alive."

"Here he is. My favorite writer." A loud, gravelly voice from her twenty-a-day habit cut through the crowd.

"Elaine, how lovely of you to come and congratulate me," said Adrian.

"I haven't yet." Bangles jangling, she smoothed her mane of bottle-red hair and gave him a Cheshire cat grin through plum lipstick. "Nice speech."

"Thanks."

"Good to see you haven't totally forgotten who I am."

"Could I ever? You're such a dynamic and persuasive producer."

"Can't compete with the woman who's screwing you, though." Elaine smiled at Carrie, who did her best not to let her mouth fall open. "Still, at least I got one BAFTA out of you before you buggered off."

"I'll never forget you for giving me my big break," said Adrian.

Elaine nodded approvingly. Cocked her head.

"And nurturing my writing into such a successful show."

Another nod. She pushed her pink-framed glasses up her nose in a prompt.

"I think that's enough, isn't it?"

"It's never enough, darling. As you well know."

And then Elaine strode off into the crowd.

Carrie felt Adrian squeeze her hand. It seemed she'd made an enemy by being married to the hottest writer in town. And signing him up to an exclusive deal with the reputable production company she'd recently started working at. They'd already come up with what she thought was a brilliant idea for Adrian's next show—about a movie star who'd been at the top of his game but through decades of extravagant spending had recently filed for bankruptcy; his latest girlfriend, twenty-five years his junior, had dumped him in disgust and he was alone, broke and struggling to function in the real world. They'd discussed it with the drama boss and channel controller at the BBC, both of whom had been *very* keen to meet them. A few weeks later it had been given the green light and was about to be officially announced.

Adrian nuzzled her cheek, his beard tickling her skin. "Hey, you and me. It's exciting."

She smiled and felt the nerves return. "Yeah . . ."

"You're not upset by Elaine, are you? Don't take any notice. Nothing's going to get in our way. We're going to develop this one together. I'm going to have one hundred percent access to your fantastic story brain; then I can go off and try to write something that isn't a load of tosh—you'll have to keep an eye on me, and hey, wake me up in the middle of the night if you get a brilliant idea—"

"Adrian, it's not me who's going to wake you up in the night."

"What? It's certainly not Elaine." He pulled a face as a less-than-savory vision floated through his head.

"I'm having a baby."

She watched as his face froze in the "in bed with Elaine" expression, then dropped.

"What?" he repeated, more slowly this time.

"I'm pregnant. Fourteen weeks pregnant."

"Four . . . fourteen *weeks?*"

"I only found out three days ago."

He looked so lost she almost felt sorry for him. But it would be okay. *It will be okay,* she mentally rallied.

"Right. But . . . you're . . . I mean, we always said, we *decided* that . . . we weren't going to . . . A family wasn't for us, right?"

She gave a small, hopeful smile.

He visibly paled.

"I see."

He was thinking of his career right now and part of her didn't blame him. The timing was awful. Everything had been going so well: the new job, signing Adrian, the green light! It was the worst possible time to be having a baby.

2

Emma sat with her parents in their pale-gray and white living room, her feet tucked under her. Her chair was some way back from where they were on the sofa so she was able to watch them as well as the television, which was broadcasting the BAFTAs live on the flat screen on the back wall.

"Oh, it won!" exclaimed her mother, Alice. They all watched as the writer, Adrian Hill, got up to receive his award.

"Good show, that," her father, Brian, said approvingly. He was on his obligatory after-dinner whiskey over ice. Her mother was nursing a glass of wine, the *Telegraph* folded on her lap, alternating between filling in the cryptic cross-word and watching the TV. They were settled, immovable, their habits and opinions long since die-cast. Not for the first time, Emma felt as if she didn't belong. Home, which had never been particularly welcoming, had become stifling.

"Must give you a bit of inspiration, Emma?" Her father turned to look at her, the badly hidden disappointment ever present in his eyes. "This fellow, Adrian Hill, good writing, wouldn't you say?" His words were loaded with expectation.

Emma bristled. She could sense her mother waiting for her response and she forced herself to stay calm, to extricate herself from her misery. She should have taken up a shift in the bar she worked in at nights, instead of staying home to watch this agony.

"Yes, he's good." There was so much more she could say, but now wasn't the time.

She immediately sensed her father's annoyance at the inadequate answer, but she felt too depressed to elaborate. It was her dream to write for television, but so far she hadn't gotten a lucky break. She couldn't even seem to secure herself an agent, and her spec script—not the one she'd originally wanted to write, that one was impossible now, but the next one—well, even she knew it wasn't her best work.

"Maybe you need to get yourself out there more," said Brian, "instead of being cooped up in the house. What are you doing all day, anyway?"

It stung. Emma knew the rest of his sentence remained unspoken: *". . . . while your mother and I are at work in real jobs."* Her father was a dermatologist and her mother a senior manager in the National Health Service. Proper jobs. Well-paid jobs. Jobs with status and a definite career ladder.

Emma took a steadying breath. "Writing, Dad. I'm in the house because I need to be at my computer to write." But the truth was, most days, especially recently, she'd felt completely uninspired. It wasn't for want of trying—God alone knows she'd started all sorts of things, but none of them was working.

"Well, it seems to me you need to change something," said Brian; then he looked back at the television, dismissing her, burying his irritation. On the screen, Adrian was holding a graciously victorious hand up to the audience as he walked offstage. Emma inwardly cursed; she'd missed the cameras cutting to his wife, something she'd wanted to see.

She stood. She couldn't bear to be in the room anymore and went up to her bedroom and closed the door. Outside the window, darkness had fallen over the salubrious south London street. She drew the curtains, then went to her desk, switched on her laptop, and loaded up her latest screenplay. She sat there, her fingers poised over the keys.

She jumped at a knock on the door. It opened before she could answer. Alice came into the room and sat down, placing a magazine on the bed.

"You know, your father only said the things he did because he cares."

Yeah, cares about the 217,000 pounds he spent on boarding school, thought Emma. An amount that she knew he—both of her parents— felt was a phenomenal waste of money. A wasted investment. For her whole life she'd felt like some sort of asset: acquired at birth and then invested in, trained, and groomed like a Thoroughbred racehorse, which was now failing to pay dividends.

"It's been two years since you graduated. And I know we agreed it was good for you to go traveling for one of those years, but since then all you've had was that short-term intern thing— three months—and they wouldn't even pay you."

Emma could tell by the tone of her mother's voice that she thought that if her daughter had been of value, she'd have been kept on and found something paid. Alice was so far removed from what it was really like for people Emma's age, particularly in the competitive, exploitative world of television, that she couldn't grasp the reality no matter how many times Emma tried to explain it. No, Alice was from a generation that was out of touch with today's graduates and she believed if you really were any good, you would've been noticed by now.

She briefly wondered what her mother would think if she knew the real reason the internship had ended.

"Only three months unpaid work in nearly a year. Perhaps it's time for a rethink?" prompted Alice, gently.

Emma's heart sank even lower.

"You've got a good degree. I can help, so can your father. We can introduce you to some people."

"But you know I don't want to work in medicine, Mum. I want to work in television. Anyway, I don't have the right degree."

"You would have the right degree if you'd taken up the offer at Oxford."

Here we go again, thought Emma. All her life she'd been channeled into being someone her parents wanted her to be. She'd taken the A Level subjects they'd wanted her to take, reluctantly agreeing to focus on sciences, on her own condition her last subject be English. Then her father had pressured her to apply to his old college at Oxford University, even writing a letter to the college master. She'd been offered a place to study medicine, and he'd never forgiven Emma for turning it down and defiantly going to pursue English Literature at a lesser institution instead.

Frustration fizzled between them like electricity, back and forth, each stinging the other.

"Look, admittedly, neither your dad nor I were thrilled when you announced you wanted to work in television, but we let you try it out. But it doesn't seem to be happening for you. Not in the way you want it to." Alice stood and sighed softly. "This is the time when you should be getting on the ladder. Building your career. Television is not a stable industry—you've said as much yourself. I worry you're frittering your life away." With that, she left.

Emma felt the remaining air go out of her as the door closed. She flung herself on the bed and stared up at the ceiling. She *was* talented; deep down she knew it. She looked over at the magazine her mother had brought up—*Broadcast*, the industry bible. Tearing off the plastic wrap, she flicked to the jobs page. It was usually pitiful, particularly in the creative, editorial area, but she'd apply for anything to get a foot in the door.

A tiny ad, almost hidden at the bottom of the single page of vacancies. Script editor on a long-running, tired series. She jolted as she noted the name of the production company.

Emma went back to her computer and started to compose a cover letter.

3

Wednesday, October 11
Five months later

Hawk pictures' offices took up the second floor of a building in Soho. Carrie walked down the corridor into the meeting room and carefully lowered herself onto the sumptuous jacquard sofa, feeling, most definitely not for the first time in her pregnancy, decidedly queasy.

At thirty-six weeks she'd hoped it would have subsided, but she was still ambushed by a sense of nausea every now and then. The latest inconvenience was the pain in her hips at night as the bones shifted in order to make space to get her baby out, and she wondered, yet again, whether pregnancy would've been a whole lot easier if she'd been a decade younger. But when she was thirty-two, she didn't want a baby, she reminded herself, brushing aside the uncomfortable thought that she originally hadn't wanted this one and sometimes questioned what had made her change her mind. Work was everything then, as it was now, but an unexpected alarm had rung when she'd discovered this accidental pregnancy. She'd had a sudden panic it was her last chance and felt a startling urge to keep the baby.

21

Carrie felt enormous; the day was unseasonably warm, and she shuffled herself farther down the sofa to get out of the sun that was streaming through the window. She was tired from being woken by the hip pain, the huge, uncomfortable bump, and the kicks. This baby had invaded her body and her life in every way possible and it hadn't even arrived yet.

Through the glass doors she saw her boss wave as she approached. Liz—svelte, perky, able to work at a natural human pace. Mother of two boys, both now at secondary school, and she had only just turned forty. She had a reputation in the business for being a bit of a powerhouse, a dynamic force who put her ambitions above everything else. You could argue that was the only way to get anything done in this dog-eat-dog industry.

Liz sat next to her on the sofa and leaned over her bump for a peck on the cheek.

"You look amazing, as ever."

"No, I don't. I look large and exhausted."

Liz tutted. "Nonsense. Anyway, soon you're going to pop. Four weeks, isn't it?"

Carrie nodded. She was more apprehensive than she cared to admit about the birth. Not just the physical act of it, but the fact that this baby would then exist, in the real world. She'd have to . . . do stuff for it. Look after it. Despite knowing it was going to happen, she couldn't quite imagine the scenario. Her life was still caught up in the day-to-day, well-known whirlwind of work. Sometimes, deep down, a thought fluttered that she never admitted to anyone. What if she'd made the wrong decision? And what if her temporary replacement couldn't cope or, worse, coped too well? She was counting on what so many of the articles on the baby websites said. She'd fall in love with her baby as soon as it arrived. Or at least stop guiltily thinking of it as an inconvenience, something to be managed before she went back to work, which she was planning to do when it was about three months old. She simply couldn't afford to take any more time off, especially not after she'd worked so hard to get this job in the first place. Up until recently she'd always been a freelancer, a producer for hire, and permanent jobs were very hard to come by. Now she had one and was taking advantage of the company's very generous maternity package, even though she'd not even been there a year. She was grateful to Liz for being so gracious about it but, despite all the assurances, couldn't relax. This was an industry in which going off sick was frowned upon, and you took your eye off the prize at your peril.

She tensed protectively when she thought about her project. She'd had a lot of success with previous shows, even been nominated for a BAFTA for one of her fact-based dramas, but this new project was the biggest yet. *Leon* was an expensive series with international distribution and it was her baby. Her *other* baby, she quickly reminded herself. If she weren't there to develop and produce her own show, particularly a show with such prestige behind it, someone else would very happily step in for her.

Which was why she was here in this room right now.

"So, your proposed maternity cover. Emma is really switched on, clever, and she's brilliant at fixing story problems," said Liz.

"Not too brilliant, I hope," said Carrie lightly, inwardly cursing at allowing her insecurities to be on display. The person they were proposing to help cover her maternity leave was the script editor on an existing long-running show that had recently been canceled.

"Well, of course, she's not in your league, but she won't . . . screw it up," said Liz. "Anyway, didn't we say you didn't want to interview for producers?"

"I don't see why I can't just carry on."

"Shout out script notes while you're giving birth?" Liz smiled. "She's only going to be there as an extra ear for Adrian if he needs it. I'm going to take care of all the producing stuff."

"Hmm," said Carrie, unconvincingly.

"Hey, I get it. No one likes the idea of someone else doing their job. Least of all a hormonal woman who's worked her backside off to get where she is. I was the same."

Carrie smiled. "Oh yeah?"

"Oh, I hated her on sight. Too good."

"What happened?"

"I came back early, got promoted, had her transferred to another department." Liz squeezed Carrie's arm. "I know you—you're still going to be working while you're changing diapers. This is just a caretaking thing in the office, that's all. And if she doesn't work out, we can come up with another plan, okay?"

A pause before Carrie nodded.

"You've not met her yet, right?" checked Liz.

"No." Her replacement had in fact been based at Pinewood Studios, which was where they'd shot the now-deceased show.

Liz smiled. "She worked for Elaine Marsh before us, but don't hold that against her. If for any reason you're not happy, we don't have to go ahead." She checked her watch. "She should be here—I'll just go and see if she's in reception."

As she left the room, Carrie sighed deeply. She was usually up for helping the newbies as much as she could. She knew how hard it was to gain a foothold in the industry and had done her share of working for eccentric and tough bosses, being required to do everything from arranging their children's birthday parties to going round to their houses and watering their plants, when really all she'd wanted was to learn about scripts and television. So when it was her turn to be the boss, instead of testing the bright young things' resilience to demoralizing tasks, she usually liked to take them under her wing, give them opportunities and encouragement.

She's just a script editor, she chided herself. *Stop being paranoid.* But the queasy feeling had resurfaced.

4

Wednesday, October 11

Emma followed Liz, Hawk Pictures' managing director, down the highly polished corridor, each clack of her heels announcing her imminent arrival, when actually all she wanted to do was quietly and unobtrusively enter the room. Her nerves were so bad she thought she might be sick; in fact, she was physically shaking and had to stop a moment to try to pull herself together.

Liz looked back. "Everything okay?"

Emma made herself smile. "Yes, just got my heel caught," she said, lifting up the back of her foot and adjusting her shoe.

She could hardly think straight, and yet she needed to be calm to get through this—there was too much at stake to mess it up. She'd also prefer to get a look at Carrie in the flesh first, rather than the other way round. It might help still those nerves, even just a little.

Then they were at the meeting room, and Emma saw her through the glass door. A middle-aged woman pushed herself up off the sofa as the door opened, and came forward to greet her. She had pale-blond wavy hair that was cut into a bob, giving the effect of a small cloud hovering around her head. She was very pretty, which Emma was pleased about even while knowing it was absurd, and she suddenly felt a rush of enthusiasm to put her plans in motion. Carrie's small stature was rendered off balance by the huge bump she was carrying, and Emma felt herself staring before quickly looking away.

Liz introduced them and Emma felt Carrie's light—*distant,* she noted—touch as she took her hand, embarrassed that her own palm was still damp.

It was a surreal moment, meeting Carrie. She'd followed her for years and watched her career closely, in part because Carrie was married to the screenwriter whom Emma had at one point admired most in the whole of television. This opportunity to work closely with them both was terrifying and serendipitous all at once. *She had to get this job.*

The call from Liz had been a miracle. After working so hard to get the script editor role on the tired show (with a few embellishments to her résumé and a fudge with her reference), she'd then worked her socks off from the minute she started, reading scripts through the night to get up to speed, making notes and suggestions, and never letting the script team want for a cup of tea the entire time she was there. It wasn't writing, but it was being close to writers and helping them with their scripts, and she had been learning loads. Then came a massive dose of bad luck—two weeks ago they learned that the show was being canceled, so there was no chance of staying on for further series, and with only a five-month stint on her résumé to join the three-month blip at her internship, it didn't look great.

Emma was dreading telling her parents she was unemployed yet again, something that she was hoping she could narrowly avoid, assuming Carrie liked her—and *God, please let that happen*, she thought, her fists clenching in desperate hope.

Carrie sat, so Emma followed suit. She briefly wondered what Carrie saw when she looked at her, which triggered another rush of nerves, and so felt she needed to say something before she completely clammed up.

"Can I just say . . . how much I absolutely love your shows. You've touched on some really important subjects, and they're all so upscale and different from anything else, and it's as if you're always defining what we should be watching."

My God, she was gushing like a schoolgirl. *Calm down. You're freaking her out.* She dug her nails into her palms hard until the pain was almost unbearable. Then Carrie was talking, so Emma relaxed her hands and made herself concentrate.

"So you've just finished on *Buried Evidence*?"

"Yes, I loved working on that show. It was good to get my teeth into something that was actually in production, and I worked with a great many different writers, some new, some very established."

"And before that, Elaine Marsh? How was she to work for?"

Emma considered the question, knowing that Elaine had a certain reputation in the industry. "She put me through my paces. I learned a lot."

Just a flicker of a raised eyebrow from Carrie. Emma wondered if she should have elaborated. She knew that Adrian had recently moved from Elaine's company and she felt on shaky ground. This business was full of political potholes.

Carrie glanced down at a piece of paper, what Emma assumed was her résumé. "You weren't there long," said Carrie. "Three months. Why did you leave?"

Stay calm, thought Emma, desperately trying to ignore the fact her heart had started racing. "It was only a three-month appointment. My contract was up."

She kept the relaxed smile on her face, maintained eye contact with Carrie and prayed she'd move on.

"So what do you think is key to the role of a script editor?" asked Carrie.

"I'm here to support the writer, represent his or her vision to the producers and the broadcaster. Also assist with research, story ideas, and script notes whenever needed."

It came out as if it was learned by rote and she

cringed inside. Emma anxiously checked Carrie's reaction to her response. An indiscernible nod. Emma's heart sank.

"Of course, Carrie is still going to be working across all her projects," said Liz. "Most likely working when she's not supposed to be," she chided gently.

They all smiled indulgently. No one spoke.

She's trying to think of a brush-off, thought Emma, hope dying inside. *She doesn't want me and she's trying to think of a way to close the meeting down. Probably say they're seeing other people or something.*

"But it would be good to have someone here in the office, keeping things moving along," said Carrie, and Emma felt her spirits soar.

Liz turned to Carrie. "What do you think of Emma starting next week, getting her up to speed?"

Carrie nodded. "Sure. Okay with you, Emma?"

"Great!" said Emma, elated. She tried to keep the tremor in her hands hidden. She'd gotten it! She'd passed the test. As she'd found out in television, succeeding wasn't just about your experience, how good you were at your job—a large part of it was about whether you were liked.

Carrie, she tentatively thought, seemed to like her. Emma felt a surge of satisfaction. God, she was going to work so hard in this job, she'd make Carrie *love* her.

5

"She's young. only twenty-four," said Carrie. she shifted around on the kitchen chair, her back aching. Really, it would be more comfortable to lie propped up with cushions on the sofa in the living room, but Adrian was cooking and she liked their evening chats.

He frowned. "That *is* young. Is she any good?"

"Has shown moments of brilliance, apparently," said Carrie, gloomily.

Adrian looked up from the potatoes he was mashing. "You're not worried, are you?"

She shrugged. "I'm about to leave my dream job." He didn't answer instantly and she knew what he was thinking: she wouldn't have to if she hadn't decided to have the baby. "The Decision" had underscored everything they'd said and done for months now, and life was a constant balancing act, walking on eggshells.

"Only temporarily," he said.

"People have short memories in this business."

"You're their hot new recruit."

"I think you'll find that's you."

She saw him preen momentarily; then he recovered, remembering what his role was right

33

now. "I'm just an extension of you. The producer who's made several critically acclaimed docudramas," he added pointedly.

"Hmm, a long time ago now."

Adrian looked across at her, incredulous. "It wasn't that long. Only a couple of years. And it doesn't take away from the fact they're all brilliant. Why are you putting yourself down? Again."

"Oh, you know me. Always think the fraud police are going to come knocking. Half the time I feel like an imposter. How the heck did I get this job anyway?"

She saw Adrian make the conscious decision not to answer, and knew it was because he found her insecurities mildly irritating. And he had a point—if she was forced to admit it, she had made some good shows, *very* good shows. But the fear it was all down to luck or timing just never went away.

"Did you see your package?" he said, nodding toward a large cardboard box in the corner of their kitchen. She looked across, knowing what it was. Easing herself to her feet, she opened it up and lifted out a Moses basket, complete with white broderie anglaise lining.

"What do you think?"

He glanced across. "Yeah, nice."

"Is that it?"

He looked again. "What do you want me to say? It's a bed. For a baby."

"Our baby. Who's arriving in the next four weeks."

There was no animated response, no light in his eyes.

"Peas or beans?" he said.

Deflated, she put the Moses basket back. "Whatever."

"I'll do both. More vitamin C for you . . . and baby." She knew it was an olive branch offered in guilt. "And you've got to stop worrying about your job so much," he continued. "No one's going to oust you." Carrie winced and he looked at her sternly. "And if they try, I'm going too."

Contractually she knew that he couldn't, but it was his way of making amends. A few moments later he brought two plates of sausage and mash over to the table. Three very well-done sausages stuck out of a mound of mashed potatoes like an alien. A pile of green vegetables was arranged to form a beard.

"All right?" he asked, waiting for praise.

She smiled. "Looks great."

It was part of their routine. He cooked while she was on her way home, commuting on the overcrowded train back to Blackheath in southeast London. They'd bought a three-bedroom Edwardian terrace house a year after getting together and gradually done it up. A childless couple's dream: white walls, open staircase, water feature in the garden. It had taken some

35

time to finance all the improvements. When they'd met, both had been working on the same soap opera; she was a script editor, he a jobbing writer. They each had ambitions to go further, but it was hard to find time to pursue anything when they were both shackled to the relentless schedule of a show that went out four days a week, every week of the year. Holidays for the staff were banned for any longer than a week, the daily hours would often stretch on into the dead of night, and God forbid you became ill. Carrie had had tonsillitis once and hadn't dared take more than a single day off to recover. If she didn't get back, her scripts wouldn't be ready to film. And despite being ill, it would be *her fault,* and it would determine whether or not her short-term contract was renewed.

She and Adrian had hit it off at a monthly story conference, recognized the bright hope in each other, and had soon fallen in love. After a night out at the cinema four weeks into the relationship, Adrian had come back to her rented flat and said he wanted to be honest with her. She'd felt a flurry of nerves, thinking he was about to confess to a wife, or a girlfriend at least, but he raised the subject of children.

"I just want you to know . . . it's not something I've ever wanted. And most women do, so I felt it's only fair to tell you. So you can tell me to get lost—if that's what you want?" He'd raised his big brown eyes to her and in them was such a look of anxiety it had squeezed her heart. She knew then that they were made for each other as she'd never really wanted children either, not after what happened when she was a teenager.

They got married at the same time they bought their house—just a year after meeting. Adrian, having worked his way up to being one of the "star" writers on the soap, had managed to earn enough to take a break from its relentless schedule and concentrate on coming up with ideas for shows of his own. Some got development funding, some didn't, but all withered and died within a year or two.

Then he thought of something so brilliant, so commissionable, it was picked up like lightning by notorious producer Elaine Marsh. She got interest from the BBC and before he knew it, he had a green light. The show, about a pupil uprising in a secondary school with tragic consequences, was an instant success, and Adrian's star was catapulted into the heavens.

Carrie, meanwhile, became passionate about telling real-life stories and got her own share of success. They both worked extremely hard and rewarded themselves with expensive holidays to exotic locations, whenever they could fit them in around their demanding work schedules. They had fulfilled dreams of diving with whale sharks in the Maldives and had even taken a trip to

Antarctica. They drank fine wine. They bought white furniture. Adrian had a two-seater BMW and bought a place by the sea, in Broadstairs on the Kent coast. They'd mapped out a lifestyle for themselves that was envied amongst their child-burdened friends, so when Carrie unexpectedly became pregnant at the age of forty-two, she was thrown by her instinctive reluctance to have an abortion. Maybe it was her body's innate last-chance need to procreate before it became barren, maybe it was because the fetus was already fourteen weeks old and was able to make facial expressions, its eyes able to squint. She didn't know, but she just couldn't go through with it.

Adrian had been poleaxed. It was so far from his vision for his life, it had taken him two whole days to even fully understand it was real. Then the recriminations had started—how had she gotten pregnant? (Forgotten to take her pill, simple as that.) She was sorry, but what was done was done. She couldn't "depregnant" herself, even though she often thought that would be a whole lot easier than the difficult decision they were trying to make, with the sand in the timer running through at a rapid pace. Eventually they both realized they'd set sail on a new ship that was going along regardless of what they thought about it and there was no getting off. Adrian had never quite reconciled himself to her decision, and deep down Carrie knew that they both had their heads in the sand, ignoring the impending third person about to join their household.

That third person suddenly gave her a massive kick to the ribs.

"Ouch," she winced.

"You okay?"

"Baby practicing football."

He nodded.

"Has no idea of the pain it's inflicting. Speaking of which, we've got 'massage during labor' tonight."

He looked sheepish and her heart sank.

"Sorry . . ."

"You're not coming?"

"I had a bolt of inspiration today. For episode four. I want to get it down while it's still fresh in my mind."

She frowned and thought: why couldn't he have got it down earlier in the day instead of during prenatal class?

"Hey, come on, don't be like that. I've come to all the others, haven't I? And I want to get this script right for the boss—she's scary." He gave her his best little-boy cheeky smile.

She found his dissembling depressing but didn't want to say so, feeling no good would come of it. This was what they were like lately: stop, start, never quite connecting. The easy harmony of their relationship had been lost somewhere in the last few months.

• • •

Later, at the prenatal class, as the only woman who'd come alone, Carrie found herself partnered with the midwife. She offered up the excuse about Adrian working, which no one really listened to, as the other mums-to-be were directing their— some attentive, some less so—husbands and partners to their best points of massage. As Carrie looked around the room, she saw that there were some women without the fathers-to-be, but they'd come with their mothers, proud women with a light of excitement in their eyes about the future grandchild.

Oh, Mum, thought Carrie, *I could do with you now,* and she felt a wave of brutal sadness that threatened to engulf her. The midwife noticed her tense up and rubbed her shoulders.

"Everything okay?"

"Yes," said Carrie brightly, the lie making her feel even more lonely, but she dared not look into the crevasse of pain that still opened up in her every now and then, even though ten years had passed. It was too deep, too dark, and all she could cope with at that moment was fending off the visceral wrench that was the physical manifestation of how much she missed her mother. *If it's a girl, I'll call her Helen,* she suddenly decided, and this did something to ease the longing.

The midwife finished the massage, then went

around the room to check on the techniques of the other partners. Carrie watched as she gave out tips to the dads. She thought of Adrian and his absenteeism. Reminded herself again of how it would all be different when the baby came. How both of them would fall desperately in love with it.

6

Monday, October 16

They spoke differently to each other now that there were three of them in the room. Gone was the intimacy of just her and Adrian lying back on the sofas, dissecting their characters, his dialogue, and figuring out where and how to make the story more dramatic. Emma sat upright in a small chair, eyes shining, pen poised. She was keen, Carrie couldn't deny her that, but she found her eagerness suffocating. Carrie had sent an e-mail to her earlier confirming their meeting time, and Emma's reply was signed off with a kiss. She'd been a little taken aback, despite the fact they were standard for the most part in the TV industry and a sign of the warmth of your relationship or your standing with your boss. No kiss, relations were aloof or you'd done something to offend the boss and could consider yourself out of favor. But generally they were doled out generously, and there were enough kisses flying around to start a herpes epidemic.

She looked at Emma sitting across from her and wished she'd relax a bit. In her experience it was usually best to come at story problems sideways. Approach the creeping tendrils head-on and you usually ended up ensnared and unable to think your way out. Adrian had written up his breakthrough on episode four and continued working through the night, delivering his script the morning after prenatal class and then promptly spending the whole of the next day in bed to recover. They'd all now read it and it was clear something wasn't quite working.

The ex-movie star, Leon, started the series filing for bankruptcy and kissing goodbye to his car collection, his village in Spain, and his submarine. Over the course of the next few episodes he battled with his own arrogance and misplaced sense of expectation, and painfully faced up to what it meant to "downsize." He struggled to deal with the everyday tasks needed to survive, such as going to a supermarket to get food. He lost his so-called friends, too, and became estranged from his family, but he started a will-they, won't-they relationship with Sally, a down-to-earth, no-nonsense girl. By episode four he was on the cusp of recovery: a job and a new closeness with Sally, who despised the shallowness of the movie business. Just as he was about to sign the job contract, his agent came knocking—he'd been offered a half-decent part in a new film alongside today's big star. The lure of a return to fame and fortune beckoned. But if he took it, he'd almost certainly sabotage his fledgling relationship. What was a guy with a dyed head of hair, who'd once owned a wine cellar the size of a tennis court, to do?

Somehow the script wasn't reading poignantly enough, and it was important to have viewers on the edge of their seats, willing him to make the right decision—whatever that might be, as many would be as torn as Leon: another chance at success, or a relationship with someone who loved him for who he was?

"I just feel there needs to be more at stake," said Carrie. "Obviously the relationship is a big deal, but there needs to be another layer, something to really encourage us to feel he's making the wrong decision when he takes the film role."

"What if Sally is pregnant?" said Adrian. "He turns his back on her and their unborn child."

Carrie glanced at him, uncomfortable with this reference that echoed their own situation, but he seemed oblivious. "Hmm, could be. Bit callous, though?"

"Doesn't have to be. He can be totally genuine about wanting to see the child, and if he does the acting gig he'll earn a lot more than the 'respectable' job, which he can argue is all for the baby."

"But ultimately she's made it clear she hates the industry and what it does to him—she'd rather have him poor and genuine than rich and full of himself. And coke." Carrie could sense Emma flicking her eyes between them as if she were watching a tennis match. She could also sense that Emma was dying to speak, and knew that if she caught her eye she'd have to acknowledge this. She decided to look her way.

"Is it okay . . . ?" started Emma tentatively. "I just had an idea. Might be silly but . . ."

Adrian threw a languid hand in the air. "Go for it."

"What if Sally was ill? Something serious. Maybe she'd found out a few days before and doesn't want to tell him, doesn't want it to influence his decision. It can't be a mercy relationship. So when he, with a heavy heart, decides to take up the part in the film, he has no idea what he's doing to her."

Carrie felt the familiar tingling on her skin when a story moved her, a sensation creeping up the back of her neck that exploded in a cascade of goose bumps. Neither she nor Adrian said anything, just looked at Emma while it sank in. Adrian, who'd been lying back on the sofa, suddenly sat bolt upright.

"I love it. Hey—maybe it's terminal, there's a chance she won't be around after his six-month stint filming in Mexico. . . ."

"But she just can't let him know this," continued Emma. "It's not just the fact she doesn't want him to choose her out of guilt; it's because she loves him and she wants him to have his chance, however much she thinks it's the wrong decision."

Adrian was on his feet now. "Bloody brilliant!" He turned to Carrie, ran his hands through his tufty hair. "She's totally unlocked it!"

Carrie, who'd been sitting quietly, feeling isolated as she watched her husband and the new girl story-riff off each other, quickly smiled. "It's a great idea, Emma. Well done."

Emma beamed at her as if the teacher in class had just praised her.

"Right, I gotta get this down," said Adrian, heading for the door. "I'm gonna work in the back office for a bit. Start seeding all this in. What do you think, Emma? Cancer?"

Emma nodded. "Could be."

He raised an outstretched arm, pointed a finger at her. "You . . . are awesome."

Carrie saw Emma give a self-conscious smile; then Adrian left the room, buzzing with the new injection of life to his script.

A quietness descended.

"I hope it was okay," began Emma, timorously, "speaking out like that?"

She saw the results—what does she think? Then Carrie crushed her churlishness. Poor girl was probably nervous.

"Of course. That's what we pay you for," she said, then instantly regretted reducing it to a transaction. What was wrong with her? She looked at her watch. "Time for lunch?"

"I'd love to."

Too late Carrie realized Emma had taken it as an invitation. Some time to sit together and get to know each other—and for Emma to understand her job more. Carrie wasn't actually that hungry; in fact, the thought of food made her feel positively nauseous. She said as much, as gently as she could to Emma, who was all graciousness and concern.

"No problem, I hope you're okay? Can I get you anything?"

"I'm fine."

"Well, let me know if you change your mind. Ginger's meant to be good for nausea. Just shout and I'll run out. Anytime."

Carrie thanked her and, suddenly wanting to be alone, heaved herself to her feet.

Emma quickly stood too. "And I meant to say—would you like to go over anything before our meeting this afternoon?"

With a lurch, Carrie realized she was talking about the meeting with the commissioning executive from the BBC, who would be coming over to the office to talk about casting. Meetings with commissioners were like a sacred audience with the Pope: rare and special and highly desired. Many a producer would keep anyone junior from attending, because if you were able to get friendly with a commissioner, you had their ear. And if you had their ear, you could pitch them ideas that they actually *listened* to and that could ultimately lead to the revered green light. Carrie suddenly realized she didn't want Emma there.

"It's all fine, thanks, Emma. And Liz will be in the meeting with myself and Adrian, so we'll probably not want to make it any more top heavy . . . "

She'd been expecting something—a look of hurt or anger—but to her surprise Emma got it straightaway.

"Oh, it's no problem. I've got plenty to keep me busy typing up these script notes."

After she'd left, Carrie felt guilty again. It was even harder than she'd thought, letting go of her job. She went into Liz's office to check over the latest budget e-mails from the accountant, which took her mind off the temp until she was distracted by seeing Emma and Adrian in the open-plan office. Emma had gotten him a sandwich and he was talking animatedly to her. Then he beckoned her into the back office and she followed him, before closing the door.

"What?"

Liz had been saying something she'd totally missed.

"Baby brain hit you already?" said Liz, smiling. "I'm just saying Kenny's a very expensive director. Fine if you and Adrian are dead set, but I do think you should meet James as well. His credits are amazing and he's available in January now the Channel 4 project has fallen through."

"Fine. Yes . . . Good idea."

"Are you okay?" said Liz, looking at her with concern. "You seem a little tired."

She was exhausted, having been woken by the agonizing pain in her hips at four in the morning and not being able to lie down again—it just hurt too much. But she didn't want to admit this, so she settled for: "A bit. Nothing an early night won't cure." And she would have one; she'd get home tonight, pull the old duvet out of the airing cupboard, and try sleeping on top of that. The extra padding might just bag her another hour or two.

Liz suddenly looked up through the window. "Luke's here," she said, standing. Carrie turned to see the BBC's commissioning executive wave to her.

"Shall I get the others?" asked Liz.

Carrie spoke quickly. "It's just Adrian. Emma's busy on something. I'll go and grab him."

"You look amazing! Such a neat bump!" said Luke as they all took seats in the conference room.

Carrie was always surprised at how many people said this as if it were a great achievement. As if a baby bump were a fashion accessory. But she smiled and looked suitably pleased, then complimented Luke on his jacket (a new one to add to his collection, which he always wore over a V-neck white T-shirt with a pair of jeans) and his recent Sunday night success—a show that had viewing figures of over eight million.

The office runner, a young graduate called Zack with a first from Cambridge, popped his head around the door to take the order for teas and coffees. Once he'd left, a quiet hush fell over the room.

"I'm *so* excited about this one," said Luke, drumming his hands on his thighs in relish. "The scripts are superb."

Adrian grinned. "Thanks."

"How's episode four?"

"Going well. Should have something to read pretty soon."

"Can't wait," enthused Luke. "So . . . casting!"

"We've had some responses," said Liz.

"Go on . . . spill," said Luke.

They were interrupted by a knock on the door. Carrie looked up in surprise as Emma came in, carrying a tray of drinks. Why was she bringing them in? It was Zack who'd come to see what they wanted.

"Zack had to run an errand," Emma said in answer to Carrie's silent question.

"This is Emma," said Liz to Luke. "She's going to be covering when Carrie goes on maternity leave."

Luke looked at her with interest, stood to shake her hand.

Carrie tensed, waiting for the "So aren't you joining us, then?" from Luke, but he was too professional, and in the awkward void she suddenly felt like an idiot—and shame washed

51

over her. Of course Emma should be there. Carrie had let the hormones and the tiredness get the better of her and she was about to invite her to stay when Emma spoke.

"Must get on. Nice to meet you." She obediently left, but as she went through the door she flashed a smile at Carrie. From her position, no one else could see.

It startled her. Was it . . . *triumphant?* Or had she imagined it?

Luke was speaking. "So . . . Leon. Our antihero. Dare I ask . . . any news on Jude Law?"

Carrie forced herself to concentrate. "Sadly, he's passed. He was keen, but there's an availability issue. His movie with Guy Ritchie films in Feb."

"Damn that Guy Ritchie!"

"Especially as he was originally set to go in April—when we would have been finished," said Liz. "His shoot's been brought forward."

"Bet he did it on purpose," said Adrian. They all laughed.

"Michael Sheen is looking hopeful," said Carrie, crossing her fingers as a twinge across her abdomen brought her up short. She breathed in sharply. Rubbed her bump.

"He would be amazing," said Luke.

"We've got a breakfast set for next week," said Adrian.

"You still around?" Luke asked Carrie.

Dead right I am. "Yes, I don't go off for another two weeks."

"Brilliant."

Enthusiastic looks crossed all of their faces except for Carrie, who was struck by another acute pain. *What is it?* And then wetness trickled down her legs and she felt it soak into the sofa. "Oh," she said involuntarily.

They all looked at her—*yes?* But she wasn't able to answer as another spasm gripped her. This time she couldn't help but let out a low moan.

Liz came to her senses first. "Oh my God, Carrie. Do we need to get you an ambulance?"

Carrie was still grimacing and unable to talk. Adrian looked shell-shocked and didn't seem to know what to do.

"I'll take that as a yes." Liz grabbed her phone off the table and rang the emergency services, talking efficiently to the operator, her other arm around Carrie's back. "They won't be long," she said, hanging up.

Christ it *hurt*, thought Carrie. Jesus, it couldn't really be labor, could it? She still had four weeks to go.

"Can I get you anything?" asked Luke, standing. He seemed out of his depth.

"Just water, please."

"I'll get it," said Adrian quickly, disappearing out of the door. Carrie wished he'd stayed with her and let Luke go.

53

No one spoke and, feeling outnumbered by females, Luke excused himself on the pretext of giving Adrian a hand. Carrie saw him stop outside in the open-plan office, collared by various members of staff who were clearly very taken with this dramatic turn of events but were trying not to glance through the glass doors too often. Emma was there, too, looking concerned.

Adrian returned and handed her a glass of water, which she suddenly didn't want. "Can I get you a blanket?" he asked.

"Why would I need a blanket?" she said, more curtly than she'd intended, but the pain was back again.

Chastened, he looked out of the window onto the street. "They're here!" he exclaimed in relief.

In a matter of minutes the paramedics were upstairs, two capable professionals helping Carrie through another spasm.

"I'll go and get your bag," said Liz, diving out of the room.

"Best get you somewhere more comfortable before the baby comes," said one paramedic kindly. "You ready to go?"

She nodded and held on to one of them as he helped her walk. As they got to the door Carrie turned, expecting Adrian to be right behind her, but he was still by the window.

She was struck by the utterly lost and fearful expression on his face. He immediately overcompensated, all arms and legs, tripping over a chair on his way to her.

As they crossed the open office to a chorus of "good luck" and "you can do it," Emma suddenly appeared at Carrie's side.

"Don't worry about anything here," she said, smiling broadly, assuredly. "I'll take care of Luke."

Carrie had no time to answer as her bag was thrust into her hand, the lift door pinged open, and the paramedics were leading her in just as another contraction took hold of her body, doubling her over in pain.

7

Carrie stared into the moses basket at the side of her disheveled bed. Inside lay her still-nameless baby, his eyes closed but lids flickering, his arms occasionally jerking in sleep. Every time they moved he was in danger of waking himself up, and that was something she dreaded. Not now. Not for . . . one hour? Dare she pray for two? Anything, anything to get some sleep, to not have to deal with the incessant crying. She took one last look at him and did her usual apprehensive search for the bond that was promised to her by the parenting books and websites. It wasn't there. Mostly she was just terrified of him.

Slowly and silently she backed out of the room. Pulled the door closed, very, very carefully. Waited, breath held. Had she made it? All was silent. *Thank God.*

She wondered what to do. Exhaustion had rendered her unable to think. And the baby was in the bedroom so she couldn't lie down there. Should she shower or just go and collapse on the sofa and close her eyes?

Adrian had moved into the spare room in order to get some sleep so he could work. Carrie glanced at her watch. It was five-thirty in the morning and still dark. She looked longingly at the closed spare room door but decided to leave him and went down the two flights of stairs to the kitchen as quietly as she could. She was just filling the kettle when there was a sound from Adrian's office.

She looked up, crossed the room, and tentatively opened the door. The rope noose that hung against the wall, Adrian's trophy prop, swung in the breeze.

"Jesus, you scared me!" said Adrian, looking around from the desk.

"Sorry. I thought you were asleep upstairs."

"Baby woke me at four. You too, I guess."

She nodded and noticed the bags under his eyes matched her own.

"You okay?" he asked.

"Yes." She suddenly wanted some company, human company from someone who didn't scream at her no matter how long she picked him up and soothed him in her well-meaning, albeit frazzled way. "You busy?"

She saw him hesitate; then he gestured to the armchair. "Just writing. Come," he said.

"Sorry. You're working . . . "

"Doesn't matter. It's nice to see you. Forgotten what it's like to spend some time with my wife without a baby attached to you."

"It's only been ten days."

"Feels longer." He quickly smiled to lighten the gloom.

"I was thinking of Rory," she said. "For a name."

"Sounds good."

"Or Toby?"

"I like that too."

"Which do you like better?"

"I think they're both great."

She felt the knot in the pit of her stomach tighten. "Do you not have more of an opinion?"

He sighed. "Sorry. It's just . . . I'm no good at names."

Her frayed nerves hissed. *What does that mean? How hard is it to pick a name? He does it every time he writes a script.*

"Rory, I like Rory," he said. "Rory Kennedy Hill. It has a nice ring to it."

She nodded. Looked over at his desk. "What are you doing?"

"Still trying to get this last episode done."

"Sorry. I know it's been hard. Baby . . . *Rory* . . . waking up every three hours."

She sounded so deflated he suddenly put his arms around her.

"It's okay," he said. "I know it's much harder for you."

His act of kindness broke the dam of tears. God, she was so *tired.*

"Hey, you're not crying, are you?" He smiled

59

at her, rubbed her face with his thumbs. "Maybe I can help. Do some feedings."

"You got boobs?"

He squeezed his chest. "Yes, unfortunately. Moobs."

She laughed. Blew her nose. "Thanks for the offer."

"What about, what is it, that fake milk?"

"Formula?"

"Yeah, the stuff you put in bottles."

"I did think about it . . . but it seems unfair somehow. The midwives keep telling me I've got the good stuff. Feels like I'd be short-changing him."

Adrian squeezed her arm. "You're a good mum."

She gave a hollow laugh. "Am I? Haven't got a clue what I'm doing."

"Rubbish. You're doing amazingly."

She knew that he didn't really know that and it felt like a brush-off. She saw him glance at his computer screen. "Do you need to get back to work?"

"It's okay," he said unconvincingly.

"I should leave you."

"It's okay if you want to talk."

"No, really, I think I could do with some sleep to be honest."

"Do it," he said, quickly. "Before Toby wakes up again."

She waited for him to correct himself, but it didn't come. "Rory," she said.

"Sorry, Rory. Course." He smiled. Banged his forehead with his fist. "Bananas for brains."

"Must be the lack of sleep getting to you too."

"Must be."

"Okay. Well, see you later."

She closed the door softly behind her and listened to him go back to his desk. Alone again, she took a deep breath and went upstairs to the living room. Plumped up the sofa cushions and lay back, resting her head in their soft cradle. *If only Mum were here,* she thought. *She always knew what to do. How to make the scary seem normal.* She closed her eyes. Wished more than anything her mother was still around. So she didn't feel so alone. She felt the blissful drifting sensation as sleep beckoned.

A spluttering cry which amplified into a full-blown wail at a pace that always amazed her. And then the return of the familiar terror that gripped her and made her feel nothing but despair.

She clamped down on the tears, got up. Went upstairs and picked up her baby. Patted his back nervously, realizing as she did so she was totally out of her depth. What in God's name had made her decide to do this?

Maybe he needed feeding. But she couldn't bear to be in this prison of a room a minute longer. She took him back down to the living room and switched on the TV. It was an old rerun of a quiz show that hadn't been made for over a decade. She took the cushions that had briefly held her head and used them to support her son's while she lifted her baggy jersey top and offered her breast, struggling to get the position right. Second attempt and he was on. A fleeting sense of achievement, mixed with relief.

She looked up to see Adrian in the doorway, watching.

"Hi. You taking a break?"

"Actually, I need to take a shower. Got to run into town."

"Something going on?"

He looked at her quizzically. "The breakfast meeting? With Michael Sheen?"

She jolted and her shock threatened to disturb Rory. He whimpered for a second and in a panic she got him latched on again.

She'd completely forgotten. What had happened to her? She was a crumbling mess, didn't recognize herself. Just over a week ago she had arranged to meet one of the best actors of his generation and now? She looked down at her baby's head.

Adrian saw her distress. "You've had something else to occupy you. Don't give yourself a hard time."

He was right, so why did she feel so desolate, so bereft?

"After . . . I thought I'd stay at the office. Get some proper writing time in."

Her mouth dropped open in dismay. "What?"

"It'll only be for the day," he said quickly. "I'll be back by seven. Six, then. Make you something to eat. We'll sit down and have dinner together. Make something of it."

Both of them knew this was never going to happen. Not with a newborn around.

"I'm just finding it a bit hard to write. And I— we—need this to be good. For all three of us." He came over to her, knelt down beside her. Tentatively touched the top of his son's head. "It's just until he's a little more sociable, okay?"

Five minutes later, she could hear the shower running.

A tiny crack of gray light was coming up behind the houses on the opposite side of the street. The beginning of another very long day.

8

Everything was slower, and planned and timed to almost debilitating levels. What would've once been the simplest thing—going to the office—was now littered with potential pitfalls: were there stairs to the station platform? (No.) Was it late enough to miss the rush hour crush so she could actually get on the train with a stroller? (Hopefully.) Could she change trains at the London terminus and get on the tube via an elevator? (Yes, she'd checked on the website and the newly revamped Tottenham Court Road had elevators aplenty, thank God.) Then she'd packed the large bag with the surprising number of essentials Rory would need, fed him, and set off, feeling as if she were abandoning the safety net of home.

It was her first trip out with him since he'd been born. Miraculously he seemed to sleep the entire way, perhaps lulled by the movement of the trains, something she was deeply relieved about. At the same time, she was consumed with trepidation that if he was sleeping now, as soon as they got to the office, he'd open his lungs. But faced with another bleak autumn day in the house, Carrie had decided to take Rory into work for the obligatory office introduction—and at the same time she'd find out how the meeting had gone with Michael Sheen.

As she pushed the stroller through the doors, struggling to hold one open, heads turned round and eyes lit up and she was glad she'd come. She and Rory were showered with compliments, and she actually looked when the girls said he was adorable and thought he did look sort of sweet in his green-and-blue-striped pixie-style hat.

Carrie glanced toward Liz's office and saw it was empty.

"They're still out," said Zack.

"At the breakfast meeting?" She looked at her watch—it was past ten. She would've thought they'd have returned by now. People were drifting back to their desks and she decided to log in to her computer and check her e-mails. Her desk was toward the back of the small open plan area, near the window. She switched on the computer and started typing her login.

"I really don't think that could have gone any better," said Liz, coming through the door, followed by an exuberant Adrian and Emma.

"What was it he said? He wanted to 'work with nice people.' Seems like you passed the test, Emma," teased Adrian.

"Yeah, well, there are enough tricky customers in this business and life's too short," said Liz.

"He seemed very impressed with you, Emma. I have to say, you've only been with us a couple of weeks and you've got those scripts nailed."

Carrie had stood up the moment they walked in, but so far none of them seemed to have noticed her. Suddenly Emma looked across the desks and the exhilarated expression on her face slipped momentarily before she recovered. She walked over.

"Carrie! How lovely to see you!"

Then they all came: Liz, throwing her arms around her, admonishing her for not letting anyone know she was coming; Adrian, brushing her cheek with a kiss.

"Oh my God, he's devastating!" exclaimed Liz, gazing into the pram. "He looks just like you."

Carrie wasn't sure he did. He just looked like a newborn, and they all were alike at this age she'd noticed, one just occasionally had more hair than the next.

"So it went well, then?" said Carrie. It felt strange having to ask.

"It went brilliantly," said Liz. "He's on board— we have a verbal commitment. And we're not a million miles off on the deal, so it should all be signed and sealed very soon."

"That's fantastic."

"Emma here did a great job. She didn't let you down."

Carrie exchanged a smile with Emma but didn't quite meet her eyes. Emma looked away first.

There was an unfilled silence.

"Right," started Adrian in a jolly tone, "best get to work." He turned to Emma. "Shall we have a chat about those script suggestions Michael's made?"

"Oh, what are they?" asked Carrie, aware she was the only one who didn't know.

"I can type them up for you if you like," said Emma quickly.

"Or I can just join the script meeting now."

"Oh yes! Of course!" agreed Emma.

Liz tapped Carrie's arm. "See, workaholic. You're meant to be on maternity leave."

"Doesn't mean I have to forget about my show, though," she said pointedly.

She faced the polite smiles with the distinct sensation of turning up to a party to which she wasn't invited, something she knew she had brought upon herself with her possessive undertones.

Emma was the one to break the silence. "Okay, cool. Shall I make some coffees?"

"Great," said Carrie.

"I'll see you in there," said Adrian as he turned toward the back office.

"Adrian," said Carrie, and he looked back, mildly quizzical.

Does he not know?

"You haven't said hello," she admonished lightly.

He looked even more puzzled—but she wasn't talking about herself. She nodded toward the stroller. Enlightenment crossed his face. "I didn't want to wake him," he said, and she knew he'd made it up on the spot. Emma, who'd been hovering, looked embarrassed and quickly headed away to the kitchen.

He peered in. "Has he been good for you this morning?"

"Good as gold," said Carrie, suddenly feeling as if she had to prove to herself that the last ten days of misery had never happened. Adrian looked at her strangely, but she ignored it; then Rory decided to wake. A tentative grumble at first, eyes still closed. Carrie quickly pushed the pram back and forth, but he was having none of it. She glanced at her watch—it had been three hours since his last feeding. Once again she was required to get her tits out or all hell would break loose.

"Meeting room's free," said Liz, and Carrie knew Rory was making so much racket now, she had no choice. Frazzled and self-conscious, she quickly wheeled him away and into the meeting room, choosing a chair that let her sit with her back to the glass door. Draping herself with the breastfeeding scarf, she fed him as quickly as she could, but it was still forty minutes by the time they were done. He was resting on her shoulder, winded and content, and Carrie decided not to give up. She left the meeting room and, carrying her baby, went to the back office. She stood outside a second, wondering if she should knock, then thinking that was ridiculous and why had her confidence reached an all-time low, she opened the door.

The room was empty.

It took a moment for it to sink in and she looked over her shoulder, bewildered, wondering if she'd missed them. Zack was at the photocopier.

"Zack, do you know where Adrian and Emma are?" asked Carrie.

"They went out to get a coffee. We ran out of the instant stuff."

"You know where?"

He shook his head. "Sorry."

Carrie looked around at the low buzz of the office, people working, getting on with their day, being purposeful, not noticing her. Through Liz's window she could see she was in deep conversation on the phone. She quickly got the stroller, tucked Rory in, and with a brief wave at Liz, signaling some pretense of needing to get away for a baby-related misadventure, she left.

Out on the street she tried to pull herself together. It was because she was tired, that's all; she felt everything so keenly because she was so goddamn tired. She looked around at the busy

Soho cafés near the office, glancing into one or two windows, but couldn't see her husband or Emma. Someone needed to get past her and the stroller was in the way. She shoved it farther up onto the narrow pavement, but the passerby was on his phone and didn't even acknowledge her, let alone offer his thanks.

Suddenly she just wanted to go home. She quickly pushed the stroller up the street, heading for the tube.

9

Thursday, October 26

Emma took a sip of her cappuccino and listened to Adrian, marveling at how much he could talk about himself. He had an insatiable appetite for the subject of "Me," often halfheartedly dressed up as the show or the industry at large.

Boredom aside, she didn't mind, in fact it helped her cause quite a bit. It must be tough for Carrie, though—she'd seen how he'd been so self-engaged he'd barely noticed her or their son and she'd felt Carrie's embarrassment and hurt, exacerbated because it was so public.

She let her eyes wander over to the window of the café a moment, onto the Soho street outside, and her focus sharpened. Was that Carrie outside, across the street? She watched as the woman turned; then she saw her face—it *was* Carrie.

Emma went to tell Adrian, but he was midflow on Michael Sheen's brilliant and insightful understanding of the character Adrian had managed to create. Damn, could he not shut up, just for a moment? She went to put her hand on his arm, but then Carrie started walking off and at the pace she was going, she was soon out of sight. It was too late.

"Something wrong?" said Adrian, finally realizing he didn't have her full attention. He glanced over his shoulder out of the window.

She decided not to tell him he'd just missed his wife. "Tell me about *Generation Rebel*," she said, smiling. "If you don't mind? I'm such a fan of the show and I feel very lucky to be sitting here with its creator."

He gave a cheesy grin. "You'll make me blush." But then he quickly added: "What do you want to know?"

Everything, thought Emma.

"It's such a brilliant idea," she said, "totally captured the zeitgeist of the moment. How did it come about?"

"I was just struck by how hard life has been for young people in this country for so long. An ever-changing school curriculum, designed to push them further, and yet funding in schools is at an all-time low. And a massive debt to look forward to for the next few decades, either their university fees or the nation's deficit—or both."

It was the story he'd peddled for all the listings magazine and media pages of the newspapers, she noted.

"And then that surge of revolution during the last election—backing Labor and Corbyn. It really inspired me."

"But the election happened after you wrote it."

He frowned. "Yes, but . . . "

She left him hanging just a fraction of a second. "Guess it was prophetic."

He laughed, pleased. "Well, I wouldn't put it quite like that."

Oh, but you'd love to.

She smiled. "I think it really touched on something, chimed with a million disgruntled voices—"

"Eleven million."

"Sorry?"

He grinned. "Ratings. Eleven million with consolidated."

"Wow. You got the youth of the characters so well. They seemed like people I knew, had been to school with. I could even see myself in them! Brilliant," she enthused, "just brilliant. Where did you get your character inspiration from?"

He shrugged modestly. Tapped his forehead. "Just made it up really. Dug deep enough to reengage with my younger self." He grinned. "It was a big shovel."

She laughed. "You're not that old."

He laughed with her, gratified, she saw, that he could still appear youthful to a twenty-four-year-old. It made her uncomfortable suddenly, the way he was looking at her as if they were of the same generation, bonded in some way. She thought of his wife.

"It was nice to see Carrie today," she said. "And your beautiful baby."

A cloud of guilt drifted across his face. "I was surprised she came in. She was tired," he explained.

"Maybe she needs a little pick-me-up."

He didn't understand.

"Something to brighten her day?" She hesitated, not sure if she was going too far. "There's a boutique next door. They have the most beautiful hand-painted Italian silk scarves."

"Oh, right?" he said, casually, as if he wasn't very interested, but she knew he'd be slipping out of the office later to get one and he'd claim the idea as his own. Another demonstration of his slipperiness.

She wondered if Carrie knew what a total piece of shit her husband really was.

10

Thursday, October 26

Carrie hadn't been able to stay cross with him long, not when he'd surprised her with an exclusive box, inside which was the most stunning, luxuriant yellow, turquoise, and white scarf. He tied it around her neck, looping it through at the front.

"Does it look good?" she asked, tentatively.

He smiled. "Go and see for yourself."

Carrie went upstairs into the living room and glanced in the mirror that hung over the fireplace, an action that had not produced the best of results lately. Her eyes lit up. This scarf had magical properties, she could swear. The dark circles under her eyes and the ghostly pallor receded, and for a brief moment she felt like her old self and she had a mental chat with the Carrie in the mirror. *Maybe it's not so bad. Everyone says it's hard the first few weeks. Maybe things just need to even out a bit.*

Glancing down at the fireplace, she saw the new baby cards still displayed, including one from Adrian's sister in Australia, who couldn't come and visit as she had three children of her own to look after. His elderly parents lived in Spain, and Carrie's father had died two years before her mum. She briefly reflected on what it would be like to have an extended family around to help, but that was one of the many things you lost when you decided to have your baby so late in life.

Going back down to the kitchen, she was relieved to see Rory still asleep in his bouncy chair. She kissed Adrian on the lips.

"Thank you," she said, softly. "It's very thoughtful of you."

He appraised her, admiration in his eyes. "Looking good."

"Do you still want me?"

"Dead right. Wanna go upstairs?"

She laughed. "Maybe not just yet."

He put his arms around her and they shared a tender kiss. It had been a long time, thought Carrie, and there was a novelty to it.

"I love you," he said.

"Love you too."

"Hey, I was thinking. Maybe we should plan a little break for when the shoot's finished in spring."

Carrie considered. "Where?"

"Somewhere not too far. We have to fly with the Decibel Breaker, after all. Greece, maybe? It'll be warm. We can get some you and me time."

Carrie wasn't quite sure exactly how that would happen, but she appreciated the sentiment.

"We could go to that place in Crete. You know,

that villa in the White Mountains we saw in the article about escaping the crowds or whatever it was. The place with the awesome hot tub."

"Sounds good," she said, thinking it might actually be possible. Rory might be in more of a routine by then. Suddenly the future felt a little brighter.

She watched as he chopped vegetables for the curry he was making. "I came to find you this morning. In the office, after I'd fed Rory."

He thought back. "Oh, we went out for a coffee. Talked over Michael Sheen's notes. She's so good you know, Emma. She's got a real intuitive sense about character."

The warm, optimistic feeling seeped away.

"And she's had some great ideas on who'd be good opposite Michael, to play Sally."

Is there anything this girl can't do? thought Carrie.

Adrian looked up and smiled. "She reminds me of you. Something about her sense of ambition."

As a compliment, it was misjudged. All it did was make her feel more unnerved, more insecure.

"Do you have to say that?"

"What?"

"How brilliant she is."

"Not as good as you," he quickly remedied. *"Obviously."*

She stood there, feeling miserable.

"Hey, come on." He was trying to make light of

it. "You're not threatened by her, are you? You're in a different league."

Carrie pursed her lips, aware she was being childish, needy. She took a deep breath, tried to lighten up.

"So what other great ideas has she had?" It had been meant as a throwaway comment, but she was taken aback to see his eyes slide downward toward her neck. He averted his gaze almost immediately, but she *knew*.

"You are joking."

"What do you mean?" he said, acting surprised.

She tugged at the scarf. "She told you to get this for me?"

"Of course not!"

But she knew by the level of bluster he was lying.

"It was my idea, one hundred percent," he insisted, and she looked at him, hurt and confused. Why couldn't he see he was adding salt to the wound?

Their eyes were held in a deadlock. So much unspoken. It was broken only when Rory started to wail.

11

As she walked in the door of her parents' house, Emma was surprised to hear their voices coming from the kitchen at the relatively early time of six. She was even more surprised to hear a third, unidentified voice.

"Oh, Emma, you're back!" said her mother as Emma went into the large, gleaming white eat-in kitchen, lit with spotlights, floor lights, and under-cupboard lights. "I left you a message—did you get it?"

She'd been on the tube and hadn't picked it up.

"This is Rebecca, a friend of your father's," her mother said, indicating the woman with tightly curled auburn hair, sitting on a bar stool and holding a very large glass of white wine. She was the kind of person who had a knowing, confident smile permanently on her face.

Emma could sense her father watching her carefully as she said hello to their guest and wondered why.

It became apparent over the beef stroganoff. Rebecca was her father's management friend in the NHS, parachuted in to assess his failure of a daughter and see if there was anything that could be done to save her, and his reputation.

"Brian tells me you work in television," said Rebecca.

"Yes, I'm doing maternity cover for a producer."

"It's a temporary role," said Alice, by way of clarification, and Emma frowned. That was obvious, wasn't it? Why reinforce it?

"Most television jobs are, Mum," she said shortly. "Maternity cover or not." She'd made this point several times in the past.

"Means it's hard to make plans," said her father.

Emma bristled. She didn't appreciate the subtle attack. It was made worse by the fact that her father was right. She couldn't ever book a holiday or, more importantly, move out because she just didn't know if she'd have any income beyond the next few months.

Getting her own place was something she was dying to do. It was funny how things had changed. When she'd first been sent to boarding school at the tender age of seven, she had longed to go home, spending hours lying awake in her narrow bed, the dark a large monster that watched and waited for her to fall asleep so it could attack. She'd cried and begged and pleaded, but it had made no difference, and she was told she'd thank them when she was older.

Emma would live for the weekends when her parents visited. Saturday afternoons were everything to her, a time that she longed for so much it was like a physical pain, and she would launch herself at them as they came through the door of the common room. She remembered their first visit as if it were yesterday. She'd flung herself at her mother's knees and, to her own surprise, had started sobbing uncontrollably. Her mother pulled her away and Emma saw her brush at the wet patches on her skirt.

"What's going on?" asked Alice, puzzled. "Are you hurt?"

Emma, quiet now, shook her head.

"It's such a beautiful place," said her father, gazing around at the eighteenth-century wooden panels with pride on his face. "Reminds me of my old school."

She sensed that it would be churlish to complain, and deep down was longing for their approval, something that she knew would be kept in check if she started to sound ungrateful about everything they'd provided for her. She knew it was a prestigious school, the head teacher said as much at every assembly.

They'd made it outside to the grounds. "Oh my goodness, they're out riding," said Alice, pointing in delight at two girls on ponies heading down to the lake. "Have you had a chance to do that yet, Emma?"

In truth, she had, and she'd loved it. She nodded.

"You're so lucky," said Alice, pointedly.

Emma nodded again, mutely.

"What else have you done?" asked Brian.

"Tae kwon do."

"And what about lessons? Are you doing well?"

She didn't really know but did know the right answer was yes, so she said so and felt a flutter of anxiety in case she wasn't telling the truth. She sometimes found math hard, and occasionally it was pointed out that she wrote her threes the wrong way around, but she didn't dare admit this to her parents.

The visits each weekend would all take the same shape, with Emma staying glued to her parents the entire afternoon, not daring even to go to the toilet for fear of their not being there when she came out. She noticed the disapproving looks they gave each other over the top of her head but ignored them.

When her parents left she would retreat into herself, watching the other girls play at break time, unable to understand their exuberance, feeling as if she were a different species. Lessons were much the same and she felt detached from all that was going on around her and would look out of the window at the birds wheeling in the sky, then disappearing over the tops of the trees, envying them their freedom. Over the weeks, unsurprisingly, her work began to suffer.

One weekend, she was waiting for her parents in the common room as usual. One by one, other girls' mothers and fathers came to pick them up and take them out for the day, and as the crowd dispersed, she began to get anxious. Then she saw a woman she recognized from the school office come and speak to her house mistress, Mrs. Jackson, who then glanced in her direction, a look on her face that struck Emma with dread. The woman from the office left, and Mrs. Jackson gently approached and asked her to go into her room for a moment. Once inside, she sat next to her on the sofa, a gesture of compassion that filled Emma with anxiety.

"I'm afraid Mum and Dad can't make it today," said Mrs. Jackson, as kindly as she could.

Emma's throat closed up in terror. She stared wild-eyed at her house mistress, not understanding, not knowing what had gone wrong.

"Why?" she managed to blurt out, her voice warped with hurt.

Mrs. Jackson wrestled with her response. "Your parents . . . feel as if they're being a bit of a distraction," she eventually said. "And that maybe you need a little more time to focus on your grades. . . ."

She stopped then as Emma was weeping silent tears, looking up at her in utter bewilderment. Mrs. Jackson wrapped an arm around her, but Emma never really recovered from the brutality of her parents' rejection. She became closed off, the hurt burying itself deep into her psyche. Ironically, she did work harder, but it was because work numbed the pain. When her parents materialized again a few weeks later, they were delighted with her progress, and with their psychology that had instigated the turnaround.

Although she still needed them and still her heart leapt every time she saw them, it was never in quite the same way. Her heart would fall as quickly as it had risen, bereft and fearful they'd take away their love at any point.

As she hardened, she would lose herself in fantasy. She would think she was in truth destined for Hogwarts and would stare out of the large Victorian dormitory window, picking out the black boughs in the winter night, searching to see if an owl was perched on any. She longed for that letter of invitation almost more than she'd longed for her mother, but neither ever came to take her away. So she began to create her own escape. Pictures playing out in her mind that seemed so real, she half thought they were. One night, she'd lain in bed, unable to sleep. Closing her eyes tightly, she'd imagined a film playing out, one she was a part of:

FADE IN:

INT./EXT. SCHOOL DORMITORY—NIGHT

EMMA sits in her pajamas on the windowsill, looking out at the dark school grounds, wishing an owl would appear with a letter. Her three other dormitory mates are all sleeping. Suddenly one of the top branches of the tallest tree starts to grow. It stretches long and far toward the window and opens it, beckoning an amazed Emma.

She carefully climbs onto the appendage, soft with moss, and it lifts her up into the warm night air, handing her over to the top branch of another neighboring tree. Soon all the trees are waving their branches, carefully handing her from one to the other as they carry her away from the school.

Emma looks up in amazement as a flock of pink flamingos (Emma's favorite bird) flies over her head, their feathers dazzling in the starlight. They sparkle with pink and coral and orange, and take care to keep up with her. Then one of them looks down, winking at her, and she knows she's free and she's safe and she's loved.

CUT TO:

This fantasy would manifest itself in both her sleeping and waking hours, and if she stared hard enough at the trees when she was inside the classroom, she would actually think she could see them secretly stretching their branches toward her. No wonder her teachers always wrote in her reports that she had an overactive imagination.

87

"Emma?"

She started, realized she hadn't heard her father speak.

"Wouldn't it be better to get something more stable? A permanent job with a proper pension?"

"My job won't be temporary forever," she said brightly to her small audience, privately thinking: *why can't they just be pleased for me?* "As you prove yourself, you get offered more. Work your way up the ladder."

"Have you been offered something after this contract, then?" asked her father. Rebecca listened keenly.

"Not yet," said Emma, keeping her voice level. "But they're really pleased with how it's going. I'm getting included on everything—we met with Michael Sheen today."

"Oh, is he the one from *The West Wing*?" exclaimed Alice, sounding impressed.

"No, that's Martin Sheen," said Emma.

"Oh. Who's this Michael Sheen, then?"

Emma was about to explain he was one of the best actors ever to come out of Wales when her father spoke again.

"But aren't you covering for this producer?"

"Yes . . ."

"So shouldn't you be in on the meeting, anyway?" Emma saw him turn and look at Rebecca as if to say, *I'm not missing something here, right?*

Emma's eyes flickered down. They'd never

understand because they just didn't want to. Even if she were collecting a bloody BAFTA, it would never be good enough. It would be a jokey, *"It's been a long time coming!"* or *"We thought she'd never get there!"*

"We just don't want to see you put everything into a job that doesn't reward you properly," said Alice. "You need security, need to make the most of the education we gave you. There are other options out there. Rebecca here, for example, could talk you through some schemes she's aware of."

"If you're interested," said Rebecca, "although it does seem to me you've already got your heart set on TV."

Emma looked up sharply but couldn't tell if her tone was disapproving or not. Who cared, quite frankly.

She excused herself up to her room, her only remaining vestige of privacy, as soon as wouldn't be deemed impolite. She fell onto her bed and wondered what it would be like to have parents who backed you, who didn't see you as a disappointment, a wasted investment.

As she lay there, she knew part of what they were saying was right. She desperately wanted some longevity to her job, some financial stability. She couldn't wait to get out of this house. She *needed* to get out.

12

Monday, November 20

There was an abundance of ladybirds painted in a bright, cheery red right from the sign at the entrance gate. They continued on the exterior walls of the building and again inside. It was one of the reasons Carrie had been drawn to this nursery. Her mum had loved nature and in particular had a thing about ladybirds. She adored them and they'd appear in all sorts of guises around the house—on a mug, in a silver and enamel necklace, on a tea towel.

Carrie was met at reception by the nursery manager, Sherie, who cooed over Rory strapped to her chest in his baby carrier. It was the best in the area, rated outstanding by Ofsted and supported by dozens of glowing reviews on various mum's social media sites. A few of her prenatal class friends had also heard good things, including Hannah, whom she was meeting for a coffee afterward.

"How old is he?" asked Sherie.

"Five weeks," said Carrie.

"Aah. Not long until you'll be getting your first smiles."

Carrie had heard about this milestone and what

a wonderful moment it was supposed to be, something she couldn't imagine. She didn't want to let on to Sherie, though, and nodded.

"Ready for the tour?" asked Sherie.

Carrie was led into the playroom, a chaotic place full of plastic toys, some enormous, some small enough to chew, throw, or sit on. A number of small children ran around and Carrie tried to count them, both appalled and fascinated by how few were needed to make such a cacophony of noise, but they didn't stay still long enough.

Sherie continued to the other end of the room and out through a door. "And this is our outside area," she said.

More plastic toys, these faded due to being outside in all weathers.

"We try to get them in the fresh air for at least half an hour every day, even if the weather's bad. It's only if it's torrential we'll stay inside."

It was freezing, with an icy wind cutting across her cheeks and making her eyes water, and Carrie instinctively put her hand on the back of the baby carrier.

Next stop was the kids' toilets, plastered with large, laminated picture posters instructing them to wash their hands or a cartoon germ the size of a small rodent would—do what?—it wasn't clear, but it implied something threatening. There were also notices for the adults, reminding them to use the readily available blue plastic gloves when changing diapers, something that struck Carrie as very clinical, but she reasoned with her unsure self that it made sense and good hygiene was for the benefit of the children.

"And here is the dormitory," said Sherie, her voice a whisper. She held a door ajar and Carrie looked in. A row of about a dozen cribs filled the room, lined up against opposite walls. Nearly all of them contained a baby, fast asleep.

It shocked her. There was something about the way they were all there, so many babies in a uniform line, that reminded her of an orphanage. One of them began to stir.

"That's Asher," said Sherie, going over and picking him up. She spoke to him in the upbeat, bright way Carrie had heard her address some of the other children. No soft murmurings, no gentle caress, despite the fact he'd only just woken up. Sherie led them out of the room as Asher squinted against the instant light, rubbing his hands over his eyes.

Carrie glanced back at the rows of sleeping babies, still mesmerized by them. She wondered who their parents were, what they were doing right now.

"When did he come here?" she asked, indicating Asher.

"Mummy dropped him off at seven-thirty and she comes to get you at seven, doesn't she, Trouble? Earlier, if the traffic's not bad."

Just before it's time to go back to bed, thought Carrie, at the same time chiding herself for her thoughts. Wasn't she about to do the same thing?

"So, I think you mentioned on the phone you were looking for somewhere when Rory is three months?" asked Sherie.

"Actually, things have changed," said Carrie, fighting the unexpected reluctance in her voice. "I need somewhere sooner. In the next week or two."

"We do have a waiting list, but I think someone's recently dropped out," said Sherie. She smiled. "You could be lucky. We'd love to have you, wouldn't we, Rory?" she said, stroking his cheek with her finger. Carrie watched as he frowned and batted at his face with his hands. Sherie didn't seem to notice.

As they went back along the corridor, they passed the lunch room and Carrie glanced in. Several small children sat at half-size tables in half-size chairs. Some were thrusting food haphazardly into their mouths. More than one seemed to be overwhelmed, despite the cheery presence of the staff, looking bewildered at their plates of food and plastic cutlery.

She forced herself to look away and moved on.

13

Monday, November 20

Emma was thankful for her premium brand coat's wind and waterproof capabilities as she stood on the railway platform waiting for her train. She looked around for something to distract her from the cold and saw an open window on the third floor of the block of flats opposite the station, a plume of smoke drifting into the air and a torso-less arm flicking a cigarette's ash down to the ground. The smoker suddenly stubbed out the cigarette against the wall and tossed it, at the same time shouting angrily to someone who was inside the flat.

"Shut up! Fucking shut up!"

A wail came floating down on the cold air.

"I said shut your fucking mouth!" screamed the woman. Her voice was brutal, dangerous, and Emma gave an involuntary shiver. One or two other people looked up and there were a few disapproving tuts.

The child began to cry louder and its voice was cowering. "Please, please no—"

"You're still fucking crying," threatened the woman.

The child cried even louder. "Stop," it begged.

Deeply uncomfortable, Emma looked up again, saw several people frowning and staring up at the window.

The woman began to count. "One!" The crying continued. "Two!"

"No . . . !"

"Three!"

Emma was starting to feel sick with apprehension. Her hands moved agitatedly in her pockets, fingers tapping against themselves with horror.

"Four! Five!"

"No . . . " begged the child.

"Leave your kid alone," muttered Emma under her breath.

She saw the man standing next to her had heard and he smiled ruefully.

"Six!" screamed the woman, her voice bloodcurdling with its threat.

"Leave your kid *alone,*" repeated Emma.

"Yeah, leave your kid alone," agreed the man. He looked at her and she saw the disquiet in his eyes, echoing her own. It emboldened her.

"Leave your kid alone!" she suddenly shouted up at the open window.

"Seven!"

She hadn't been loud enough. "Leave your kid alone!" Emma shouted again. The man suddenly joined her. "Leave your kid alone!" he bellowed.

Then there were others: an elderly lady, a man in a leather jacket, and soon several people on the platform were joining in her chant and it elevated in power and volume. *"Leave your kid alone!"*

A woman's face came to the flat window. She looked down, peeved. "What the fuck are you lot going on about?" she spat.

They kept on chanting and she shrank back at the force of their voices.

"Or we'll call the police!" the elderly woman called out.

The woman's face fell and she pulled back from the window, shutting it.

Emma breathed deeply, still shaken by the vitriol in the woman's voice. She hoped the child was okay. A collective sense of relief and tentative triumph was felt up and down the platform.

They were recceing locations today. When Leon, the ex-film star, hit rock bottom he was forced to take a job at a car wash (something he did abysmally), and the production's location manager, Jake, had lined up several for her, Adrian, Kenny, the director, and the production designer to take a look at in various places across south London.

"This one's definitely larger," said Adrian.

"More run-down-looking too," enthused the production designer.

"Cast and crew base would be across the way in the timber yard," said Jake. "There's plenty of room for all the trucks."

It wasn't the most glamorous location to be

checking out, but it was still immense fun and Emma was excited to imagine scenes from the scripts coming alive as she gazed around the forecourt. Many of the locations that would be used regularly, such as Leon's house, would be built as sets at Pinewood Studios, but if they only had a few scenes to shoot somewhere, it was cheaper to find a live location.

Kenny, the director, was walking around waving his arms about as he played out the scenes in his head while the rest of them huddled in the cold, waiting for him.

"Have you got any thoughts on the Spanish Village?" Jake asked Adrian.

"Damn!" exclaimed Adrian. "I left my drawings at home."

The Spanish Village was a key location as it was where Leon first met Sally, his potential new down-to-earth girlfriend, who was there on her first holiday in years. Emma had learned that Adrian liked to dabble in art, and he'd clearly been getting his vision for the show down on paper.

"Can we just talk them through?" asked Jake.

Adrian looked dubious. "Not really. I think the drawings capture something that's hard to explain."

"Could Carrie scan them and e-mail them over?" suggested Emma.

"She's out. Spending the day with a friend. I'd

go and get them," added Adrian halfheartedly, "except we've still got one more garage to see, haven't we?"

Jake nodded. "We've got time after, though. I'm going to need to take the car as I have to get back to make some calls but there's plenty of time for you to drop in at home before we meet back at the office."

"You reckon?" mumbled Adrian.

"I can go," said Emma. She saw his eyes light up.

"Really? You don't mind?"

"It's fine. I don't really need to see the next place, so I might as well get a head start. Meet you back at the office?"

"I'll have Soho's finest cappuccino waiting for you," said Adrian, and she could see he was delighted someone else had volunteered to travel all the way to Blackheath and then back into town.

As Emma set off she felt Adrian's keys through the lining of her coat against her chest, held tight in the zip-up pocket. Their constant presence poked at her, fueling her excitement and nerves. This was the opportunity she'd been waiting for.

14

Monday, November 20

The row of terraced Edwardian houses just minutes from Blackheath station were penned in by glossy black railings beyond which flights of steps led up to equally glossy front doors in regal colors of deep green, blue, or pillar-box red. Emma went up the steps of Adrian and Carrie's house, past the matching bay trees acting as foot soldiers at the top, took Adrian's keys out of her jacket pocket, and placed the Yale smoothly in the lock and turned.

It opened onto a light, inviting hallway with real wood floors and a cream and red patterned rug. She slipped off her shoes and lined them up carefully with the others on the wooden shoe rack. The house felt warm, not just because she'd come in from the freezing November wind, but because under her socked feet she could feel the radiant heating.

Adrian had told her his study was on the lower ground floor, and she could see the modern glass staircase ahead of her but couldn't resist a peek in the living room immediately off to her right. As with the hallway, it was immaculately decorated, the Edwardian ornate black iron fireplace gleaming, the paintwork a carefully chosen shade of period duck egg blue. She went over to the mantelpiece, drawn by the collection of framed photos she could see half-hidden behind a plethora of baby cards.

Plucking one out, she recognized Carrie and Adrian in scuba gear on a small boat, the sea behind them an impossible hue of aquamarine. He had his arm around her shoulders and she was laughing at something. Emma put it down, seeing the one next to it was of their wedding. She looked closely, studying every square inch of the picture, the dress, of course, but also Carrie's expression, the backdrop, trying to learn as much as she could. They were standing under a tree in a large garden, perhaps that of a stately home.

Then she saw another photo, smaller this time, which was almost completely covered by a card with a blue stork on it. This one took her breath away for it was Carrie many years ago, when she'd graduated, on the steps of her university. She looked so young, thought Emma. She stared at it for one last time, then put it back carefully, making sure she didn't dislodge any of the cards.

Sighing, she stepped back and looked around the room. What else was there? A modern painting over the sofa which she instinctively knew was Adrian's—bold primary brushstrokes on a white background. A set of coasters on the side table that were carved—by hand it looked like—in a light-colored wood. Each was of a different African animal, the Big Five, perhaps a souvenir from another holiday.

She left the room and hesitated in the hallway, undecided whether to look around upstairs first or go down to the lower ground floor. Down won out and she went carefully down the glass steps, which wound round on themselves until they deposited her in a large modern eat-in kitchen. At one end were floor-to-ceiling windows that led out onto a courtyard garden, at the other end, a wooden door behind which Emma knew was Adrian's study. Then something that made her gasp with delight—the length of one entire wall of the dining area was covered in books. Shelf after shelf of them, the top ones only accessible by the rolling ladder that moved across. Emma had always wanted a bookshelf like that and one day, when she had the right job, that was what she was going to buy herself.

She started with the fridge: bottled smoothies, olives, a fancy French brand of sparkling mineral water. French cheeses, too, and expensive sliced meats from a deli, not the supermarket. The pullout larder was full of tins of tomatoes and beans with Italian labels, unusual shaped pasta in authentic paper packaging, some boxes of organic granola, one of which she recognized as the brand she herself liked, which gave her a wave of pleasure. A washing basket piled high with ironing sat on one of the worktops. She laid her hand on it, touching one of Rory's fleecy jumpers, blue with a small cream penguin on the front.

She moved over to the bookshelves and, once again, was pleased to recognize a number of titles in the collection that she also owned. She was going to browse further when she checked herself. *Mustn't get too distracted.*

Going into Adrian's office, the first thing she saw was a noose, hanging on the wall which swung in the draft from the opening door. Emma recognized it as a prop. The rope the children ultimately hanged their headmaster with. Next to it was a large stylized print of the cast of *Generation Rebel*, signed by each of them. She read some of the messages: *"Thanks for creating our show!" "To the writer of our generation,"* but didn't smile at the generous acknowledgments.

She went over to Adrian's desk under the window. Above her she could see legs of people as they walked by on the street outside. The drawings were exactly where he'd said they would be, in a pile on the left side of the desk.

She didn't pick them up; instead she opened the set of drawers underneath, top one first, but it was just full of pens, staplers, a bar of fine dark chocolate. She methodically worked her way through the others, rifling through printouts, magazines, all dull, boring stuff. *Where did he keep the important paperwork?* She moved over to a set of shelves and stopped dead when she saw, next to a pile of books, a small bronze mask. Adrian's BAFTA. It was a moment before she could pick it up, but then she felt its weight, held it aloft, closing her eyes—

"What do you think you're doing?"

Jesus! She nearly dropped it as she spun around to see Carrie standing in the doorway, Rory in her arms.

"Sorry, I was just . . . I came to pick up some stuff for Adrian," she stammered, quickly replacing the BAFTA and grabbing the drawings from the desk.

"Who let you in?"

"He gave me his keys. He's . . . we were on a recce and he'd forgotten the designs and so I offered. To come and get them. So he could continue."

Carrie gave the tiniest nod and Emma was mortified. "I'm sorry if I scared you. He—Adrian—said you were out with a friend."

"I was supposed to have been. She canceled."

"Oh, right. Like I said, I'm really sorry. The last person I'd want to upset is you."

Emma saw Carrie's frown of annoyance—and bafflement. She wished she could take her words back.

"Emma, do you have my phone number?"

"Yes."

"Maybe do me the courtesy of letting me know next time."

"Oh yes. Of course."

They stood there looking at each other and Emma felt a desperate urge to leave. "I'd better get these back. Location meeting starts in a bit. The recce went well this morning, found a good garage," she babbled.

"Great," said Carrie.

Emma clutched the pictures to her chest and, walking awkwardly past Carrie, assured her she could see herself out.

Closing the front door behind her, she took a deep breath. She'd gotten away with it.

15

Adrian had texted to say he would be home later than usual and it wasn't that bad, only nine o'clock, but Carrie's irritation had steadily grown from the moment his message came through. He obviously knew about her run-in with Emma by now and he'd said nothing. Her anger was made worse by the fact she'd only had four hours sleep the night before and had been alone with Rory all day, and she was exhausted.

He kissed her and she smelled booze.

"Where did you go?"

"Only The Crown, you know, opposite the office."

"Many of you?" She tried to remain casual.

"Me, Jake, Kenny." He had his head in the fridge, looking for something to eat.

"Was Emma there?"

"Emma? Oh . . . yeah," came Adrian's muffled voice.

She waited for a bit, getting worked up as the silence continued. Seemed like *she'd* have to bring it up. "Did you not think to call me once you'd handed over your keys to our house?"

Holding a foraged Tupperware of leftover

pasta in his hand, he shut the fridge door. He was looking at her, evaluating her level of annoyance, judging how much peacemaking needed to be done.

"I'm really sorry," he said. "It was just a spur-of-the-moment thing. I was running around like the proverbial blue-arsed and Emma just offered to help out. I thought you were meeting someone—Hannah?—for lunch."

"She canceled. Little Molly's got a cold."

"Okeydoke. You eaten?" he asked, holding up the box of pasta.

She nodded. He headed to the microwave, beeped a few buttons; then the hum of the machine started.

"She was holding your BAFTA," said Carrie. "When I walked in on her."

Adrian chuckled, a self-congratulatory amusement that indicated he understood other people being fascinated by such trophies. "Was she?"

"Sometimes . . . I'm not too sure about her."

"How do you mean?"

"Well, she's so . . . fawning . . . sycophantic really."

"You're an amazing producer. She looks up to you."

"I've produced three docudrama serials."

"One of which was BAFTA nominated."

Not winning, she thought.

"Still much bigger fish to admire out there. Maybe she's so effusive because she thinks I can help her out. I'm—or rather my job—is useful to her."

"Probably helps the résumé," he said, casually.

She bristled. He was totally missing the point, and why did he have to be so goddamned good-natured all the time?

"How's she getting on?" she asked.

"Yeah, good. Really good. Had some brilliant ideas on the interview storyline, you know, the one we were getting stuck on."

"Did she now," she said, snippily.

Adrian had turned around, his impatience finally surfacing. "She's just trying to do her job."

"You mean, my job."

"Yes, your job. And it's still *your* job."

He put his plate of pasta down and came over to her, wrapping his arms around her neck.

"I'm sorry, okay? I should never have given her the keys and not let you know."

She considered staying annoyed, but it was nice, this tiny moment of closeness, something they'd not had in a while. She allowed his apology to soften her mood and rested her head on his shoulder. Felt as if she could go to sleep right there.

He kissed her, nuzzling her neck. "Am I for-given?"

"Suppose." She smiled.

He kissed her again, more lingeringly this time. "Wanna go upstairs?"

She immediately deflated, a total wave of exhaustion flattening her. Did he not understand anything? She was in a constant state of worry. Just this morning, Rory's entire body had gone into bi-tone, the right side of him red and the left side incredibly pale. She'd been petrified but on calling the midwife learned it was perfectly normal—something to do with his tiny new blood vessels still being sensitive to even slight changes in temperature. If it wasn't Rory, it was her relationship and what was happening to it. Or her job, which she was convinced Emma was out to get. Carrie had seen the hungry, ambitious look on Emma's face as she'd held up Adrian's BAFTA. It was as if she'd owned it herself. People had short memories in TV and were dazzled by shiny, new things, so the threat of being replaced by a brilliant, child-free twenty-something who had all the time in the world to dedicate to the company she worked for was a very real one.

She couldn't relax. The very idea of sex, of someone else needing a part of her when she was emotionally chopped up into so many pieces, made her nearly panic.

"You're joking, aren't you?" she said.

Adrian was doing his little-boy hurt look. "Actually, no."

"I've had four hours' sleep, Rory's finally dropped off, but I know, I just *know* he's going to wake again around midnight and last time it took me two hours to feed him and put him down again. Then it's going to happen all over again at about three-thirty."

They hadn't had sex since before Rory had been born, but she could barely muster the strength to climb the two flights of stairs to bed. Her outburst had sucked the energy out of the room and they looked at each other, neither knowing what to say. She shook her head.

"Sorry. It's just hard at the moment, you know?"

He nodded and she left the room, not daring to look back. She knew there would be an expression of utter disillusionment on Adrian's face and she couldn't bear to see it.

Somehow she needed to regain control of some part of her life. Rory was a law unto himself and she was afraid to admit that the problems in her marriage ran deep, ever since she'd decided to have a baby.

But Emma getting her job? Over her dead body.

16

"I want to come back." Carrie sat in Liz's office, across the desk from her. Rory was next to her, miraculously asleep in his stroller, and she could hear his little snuffling noises.

"What . . . ?" Liz's eyes opened wide as she tried to comprehend. "You mean . . . ?"

"Yes. Now. Or rather Monday. I want to come back to work."

"But we discussed three months. Rory's only six weeks old."

"Five. And I've changed my mind." She mentally blocked out the feelings of guilt that had been a constant torment, ever since she'd made her decision. *Keep looking ahead,* she instructed herself anxiously, feeling an impromptu desire to cry. If she looked at Rory, it might make her change her mind back again.

Liz shook her head, a leveling movement to try to make sense of what Carrie was saying. "Why?"

"I'm missing it." Carrie bit her tongue at the half-truth.

Liz laughed. "You've only just given birth! You're not thinking straight."

"I've found a nursery for Rory and they can

have him from next week." She saw Liz start at the suddenness of it all and felt a pang of anxiety. *Why am I having to fight for what is rightfully mine?*

Liz frowned. "Is it Emma? Are you worried she's not handling things? Because I can assure you, you've got absolutely *nothing* to worry about in that department. She's doing an amazing job and in fact is surpassing all our expectations. It's quite extraordinary really, considering how young she is."

"For God's sake, Liz, I'm coming back to work and there's nothing you can do to stop me!"

She hadn't meant to shout and Liz flinched; then her eyes rose to the glass window behind Carrie. Carrie turned and saw Emma walking past with two teas. She'd stalled at Carrie's outburst, clearly overhearing, but quickly hurried on again, eyes straight ahead.

Carrie turned back to find Liz watching her carefully.

"So . . . as I was saying . . ." said Liz as she smiled supportively, "you are okay with Emma, aren't you? Happy with the work she's done? I'd hate for you to be sacrificing your time with Rory because of any concerns. You can tell me anything in confidence."

"Oh yes, more than happy," said Carrie, forcing a smile. "She's been amazing. And her work on the scripts—brilliant." She didn't have to lie about that—Emma was exceptional. Carrie perfected a casual shrug. "I just want to come back to work, that's all. Want to get plugged in again. Going mad stuck at home with a small baby all day."

They laughed together and Carrie felt ashamed.

"Okay, if that's what you want," said Liz.

"It is, it really is. Thank you. Only . . ."

"Yes?"

"I'd like to work part-time. Still see a bit of Rory." The truth was she hadn't quite the heart to put him in the orphanage nursery for the whole week.

"I completely understand."

Carrie nodded in relief.

"Except that this isn't really a part-time gig. You know that . . ."

"I believe I can make it work."

Liz couldn't help laughing, a sound of incredulity, mixed with just the tiniest shade of disdain, of not quite believing what she'd just heard. "Carrie, the show is about to go into production . . ."

"I know, but—"

"It won't work."

Carrie almost decided to put Rory in the orphanage full-time, but she couldn't bring herself to do it. Instead she churned inside while she thought of ways to persuade her boss to agree to the impossible.

Liz softened her voice, but her message was clear. "I'm sorry, it's full-time or it just can't work. Not with filming about to start. Do you want to think about it?"

Crushed, Carrie nodded, then got up from the chair and left.

17

Emma knocked on Liz's door and awaited her invitation to come in. Then she entered and closed it softly behind her.

"I couldn't help overhearing . . . and it's fine. I know I'm contracted until the New Year, but if Carrie wants to come back sooner, then it's okay." In truth the possibility frightened her deeply, to lose another job, but alienating Carrie scared her more.

Liz smiled. "So you did hear. Well, it's not settled yet. There's an issue over hours."

Emma thought. "You mean, Carrie wants part-time?"

"Uh-huh. But that's not going to work. Anyway, I shouldn't be discussing this with you."

Liz looked away, as if the conversation were over, but Emma suddenly had something she wanted to say. "I . . . um, tell me if this is completely out of the question but . . . do you think Carrie would consider a job share? I mean, I'm not saying I should be a producer or anything," she reassured, quickly, "but I could stick around for the days she's not in—if that helps at all?"

Liz was watching her, pondering her proposal.

"Do you know, I think you might actually be on to something here. We've all noticed how well you've fitted in—and shown an aptitude beyond script editing. You've even taken some of the producing tasks over for me, dealt with them well." Liz paused. "Would you be interested in taking on more responsibility? Actually stepping up to producer? Carrie would still lead, but if you held the reins when she wasn't here, I think she could get what she wants."

Emma could not believe her luck. To think she'd come into this place as a humble script editor just a short time ago and now she had her first bite at the producing cherry.

"I'd love to."

Liz smiled. "Good. We'd make it official, and in recognition of your increased responsibility and input, there will be added remuneration."

"Wow . . . thank you."

"I think it would be best if you still did the full five days so you'll be working alongside Carrie. And between you and me, babies can be unpredictable. I've no doubt there'll be times when Carrie's called away. I'll have to clear all this with her, but I don't anticipate any problems. She's been singing your praises too."

Had she? Emma's heart soared.

For the rest of the day she could barely contain her excitement. She was going to be a producer!

18

As she journeyed home, Emma held her news close, letting the joy of it bubble over again and again. She became aware she was attracting curious looks—complete strangers were catching her eye and offering intrigued smiles. Lost in her own thoughts, she would be surprised by the attention and smile back.

I have a promotion!

Carrie likes my work!

What would her parents say? She couldn't wait to tell them, to see their faces light up. She was going to be a real producer on a real show. She was going to get a credit! Her mum and dad could watch TV and see her name, which would come up in one of the prestigious positions right at the start of the program. She'd never expected her offer of job sharing to be taken seriously, but how right she'd been to speak up. Everything was working out just as she'd hoped it would.

She jumped off the train and hurried the few streets in the dark to her house. A welcoming light was glowing outside. She let herself in and took off her shoes, hung up her coat, then went into the kitchen, brimming with excitement and anticipation.

Alice looked up from stirring something on the stove, an apron over her blouse and navy skirt. "Oh, hi, Emma. Is it still raining?"

"No, not anymore."

Brian was setting the table. "You joining us?"

"Yes." She was put off balance by the question—she always did unless she called ahead to say she'd be late—but decided to bury the vague sense of not being included.

"Good day?" asked Alice.

Emma felt the joy surge in her again. She beamed at them, but her mother was adding salt and her father was inspecting the cleanliness of a wineglass.

Go on, tell them! Oh God, she was nervous as hell.

"Actually, I've had a rather spectacular day."

Both of them looked at her, surprised. Suddenly noticing her excitement.

"I've officially been asked to job-share as a producer."

It took a moment for this to sink in; then Alice's face tentatively lit up. "Really? How come?"

"The woman I've been covering for is coming back from maternity leave but only wants to work part-time—and so I'm going to be doing the role with her."

"So, you'll be part-time too?" asked Brian, dubiously.

"No." Emma couldn't keep the triumphant note

out of her voice. "They want me full-time. That way I can support the lead producer more."

"Well . . . seems like you've made quite an impression," said Alice, breaking into a full smile and coming over. She gave Emma a delicate hug. "Congratulations, darling."

Emma grinned. "Thanks."

"Yes, well done, Emma," said Brian, and although Emma could detect the note of surprise in his voice, she didn't care.

Brian suddenly let the good news take hold and went to the fridge. "This calls for a celebration." He pulled out a bottle of champagne. Away went the dubiously clean wineglasses and out came the flutes.

"So what exactly does this mean you'll be doing?" asked Alice, holding her glass out as Brian filled it. She clinked Emma's glass.

"I'm going to be coproducing," said Emma, still relishing the sound of her new position, "on a show for the BBC."

She saw her father puff up with a carefully measured, very restrained approval and her heart swelled.

"The BBC," repeated Alice, looking at her daughter in a new light. Emma knew she was already thinking about which of her friends she could tell this piece of news, just subtly dropped into conversation. "And you're producing, you say?"

Her mother was checking the facts for her story. "Coproducing," Emma corrected.

"It's still being a producer, though?" confirmed Alice.

"It is. I'll be the junior half of the team but—"

"Don't put yourself down. No one ever gave out prizes to those who declared themselves not winners," said Brian.

She wasn't putting herself down, just being accurate, but Emma didn't feel like laboring the point.

"To think we'd almost given up on you," he added jovially.

Emma smiled briefly.

"Did you get good terms?"

"Yes, more than fair salary."

"Holidays?"

"Well, I probably won't be taking any as it's going to be full on until we shoot; then it's almost impossible once you start filming, but yes, on a pro rata basis."

"Pro rata?" said Brian. "I thought you said it was full-time?"

"It is. But it's still a contract . . . fixed term . . ." She tailed off as their faces contorted with confusion.

"Fixed term?" asked Alice.

"Yes."

"So it's not a *permanent* job, then," said Brian, flatly.

"No . . . Not many are in this business."

"But the person you're covering for—hers is a permanent job?"

"Well, yes, but . . ." Emma felt all her earlier excitement evaporate. "This is a big deal, you know, to be offered such a step up." She felt angry with herself for sounding like a child, for pleading with them.

Alice waited just a moment too long for it to sound authentic. "Oh yes," she said, "we can see." She suddenly went back to stirring the contents of the saucepan, tutting as she realized she'd left it too long and it had stuck on the bottom.

Emma looked at her father. He, too, had turned away and was continuing to set the table.

She was about to say something else, to angrily defend herself, but she'd seen the looks of frustration and embarrassment on her parents' faces and closed her mouth abruptly. As she did, everything became crystal clear. *How could she not have seen it before?* These people would never be satisfied unless she did exactly what *they* perceived was successful, a certain career, a certain pathway to obtain it. She could win a dozen awards, make a huge amount of money, but it would never be good enough.

A little part of her soul changed its molecular makeup forever, became as hard as a stone and settled in the pit of her stomach.

19

Wednesday, November 22

Carrie was incandescent with rage. she stomped around the kitchen but in a controlled, muted way as Rory was asleep in his Moses basket on the dining table. All she wanted to do was kick and shout, but instead she gripped the edge of the work surface and let out a strangled, muffled scream of frustration.

How dare she?

It was obvious now, what had been going on. Emma wanted her job and had been doing everything she could to get it.

Well, she wasn't having it.

Except Carrie would now have to job-share, an idea that made her feel so impotent, it physically weakened her. It was *temporary,* she reminded herself and breathed deeply, again and again until she could regain some composure. The deep inhales began to make her feel dizzy and she quickly sat down at the breakfast bar as the room spun. A jar of utensils seemed to move across the worktop, and she realized she was hallucinating now from the lack of sleep. She held her head in her hands until the room settled.

When Liz had suggested the new arrangement, Carrie had had no choice. Liz was keen, Adrian delighted, and she'd walked right into it by pretending she had no issue with Emma. She'd casually tried to suggest someone else, but it was pointless and made her sound stupid, as Emma clearly knew the scripts inside out. Liz had presented what she said was a choice but they all knew was a fait accompli, and Carrie had to smile and nod and agree how serendipitous it all was, how lucky they'd found such a good replacement to enable her to "have her cake and eat it."

She looked across at Rory and once again felt the helplessness, the painful guilt at resenting the fact his presence meant she could no longer do her job the way she wanted to do it. But the alternative was putting him in that nursery from seven in the morning until seven at night, five days a week, something that made her feel hopelessly sad.

Carrie had another flurry of disquiet—maybe Emma *was* singularly brilliant. She stood up, nerves in the pit of her stomach dislodging her from her seat.

One thing she was certain of was that Liz wanted people around her who would make her look good, such as Adrian, the superstar writer, or Emma, the new, bright, young thing. It was a business of self-preservation and self-advancement.

And if Carrie knew what was good for her, she would shut up and put up.

Even if there was a better way of handling it, she had no idea what it was. She was just too tired to think.

20

They had a desk next to each other in the open-plan area and Carrie calculated that on her workdays, she spent nine of her daily waking hours in close proximity to Emma, more than her husband and certainly more than her son, whom she dropped off at seven in the morning and didn't see again until she picked him up in the evening, only to put him to bed. She kept up civilities, though, especially as now she was back in the office she could see just what an impact Emma had made.

Liz would joke with her, ask her opinion on new pitches that came in from various writers, just placing a printout on her desk with a casual, "What do you think?" which was really an invitation for Emma to voice her opinion in the inner sanctum, and Carrie knew by the way the proposals kept coming—some, she noticed as she glanced over, created by very reputable writers—that Emma's opinion was very highly valued.

Emma was careful not to alienate her, though, noted Carrie, and was almost obsequious with her attentive behavior, following her around like a puppy, always under her feet. Carrie kept the relationship professional, making sure Emma was in the loop on information and decisions (albeit occasionally choosing precisely when to impart certain things, just for the hell of it). There was a coolness, though, in the way Carrie spoke to Emma, something that was noticed in this easygoing business in which hugs were free flowing and people often addressed each other as "darling," "gorgeous," "wonderful," or some other gushing form of address. Whenever Liz noticed and looked at her askance, she'd turn up the thermometer a little, keep her resentment deeply hidden.

She couldn't bring herself to relax fully around Emma, though, suspicious as she was of her, and once Liz had asked: "Everything working out with you and Emma?" It had been said casually enough, but the question was as loaded as a Kalashnikov and just as deadly.

"Fine," said Carrie, "we're really getting into a rhythm together."

Liz was approaching their desks now and Carrie looked up, piqued by the fact Emma's was closer to the walkway, and therefore she was always at the forefront when receiving news.

"Hi, guys. Luke's asked for a meet to catch up on everything, seeing as we're a month from filming," said Liz.

Carrie made sure she replied first. "Great. When?"

"Next Thursday," said Liz, wrinkling her nose in a gesture of mild sympathy.

What? She didn't work Thursdays! "Can't we look at another day?" Carrie asked, trying to remain cool. She felt deliberately excluded. Why had this date been agreed on?

"He's off for two weeks to the Caribbean, then it's New Year's—and that's just too close to filming."

Carrie grit her teeth. "What about before?"

"I've tried, but his assistant says he's back to back. Getting everything in before he goes away." Liz paused. "I've mentioned it's difficult for you, but he's happy if you can write up a report and then Emma and I can just meet him to go through everything. Adrian will be there too."

They'll all be there. Everyone but me. Carrie's insides churned and she felt her smile falter. She was clearly the inconvenience, worse, the one who was dispensable. The meeting with the channel commissioner about her show could take place without her.

Emma's silence was telling—no doubt she was looking forward to stepping into her shoes, thought Carrie, darkly.

She suddenly sat up in defiance. "Fine. I'll just bring Rory."

Liz looked alarmed. "What?"

"He's getting into a routine now. What time's the meeting?"

"Ten-thirty."

"Perfect! Rory sleeps between ten and twelve."

"I'm really not sure that's a good idea."

"It's just for an hour or so. It'll be fine." Carrie had a flinty note to her voice. "He's not going to be in the room. He can be in your office and if he wakes, which he won't, then I can just pop out for two minutes."

She knew the madness of it even as she was speaking but refused to back down. She was damned if she was going to miss this meeting.

Liz, she saw, was tight-lipped but wasn't going to argue anymore.

"Excuse me," called Zack, from across the bank of desks. "I've got Michael Sheen's agent on the phone. Wants to talk to the producer of *Leon*."

"Fine, put him through," said Carrie, turning to her phone.

"Um . . ." Zack blushed. "He's actually asking for Emma."

Carrie was struck dumb for a moment, and it was as if they had all stalled in some sort of freeze frame.

Emma was the first to recover. "Put him through to Carrie. She's the lead producer."

She sounded so authoritative, her words actually had the opposite effect, and humiliated, Carrie

132

felt like the junior individual as she picked up the phone.

As she began to speak, Emma tactfully moved away.

Despite the torrential rain, Carrie had decided to walk to BAFTA, where she regularly held meetings when she needed a change from the office. Her shoulders had been rigid with tension ever since the morning's events and desperate to get out, she'd left early. The journey was a constant battle with the wind and rain, which had left her even more worked up than when she'd departed, and she half stumbled into the quiet sanctuary of 195 Piccadilly with a sense of exhaustion.

Someone took her wet coat and umbrella running with rivulets of water; then she found her writer—a woman she knew from one of her previous shows—and they took two coffees to a table by the window. The bar was on the first floor and was light and airy with huge windows overlooking Piccadilly's seventeenth-century creamy white buildings, the tops of the red buses gliding past beneath them. She began to relax and they spent a pleasant time chatting over possible new ideas to explore together. The writer had to rush off after an hour, but Carrie stayed on and checked her phone, answering a few e-mails rather than going back to the tense atmosphere of the office.

Craving another coffee, she got up to go to the bar and bumped straight into a formidable redhead.

"Elaine!"

"Well, if it isn't TV's most popular producer. Aren't you supposed to be pregnant?"

"Rory was born seven weeks ago."

"A boy. Congratulations." She looked around the room. "Where is he?"

"At his nursery."

"You palmed him off already?" Elaine smiled broadly. "Needed to get back to the job, eh? Never know who might be waiting in line to nobble your spot."

She always knew just how to get under my skin. Outwardly, Carrie ignored the jibe. "Life treating you well?"

"If you count having to wait nine damn months for the BBC to get back to me on a submission, then it's marvelous. I don't have your instant commissioning prowess, you see. Not anymore."

Carrie knew it couldn't be as bad as Elaine painted it. Elaine had been in the business for several decades; she was a survivor who always had something up her sleeve.

Elaine started to move off. "Well, lovely to gossip . . ."

Carrie suddenly remembered something, placed her hand quickly on Elaine's arm. "Just one thing . . . you had an Emma Fox working for you a while back. Last year?"

Uninterested, Elaine continued to make a bee-line for one of BAFTA's quintessential turquoise high-backed chairs. "Don't remember."

"Tall. Blonde. Very bright."

Elaine stopped, her face registering. "Oh yes. The intern."

"Intern?" said Carrie, surprised. "I thought she was an assistant script editor?"

Elaine laughed, a hearty guffaw. "Is that what she called herself? The little fibber. She made tea and photocopied. Shame really, she showed potential, but she seriously fucked up. Had to get rid of her."

Carrie's heart leapt. "Why, what did she do?"

"Russell!" gushed Elaine, striding over to the entrance without even a second thought to Carrie. Her writer had clearly arrived, and Carrie noted wryly he was a big player—Elaine was still doing okay. She was desperate to ask Elaine more about Emma but knew she'd not get anything else out of her today so, with a last-longing look back, she left the building. Out on the gray rain-soaked pavements of Piccadilly, she opened her umbrella once more and hurried back to the office.

At her desk, Carrie returned Emma's welcoming smile and willingly accepted her offer to make them both a cup of tea. As soon as Emma was in the kitchen, Carrie dug out the folder with the crew résumés. At the bottom was Emma's, which Liz had handed to her all those weeks ago.

Her eyes scanned down—there it was. Assistant script editor working across various developments for Elaine Marsh's company. She stuffed the résumé into her handbag as Emma came over with two steaming mugs.

"Thanks," she said, smiling more warmly than perhaps she had in a long time.

Emma was hiding something. Not just the little expansion on her job title, a common enough crime in such a competitive industry, but the reason she'd left. She'd told them her contract was up. Not true, according to Elaine.

Carrie felt herself regain something of a foothold on her crumbling position. Maybe Emma wasn't the golden girl everyone thought her to be. What was it Elaine had said? She'd "seriously fucked up."

Carrie glanced at her cohort out of the corner of her eye, her mind wondering.

What had she done?

21

He loved his baths. Carrie held Rory while he kicked his legs in his own uncoordinated way, surprised and fascinated by the wet stuff that seemed to appear out of nowhere and land on him. Her back ached from leaning over the tub and Carrie creaked as she stood. Her body had never felt so battered, not just from giving birth, but from the inability to get enough rest to recover properly, and she reflected again on how childbirth was a young person's game.

She wrapped Rory in a towel and got him ready for bed, finding herself giving a running commentary on everything as she did it. *"Let's pat you dry," "Diaper time!" "Where's those arms?"* She sometimes wondered if this was part of the natural progression of slipping into madness.

As she snapped up his sleepsuit, eternally grateful for the baby changing unit so she didn't have to kneel on the floor, she gave him a smile just before she picked him up. Then something totally unexpected happened.

He smiled back.

She stopped still, thinking she'd imagined it. There was only one way to find out for sure.

She smiled at him again.

Again, he returned it.

She let out a laugh, a mad, bewildered peal. Then scooped him up and hurried down the two flights of stairs, the smell of a beef casserole growing ever stronger as she descended to the kitchen.

Adrian looked up from peeling potatoes, unused to her moving with such energy.

"What's wrong?" he asked.

"Guess what?"

"What?"

"Rory *smiled*. He actually smiled."

Adrian put down the peeler with interest. "Oh yeah?"

She held Rory upright in her arms, so he faced Adrian. "Go on, show Daddy." Rory seemed oblivious. Carrie looked up at Adrian. "You have to smile at him first."

Adrian hesitated and then under her insistent gaze moved closer and waggled his fingers. "Hello, mate."

Rory started to grumble, rubbed his eyes with his fists.

"Go on, again," said Carrie, encouragingly.

"Hi, Rory. Woo-hoo." Adrian waved at him again.

Rory started to cry.

Adrian shrugged. "Guess he's all out of smiles."

"He's just tired," said Carrie quickly. She'd seen the distance in Adrian's eyes, hated the feeling of panic it raised in her. "I'll put him down," she said, "then come and help you with the mash."

She walked back up the stairs, rocking Rory as his crying had started in earnest now. A combination of patting him on the back and a continuous shushing noise at a volume loud enough to make her throat sore meant he was starting to drop off once she'd reached her bedroom. She carefully laid him in the Moses basket, let her warm hand rest on his tummy for a moment, then slowly took it away and backed out of the room.

A pair of hands rested on her waist. She jumped.

"Wanna get freaky?" Adrian said in her ear, and led her to the spare room.

They kissed and his hands roamed. She knew the curtains were open and the room faced out onto the street, so she broke away and went to close them, realizing she was nervous and taking her time.

"Don't worry about that," said Adrian, impatiently.

"We're not giving the neighbors a free show," she said.

When she turned around, he was already naked on the bed and she giggled. He patted the sheet next to him. She slipped off her dress, conscious of her post-pregnancy body, and then got quickly under the covers next to him.

They looked at each other, reacquainting themselves with the prelude to intimacy, something that hadn't happened in so long it felt strange. They kissed again and hands touched bodies, stroking, caressing. With a sense of joy and relief, for a part of her had been dreading this moment, Carrie began to get into it. Her hands moved lower and she was surprised to find he wasn't ready. She sensed his embarrassment and tried to reassure him with her hands, but after a few more minutes, he rolled away.

"Guess I wasn't in the mood."

He was staring up at the ceiling and she moved closer to him, putting her hand carefully on his chest. She could see he was frustrated.

"Been wanking furiously the last few weeks. Thinking about nothing except this—us—and now . . ."

"It's okay," she said.

He got up, started to put his clothes back on. "Better get the spuds on or we'll never eat. It's getting late."

Carrie glanced at the clock. It was seven-thirty. Not late at all. Not unless you were in bed at eight-thirty because you had to get up several times in the night for a baby.

Back in the kitchen, they worked together, mostly in silence, just exchanging the odd practicality: "Please can you grab the butter from the fridge?" "Water or juice?"

Once they were sitting at the table, Adrian looked up at her, apologetic.

"I might go and work at the beach house tomorrow."

Dismay gripped her. "But . . ."

He responded before she could really say anything. "It's just hard, you know? Being able to concentrate. And I don't want to be a grump—Rory's only small, of course he's going to cry—but I just need the space to crack on."

She'd been looking forward to her day off and being at home with both Rory and Adrian, and briefly thought about trying to persuade him to stay but was suddenly exhausted by it all. The gulf between them was widening faster than she could close it.

Her original vision for this period in their lives was being able to spend more time together. Instead of her working long hours every day in the office and Adrian writing at home, she'd had this cozy, romantic notion of her pottering around the house with their baby, him coming out for breaks and draping a protective arm around her shoulders, drinking in the scent of his newborn son's head. The three of them together. It was almost laughable how she'd got it so wrong.

22

Adrian insisted on picking her up at the station, and as Emma came out into the road outside she had no trouble finding the silver BMW he'd texted her to look out for as it was in the parking space directly opposite; the only shiny thing amongst the gray tarmac and furiously scudding dark clouds. He waved as she appeared and she crossed the road, the wind propelling her over; then she opened the car door, her coat sliding smoothly across the leather seating as she got in. She was immediately enveloped in a warm, luxuriant cocoon. Outside she could see other passengers battling against the wind as they walked, eyes screwed up and shoulders hunched against the cold.

"Thanks for coming down," said Adrian, raising his voice over the radio, a funk tune courtesy of a youth-orientated, cutting edge music station.

"No problem." Emma put on her seat belt and looked around at her sporty surroundings. She glanced over her shoulder, noticed it was a two-seater. No room for baby seats.

They set off down the main road toward the town center, which was strung with Christmas lights, unlovely and characterless until dusk; then she saw the sea, glimpsed between the buildings, a heaving gray mass flecked with shards of turquoise when the sun escaped through the clouds for brief seconds.

Emma had had no idea Carrie and Adrian owned a second home by the sea until he'd called her that morning saying he needed her to work over some scenes, and if it wasn't too much trouble, could she get the train from London, fully reimbursed of course. As she hung up, she wondered about this new place, whether it was somewhere Adrian escaped to write. Whether it was somewhere he kept his private documents, and she felt a cold thrill as she sensed new possibilities.

They drove through the town, Emma catching glimpses of the sea between the buildings; then they turned north, along residential streets. After a few minutes, Adrian pulled into a wide, quiet road, where up ahead two large metal posts blocked both the entrance and exit ways. A large sign across the central brick barrier announced they were entering the North Foreland Private Estate and that CCTV was monitoring those who entered.

The entrance barrier obligingly descended into the ground as Adrian drove over a metal plate in the road and Emma sat up, taken aback by the size of the properties. She caught glimpses of grand houses hidden behind six-foot-high fences or large, tightly planted evergreens, a breathtaking tease at something majestic that was immediately hidden from view again as they moved on. Not all of the houses were concealed. Some displayed their ostentatiousness proudly: a white cubic mansion with full-length glass balconies, a three-storied mock Tudor manor.

They drove toward the sea, closer and closer until Emma thought they'd go right over the cliff edge, but then the road swung left and they followed the cliff top, the edge vertiginously close. The road curved around, hugging the line of the chalky cliff, and at each bend Emma could see the drop, a sheer plummet to the beach and the churning waves below. Adrian stopped the car and reached over to the glove compartment with a polite "Excuse me," then pulled out a remote control that parted a set of iron gates, flanked on either side by huge, dense pine trees.

They drove up a wide brick driveway and Emma caught her breath at the sprawling, imposing dark-brick house ahead of her. Just off its center was an Arts and Craft style roundel, the more noticeable as it was rendered white. The windows were large and made up of several smaller panes, and when the sun caught them they reflected the sea back at her. This house had one of the lucky positions facing directly out to the Channel.

Adrian turned off the engine, and Emma got

out of the car and was immediately caught in a gust that tried to whip her head off. She pulled at her coat and deliberately faced into the enemy. It was coming from beyond the road, from the vast expanse of open air and slate-gray sea that she could glimpse through the gates and beyond the cliff edge. Then she looked behind her, holding her pummeled hair away from her eyes, and saw a white octagonal lighthouse on the higher ground just outside the estate.

"The North Foreland Lighthouse," said Adrian; then he pointed southward down the coast. "And just a short way down there: Bleak House." He spoke with a note of pride in his voice. "Dickens's residence when he wrote *David Copperfield*. And here on this very estate"—he waved his arm with a flourish—"The Thirty-Nine Steps. As in John Buchan. A hidden staircase that goes down through the cliff into the sea. The book was written here where he lived," he added, and threw his arms up into the wind with a self-deprecating grin. "A town of genius writers!"

He might be pretending to joke, but Emma knew he secretly wanted to consider himself in this category and so she laughed obligingly.

"Want a tour?" asked Adrian.

Emma looked up at the house. "Sure."

"No, I mean the steps. All us residents have a private key. Come on!"

He led her out of the driveway and back down

the road they'd just driven along. The cliff edge was to Emma's left, just a few yards from some tufted, windswept grass, and there was no fence, she noted, and kept her distance.

"Tide's coming in," Adrian said, peering cautiously over. "We'll have to be quick."

The wind whipped her face, its roar mixing with the crashing waves and the screech of seagulls. After a few minutes they came to a wooded area, a tiny copse grown out of the tufted grass. It was surrounded by a metal fence and Adrian led her to the entrance gate and, pulling a key out of his pocket, opened it. A large yellow hazard triangle with a picture of a falling man warned of the imminent slipperiness. Another sign declared the area dangerous and stated that the authorities washed their hands of any injury during use.

Emma could see the first few steps heading down into a door-shaped hole in the rock—a dark, cavernous mouth that led into the belly of the cliff.

"Does it go all the way down to the beach?" she asked in awe.

"Yep, some people say it was used for smuggling back in the day," said Adrian. "Come on."

He bounced down the steps in his eagerness to show her, his slight, wiry body navigating the stairs easily.

"We're going down?" asked Emma.

"Course."

"But what about the sign?"

"Sign schmign."

Emma cautiously followed, realizing quickly that Adrian had disappeared into the darkness. Suddenly a light came on ahead—he'd switched on the flashlight on his phone.

A damp, salty smell enveloped her as she descended, and she touched the walls of the stairwell, shivering at their cold clamminess. Because Adrian was pointing at the beam ahead, she couldn't see her footing properly and found herself slipping more than once, grabbing a rusty handrail to steady herself. Some of the steps were crumbling and she once again questioned the sanity of going down there, but Adrian was determinedly striding onward. After a while they came out of the shaft and into a tunnel section, where up above her Emma could just glimpse the remnants of light fixtures in the shadows. It seemed to go on forever, step after step after step, zigzagging through another shaft and two more tunnels. The darkness was claustrophobic; the cold, dank air stuck in her throat. As she descended, the sound of the waves grew ever louder, echoing up through the stairwell, and then finally, a glimmer of gray daylight ahead. Emma took the last few steps especially carefully as they were strewn with wet seaweed; then she was spat out of the chalk tunnel and onto the beach.

Adrian was beaming at her, delighted with his

adventure. "There are more than thirty-nine of the buggers, eh?"

She smiled tightly and assessed the tide. The sea was crashing up onto the beach, the waves nipping at their ankles. As she cast her eye up and down the coast, she realized there was no escape. The only way out was back up the steps.

On the road once more, Adrian was still on a high as they returned to the house. Emma was shivering from the cold.

"Let me get you a coffee," said Adrian as he led her inside. She watched as he keyed in the code to the alarm and went bouncing into what she saw was the kitchen. A radio station had been left playing and Adrian did some moves as he got two mugs out of the cupboard and filled them with coffee from a shiny chrome machine on the worktop.

"Nice place," said Emma, admiring the spacious, modern kitchen. It was huge, all gleaming black work surfaces and rich oak cupboards. A silver fridge the size of a double wardrobe barely filled a wall; next to it was a floor-to-ceiling wine cooler.

"Thanks. *Generation Rebel* paid for it."

Did it now. Emma smiled. "That's nice of *Generation Rebel*."

"Nice of the Americans to buy the format. Hey, look, we have our own pizza oven," he said, opening a stainless-steel letter-box-shaped oven door and demonstrating by taking a long-handled wooden pizza peel and pretending to shimmy in a pizza.

Emma kept her smile in place and continued to do so throughout the "casual" tour, Adrian blithely reeling off rooms with a waft of his hand, but she saw the lingering pride in his eyes as they flickered over his very own beach house. It was magnificent, the kind of property that would feature in magazines. The dining room table seated twelve comfortably; you could sit in the white oval bathtub and look out to sea. There was even a games room and a bar. From the landing window, Emma could see a pool, covered for winter, which took up a fraction of the large garden.

"And here's the office," he said, coming to a sizable room on the first floor in the roundel. It was dominated by a large telescope, which pointed out of the window toward the sea.

"Go on," he insisted.

Emma leaned over and put the glass to her eye. Suddenly the heaving waves seemed within touching distance. She swung the telescope back onto the estate, stopping when she picked up the small, wooded area just a short distance from the house, almost on the cliff edge itself. There were his thirty-nine steps.

Adrian took a seat at an enormous desk, a place designed to pull back shoulders and flex arm muscles. He was like a concert pianist preparing to conquer his instrument. His fingers struck at the keys of his computer.

Emma sat at the window seat: found she liked to look out, was mesmerized by the cold block of churning water.

As Adrian started to talk through the script, she listened, interjected, suggested, all the while realizing how reliant he seemed to have become on her. Maybe it was second project nerves; after such a mammoth hit, they were all aware of the pressure to deliver, none more so, she knew, than Adrian. As they worked, Emma took in the room. The leather sofa, the handmade oak bookcases that fitted into the snug corners of the roundel, the comic book canvas prints of Wonder Woman and Superman on the walls. She couldn't see from where she was sitting, but there were probably drawers underneath the titan of a desk. Drawers that she'd like to look through. There was also an oak unit to her right, again curved with two doors either side of a set of three drawers. If only she had Superman's x-ray vision so she could see inside. There was also, bizarrely, a framed pair of handcuffs hanging on the wall. He saw her looking.

"From the set," he explained, gleefully. "Used to cuff the Headmaster. They're the real McCoy. We had to have a special advisor on set, just in case he needed to get free quickly."

After a couple of hours, they'd discussed enough for Adrian to be able to continue writing, and Emma knew he preferred to be alone for a bit.

"How about I go and fix us some lunch?" she suggested.

Adrian pulled a face. "There's nothing here. House has been empty a while."

"I can go to the shop? If you point me in the right direction."

Adrian pulled something out of his pocket and tossed it to Emma, who caught it deftly.

"Take the car," he said with a grin, and she looked down at the set of keys. "The one with the green cap is for the house so you can let yourself back in. The car's self-explanatory."

"Are you sure?" Emma could tell the BMW was his pride and joy.

"You have a license, right?"

"Of course."

"Then you're insured. Go for it."

"Okay." She smiled and took the two twenties Adrian gave her and was about to leave the room when he spoke again.

"Thank you, Emma."

She turned back, puzzled. "For getting lunch?"

"No, for coming out here, being so good on the scripts. They've . . . really gone up a level. I can't tell you how brilliant it's been since you've joined."

She could see he was deeply grateful, and she

thought she could even detect a hint of relief. "I enjoy it," she said matter-of-factly. "And I like working with Carrie. She's an amazing producer. I find her inspirational." She didn't know if he believed her or not.

The wind seemed to be pushing her away as she fought it down the drive to the car and she looked back once to see if Adrian was watching her, but the window she'd been sitting at five minutes before was empty.

Emma drove down to the gates and remembered they were electronic. She fumbled in the glove compartment for the remote and after a click they started to glide open. She headed out of the estate, the steel bollard disappearing into the ground as she drove over the pressure activated plate. As she checked the public road for traffic, a car pulled into the estate, slowing as the driver saw her face. It was an older, well-dressed woman, perhaps in her late sixties, and she stared at her, frowning. A small pug was in the passenger seat, also giving her a baleful glare. Emma wound down her window.

"Is everything okay?" she asked, politely.

The woman looked a bit taken aback but recovered quickly. "I was just wondering," she said, "who you were as you are driving my neighbor's car."

I stole it, Emma felt like saying but had a sense the joke would fall flat on her audience. "I work for Adrian. He's at the house writing and so I'm just running out for some lunch." The woman appeared to mellow at the mention of Adrian. Emma smiled. "It's good to see everyone looks out for each other here. I'm Emma, by the way."

The woman nodded and then, seemingly satisfied, drove on her way. *Don't introduce yourself then,* thought Emma as she watched the woman disappear into the estate from her rearview mirror.

She headed for the town center and, finding a deli, got warm quiches and some soup. As an afterthought she added two large chocolate brownies.

As she walked back to the car she took a little detour, crossing the road to a reheeling place she'd spotted on the way down. She hovered outside for a moment, looking through the tinsel-framed window. She'd considered her options again and again that morning. There was no other way. Emma went in and asked the man behind the counter to make a copy of the key with the green cap. It only took a few minutes; then she left.

"Smells fantastic," said Adrian, bounding down the stairs as he heard her come in. "Car okay?"

"Slight dent on the offside front wing when I hit one of your neighbors' cars. Blue Volvo? Older lady, green hat with a feather, small pug on the front seat, both with a look of suspicion?"

"Geraldine?" There was a millisecond of alarm. "I take it you're joking?"

She grinned and he relaxed. "You know her, then?" she said. "She seemed quite perturbed to see me driving your car."

"She's a nosy old thing. Lives in the road behind us. Her plot backs onto ours. She probably wondered who you were." Adrian looked inside the bag of food. "She'll be thinking I've got a bit on the side."

Emma stopped still, taken aback, her insides curdling at his words. Why would he say that? Deeply uncomfortable, she looked at him, but he was unpacking the lunch. He glanced up. Smiled.

"Do you mind getting a couple of glasses out of the cupboard?" He pointed behind her.

Flustered, Emma reached back and opened up a cupboard door.

"The next one," said Adrian, and she opened another and was faced with a row of gleaming glasses. She collected herself before she turned back again, but now he was getting some cutlery out of the drawer. Had she been mistaken? At the time she'd had the feeling he'd known what he'd said, had in fact said it deliberately, thrown it out as a hook to test her. But maybe she'd been wrong.

"What would you like to drink?" she asked.

Adrian wistfully patted another chrome machine. "I'd do you a juice, but we've no fruit. I've got rum," he said. "That's something I never run out of. Better not get started on that, though—no idea where it'll lead us." He laughed and looked her in the eye.

Uneasy, Emma turned her back and filled two glasses from the tap, looking out into the garden. "It's a lovely place you've got here. Be great when Rory's older—bring him to the beach."

He was silent so long she thought he might have left the room. She turned and he gave a tight smile.

"Yeah, can't quite imagine that now. All he seems to do is cry, eat, sleep."

"That's like all babies, isn't it?"

"Is it?"

Well, she didn't know, but he should—he was the one with a child. She hid the thought and smiled. "I'm not an expert, but that's my general understanding."

"I'm no expert either." He was smiling back conspiratorially at her and she was uncomfortable with how he seemed to want to align himself with her.

Adrian sat at the table, opposite her, and cut a mouthful of quiche. "So how about you? Have holidays by the seaside when you were growing up?"

"Sort of. My parents have a place in Italy, on Lake Maggiore. So it was a lake beach as opposed to the ocean."

"The Italian Lakes? Nice."

"Yeah, they'd both done well in their respective careers before I came along."

"Late addition?"

"My mum was in her forties."

"And your dad?"

"Same."

"So were you . . . I mean, had they been trying for a family for long?"

She raised her eyebrows.

"Sorry. I've overstepped the mark."

"It's okay. My parents had trouble conceiving."

"Didn't give up, though. Must've been keen to have a child."

"They were. Extremely. They went to great lengths to have me."

He exhaled heavily. "Wow. It really hits some people hard, eh. That need to procreate. But it's good," he added, seeing her face. "Good that they were both happy to have a"—here he took a large intake of breath—"massive change of lifestyle."

"For a while. I was sent to boarding school," she explained.

"Ah. Guess that's always an option for Rory," he joked.

Don't you dare, thought Emma. "It was pretty miserable," she said lightly.

"And your parents?"

"What about them?"

He hesitated. "Still together?"

She looked at him. He made her skin crawl. What a shitbag. Discussing all this, albeit in a shoddy veiled way with her. But she smiled warmly, almost encouragingly, and said, "Very much so."

23

Thursday, December 14

"Marsh Pictures," singsonged the receptionist.

"Hello, could I please speak to Elaine Marsh?" asked Carrie. It was the fourth time she'd called since she'd bumped into Elaine at BAFTA, just over a week ago. Each time she'd gotten through to her assistant, Leanne, and then been fobbed off with some lame excuse. She knew they were excuses, as even Leanne was starting to sound embarrassed. Carrie grit her teeth, waiting to be put through, knowing she was deliberately being made to sweat. She was being punished for stealing Adrian away.

"Hello?"

"Hi, Leanne. It's Carrie Kennedy again. Is Elaine around?"

"Just a minute."

Again, Carrie heard the tell-tale self-conscious note in Leanne's voice that told her Elaine was likely sitting in her office, a couple of yards from her PA.

As she waited to learn if she would be graced with Elaine's phone presence, she continued to push Rory's pram, back and forth at the top of the stairwell. This wasn't a conversation she could have in the open-plan office, and her husband occupied the conference room, so she'd been forced out here to try and talk to Elaine at the same time as trying to get Rory to sleep after his feeding. At the moment Rory was being the more compliant.

"I'm really sorry, Carrie, but Elaine's on another call at the moment."

Carrie bristled. "Bull*shit*."

"I . . . You what?"

"I know perfectly well she's not, so don't waste your breath lying for her. ELAINE, I KNOW YOU'RE LISTENING IN TO THIS CALL," Carrie shouted into her phone, "AND SOONER OR LATER YOU'RE GOING TO HAVE TO TALK TO ME."

A wail started up from the pram. What the hell had she been thinking? She quickly pushed Rory up and down the short landing and he began to settle again.

"As I said, Elaine's . . . otherwise engaged," said Leanne, curtly. "Can I take a message?"

Carrie hung up. She took a few deep breaths. Luke from the BBC was arriving soon and she had to be at the top of her game. She lifted and dropped her shoulders several times, trying to release the tension, the tiredness. Glancing down at the stroller, she saw Rory was asleep and, now that he was getting into a routine, should remain so for the next two hours. At least something was going to plan.

She carefully wheeled him back into the office and then into Liz's room. Checking he was settled, she then hurried back to her desk to look for the casting DVDs for the meeting. Her desk seemed to be a pile of papers and she rummaged frantically but couldn't find them.

"Are you looking for these?"

Carrie glanced up to see Emma holding up the DVDs.

"I've gone through them and marked the time codes of our frontrunners," said Emma. "Make it easier when we're playing it for Luke."

"Thanks," said Carrie tersely. *Why does Emma always have to undermine me?*

"And I've just spoken to the art department. They're finishing up Leon's living room as we speak—got some great kitsch props from his time as a hot-shot actor, so that should be fun to see. They've even got a grass-topped coffee table!" Emma laughed and Carrie bit her tongue and forced the briefest of smiles in return.

Emma faltered. "Is there something wrong?"

"No. What could be wrong?"

"I don't know . . . It's just . . . sometimes I feel that I'm not supporting you the way you'd like me to."

Carrie looked at her. "Luke's going to be here in a minute. Are we ready?"

"I'll just go and check the TV's working in the meeting room," said Emma, heading away.

161

Carrie sat down abruptly. She had to get a grip. They needed to be able to work together, and she certainly shouldn't let something as petty as Emma's enthusiasm get her down. It was a waste of energy. Let her do the checks, the grunt work. It was useful. Carrie got up to see how the conference room was looking—and to prove to them both that she could be a little more pleasant to be around.

She saw Emma first through the glass window. She was bent over the DVD player, pressing buttons, making sure everything was coming on. Adrian was sitting on the sofa going through his script—except his eyes weren't on the page; instead they were looking at Emma's shapely backside, clad in black jeans.

Neither had any idea Carrie was there. She hesitated a moment and then jumped as she heard Luke's voice ring out. She turned to the reception area to greet him.

"He's brilliant," said Luke, as the actor reading for the part of Leon's agent went through his lines on-screen. "Got a really good ruthless quality to him."

"He does," agreed Carrie, "and I liked him in that Netflix crime drama."

Everyone chimed in agreements as the DVD played on; then the actor disappeared with an abrupt cut to black. Emma paused the DVD—

162

they'd watched both of the contenders now.

"So we're debating between these two," said Adrian. "Eddie, the actor we've just seen, or Simon."

Luke crossed his legs, sat back. "It's hard. Both delivered a fantastic audition." He stroked his chin. "Like I say, I think Eddie's got the edge on scariness—he's got that don't-mess-with-me quality. But Simon has more charm."

"He's definitely sexier," said Liz.

"Those eyes!" swooned Luke, which was met with laughter.

"But don't we want our lead to be the sexy one?" said Carrie. "He's taken this quality for granted and now he's lost it—gradually gets his mojo back? And Eddie's brutal ruthlessness will really add to the pressure; both when our lead loses his job and when he's torn about returning to acting."

Various "hmms" and nodding.

"I'll admit, if my hand were forced, I'd probably err on the side of sexy Simon," said Adrian. "I like his devil-may-care quality."

"I prefer more contrast," said Carrie. It was said light-heartedly, but their difference of opinion made the room feel gladiatorial.

"What do you think, Emma?" asked Luke.

A ripple of surprise rolled over the room and Carrie saw Emma shift uncomfortably in her seat.

"It's not really my call," she said.

"Still like to hear your opinion," said Luke.

"Okay . . . well, I think Carrie's right—Eddie's steely quality will help up the pressure . . . but Simon's charm is also very manipulating."

"She's sitting on the fence!" said Luke, smiling. He wagged his finger. "Not allowed."

Everyone was looking at Emma. She took a deep breath. "There's something about Simon that I think is more interesting. I think his persuasive charm also comes across as very dark, very threatening."

Carrie kept the pleasant look on her face, but inside she was furious. Then, faintly, came a sound that set her nerves on edge. A wail, intermittent at first but quickly picking up. Every muscle tensed in her body. She knew she had to get up, to go and see to Rory. She looked across at Adrian, expecting, what? An empathetic smile, a knowing look? But he wouldn't even meet her eye. *Why don't you go for once,* she thought. *Why can't you just help?*

The resentment held her in its grip, rendering her rigid and she didn't move. The crying got louder. Out of the corner of her eye she could see a couple of the staff glance tentatively over at Liz's office. Adrian finally flicked a look over to her: frustration mixed with an urgent dismissal.

Rory amplified his yells.

"Is there a baby here?" asked Luke, looking around.

An awkward hiatus settled over the room. Carrie could sense Liz getting irritated.

He's yours, Adrian, thought Carrie, angrily. *He's yours, too—admit it!* But the silence reigned until, suddenly, Emma stood.

"Will you excuse me just a moment," she said, and left the room.

Carrie stared, openmouthed, as Emma went to Liz's office. She was on her feet and following, just in time to see Emma pick Rory up out of the stroller.

"Give him to me," she snapped.

Emma obeyed and Carrie tried to calm her son.

"Bad idea," hissed Adrian, suddenly coming up behind her as he pulled on his jacket.

With one look at them both, Emma slunk off.

"Thanks for the support," hissed Carrie.

"Me? What about you? Why's it my job to sort him? You're not even supposed to be here today. It's meant to be your day off."

"That would've made it easier for you to get the actor you want."

"Your opinion would still be counted."

"My opinion is worthless when you gang up with Emma."

Adrian expelled a frustrated sigh. "We weren't ganging up. We just happened to agree, that's all." His eyes were ablaze. "I never signed up for this, Carrie." Then he walked away.

She saw Liz approach. "Carrie, I think it might

be better if Rory doesn't come to Pinewood," she said, and Carrie could do nothing but nod. She gently kissed the top of her now-quiet son's head and watched as they all left the office without her.

24

She just couldn't seem to get Carrie on her side. Emma had only meant to help, but Carrie had been livid when she'd picked up Rory, as if she couldn't bear for her to touch him. He had been so light, so tiny, and she'd felt a rush of warmth for the few seconds he'd been in her arms.

She glanced across at the set designer, who was enthusiastically pointing out the grass-topped coffee table to Luke.

"Is it real?" asked Luke, amazed. He touched the cool green blades.

Adrian handed him a small contraption.

Luke grinned. "Get out of here."

Adrian pushed a button on the side of the miniature lawnmower and placed it on the tabletop. It began to slice off the top of the grass and Luke clapped his hands in delight. Adrian and Liz smiled, pleased at his response, and Emma had to admit, as props went, it was pretty cool. But she couldn't concentrate properly on any of it. She was angry at herself for her part in the scene that had taken place in the office. Perhaps she should've just sided with Carrie on her choice of actor, but she'd genuinely thought the other was better.

Maybe that didn't matter. The thought of alienating Carrie was too terrifying. This job, this *connection* was all she had right now. Emma had plans beyond this job. If she was going to be a successful writer, she'd need a producer to champion her work. She could think of no one more perfect than Carrie. For all kinds of reasons.

She shook off the unsettling feeling and glanced up. Adrian was playing the fool and trying on a Viking hat. If only she could show him for who he really was. She needed to work harder, search deeper. There must be something hidden away. At the beach house, possibly. She needed to go back.

25

Friday, December 15

A man in a red santa suit was beaming at several delighted children outside Hamleys, the world-famous toy store. He handed out balloons as they thronged forward, shiny eyes tilted upward, drawn to him like bees to nectar. Carrie was unable to pass and she was brought out of her internal reverie, mildly confused by what was going on.

She glanced around, taking in the scene. *Christmas.*

She'd known, of course, somewhere deep in the back of her mind, but somehow the noisiest holiday of the year had not fully penetrated her consciousness until now. Christmas! It shocked her how she'd managed to get to the middle of December without being truly aware of what was going on around her. It was another reminder of how tired and dazed she was, how stressed. How her life had been so dramatically and irrevocably changed, something that scared the living daylights out of her if she allowed herself to think about it too much.

Thoughts of the previous year drifted through her mind, wistful images of a life now gone: She and Adrian in a wooden bungalow over a clear lagoon with steps that led down into the waist-deep water. Snorkeling along the reef, then later exchanging gifts on the beach over dinner. They'd been so close then, so content. He'd certainly never looked at other women. Carrie had carefully questioned him on the way he'd been staring at Emma's backside the day before, but he'd vehemently denied it. Said she'd had his line of vision wrong. She'd felt a rush of anger not just at him, but at her too. Ever since Emma had come along, everything had gone wrong. She had nearly pressed it with him, but it would have only led to a full-blown argument, something she couldn't face. It didn't help that he had come home late—around eight—by which time Carrie was already in her pajamas. Neither of them had mentioned the disastrous end to the meeting.

A child no taller than her hips bumped into her in his rush to get some of Santa's balloon stock before it ran out. She placed a hand on the baby pouch strapped to her chest as she navigated the excited children. She hadn't spoken to Adrian about what they were going to do this year—and nor had he brought it up. They'd probably stay in the house in London, the day playing out with its feedings and naps, exactly the same as any other day.

Carrie continued down the brightly lit Regent Street, turning off into the southern end of Soho and heading for Golden Square. She could see the glossy red door that led to Marsh Pictures' offices just ahead and prayed Rory would stay asleep long enough for her to have a direct conversation with Elaine. It was rather dramatic, door-stepping her, but it was the only way she could get Elaine to actually speak to her.

There was a green and gold holly wreath hanging on the door that only served to remind her she'd put no thought into decorating their home (neither did she have the energy to do so); then the door suddenly opened and out walked Elaine herself, with a small dog on a leash.

Carrie's heart jumped and she hurried forward— they'd have the conversation in the street if they had to, and she was about to shout out when she saw Elaine was on the phone and marching north in her orange heeled boots, her pink floral scarf flying behind her in the cold winter wind. Carrie clutched Rory and quickened her step. Elaine dodged through the narrow Soho streets, going at a pace that belied her heels. Carrie broke into a half run, began to gain on her, and then finally in a last thrust, she dodged around a parked car and landed on the pavement right in front of Elaine.

"Jesus Christ!" shrieked Elaine, clutching her chest. She gasped and told the person on the other end of the phone she'd call them back.

"What in God's name are you doing?" said Elaine, still breathing heavily.

"Are you okay?" asked Carrie.

"I will be. It's nothing. Despite what the doctor says."

"I need to speak to you."

"So you're stalking me?"

"Wouldn't be necessary if you took my calls."

Elaine gave a glimmer of a smile. "Ah yes. I did get a message."

"Four hopefully."

"Four?" Elaine raised her eyebrows disingenuously as she lit a cigarette. "Must be important."

"Cut the crap, Elaine. I need to know what Emma Fox did that made you fire her from your company."

"Ah, so that's what this is about."

"What was so bad? You said something before about her seriously fucking up."

"I'm sure there's some confidentiality law about not disclosing staff behavior."

"Please, don't make me beg. We're two professionals. This business is built on shared info."

"Are you thinking of hiring her?"

Carrie paused. "We already have." She considered; might as well swallow her pride. "She's job sharing with me."

Elaine stopped mid-drag, cigarette held aloft. It was the first and probably the only time Carrie had seen her discomposed, something that made the hairs go up on the back of her neck. It only lasted a second; then Elaine was back to her acerbic self.

"Wow. Job sharing. With *you*. Are you telling me she's some sort of *producer?*"

"Liz's very impressed by her."

"She's impressive. But I wouldn't trust her an inch."

Carrie bristled. "Why did you give her such a good reference, then? You know, it's one thing being a bit annoyed with me for supposedly stealing my husband from you, but totally out of order to go and deliberately sabotage my show."

Elaine looked at her strangely. "I didn't."

"Didn't what?"

"Give her a reference. Nor would I try to sabotage your show. Looks like you've gone some way to doing that yourself, anyway." She mused. *"Producer?"*

"Well, someone spoke to Liz."

"It wasn't me."

Carrie narrowed her eyes.

"Oh, stop being so bloody ridiculous," said Elaine. "This business is full of bullshit. People find unscrupulous ways to inveigle their way into jobs all the time. Maybe she got someone else to do a reference on my behalf. And if I ever find out who, I'll kill them. And her," she added.

Carrie knew she was telling the truth. "Okay. Sorry," she mumbled.

"Pardon?"

Carrie grit her teeth. Spoke louder. "Sorry."

Elaine smiled. "Accepted."

She started to head off, but Carrie put her hand on her arm.

"You still haven't told me what she did."

"Oh. Yes." Elaine cocked her head, curious. "She was very interested in your husband."

26

Friday, December 15

The wind was bone-cracking cold. it pierced through Emma as it came blasting off the dark sea and over the top of the cliffs, the gusts trying to dislodge her as she waited. She huddled against the iron railing fence that surrounded The Thirty-Nine Steps, trying to take shelter by squeezing next to an overgrown straggly bush. It couldn't be much longer. Adrian would want to get back to London before it got too late.

He'd asked her to come down to Broadstairs so they could work on the scripts together, and she'd been torn. It was another opportunity to look around the house, but on the other hand, she didn't relish the idea of being alone with him again, not after he'd come on to her last week. She'd been relieved that today had remained professional; they'd worked through until late afternoon, Emma hiding her impatience for them to finish so he would leave the house. Eventually he'd called it a day and she'd graciously refused a lift, saying it was quicker for her to get the train as she was meeting friends in town and was wary of getting snarled up in Friday evening traffic.

Night shrouded her, the only light coming from

the streetlamps on the other side of the road, within the compound of the North Foreland Estate and a weak half-moon, hanging over the sea, sporadically visible whenever the wind sped the clouds along the charcoal sky. From her windswept hidey-hole Emma could also see the periodic red and white beam of the lighthouse. She'd been stowed away long enough to count its rhythm, five bursts every fifteen seconds, a radiant glow that carried out to sea, illuminating the ghostly turning blades of the off-shore wind farm before being lost somewhere out in the ocean.

Her teeth started chattering. She should've brought more clothes, a scarf. She looked around, trying to take her mind off the needle-sharp wind penetrating through to her bones. She could see the entrance to the steps, dark and fathomless. For want of something to do, she pulled out the flashlight she'd brought and with numb fingers switched it on and directed it toward the black space, trying to look down the steps through the cliff. The beam didn't reach far enough.

Suddenly a car came down the road and she quickly flicked off the torch. She crouched behind the bush, peering out as the car passed by. It was Adrian. Pulling the hood on her coat right over her head, she hurried back towards his house.

Emma glanced up and down the road, checking for faces in windows, die-hard dog walkers, but it was quiet and empty, everyone probably cozied up in their houses out of the cold December night.

She threw her bag over first, hearing it land with a thud on the driveway. Then she leapt against the gatepost, her hands grabbing the top of the bricks, their cold grit painful against her skin. Pushing her feet against the side, she managed to leverage herself up and over.

A security light immediately popped on and she instinctively shrank back. After a few seconds it turned itself off again. She knew the minute she moved it would once again illuminate the driveway, but no doubt foxes triggered it all the time. She would just have to be quick. She hurried up to the front door and, using the key she'd got cut the week before, put it in the lock and turned. In seconds she was inside. She remembered the code for the alarm from her last visit to the house, when she'd watched him type it in. A few taps to the keypad and then the house was silent.

Emma took a second to catch her breath, still her pounding heart. Standing there in the dark, grateful for the warmth, she thought she'd be there an hour at most; then she could get the hell out and make her way home. Keeping the flashlight low, she climbed the stairs to the roundel and went into Adrian's office.

Going over to his desk, she sat in his chair

and opened the drawers. The top two were full of miscellaneous knickknacks, more of the bitter dark chocolate. The bottom one was deeper and full of papers piled up on one another. She heaved them out and placed them on the desk, flicking through methodically, careful to keep them in the same order. They were all notes or documents relating to *Leon*; pages of scripts that had been scribbled on, character biographies, synopses. It took longer than she thought to go through them, but finally she placed them all back in the drawer, heart beating fast. She didn't like being in there but knew she had to check the oak unit before she could leave. She went over to the other side of the room and opened its doors, nearly losing heart at the piles of paper stacked inside. Did this man never throw anything out?

She worked from left to right, pulling out each pile and carefully going through the papers on the wooden floor, her back against the leather sofa. As she flicked through, illuminating the pages with her flashlight, she grew ever more despondent and anxious. More stuff on *Leon*. Then suddenly the content began to change. Script pages and notes from *Generation Rebel*. Encouraged, Emma sat up straighter, flicked through with a new energy.

It had struck her several times before tonight that there was probably nothing there and the evidence she was looking for had been long since destroyed, but a part of her had to search, had to find out for sure.

The documents began to get older, e-mails dated from a couple of years ago, with notes on *Generation Rebel* scripts from various executives. The hairs went up on her arms as she recognized the fictional people, she knew them as well as she knew herself. Then outlines of stories—again ideas she recognized. Emma found herself slowing down to read the old drafts, before chastising herself. These weren't relevant.

There was one pile left. With a deep breath she pulled it out of the cupboard and onto the floor.

That was when she heard the front door snick shut.

27

Emma froze, her heart pounding in her chest. had she been mistaken? She felt sick and in a panic leapt to the window, keeping out of sight as she edged open the curtains. Down on the drive was Adrian's BMW. Fuck. Fuck, fuck, fuck.

She wildly looked down at the papers on the floor. Frantically, she stashed them back in the cupboard, trying to remain quiet, trying to listen to the house. She flicked on a side light and then grabbed her phone from her bag; fingers stumbling over the keys, she quickly sent a text. She stood up and faced the office door, just as it slowly began to open.

The look on his face morphed from surprise to a barely registered flicker of lust to suspicion. "Emma! What are you doing here?"

"I left something behind," she said, breezily.

He switched on the main light and she squinted in its brightness. "How did you get in?" he asked.

She thought quickly. "The window. In the kitchen. It was ajar."

Adrian frowned. "I didn't open it."

"No . . . I did . . . earlier. To get rid of the smoke. The bacon sandwiches, remember?"

"And the alarm?"

She had the grace to look embarrassed. "I . . . er . . . I'd seen you key it in."

He raised an eyebrow. "Is that right?"

She saw him look around the room, mistrustful, trying to work out what was really going on. Then his phone beeped. He checked it out. Emma knew what it was—the text she'd sent moments before.

He looked at her, held up the screen. "Hi, Adrian, please can you call me?" he read out.

"Yes, to explain. About the window. Having to come back."

He nodded. "Emma, you'll understand why I think nothing of what you're saying is true."

She swallowed. Kept quiet.

"In fact, I'd go as far as to say you were covering something up."

She smiled weakly, innocently, she hoped.

"You see, I was driving home along the M2 when I got a call about half an hour ago from Geraldine . . ." *The nosy neighbor*, thought Emma, heart sinking. "She'd been out walking her dog," continued Adrian. "Said there was a small light flickering in the office here, as if someone had broken in, was searching the place, so of course I came straight back. You want to tell me what's really going on?"

Emma felt the sofa pressing against the back of her legs. Weak, she sat down. Remained silent.

Frustrated, Adrian waved his phone around. "This isn't cool. I thought we got on, you and me. I thought we worked well together, trusted one another."

"We do."

"Newsflash. You've just broken into my house."

"I told you . . . the window—"

"Bollocks. Emma, don't treat me like a dick." He pushed his hand through his hair. She saw him mentally work out what approach to take with her. Then he sighed. "I'm putting my everything into this show, shitting myself in actual fact because there's always the possibility it might not work out. Something that perhaps only you really know. Certainly Carrie isn't aware of how much I'm cacking my pants." He paused. "I don't need to tell you how important it is that I get it right. And as much as I love you being a part of it—goddamn it, you're so bloody brilliant sometimes I feel like you could write it yourself—that feeling is not going to stick with me if I'm checking over my shoulder to see if you're stabbing me in the back. Or whatever the fuck it is you're doing here in the dark without my knowledge. Now I'm not one for threats, but please, Emma, give me something that makes this"—he waved his phone arm between them both—"our brilliant team of you and me, keep going. 'Cause apart from anything else, it's going to be a right pain in the arse to go looking to hire somebody new."

Emma sat still, her body rigid. She had no idea how to get out of this. She looked up at Adrian and knew she had to give him an answer. Something. She couldn't lose her job, not for several reasons. It was unthinkable. She saw the hope in him start to flicker away, and knew in a few more moments, everything would be lost. Everything that she'd hoped for, had been yearning for since she was a little girl.

She nervously crossed her legs and saw his eyes follow this action, saw the glimmer in them.

He held up his phone. "You know what? I think this might be one for the police."

No!

"Unless you can give me a reason not to." He paused, softened his voice. "A very good one. Only I see you here, in the privacy of my office, and you've just sent me a text so you can tell me you're back at my house . . . Someone could mistake that for an invitation."

He smiled and she felt sick to the pit of her stomach, hardly able to take in what she'd just heard. She should—what? Tell him where to go? Get fired? Never work in TV again? She couldn't think straight. All she could feel was fear. A deep, consuming fear that she knew would engulf her if he cut her from the life raft that was her work.

Adrian held his thumb poised over the keys, eyebrows raised in anticipation.

Later she would think it was the diabolical fear

that had robbed her of her courage. That and the unspeakable loneliness. She couldn't face it again.

She rested her trembling hand on the empty seat next to her. Smoothed it over the soft leather. "The reason I texted . . . the reason I wanted to speak to you is . . ." She couldn't continue but she didn't have to. He'd dropped his hand to his side.

She forced herself to make eye contact with him again, an animal caught in a trap, and felt herself cross over to a place from which she'd never be able to return.

She saw his face light up, soften. Then he slowly placed his phone on the desk and went to join her on the sofa.

28

Monday, December 18

Emma lay in bed listening to her parents get ready for work. The cheerful, optimistic smell of freshly ground coffee wafted up the stairs, and under her door she could hear "O Come, All Ye Faithful" on the radio being belted out by a large chorus, accompanied by her dad's admittedly rich tenor, her mother's descant voice chiming in singing choirs of angels. It reminded her of school. Four hundred girls in chapel, all following the careful baton of Miss Barkham, the music teacher.

She listened as the carol finished downstairs and the *Messiah* started its opening bars. She wished they'd hurry up and leave so she could return the house to silence.

At least it was better than the usual overplayed rock and pop fare, songs she'd tired of since they'd first appeared on the radio in October. But after having to listen to them in Adrian's BMW on the drive back from the beach house Friday night, she would never be able to hear them again without their making her heart plummet to depths she didn't know existed.

It had been an excruciating drive—having to

sit so close to Adrian after what they'd done. Regret and self-loathing growing inside her until she was rigid with misery. He'd been quiet on the way home too, and the silence was filled with the overbright screeching of Wizzard's "I Wish It Could Be Christmas Every Day." Adrian offered to drive her all the way home and she'd protested at first, saying he could drop her at a London station and she'd find her way from there, but he'd insisted, had been quite caring in fact, and in despair, she'd hadn't known how to argue with him. He'd asked her twice if she was okay, concerned perhaps, by how quiet she'd been and she'd said she was fine, even giving him a quick smile, anything to get him off her back.

When he dropped her at the end of her road (she'd insisted, not wanting him near the house, but had felt even more sullied by this skulking action), he'd turned the engine off, a sign, she knew, for them to talk.

It was the absolute last thing she wanted to do, to speak about what had happened between them, and she'd opened the car door.

"Wait . . ." he'd said, a small, concerned frown on his face, and she'd stopped midway out of the car. "Are you sure everything's okay?"

It had taken a lot of effort, but she'd smiled and nodded.

"You and me. We're still cool?" he'd asked tentatively.

"Course."

"I know it might be difficult now, with Carrie . . ."

You don't know the half of it, thought Emma, miserably.

"And I'd appreciate it if . . ."

She looked at him, astounded. Who did he think she was? "I wouldn't *dream* of saying anything," she said, aghast.

He blushed. "Sorry. Of course. I know that."

"I've got to go." Emma stepped out of the car as he leaned across the seat, smiling at her as if everything were normal.

"Have a great weekend. See you on Monday."

She'd nodded, but now it was Monday and she had no intention of going into that office. She couldn't bear to see him, couldn't look at him knowing he'd seen her naked, touched her. Worse, it was one of Carrie's workdays and she just couldn't face her.

She'd ruined everything. There, she'd admitted it. That was the thing that devastated her the most. And she hadn't even managed to find the evidence she'd been looking for. She'd derailed her whole plan because she'd been stupid enough to get caught in their house. Tears of self-pity started to flow, but just as the dam opened up, there was a knock on her bedroom door. Emma quickly wiped her face as her mother came in, dressed in a light-gray trouser suit and a pale-blue shirt.

"Still feeling poorly, Emma?" she asked.

"Yes."

"Do you want any breakfast? Dad's made scrambled eggs."

"Sorry, just can't face it," mumbled Emma from beneath the duvet.

"Are you sure? Toast is still warm."

"No, thanks."

"Oh, well, never mind." She sounded disappointed. "So you're not going to work today, then?"

"No."

Alice hesitated. "Well, maybe you'll be better later. Take care of yourself," she said, and Emma looked up, surprised by the solicitous tone, but her mother had already closed the door.

Emma reached out for her phone and composed an e-mail to Carrie, informing her she'd caught a bug and wouldn't be at work. It was short and matter-of-fact. Not long after that she heard the radio switch off downstairs and her parents leave for work.

She went down into the kitchen, pulling her dressing gown tight around her because the heating was on a timer and had gone off for the day. Ever conscious it didn't feel like her house, it seemed indulgent, almost disobedient to switch it back on, so she made herself a coffee and sat at the breakfast bar, her hands wrapped around the cup. She stared out through the patio doors, the frost on the tiny patch of grass, the sky not fully light. Her phone beeped. She glanced down—Christ, it was a message from Adrian. She pushed it away, but it tugged at her until, furious, she had to read it.

Hope you're okay? Worried illness has something to do with Friday???

Oh, for God's sake. She didn't want to answer, didn't want to engage, wished he'd just *disappear*. She pushed her phone away, picked up her coffee, and went back up to bed.

Despite indulging in a day of moping, Emma made sure she was showered and dressed by the time her parents came home. Her mother appeared first, pleased to see her daughter feeling better, and delighted—even relieved—she was able to join them for dinner. Alice had texted during the day, too—twice—just to check in, and Emma was puzzled by all the attention.

They broke it to her over dinner. With both of them turning sixty-five the following year, and solid pensions to support them, they'd decided to retire.

Emma had been warily pleased for them. "That's great. You've worked so hard for so long." She smiled. "You're not going to know what to do with all your new spare time."

"Actually . . ." started Alice.

"We quite fancy a change," said Brian.

Alarm bells started to ring. Emma looked from one to the other.

"We've never really spent enough time at the lake house," continued Brian.

"And we'd like to. Get to know the area—and the neighbors—properly."

"How long for?" asked Emma, uneasily.

"A while," said Alice.

"Months?"

Brian put down his knife and fork. "For the foreseeable."

Emma quashed her rising panic. "And this place?"

Her father paused before speaking. "We're going to rent it out."

Her stomach twisted and she looked at both her parents, crestfallen.

Her mother was sympathetic. "I'm sorry, Emma, but we'll need the income. You know there's no central heating at the villa and we'll have to get that fixed. And the windows need replacing."

"What about me?"

"Of course we'll help set you up. Contribute toward your first rent," said Brian.

"And after that?"

Neither of them answered her and Emma saw them exchange a wry glance.

"I know it seems hard but . . . well, I'm sure you want to stand on your own two feet, don't you?" Alice smiled.

Tears threatened, but Emma kept them at bay. Her eyes blazed. "So this is your latest plan. To manipulate me into somebody you want me to be."

"What?" said Alice.

"Will you only be happy if I become the person you think is good enough?"

"I don't know what you're talking about," said Brian. "We've always been very happy to discuss all options with you."

"You've discussed nothing. It's all been one-sided. You've made it perfectly clear what you want me to do."

"That's not true—" started Alice.

Emma stood abruptly, her chair scraping back. "How long?"

"What?"

"How long until you rent this place out?"

Alice looked at Brian. "Well, we were thinking . . ."

"February," said Brian.

Jesus! "Fine, I'll be out by then."

"Emma . . ." Alice stood.

But Emma didn't stop. As she left the room she heard them speak sotto voce to each other.

"She'll come round," said Brian. "Rebecca's still got a position open for her. She's bloody lucky. We can't let her ruin her life on some whim. My God, she could be so brilliant, if only she'd see what was in front of her nose."

193

Alice sighed. "I know. Whoever knew bringing up children was so hard?"

Emma silently climbed the stairs and went to her room.

She closed the door and leaned back against it. Her life was falling apart. She had no time to wallow in the misery of the other night. She had to fight back.

29

"Let's get one thing clear: it was a mistake. we shouldn't have done it and it won't ever happen again."

"You got it."

Emma stared at Adrian; his casual attitude was irritating. Now he was smiling at her, his head tipped quizzically to one side.

"So why were you there?" he asked. "As flattering as it is to believe you climbed through my kitchen window and arranged our little tryst, I can't help feeling there was something else going on."

Emma held his gaze, suppressing the fear in the pit of her stomach. He mustn't know what she'd been looking for.

"Nothing else." She shrugged. "You underestimate yourself."

His head tipped again: *explain.*

"You're very clever, a very successful writer. It's attractive."

She saw him preen and held back the impulse to gag. She needed to get to the end of this grueling conversation. They were in the back office on borrowed time—Carrie would no doubt miss

195

them in a minute and come looking, and Emma wanted this out of the way and forgotten as soon as possible.

"So we're in agreement. Big mistake. Not ever going to be repeated?"

Adrian looked at her. "It's okay. I get it. We've all got jobs to do. I have a wife . . ."

"And child."

He hesitated. "Yes, one of those too." He lowered his voice further. "I am not intending to jeopardize this show or anyone's career. So please don't worry."

She examined his answer carefully, scrutinized his face.

"Trust me, Emma. I have more to lose than you."

I don't think you do, she thought, but said nothing. A rap on the door made her jump.

Carrie came in and looked between them. "Everything okay?"

Adrian held up a DVD. "Emma just dropped off this composer's reel. Mark Williams. Have you heard it yet?"

"Yes," said Carrie.

"Any good?"

"I like him."

"Cool. Let me check him out." He put it into his laptop.

Nervous about being in such close proximity to both of them, Emma saw her chance to escape and quickly left the room.

30

Carrie watched through the open doorway as Emma went back to her desk. She didn't understand why the door had been closed if Emma was just dropping off a DVD.

She glanced back at Adrian, with the distinct impression she'd interrupted something, but he had his headphones on and didn't take his eyes off the screen.

She left the room and went to the kitchen to make herself a coffee. It had been four days since her conversation with Elaine, but she couldn't get it out of her head. Especially as Adrian had spent the whole of Friday working with Emma at the beach house.

They'd stood in the cold outside Elaine's office as Elaine had regaled her with what had happened all those months ago when Emma had been fired from Marsh Pictures.

Elaine had caught Emma snooping. Looking at confidential documents. She'd left Emma in her office with instructions to hunt out a particular draft of a script and had walked back in half an hour later to find her looking through the contracts file for *Generation Rebel*—specifically Adrian's contract.

It was something she kept in a separate cupboard. So Emma had very little with which to defend herself. Strangely, she hadn't even tried, apparently, just put the contract back on the desk and went to get her things. She'd been out of the building less than ten minutes after getting caught.

"Maybe she was looking at your husband's fee," Elaine had said, "to see how much he cost. Then she'd know what someone would have to offer."

"We all know it's the channel who pays, not us producers," said Carrie.

"Still gotta raise it, though, haven't you?"

Carrie had mused on this theory darkly. It goaded her that Emma and Adrian worked so well together—maybe Emma was already drip-feeding new ideas into his ear. Well, she could go to hell—Adrian was signed up for three years with her. Three years that she anxiously knew she couldn't fulfill, not the way she'd originally planned it. There was plenty of room for Emma to inveigle her way in.

"Ambitious, is she?" asked Elaine, knowingly.

Carrie shrugged.

Elaine let out a peal of laughter. "Oh, you're to die for. So transparent. Must feel threatening, someone so set on doing well, taking over half your job."

She refused to rise to the bait. "Did they ever meet?"

"No, Adrian was already cooking up ideas with

you by the time Emma had her short stint with us." Elaine leaned in. "I've seen it before, you know. Producers circling like sharks. Whispering poisonous thoughts into writers' ears. 'You deserve this, you should be allowed that, are you sure you're getting the right respect . . .' Subtle words designed to look like magnanimous support. When all they want is to drive a wedge between the writer and his or her current producer of choice." Elaine's eyes glinted. "I'm sure you didn't ever say anything like that about me. . . ."

"Of course not," said Carrie.

"Hmm. Christ, every producer in town would dig out their own eyeball to bag Adrian. He's got green-lighting power."

"You really think she's trying to set something up with him?"

"Why not?"

"She's so young . . . I mean, this is her first producing gig."

"And a pretty impressive one at that. Do you ever stop to think she's in the office more than you? She's doing five days a week on *your show*—you're doing three. You've practically handed it to her on a plate."

Carrie balked. She was so naïve. Why hadn't she made this basic observation?

Elaine smiled. "But you'll be able to keep her at bay. Just so long as you and Adrian are getting on."

Carrie's eyes flickered. She instantly regretted it, but it was too late.

"Oh my. Better paper over those cracks before she steals him while your back's turned changing diapers."

Elaine put a comforting hand on Carrie's arm. "Don't look so down. Anytime you need to talk, I'm here. I know what it's like, remember!" Then she removed her hand from Carrie's arm and walked away.

It had been a disturbing conversation that had plagued her all weekend. Adrian and Emma spent enough time working together alone for Emma to cook up anything. And then there were the private conversations like this morning, the closed doors.

Carrie took her coffee to her desk, opened up her e-mails. There was one from the head of costume.

She looked to her right where Emma was working. "Did you get this? Jill's got some outfits for us to look over. Wondering if we're free to go over to the production office at Pinewood this afternoon."

Emma looked apologetic. "I'm sorry, Carrie, but I think I'm going to have to bow out. I may have come back to work too early . . ." She rubbed her stomach. "Still feeling a little queasy. In fact, would it be all right if I . . . ?"

She did look pale, thought Carrie. "That's fine. You go."

"Thanks. Sorry again."

Carrie watched as she gathered up her things and left the office. There was definitely something about her she didn't trust. Maybe Elaine was right—Emma was planning to oust her. She didn't know yet, but she was certainly going to find out.

31

Tuesday, December 19

Emma didn't go home. instead she headed to Victoria station and then took a train to Broadstairs, finding a quiet seat by the window. There were only three other people in the carriage and everyone sat in contented silence. The train wound through the Kent countryside in the bright, cold winter sun, many of the fields dark and restful, sheep and cattle dotted on those that were still green. As she neared the coast, she'd occasionally catch a glimpse of the sea, a pewter sparkle when the sun caught it.

Emma walked the two miles to the North Foreland Estate, through the town and then along the clifftop road, watching the seagulls swoop and dive down to the beach below. The tide was out, revealing countless rock pools, populated with unlucky winkles, their fate sealed as the seagulls stood mercilessly on the edge, plucking them from the water.

The estate was quiet. Emma looked around, trying to see beyond the trees and high fences, where there were glimpses of houses, spying on her she felt, and she wondered which one was Geraldine's. The windows she could see were blank, the driveways empty. Emma lifted herself over the wall, walked up to the front door, and let herself in. Alarm off, she wasted no time in going upstairs to the office. She faltered briefly as she opened the door, but gave the sofa a wide berth and opened the oak cupboard, pulling out the last pile of documents she hadn't searched. She checked her watch. She had hours if needed as Carrie and Adrian would only just be arriving at Pinewood. But she wanted this done as quickly as possible and so she set to work, turning each paper over as she searched. She knew there was a good chance there was nothing, that this, like the last time, was a wasted trip. One that had cost her dearly. Everything she was looking through still related to *Generation Rebel*, so her heart could not help but hold some hope.

She stopped abruptly as she came across a large white envelope. It was addressed to Adrian, via his agent, an address she remembered she'd looked up online. The bright orange stamp she'd stuck on had now been darkened by a postmark, the date from nearly four years ago. Tentatively she opened the worn flap, wondering if the original contents were still inside. She slowly pulled out several sheets of paper. A bittersweet smile of triumph. She could remember writing this letter, she thought ruefully. She could remember her naïveté. She didn't stop to read any of it; instead she put the papers back in the envelope, returned the other documents to the cupboard, and after resetting the alarm, left the house.

As she walked back along the cliff road, she smiled to herself. Her bag was pulled close to her body, the envelope carefully placed inside.

32

The wind blew her along and she laughed joyully. The world suddenly seemed brighter somehow, its colors more vibrant, more radiant. Her secret, so long a tiny, private smolder, was now a rampaging inferno inside her, and as she passed Bleak House with its solid, fort-like strength, she gave a little nod to the ghost of Charles Dickens. He'd appreciate the twist in this tale, the wronged individual getting a piece of luck, luck that had the power to change the narrative. Yes, indeed! She continued walking until she came to Viking Bay, its glorious golden crest of sand before her, and suddenly felt the urge for spontaneity. A celebration!

"A strawberry and chocolate double scoop in a cone, please," she said, then paid for her ice cream and took it down to the beach. She sat on the cold sand, looking out to the water, grinning between licks. *What a stupid idiot he is,* she thought. She'd hoped, somewhat in a fantasy world, that she might find something, anything to vindicate what she'd been harboring, not really believing she'd get anything—but *this!* God, this was something he was going to regret.

Justice, she thought. Justice needed to be carried out.

A Frisbee landed a few feet to her right and she looked up to see a little girl, dressed in her school uniform, running along the sand. She was followed by her mother, who was wrapped up in a huge, puffy coat, a scarf poking out of the top, her daughter's school bags braceleted over her gloved hands. The mother put the bags on the sand and joined in the game, shrieking with laughter as much as the little girl did as they ran for the Frisbee, often both of them diving for it at the same time. The girl was about seven, Emma guessed. Around about the age she was when she'd been sent away to boarding school.

She watched them playing together for a while; then the girl looked across and Emma raised a hand and smiled, but the girl ran past, the wide grin on her face full of the simple joy of freedom, and Emma realized she hadn't been looking at her at all—she'd been following the line of the Frisbee.

Feeling foolish, she stood up and brushed the sand from her backside. She left the beach and headed up to the station. On the train she picked a seat that was away from anyone else and once it had pulled away, she took the envelope out of her bag, lifted the flap, and pulled out the contents.

Dear Adrian Hill,

I am writing to ask if I might be able to seek your advice. I am a student at Exeter University in the second year of my English degree. I am also a television drama nut and watch everything (!) from the US drama imports to the brilliant shows that are made here in the UK. I absolutely loved your recent episode of IN GOOD FAITH—it's the best soap on TV. It was so fresh and surprising, and the twist at the end when Jonah revealed his second wife blew me away. I love to write in my spare time and eventually would like to have a career as a television screenwriter, much like yourself.

My understanding is that in order to get taken seriously, I will need an agent and I was wondering if you would be able to advise me on how best to choose the right agent to contact. My style is still evolving, but I am currently working on a series set in a school in which the children rebel against the establishment. After years of being forced through the education machine like sausages, being bullied and pressured to do even more advanced learning (to keep up with the Chinese), they finally crack. Demands made to the authorities are laughed off and so the kids form an uprising until they ultimately hold the teachers hostage, leading to tragic consequences for one. I see it as a modern-day *Lord of The Flies* and a comment on today's education system and its part in the rise of mental health issues in children. I have enclosed a full outline, should that be of interest.

I hope you don't mind me contacting you, but I am such an admirer of your work. Any pointers you can give me would be very gratefully received.

Best wishes
Anna King

She remembered being gripped by nerves at the last minute and choosing the false name. The entire letter was handwritten, a deliberate choice in the hope that by giving it a personal touch, she would receive a reply.

She never heard back. Two years later it became perfectly apparent why.

Emma put the letter away and stared out the window. She had the proof. Now she had to decide what to do with it.

33

Wednesday, December 20

It was always the trucks that got Emma first, the sheer size and number of them. Gleaming white, full of shiny silver boxes of equipment, hauled out by efficient armies of men, reeking of masculinity, with tool belts strapped around their waists, which she knew were full of gizmos that were actually used, not just for show.

Early for work, she'd made her way along 007 Drive, past the Stanley Kubrick Building to the north lot. Her pass had let her into the studios, but she deliberately kept a low profile while she wandered around, became immediately purposeful, and moved on whenever she saw security looking her way. She loved being out here; often the soundstages were screened off, but glimpses of a snowy village or a 1930s New York street could still be found. She'd see cranes being erected, dolly track laid, lights going up. Sometimes, actors were hanging around, remarkably on their own, free of paparazzi or entourage, as they waited between scenes, having a cigarette or coffee break. The energy of a film set was electric to her, and even though much of a day's filming was painfully slow, waiting for each department to be ready, for the director to block the scene, the actors to rehearse, she couldn't get enough of it. She'd struck up conversation with one of the technicians—Ray—who had befriended her. He was the one who told her that there was a James Bond film currently being shot at the studios, along with a movie on the life of Marco Polo—earlier she'd taken a peek at the exterior tank stage, where a mediaeval ship packed with men with swords and live horses was afloat in front of an enormous green screen.

Someone tapped on her shoulder. She jumped, thinking it was security telling her to move on, but Adrian was standing there, carrying two coffees. She forced herself not to recoil as he handed her one.

"Thought we could make a start on episode six—the notes from Luke. Then I can write the changes over the next couple of days, get the last of the scripts out to the cast just after Christmas. It'll give them a few days to look over them before the read-through."

The read-through was set for the first day back after the Christmas break. It was a marathon event that would bring the cast together for the first time, and in which they read aloud all six scripts to an audience of the senior producers and the channel executives. Emma loved read-throughs, loved hearing the words come alive, as the actors

became their characters. It didn't matter they were all sitting in a boardroom; she could imagine the cast in costume and in situ. It also gave her a sense of whether the script that had been labored on for months was truly working.

Emma already knew Luke's notes by heart. "They're not too bad," she said. "He's gone easy on us. In fact, he's been pretty good for the entire series. Was he like this for *Generation Rebel* as well?"

"Yep, scripts were in good shape so he let us off lightly."

"It's the authenticity that impressed me. Your knowledge of the education system and how it had affected those characters."

Adrian smiled modestly.

"Did you get your inspiration from anyone in particular?" she said casually, watching his face.

He seemed to be focused on a crane, loaded with a camera that was panning across a set, and didn't meet her eye. "Just through talking to friends. Hearing about their experiences with their children."

"Well, it's brilliant. Almost as if you'd just gone through school yourself."

He glanced at her and she smiled in admiration. "Glad you liked it."

Adrian suddenly blew on his hands. "Right, better get back."

He set off in the direction of the TV stages, not waiting to see if she was behind him or not.

She watched him go, loathing him.

Adrian was taking off his jacket when she came into their shared office.

"No Carrie?" she asked.

"She's still dropping off Rory," said Adrian.

"You want to wait for her?"

"She's already given me her feedback on the notes."

Emma nodded. She worked through them with him, discussing how they might implement the changes Luke had suggested. It didn't take long and after an hour, he left to find a quiet room to write them up.

Carrie arrived soon after. Emma watched as she put down her bag and switched on her laptop. She'd said nothing to her other than the absolute minimum, a courteous greeting. It made Emma nervous; surely Carrie didn't know anything about the night at the beach house. She sat at her desk, too self-conscious to work, aware of Carrie's every move.

"Did you go through the notes?" Carrie suddenly asked, breaking the silence.

"Yes, Adrian's writing them up now."

"Good." She paused. "Do you know what he's going to do next?"

"Well . . . no. I'm guessing these rewrites

are going to take the rest of the day—longer probably."

For the first time since she'd arrived, Carrie looked her straight in the eye. "I mean, his next project."

Emma was perplexed. "Um . . . no . . ."

"It's just that lots of producers would like him to write for them. I know he gets calls."

Emma nodded vaguely, wondering where this was going.

"Except he's got an exclusive contract with Hawk Pictures."

She knew about this. "Yes."

"That I negotiated."

The threat was clear.

Emma's mouth dropped open. "What do you mean?"

Carrie stayed silent.

"Do you think I'm . . . developing something else with Adrian?" she said, incredulously. The thought made her feel nauseous. The intimacy of all that intense time together. The hours and hours required for the two of them to be alone, resident in a world of only their creation. It was all she could do not to gag.

"I wouldn't . . ."

"Really? It would be quite a coup."

Carrie doesn't believe me. Emma's faced burned with mortification. "Maybe he's not as good as he says he is," she blurted out.

Carrie's mouth dropped with utter astonishment. "I beg your pardon?"

Emma bit her tongue. Wished she could take it back.

"I can't believe you just said that. . . ." Carrie was staring at her, astounded at her audacity. Then Emma saw something click in her mind.

"Are you serious?" Carrie said, coldly.

"What?"

"You're really trying to make me think my husband is a substandard writer so that I don't mind when you steal him from under my nose?"

Emma blushed. "What? No! I don't know what you mean."

Carrie lowered her voice. "I won't have it, Emma. You might have inveigled your way into my job, *this* job, but that's where it ends. As soon as this show is finished, there will be no more working with Adrian."

Emma opened her mouth to speak, but Carrie was already out the door, though not before Emma got a glimpse of her face, riddled with sadness and exhaustion.

She sat there in the quiet room, shocked at Carrie's accusation, her mind writhing with regret. None of this was going the way she'd planned. A flutter of panic rose up inside her. Somehow she had to get everything back on track.

34

Friday, December 22

It was the last day of work before the Christmas break and Emma still hadn't confronted Adrian. There was a sense of the holiday season in the air. Packets of mince pies lay open on filing cabinets for people to help themselves, and more than one member of the crew had found an innovative way of wearing tinsel: round their head, neck, backside.

They'd most likely finish early, everyone going back to their families for the holidays. Emma would be going home, too, to a strained Christmas with her parents. It would be some relief to all of them that Brian and Alice were going to Italy on Boxing Day. Emma had been invited but had declined. She did not want to be around conversations on how the lake house needed to be renovated, when she was soon to become homeless. Christmas was a bad time to be looking for rooms in flats in London, Emma knew, and this only fueled her growing anxiety that she would have nowhere to live in a matter of weeks. She couldn't even stay on at her parents' house, as it had already been rented, a family was due to move in at the end of February. Both her parents would periodically check in with her on the success of her search, her mother in particular hiding occasional bouts of concern at her daughter's prospects, but neither one would budge from their position. Emma knew they both secretly thought it would be the making of her.

Emma looked over to where Rory was in his stroller in the corner of the office. Carrie had popped in, bringing small gifts for all the crew, and was down in the studios handing them out. As soon as Carrie had left the office, Adrian hotfooted it out of the room, leaving Rory alone with Emma.

She could hear him gurgling happily but couldn't see into the stroller from where she was sitting. She got out of her seat and walked over to him, curious. As soon as she came into his view, he looked up at her, unsure. She smiled at him, waved her fingers.

"Hi, Rory. Have they left you all alone?"

She watched as he appraised her, his huge blue eyes wary.

"How could they leave you?" she murmured, then reached into the pram and picked him up. He didn't protest and in fact she thought he seemed pleased to have a change of view. He gazed around the room as she bounced him gently in her arms, enjoying being able to study him.

His blond hair was so fine it was barely visible, and she smoothed her hand over his head,

218

marveling at how soft it was. She then touched his tiny little hands, staring in wonder at the doll-sized fingernails. She sniffed the top of his head, taking in the sweet baby smell, and nuzzled his soft, minute earlobes. He was a perfect mini human being.

Then he looked directly at her and she felt her heart squeeze. She laughed in delight.

"Hey, you. Shall we be friends?"

He smiled at her.

"Because," she said softly, "I know what it's like to have absent parents. If you need someone to talk to, I'm here." She held him close. "And if it ever gets really bad, I'll come and get you. We'll run away together. Eh? Won't we."

Rory began to rub his eyes with his fists and Emma gently kissed him on the forehead. She looked at him one last time, then, with great care, laid him back in his stroller. She tucked him in and smiled tenderly at him. She pushed the stroller back and forth, and his eyes started to close. Soon he was asleep.

Now was the time. Before Carrie came back.

Emma walked down the corridor to the small office where Adrian had escaped to, and knocked gently.

"Yep?" he called.

She opened the door. "Sorry to bother you, but there's an Anna King down at reception for you."

219

He frowned. "Who?"

"Says she has a meeting with you at one o'clock?"

"Don't know anything about it."

"I didn't think you'd mentioned it. But she's downstairs. Shall I bring her up?"

He pondered. "Okay."

"I'll take her to our office. Can I get you a coffee while I'm passing the machine?"

"Love one."

Emma went directly to the coffee machine in the kitchen, made two Americanos, and brought them back, without going to the reception area. She placed them both in the office, then returned to the room where Adrian was writing.

"She's here," she said, putting her head around the door.

He smiled as he got up. "She say what this is about? I could do with a bit of a heads-up, make sure I don't embarrass myself."

They walked down the corridor. "She said she knows you from years ago," said Emma.

He frowned. "Where?

"Not sure."

They came to the office. Adrian looked in, perplexed. "Where is she?"

Emma ushered him in. "Coffee's on the table."

"Great, thanks." He looked around, then picked up his coffee, took a seat on the sofa. "She gone to the ladies' or something?"

Emma sat down opposite him. "She did mention one thing. She went to Exeter University."

"Oh, right. So where is she now?"

Emma stilled the butterflies in her stomach. Crossed her legs.

"Emma?"

"She wrote to you on the eighteenth of February 2014, to ask you for some advice."

She watched him carefully as his memory started to throw back great burning cannonballs at him. He shifted uncomfortably in his seat.

"I don't really have time to meet her," he said. He stood suddenly and went to the open door, but she was already there, closed it.

He looked at her, puzzled.

"You still don't get it, do you?" she said.

He frowned. "Get what?"

She smiled coldly at him. Like a damn bursting, an idea of preposterous awfulness seemed to flood his brain.

"*Jesus!*" He stared at her, horrified. "Are you telling me . . . you . . ." He continued spluttering and running his hand through his hair in disbelief.

Emma decided enough was enough.

"Yes, Adrian," she said with great patience. "It was me who wrote you that letter. Me who sent you the school series idea. I am Anna King."

35

Friday, December 22

"You're lying."

Emma remained calm. "Why would I lie?"

"You're not Anna King. I don't even know who Anna King is."

"Which is it, Adrian? Make up your mind."

"What do you want? Is this some sick way of blackmailing me? My agent warned me about people like you."

Emma got her letter and documents out of her bag and held them up.

Adrian's eyes widened in alarm. "Where did you get those?" he snapped.

"You do recognize them, then? I got them from where you left them, in your office at the beach house." She paused. "I'd like to know why. Why did you feel you could just steal my idea? Is it because I was only a student? Did you think I was an easy target?"

She could see by his face that this was true.

"It's my idea," she repeated. "My characters. My stories. My entire series."

Adrian's face hardened. "You haven't got a clue," he said. "I wrote the damn thing. I *created* it."

Emma bristled. "No, I created it. You took my creation and ran off with it. Made yourself a load of money and a reputation. Did you ever stop and think of me? While you were coasting along with my idea? Did you ever think of how I wanted to write up that show, that it was my *right* to?" The frustration of the last few years, of being unable to write anything new because of the searing sense of injustice boiled over.

"Did you ever feel *guilty?*"

He was stony-faced. She waited for an answer, but none came.

"I want you to tell Carrie what you've done. How you stole my idea. And I want it all to come from you. This"—she pointed between them— "this conversation never happened."

Adrian contemplated her for a moment, then walked across the room. "Why would I feel guilty? You think this has never happened before? People adapt—"

"Steal."

He ignored her. "Ideas all the time. There's no such thing as an original idea. In fact, how do you know I wasn't already working on something set in a school? I made it happen. You know how this business works. You would never have been commissioned to write it, not a complete newcomer."

"That's not the point—"

"What experience do you have? You haven't done anything."

"It's not about the exp—"

"You've seen what I've accomplished and thought it was easy. There's no way you could've come up with the goods. What have you written in your life, Emma? Nothing. Zilch. You're not a writer. You're just a wannabe."

Emma caught her breath, floored by his breathtaking cruelty.

Rory was stirring in his stroller, disturbed by their argument. His cries quickly became louder and Emma looked across at him. His little face was screwed up and his yells came between breaths. She turned to Adrian, accusation in her eyes.

"Why don't you pick him up?"

"He doesn't like it when I do."

"That's because you never do. I bet he hardly knows you. Pick him up."

"Keep your nose out."

"Pick him up."

Adrian stared defiantly at her.

"I mean it, pick him up and soothe him. Before Carrie hears him from halfway across the studios. Give her a fucking break, you prick." She folded her arms, fury in her eyes, and he tentatively went over to the stroller. He clumsily picked up the baby and attempted to rock him, while holding him at arm's length.

Miraculously, despite Adrian's ineptitude, Rory stopped crying. Adrian took full advantage of this and immediately put him back in the stroller.

Emma was still seething with anger. "What is wrong with you?"

He didn't bother to reply. He picked up his coffee and turned to leave.

"Children are a gift, you know," said Emma.

"Not one I ever asked for."

She slapped him across the face then. He put his hand to his cheek, and shocked at what she'd done, she turned and left the room.

36

There were numerous presents under the tree; a towering pile of gift-wrapped shapes in shiny colored paper, adorned with ribbons and bows. Carrie couldn't help but feel a burst of excitement when she first saw them, out of habit formed in childhood that would probably never diminish, even when she was an old lady.

Except when she looked through these presents she recognized the paper on all of them. This was because she'd wrapped them for Rory, which meant there wasn't one for her from Adrian. She bit down on her disappointment, then felt a murmur of hope: perhaps he was keeping it somewhere else?

It was midmorning and she'd been up since half past five with Rory. He'd already completed his first nap of the day and when Adrian surfaced, she felt as if she had been catapulted ahead in time, as if she were living in a different time zone from him.

"Happy Christmas," he said, kissing her briefly on the lips; then he promptly began to make himself a bacon sandwich for breakfast, which made her wonder when they might be eating

Christmas lunch. She was already hungry, having had her own breakfast at seven, and again felt as if they were living on different continents.

It was only when he went to the fridge that he noticed the gifts under the tree.

"Bloody hell, who are all those for?"

"Well, Rory mostly."

Adrian stared, openmouthed. "He's not even one. He won't have a clue. How much . . ."

He didn't finish the question, but the bah-humbugness was apparent and she bit back a sharp retort. At least she was *trying*. If he'd actually come downstairs last night and helped her wrap, he would've known all about the presents she'd bought their son, but he'd taken himself up to the living room soon after dinner. He'd taken his phone with him, too, slipping it into his pocket in a secretive sort of way, as if he was conscious of it betraying him several times during the evening, publicly announcing the receipt of messages, which brought a tense frown to his face. She'd asked once, casually, who it was, but he'd brushed her off with a vague explanation of an old friend.

Carrie poured herself some coffee and tried not to let disappointment settle over her. Here they were on Christmas Day in their London house, just the three of them. Apart from the presents under the tree and the large, as yet uncooked free-range turkey in the fridge, it was like any other day off from work. The thought depressed her and she shook it off. Time to get into the spirit!

"Let's open some presents!" she declared.

"You do it," said Adrian, still eating his sandwich. "I'll watch."

"But . . ."

He looked at her questioningly and she tried her utmost to keep a calm and pleasant expression on her face. Didn't he realize she'd *wrapped* them all so she knew what was in them?

Rory started to fuss in his bouncy chair and she began to make up his bottle, scooping powdered formula into some boiled warm water and shaking it vigorously. As she turned around she suggested Adrian might like to give it to him.

He was over by the tree, his inner child having conquered his middle-aged Scrooge and he was holding up a present and shaking it.

"What's this?" he asked, and the look of anticipation and delight on his face made her smile and tell him to open it. She watched as he did and so ended up feeding the baby.

He pulled out a box and looked at it, mystified.

"It's a baby gym," said Carrie. "Rory lies under it and reaches up for all the toys."

"Oh, right. Cool. Shall I do another?"

He went on to open the remainder of the gifts until the floor was full of boxes depicting baby toys in bright primary colors.

"Wow, he's got a lot," said Adrian, looking at

them. She could almost hear envy in his voice, but then thought that was ridiculous, a grown man envious of a tiny baby.

"There's something for you too," said Carrie, pulling a small envelope from among the branches of the tree she'd decorated only the day before.

He opened it to find two tickets to see his favorite rock band in concert.

"Oh, wow! Thank you." He kissed her. "How did you get these?" he asked in wonder. They'd sold out almost instantly.

She'd set an alarm on her phone to make absolutely sure she wasn't distracted by something baby-related and had then gone online the second they were released, trying again and again despite the fact the system was near crashing from overload. Her tenacity had paid off. "Oh, you know. Just told them you're their biggest fan."

He grinned and then there was an expectant pause in the conversation. "I've got something for you too," said Adrian. "It's upstairs."

She smiled, but he didn't immediately go and get it; then his phone beeped.

He moved away from her as he read the message and she tried to look at his face, but he had his back to her.

"Who is it?" she asked.

"Oh, nothing. No one important." He tossed the

phone down on the kitchen counter, as if to prove the point.

It's Christmas Day, she thought. *Who's texting him on Christmas Day?*

They looked at each other and she wanted to ask more but didn't know how without creating an atmosphere, and in her hesitation, he made his escape.

"Right, present. I'll be back in a minute." And then he was gone.

She burped Rory, waiting for Adrian to reappear, but the time dragged on. She could hear him through the ceiling, a muffled sound as he moved around. Maybe he was still wrapping her present. She looked over at the phone he'd left on the worktop, pondered for a moment. It wouldn't be right. . . .

She got up and, with Rory over her shoulder, went to it. Only take a few seconds . . . She quickly unlocked it and then looked at the last text—a deep intake of breath when she saw it was from Emma.

You need to tell her. It's only fair.

Her? Carrie knew who Emma meant—herself. *Tell me what?* But deep down, she knew. She tapped on the message, then scrolled through. Emma had sent him two other messages over the last couple of days.

Saturday December 23. 15:09
Have you told her yet?

Sunday December 24. 09:54
You need to speak to her. Tell her it was my idea.

She was stung with hurt and humiliation. What was this? It almost sounded like it could be . . . she could hardly bring herself to say it, but . . . an *affair?* Or was Elaine right, Emma and Adrian were working on an idea together?

Rory was starting to get tetchy and on checking the clock, she saw it was time for his nap. She climbed the two flights of stairs to the bedroom and put him in his Moses basket. Then she lay down on her bed, exhausted. Tried to make sense of what she'd just found out and how best to handle it. Tried not to let the betrayal floor her too badly—she knew she had to stand up and fight, but she was tired. So very, very tired.

She woke to the sound of Rory waking and realized, with much surprise, she'd also been asleep. As she sat up and looked into his basket, she was rewarded with a smile. She then caught a whiff of roast dinner.

"Hey, sleepyhead," said Adrian, as she went down to the kitchen with Rory over her shoulder. "Good nap?"

"Yes, I hadn't realized I'd dropped off."

"I came to check on you and you were dead to the world. Clearly needed it," he said, indulgently. Then he indicated the stove. "Thought I'd crack on with our Christmas lunch. Your timing's perfect. Turkey and spuds are done. And we've got red cabbage with bacon, stuffing, chipolatas, broccoli with chili, and peas." He waved his hand over the oven with a flourish.

Carrie took it all in. Adrian had gone to a lot of effort.

They sat down at the table he'd laid, poured a glass of red he'd already opened so it could breathe.

"Cheers," he said, lifting his glass. She returned the toast.

"It's delicious," she said, taking a small bite. "Thank you."

It was burning on her mind, and she knew she had to ask. "Adrian, is there anything you want to tell me? About you and Emma?"

His face contorted with guilt before he hurriedly pulled himself together. Too late: she'd seen it.

He laughed, a deliberately perplexed chuckle. "What do you mean?"

Which question should she ask? "Have you been working together? On a new project?"

He was staring at her in amazement. *Did you really think I wouldn't find out?* she thought.

"It's nothing," he said. "She's . . . she's tried to pitch me a couple of things but, well, you know what it's like with these young, ambitious kids. Got no principles. Sell her own grandmother if she could." He reached across the table and squeezed

233

her hand. "Don't worry. She's no match for you."

Carrie looked at him carefully and he sensed her hesitation.

"I promise you, Carrie. I'm not about to start a new project, now or anytime soon with Emma."

He said it with such conviction that she knew he was telling the truth. *But the texts tell a different story.* She suddenly couldn't face confronting him about them. Not now.

They continued with their dinner and then sat in front of the TV for the rest of the day, Carrie dozing off again at one point.

It was only when she was in bed later that night she realized Adrian hadn't given her his present.

37

The sun shone down on Wandsworth Common, making sculptures of the bare branches of the trees and casting the large numbers of post-Christmas walkers in a picture-perfect winter glow.

Emma had needed to get out. Christmas Day had been a trial, she and her parents the only three around the table, Emma feeling outnumbered in every way. She'd felt suffocated by their annual routine and had attempted to suggest a couple of changes, perhaps something other than turkey for dinner or to maybe play a different game from Monopoly, but her parents' response had been one of incredulity that she should *want* to do anything different. It was a tradition, it had worked for years, and would work thus for many years to come.

At church, her father thundering out the carols, her mother self-consciously satisfied at their pew position (warranted due to the amount of time they dedicated to the community), Emma found herself unoccupied. The devil makes work for idle hands and she sent—yet another—text to Adrian. She didn't expect a reply, not on

Christmas Day, and when one didn't come she was actually relieved. perhaps it would be best to keep Carrie in the dark for now.

It didn't excuse Adrian for not telling her prior to now, though, and she was beginning to get angry at the way he was blanking her.

This morning, once her parents had left for the airport, she was overcome with such a sense of loneliness she'd forced herself outside for a walk. As she strolled around under the bright blue sky, she pondered what to do over the next few days. A friend from university, Amy, had invited her up to her place in Hertfordshire to stay and she was sorely tempted to get out of London for a bit, but she had an appointment to see a room in a flat on Thursday. Something had unexpectedly become available through a friend of a friend. It was in a reasonable area and sounded nice, which meant it would be snapped up quickly, so she didn't dare leave it until the New Year.

"Well, well, if it isn't Emma Fox."

She turned to see a woman with flame-red hair under a bright green beret and her heart began to beat rapidly.

"Don't tell me you live around here?" said Elaine. "All this time and to think we're neighbors."

Emma smiled politely, trying to cover up her anxiety. She knew she was worthless to Elaine and so something must have happened to make her stop and talk, rather than turn and walk in the other direction.

A small dog, low to the ground, fluffy, with no eyes visible, came running up to Elaine and deposited a ball at her feet.

Elaine bent down. "Good boy, Monty," she said, and threw the ball again. Emma watched as the dog, presumably able to see through all the fur, took off in the same direction.

"Nice Christmas?" asked Elaine.

"Yes, thank you."

"I hear you're working over at Hawk Pictures, with Carrie and Adrian."

"That's right."

"Unusual for someone to take you on without a reference. Must have been blown away by your interview."

Emma was churning with discomfort but said nothing. If Elaine already knew she'd faked an e-mail address—and a reference—then she certainly wasn't going to confirm it.

"Enjoy working with Adrian?" asked Elaine.

Eager to follow any deflecting line of conversation, Emma smiled broadly. "Very much so."

"You've got a soft spot for him."

"What? No." Her denial bounced out of her mouth too quickly.

Elaine smiled. "I didn't mean like that. I meant his work, his talent."

Emma could feel the heat in her cheeks. *Christ, go down, go down*, she silently implored.

Elaine was looking at her curiously. "Oh my word, you *do* like him."

"Don't be ridiculous."

"Those red cheeks are not down to the cold weather, m'dear." She laughed. "Well, who'd have thought. Bet he loves it, young girl, fancying him."

"I do *not* fancy him," said Emma, through gritted teeth.

"He's a bit of a flirt, in my experience. Tried it on with our production secretary. Had to give him a stern talking to. Hard, though, not to feel something for someone when you're working closely with them, day in, day out." She narrowed her eyes. "I hope he's been behaving himself . . . ?"

"Of course he has," snapped Emma, instantly regretting her brusqueness. She suddenly felt a rising panic at her inability to handle the conversation and started to walk away.

Elaine's eyes widened in salacious delight. "He *hasn't,* has he . . ." she said, following her, taking her arm.

Emma shrugged it off furiously.

"What's he done? Or more to the point, what have you done? Together?"

Emma whirled around. "Shut up. You don't know what you're talking about."

"Just trying to ascertain the truth."

"It's not the truth. It's nothing but gossip. Nasty, malicious gossip."

"My dear, I find nine times out of ten, gossip is gospel. You told his wife?"

Emma cast her a look of loathing and then walked away again.

" 'Cause she'll find out, you know," Elaine called after her. "Business is too small for secrets."

The blood was pounding behind Emma's eyes. She was seething with fury. How dare that woman *presume* . . . Except of course it was all true. She felt sick to the pit of her stomach. If Carrie found out, she'd . . .

Emma shuddered. It didn't bear thinking about. Elaine had just better keep her mouth shut.

38

The rich, buttery smell of pastries beckoned from across the room, piles of untouched croissants and Danish whirls. Competing with them was the toasted, homely scent of fresh coffee. As the great and the good of *Leon* turned up for the read-through, they migrated over to the breakfast table and devoured its contents.

Carrie looked on in satisfaction; she'd been one of the first to arrive and so far everything was running according to plan. All the cast would be here today, as would the executives from the BBC, and the senior crew. Currently circling the room, getting to know the cast and welcoming them, was Emma.

Carrie had quietly watched Emma ever since she'd arrived. She'd watched her husband too. And she had the distinct impression Adrian was avoiding Emma. He subtly moved away anytime she got close as she made her rounds, meeting and greeting. In fact Adrian had stuck to her, Carrie's, side for most of the morning in an unusual act of solidarity.

She never did confront him about the texts. As much as she hated to admit it, she didn't trust him to tell the truth and couldn't bear what the lies would do to their already fragile marriage.

Instead she would keep watching, keep waiting, but she was wary.

Something was going on and she didn't like not knowing what.

39

Tuesday, January 2

Emma took her coffee and a chocolate croissant, and found a seat next to an actress who was playing a lesser part: she didn't want to ruffle any feathers by taking a prime spot next to one of the stars. Anyway, those were rightly Carrie's and Adrian's places, not hers.

She looked across at Carrie, who was chatting to another member of the cast, totally engaged. Adrian was by her side, as he had been all morning. It was as if the dynamic duo were back. They exuded authority and togetherness as they sailed around the room.

For much of the morning, Emma had felt invisible. She knew Adrian was avoiding her and almost certainly wished she wasn't there. She'd heard nothing from him over the Christmas break; he'd not replied to any of her texts. His arrogance astounded her, and a ball of anger was growing deep in the pit of her stomach every time he refused to meet her gaze or moved away as she approached.

Emma watched as Adrian and Carrie sat down, next to the two stars of the show. She carefully assessed Carrie from the other side of the room.

She couldn't see any indication that Adrian had owned up to her about his theft, but then Carrie was a consummate professional, so perhaps she was keeping it well buried. Likewise, there didn't seem to be any hint that Elaine had spoken to her, for which Emma was deeply relieved.

"Right, shall we all take our seats?" said Carrie, and people began to fill the remaining places around the large conference table. Emma caught Adrian's eye—the first time all morning. He held her gaze for a nanosecond, then looked away. Unresponsive, as if he didn't know who she was.

Stung, she glanced down at her script so she wouldn't betray her feelings to those next to her. Christ, she'd worked by his side the last *three months*. She was the one who'd been at his beck and call, who'd dropped everything to go to Broadstairs, his London home, or the office, wherever he wanted really, at any time he'd needed her. She'd taken the evening phone calls, just when she'd sat down to have something to eat, replied to the weekend e-mails immediately, even leaving the cinema in the middle of a movie when he'd said how urgent it was, how much he could do with "her ear." She was the one encouraging, cajoling, listening, suggesting, sometimes even coming up with the whole damn story herself just so he could put the words on paper. Words that she would again read, edit, discuss with him to make them better, make them enticing and exciting to this roomful of people sitting down right now, people who'd been shaking Adrian's hand and telling him how amazing his scripts were.

It was the second time he'd taken what he could from her, then walked away.

No chance, Mister, she thought, furiously. *You think you're just going to get away with what you did?*

Her ears pricked up when she heard an actor sitting across from Adrian mention *Generation Rebel*.

"I *loved* that show," said the actor. "Brilliant scripts, just like these." He tapped the piles of paper on the table in front of him.

Emma watched as Adrian shrugged modestly.

"And what a hit!" exclaimed the actor. "Did you have any idea when you were coming up with it that it would be so successful?"

Adrian laughed, shaking his head. "Of course not. It was just the right combination of timing and luck."

Emma was breathless with the injustice of it all. He'd blatantly stolen her whole idea. Used it to fatten his bank account and build himself a reputation.

"Well, it was inspired," continued the actor. "A work of genius."

"One of those things no one can predict," said

Adrian. He looked across the room and catching her eye for a fraction of a second, he smiled, then turned back to the actor. "One of those freak, lucky accidents."

40

The last of the cast and the channel executives had left, driven away in their taxis, and the production team were bustling around the room, clearing away the debris from the afternoon tea that had been served to revive flagging energies at around four. The cast had put their all into the lines, and the words bounced off the page, becoming alive with the promise of the show that was to come. The actors were happy and the channel was happy, and now Adrian would go and do the last few tiny tweaks to the dialogue before filming started the following Monday. Emma had made all the notes against the scripts, ready for his last edit.

She watched as he finished up a conversation with the director; then he left the room. Now was her chance. She looked across at Carrie, who was talking to the accountant, and quietly slipped out the door herself. Down the corridor, she saw the door of the gents toilets slowly ease to a close, and followed in the vacant slipstream, into the gents herself.

"Jesus Christ, Emma!" said Adrian, cock in his hand as he stood at the urinal. He turned his back so she couldn't see, hurriedly zipped up. "What the fuck do you think you're doing?"

Emma wrinkled her nose in distaste. "Believe me, I don't find it pleasant entering the men's toilets, but we're long overdue a conversation, don't you think? And seeing as you've been avoiding me, I had to come and find you."

Adrian was rapidly washing his hands. "There's nothing for us to discuss."

"Don't bullshit me," said Emma, angrily, then reined herself in. She'd promised herself she wouldn't get upset. "There's a whole heap of stuff to talk about, but mostly, you stealing my series idea and passing it off as your own. Have you told Carrie yet?"

Adrian finished drying his hands, lifted them, palms out, in a soothing pose. "Look, Emma, I think this has all got a bit out of hand. Yes, I may have used your idea as *inspiration,* but the finished product is certainly a long way from what you sent me."

"It's the same setting, same characters, same story arcs. *Generation Rebel* is set in a school, in which the pupils, led by a once-nice middle-class girl of fifteen, rebel against the authorities, and end up hanging the headmaster in the boys' toilet." She looked around. "Much like this one."

He scoffed. "Is that some kind of threat?"

Emma ignored him. "Adrian, I'm not going to go away. I can understand why you don't want to admit to your wife what you did. It's humiliating, and it may well damage your already rocky relationship, and if it gets out, also your professional reputation." She took a breath. "I have reconsidered the situation. Carrie's got enough on her plate, quite frankly, being the only parent who's looking after Rory. You barely even acknowledge him. It must break her heart. So this is the deal. Just try and appreciate her. If you don't, then *I'll* tell her what you've done."

Adrian was staring at her, bamboozled by this change in direction. There was a hint of relief he was off the hook, but she could see he was puzzled by her demands. She kept her chin high, brazened it out.

"Why do you care about her so much?"

"She's a decent person. Doesn't deserve you, if I'm honest."

"Nah, there's more to it than that. I've seen you, the way you're always trying to please her. What's going on between you two?"

"Nothing."

"There's something you're not telling me."

Emma took a deep breath. "You're just a shit to her and she deserves more. End of. The other part of the deal . . ." She saw surprise in his eyes. *Good, now he's on the defensive.* ". . . . is that I need money."

He snorted. "Blackmail?"

"Five thousand."

"You can piss right off."

Emma looked at him coldly. "I know how much you've earned from *Generation Rebel*. I've seen your contract. I know your fee, but that's just the start. I know how much you get for international sales and how many countries it's sold to. I know how much you get for format rights and the amount the cable channel in America has paid—"

"I'm not giving you any money."

"You could add a zero, two even to what I'm asking and it still wouldn't be anywhere near what I rightly deserve."

He was looking at her as if she'd lost her mind, and it was all she could do to stop herself from flying off the handle. Adrian had become a very wealthy man off her idea and she was about to become homeless. The room in the flat she'd seen just after Christmas had been tiny but clean. Trouble was, she needed six weeks' rent as a deposit, plus a month up front, and had to pay a steep holding fee. All in all, several thousand pounds. Her job was about to finish and it was clear there was little chance of being renewed at Hawk Pictures, given the current circumstances. Indeed, it would be a long and hard search until she found anything else. She needed to keep a roof over her head and what she was asking for was mere peanuts to Adrian—and was arguably hers anyway. In fact, she'd likely be asking him for more before she could get herself settled.

"I'll tell her," threatened Emma. "She knows you better than anyone—she's seen how much hand-holding you've needed during this new show. The minute I tell her, she'll know you did it."

It was that which convinced him. Not Carrie realizing he was a thief, but having his ego pricked by her understanding he hadn't come up with all that genius himself.

The next day, five thousand pounds landed in her account.

41

Monday, January 8

"Roll camera!" called Kenny, his director eyes fixed on the scene in front of him: Michael Sheen playing Leon, about to storm into his agent's office, insisting he was the star and the studio had better give him four black Labrador puppies in his trailer or he was walking.

"Rolling . . ." replied the camera operator. "And set."

"Action!" said Kenny, and Carrie watched, enthralled as the actors played out the scene. She was transported by their performances, so much so it took a few seconds to register her phone silently vibrating in her pocket. Looking at the screen, she frowned—it was Rory's nursery. The timing was terrible, first day of the shoot, first shot of the day. She desperately wanted to keep on watching as Adrian and Emma were doing, but what if Rory had become ill? She waited until Kenny called "Cut" and then slipped out of the studios.

Back in the office with her phone pressed against her ear as she waited to be put through, she hoped Rory was okay, for his own sake, of course, but it would also be very hard to leave the set on the first day of filming.

"Hi, Carrie," said Sherie, over the line. "Just so you know, everything's fine with Rory." Carrie sighed with relief. "The reason I called," continued Sherie, "was to do with this month's fees. I'm afraid the automatic payment didn't go through."

Carrie was confused. "What? Why not?"

"The bank doesn't give us a reason. Would you be able to check it and let me know?"

Carrie reassured Sherie she'd call back as soon as she could, then went online to access the joint bank account. Her eyes widened—it was more than three thousand pounds overdrawn. She scrolled through the transactions and her mouth dropped when she saw a payment made the previous week for five grand. Five grand! It wasn't her, so it must have been Adrian. What on earth had he been buying? Then her breath stopped and an unpleasant tingle ran up her spine. The payment was to a Miss E. Fox. Emma.

Why was Adrian paying Emma five thousand pounds?

She quickly transferred some money to put the account back into credit and paid the nursery. Once she'd informed them it was just an over-sight and had apologized, she sat back in her chair.

Something was definitely going on between her husband and her maternity replacement. There was only one way to find out what.

She got up and went back down to the studio.

42

Monday, January 8

Adrian ran his hand through his tufty hair, pacing in small steps back and forth. "I . . . er . . . shit!"

Carrie watched him. They were outside in a quietish side alley, away from any passing crew members.

He rubbed his hands over his face, peered guiltily between his fingers. "I don't know how to say this. . . ."

The butterflies in Carrie's stomach fluttered around again, aching to be freed. "Just tell me."

"I can't . . . I—"

"Oh, for Christ's sake, Adrian, just tell me what you've done," snapped Carrie. She shivered and wished she'd put on her coat to come outside.

"Okay! Okay," he placated, then took a deep breath. "I had to pay Emma that money because . . . she was threatening to tell you something if I didn't."

Carrie's eyes were agog. "Wait, she was *blackmailing* you?"

"Yes."

"In God's name, *why?* What was she going to tell me?"

Adrian's face crumpled. "I'm really sorry, Carrie.

I never wanted to hurt you but . . . Emma . . . she and I . . . we had sex."

Her ears were roaring, the deafening sound of her heart plummeting. She was aware of a great pain in her solar plexus, an inability to breathe.

Adrian was looking concerned. "I'm so, so sorry. It wasn't planned, it just . . . happened and it was a mistake. A one-off. I'd undo it if I could, I really would."

She'd gathered enough energy to utter a word. "When?"

"A few weeks ago. At the beach house. I didn't mean it to happen, I . . ." He put out his hand to touch her, but she flinched.

"Where was I?"

"At home. With Rory."

She nodded. *With Rory.* Everything had changed since Rory. Her relationship with Adrian had become unrecognizable. She no longer knew what it was, who they were. And now her husband was sleeping with a girl half her age.

She was disturbed by a sound, a pent-up agony, finally released, and she looked up, astonished. Adrian was crying, not just a snuffle but full-blown weeping, tears of despair pouring down his face.

"I'm just so sorry," he repeated again and again. "I never wanted this to happen. I never wanted any of this. I love you, but I feel like I've lost you. I miss you, Carrie. I miss what we did together. I miss our house not being full of baby paraphernalia. I miss being able to go out somewhere, to just walk out the door with you."

His grief was real, and his words echoed guilt-ridden sentiments that had crept into her own mind as well. She looked at him, overwhelmed with myriad emotions when he suddenly threw his arms around her, clinging to her. Uncomfortable, and still hurting deeply, she extricated herself; pushed him away.

He suddenly seemed to be aware of his behavior and got a grip. "What do we do now?" he asked, quietly.

Carrie's heart was still in free fall, rendering her unable to think, but there was one thing she knew instinctively. "She'll have to go."

He nodded, guilt on his face. "It's not just her fault . . . seems unfair somehow . . ."

"Well, what do you want to happen? Me go instead?"

"No! No, of course not."

"Because I cannot work on the same production as that girl now you've . . ." She couldn't get the words out, so busy were they lacerating the inside of her throat.

"No, I totally get that." He hesitated. "What do we tell Liz?"

"I don't know, what do *you* think?" She resented the fact he'd put the question onto her.

"We'll think of something," he said quickly. "*I* will," he corrected.

● ● ●

It was only later, in the middle of the most grueling day, using every ounce of her energy to behave around her cast and crew as if she were having the time of her life, that a needling thought suddenly made itself heard. Adrian hadn't exactly tried to hide the payment he'd made to Emma: he'd paid her out of their joint account.

She couldn't get rid of the uncomfortable feeling that maybe he had *wanted* her to find it. Wanted her to find out Emma was blackmailing him. And the question that left her feeling deeply unsettled was: why would he want that?

PART TWO

Emma

43

Tuesday, January 9

Today was the day.

Carrie had told the nursery that she'd bring Rory in a bit later today. There had been no need really, he could have stuck to his hours and she could have spent the morning alone, catching up on work, but she'd wanted his company. She held him on her knee, supporting him as he tried to straighten his legs against her lap, babbling away happily to her, oblivious to what was going on in his parents' lives. His innocence was uplifting and worked as a salve on her deep, hurting wounds, temporarily taking the edge off the pain.

She hadn't wanted to talk to Adrian after work the previous night. By the time she'd left the set and then gotten Rory from the nursery, it was late and every sinew, every nerve ending in her body, throbbed with exhaustion. If she'd tried to face her husband's infidelity, to hear more details, she knew she'd probably just burst into tears or be viciously angry, or both.

So she'd put Rory to bed; then Adrian had sheepishly come to see her in the kitchen, but she'd made it clear she wasn't up for conversation. She'd eaten some toast, then gone to bed herself.

It was a cliché, the younger woman. Despite knowing it was a mistake, Carrie found she was comparing herself with Emma. Emma was thinner, yes, of course she was. Carrie had just had a baby and she was dubious her figure would ever recover completely, something she didn't like to think about too much. Emma's blond hair was shinier than her own, and was still free of gray. In fact, they weren't dissimilar in looks, she thought bitterly. Emma was a younger version of herself. But it wasn't just looks; it was Emma's brightness, her endless supply of energy, her enthusiastic eyes unbeaten by diabolical tiredness. In some dim and distant memory, Carrie thought she could recall being like that. At the start of her career, when she'd carried an optimism that nothing could diminish. Her grasp on the image of her previous self flickered, and she had to keep retrieving it again and again until it became too tiring.

Old. She felt old.

She slept fitfully, waking to feed Rory twice, and each time the revelation of the previous day had sunk its teeth into her again, feeling worse as things always do in the silent, dark, lonely hours of night.

Neither of them had said much this morning, both waiting for the ax to fall, unable to face a postmortem until it was done. Adrian had slunk off to the Soho office, and she had opted to spend stolen hours with her baby.

She laid Rory down on a blanket on the living room carpet so she could safely take a sip of her tea. He continued to chat away to himself as she stood rigidly by the window, looking out at the freezing January morning. A runner dressed head to toe in Lycra pounded past on the pavement, great puffs of air expelled from his mouth into the cold, hanging in the space he'd just vacated.

How did I not see what was going on? Emma had wanted the lot: her job, to work with her successful husband, and ultimately to sleep with him. Carrie felt violated, as if she were naked, exposed in her stupidity—*her naïveté.* She'd worked so hard for everything and this . . . girl, this abominable, awful, vile girl had tried to take it all from her. Just because she felt like it. She was like a stalker, no, a parasite, helping herself to someone else's life.

On the floor, Rory gave a distressed cry and she looked down to see he'd rolled over onto his tummy and gotten stuck. Quickly she put down her tea and plucked him from his blanket. As she held him in her arms again she got an image of Emma picking him up that time and felt a wash of fury and revulsion. She held him tight and, over his head, looked at her watch.

It was nine o'clock.

44

Emma looked up from the scene rehearsal to see Liz across the studio beckoning her. She quietly slipped out to where Liz was waiting in the corridor.

"Can I have a word?" asked Liz.

"Sure."

"In my office," said Liz, and Emma followed her, wondering what it was about.

As she passed the office she shared with Carrie and Adrian, she was surprised to see it still empty. She had spent the morning in the studio since breakfast, watching the filming and glancing at her watch, wondering where her bosses were.

"Have you heard from Carrie and Adrian?" she asked Liz as they entered the office.

"Take a seat," said Liz, indicating the sofa.

A bell began to toll ominously in Emma's head. She slowly sat, waiting as Liz took the chair next to her.

By the way Liz was looking at her, she was contemplating how best to break whatever she had to say, and Emma braced herself but was still unprepared for what happened next.

"Emma, I'm sorry, but considering your recent

intimacy with Adrian, I'm afraid I'm left in a very difficult position and have had to decide what is best for the show and those who are essential to delivering it. Therefore, as of this morning, I am terminating your contract."

Emma sat there, shocked, silenced. Then a deep blush of shame rose up her neck and flooded her face. Liz knew. And if she knew, Carrie knew. *Oh my God,* thought Emma, and the room suddenly started to spin. She reeled and her hand went out to the arm of the sofa to steady herself. Stricken, she looked at Liz, who was still waiting for her to say something. She was aware she should be defending herself, expressing her outrage, explaining that Adrian had come on to *her,* even made a veiled threat if she didn't sleep with him.

"I . . . It was Adrian's idea."

Liz raised an eyebrow as if to say, *Is that the best that you can do?*

"He . . . suggested that if I didn't sleep with him, then he would . . ."

Liz frowned. "What? Are you suggesting that he forced you?"

Had he? It wasn't exactly like that, but he had said something about calling the police unless she had a good reason to explain why she was in his house. Put like that, it wasn't unreasonable of him. Why had she felt so threatened, so powerless?

"Because if you are, then that is a very serious allegation."

Emma squirmed, unsure. She felt completely out of her depth.

"Are you saying that?" asked Liz. "That he forced you?"

She was under pressure to answer and it wasn't as simple as a yes or a no. All she could process was the misery of Carrie knowing about that awful, terrible night. One that had cost her dearly and now had sabotaged everything she'd hoped for.

"Emma?" prompted Liz.

"Yes?"

"Are you saying that Adrian forced you to sleep with him?"

Emma looked up at her, took in this successful woman who had brought her onto the production. This was her moment to confess everything— tell Liz how Adrian had stolen *Generation Rebel* from her. *And then what? Generation Rebel* had nothing to do with Liz. Her focus was *Leon*. All she cared about was making a success of the multimillion-pound, star-studded juggernaut that was *Leon*. Her own reputation depended on it. Nothing must get in the way of the show. That's how it worked in TV. Liz might offer sympathy, might even tell her to direct her complaints to Elaine, but she'd still be fired and Adrian would be protected. *Leon* would be made, and those still a part of it would continue cresting on its wave while she was left to fend for herself with nothing. She'd been cast adrift.

"No, I'm not saying that."

Liz nodded. "I'm sorry it's come to this, and I do feel sympathy for your situation, genuinely I do. But you had such an opportunity, Emma. Why on earth did you do something so stupid?"

Was anyone telling Adrian he was stupid? Emma wondered. She didn't answer. She needed to get back to her desk, clear her head, and think about whether there was a way to salvage any of this.

"Okay, well, if there's nothing else to discuss, security is waiting outside."

Emma sat up in alarm. "Security? What for?"

"You're on garden leave, which means I'm afraid you have to go now. Collect your things from your desk and then they'll see you off the premises."

"*Seriously?* I'm not a criminal!"

Liz shrugged. "It's just the way these things happen. It's best you go along with it." She stood, went to open the door, and Emma started as she saw a man in uniform standing outside. What was she going to do? Run past him? Wrestle him to the ground?

SMASH CUT TO:

INT. STUDIOS—DAY

EMMA is angry at how she has been made a scapegoat. She reaches for the belt around her waist and presses the metal buckle. Instantly, with great panache and fluidity, her clothes metamorphose, the jeans and sweatshirt are replaced by a kick-ass jumpsuit and silver mask. She is empowered.

Kapow! She punches the SECURITY GUARD in the face and he collapses to the floor. LIZ is staring, openmouthed. Emma leaps down the corridor and soars out of the window, her super-power enabling her to fly, up, up to the sky, where the endless space allows her to expend her frustration and sadness.

CUT TO:

Smarting with humiliation, Emma got up from the chair by Liz's desk. Her heart was pounding as she stiffly walked along the corridor to her office, conscious of the security guard following her. She threw her personal effects in her bag.

"No scripts or nothing like that," said the security guard. She threw him a dark look and continued to gather her belongings. Then took her coat and made her way down the stairs and out of the building.

As they crossed the grounds, the walk had never seemed so long. She held her head high but inwardly prayed for it to be over, and for the man behind her to disappear.

"Emma? Everything okay?"

Her heart sank as she turned slightly to see Ray, the technician whom she'd become friendly with, watching her with a puzzled expression. Keeping her mouth clamped shut for fear of bursting into tears, she gave a tight nod and continued her walk of shame until she reached the exit and was unceremoniously dumped onto the street outside.

45

Wednesday, January 10

She'd been used and chucked on the rubbish heap. no longer needed. It had all become clear once she'd gotten home yesterday. She'd lain on her bed with time to reflect on the horrible events of the morning, and that's when the thing Liz had said had hit home. "I've had to decide what is best for the show and those who are essential to delivering it." She, Emma, was no longer essential to the show. Adrian had finished with her, taken what he wanted and dispensed with her.

She was seething, fury and hatred bubbling away in her veins, coursing through her body, round and round and round, never letting up, reminding her again and again of how grossly unfairly she'd been treated.

She hated him.

Knowing Adrian wouldn't answer her calls or texts, she'd phoned Zack, the runner at the Soho office, as she still had Adrian's iPad to drop off. She'd managed to glean he would be in the Soho office this morning and so here she now was, walking up the stairs. She opened the door and Zack was on the desk. He gave her an embarrassed smile and she wondered how much he'd been told. Everything by the look on his face.

"Hi," she said, breezily. "I've got Adrian's iPad."

He held out a hand. "Great. If you could—"

"I'll go and give it to him personally," she said firmly, and before Zack could do anything, she was opening the door of the back office, where she'd spent so many hours working with Adrian.

He looked up, startled when he saw her. Emma could sense Zack coming up behind her and she shut the door in his face.

"I think we need to talk, don't you?" she said to Adrian.

"Er . . . not really. Nothing to say."

"If you don't get your coat and follow me right now out of this office, I will make such a scene you'll wish—"

"Okay, okay!" he said, irritated. He jumped up and plastered on a serene expression for everyone watching as they left.

"Why did you have to make me a scapegoat?" asked Emma. "We could've carried on working together, we were still working together, despite our . . . mistake." They were in the coffee shop on the street outside, the place where she'd given him tips on buying a gift for his wife.

He shrugged. "It wasn't my decision."

She fought to keep her temper under control. "Adrian, you're the showrunner. You could have done something, said something so I wasn't unceremoniously thrown out on my ear. After *everything* I did for you. I was a part of this, too, you know."

He briefly looked uncomfortable, pulled himself together. "I'm not saying you didn't work hard—"

"Work hard? Of course I worked bloody hard. But it was more than that. I developed this show with you, Adrian. Those characters, their stories, they're as much out of my head as yours." She could hear her voice, almost pleading with him to admit it.

He glanced down at his coffee, then back at her. "I think you're being a little unrealistic . . ."

"Don't, Adrian."

"Emma, you may have been a sounding board, but that was all."

Her throat felt tight, stuck with hurt. *What did you expect?* It was pointless, a waste of time. There was only one way to deal with people like Adrian.

"I'll tell Carrie you stole *Generation Rebel* from me. And Liz, and anyone I care to, and your reputation will be ruined."

He contemplated her. "Carrie won't believe you. Neither will anyone else. It's a waste of time."

"I've got my letter."

He scoffed. "You could've written that this morning."

"I—" she began indignantly, but he spoke over her.

"Emma, you've just been fired for having sex with your boss. A silly, inappropriate thing to do. So now you're spitting blood and you make up some ludicrous statement about your boss's previous success. Emma, the woman scorned, tries any sort of revenge, even if it means fabricating an outlandish story. Who are they going to believe? You, the newbie trying to get a foothold in the industry, or me, the established, respected, BAFTA-winning writer who can make them a lot of money?"

Emma's face crumpled as it all became crystal clear. *I've been set up.* He'd admitted to their sleeping together because he wanted to rid her of the hold she had over him with *Generation Rebel*. And now, if she said anything, it would be as he was painting it: she was seeking revenge for being sacked.

"Actually, I have a bone to pick with you," he said. "Why did you tell Carrie about us?"

"I . . . I didn't . . ." She was baffled, horrified. "It was *you* . . ."

"And why would I sabotage my own marriage?"

"To get me fired."

"Could've done that a million ways."

"I didn't bloody tell her!" She was raising her voice now; people were looking around.

"Well, who else knew? Who have you told, Emma?"

Oh Jesus, no. Could I have gotten it wrong?

A name had come hurtling into her head. Elaine.

46

The bare branches hung low, dressed in green dust that was lit to a patchy emerald where it caught in the bright winter sun. Under Carrie's feet were the remnants of the annual autumn castoff, a blanket of leaves, their crunch long gone. A crisscross pattern of long shadows lay over them, stark black lines that mirrored the branches and trunks above.

She walked through the ancient woodland of Marden Park, high on the North Downs in the Surrey Hills, Rory encased in fleece in a baby pouch strapped to her chest. It had been years since she'd come here, her mother's favorite place when they'd lived nearby in Purley. As a child she would be brought here through the seasons and had grown to love every one of them; the vivid bluebells in spring, playful butterflies in summer, glistening treasures of chestnuts in the autumn, and occasionally, if they were lucky, boughs laden with snow in winter. Then there were the ladybirds—they'd always loved the ladybirds, which would hide among the tall grass, Carrie seeking them out, exclaiming in delight when one crawled onto her hand. Her mum once sang her the nursery rhyme—"Ladybird, ladybird, flyaway home. Your house is on fire and your children are gone"—and Carrie had found it upsetting. Her mother had needed to reassure her that she'd never abandon her and Carrie was enveloped in a hug; then they'd sat for hours, letting the ladybird explore up and down her arm.

Through the branches Carrie could see the piercing blue cloudless sky, and she impulsively kicked at the leaves on the ground, releasing their sweet, musty scent. She'd thought she might get lost, it had been so long, but the paths remained the same and she enjoyed the comforting sense of familiarity as she came upon sections of the landscape she recognized. Soon she would break out of the woods onto the chalk grassland, and sure enough the view that presented itself to her five minutes later was one that still took her breath away.

Rolling green hills interwoven like dipping waves, framed by the heads of bare trees and ancient hedgerow. Nestled down in the valley was once an eighteenth-century manor, now an exclusive girls' boarding school set in several acres with a lake. Her mum had always said she liked to see the girls out in the extensive grounds during their break time; she liked to see the new generation getting ready to take on the world.

To Carrie's right was a wooden bench. She went

to sit on it, first polishing the brass dedication plate with the cuff of her coat.

Helen Kennedy 1946–2007, aged 61 years.
My Darling Mum

As she sat, she gave a quick check of the bench, which left her pleasantly surprised; it was almost in as good condition as when she'd had it put there a decade ago. A bit more weather-beaten but still strong. It faced her mother's favorite view. A place they'd stop and picnic if the weather was good enough. She remembered one such occasion, a special treat after school with just her and her mother, as her dad was still at work. They'd sat down, only to be harassed by several wasps within minutes. Carrie, being irrationally terrified of them (she'd never been stung in her life), had screamed the place down. She smiled and glanced at Rory, who was asleep, his fat cheek resting on her chest, pulling his tiny mouth ever so slightly open as he breathed steadily against her.

Carrie put her arms around him and gazed out at the hills. The vastness of the landscape was what she'd always loved, the way it made her feel as if she could hurtle down the slopes, arms outstretched, filling her lungs with a power and purpose that might even enable her to fly.

"What am I going to do, Mum?" she suddenly said out loud.

Her mum had liked Adrian well enough, at least she'd never said anything to the contrary. The only time she'd voiced an opinion was when Carrie had announced their whirlwind marriage. Helen had been surprised at the speed of it and had checked once, that her daughter was sure, was happy, and as soon as Carrie had professed herself deeply in love, Helen had buttoned up and been nothing but supportive. She'd only known him a few years before she died, and since then Carrie had always imagined that her mum's relationship with Adrian would have continued to grow and she'd have become close to him.

Except now, after everything that had happened, she felt as if she'd been fooling herself. Maybe her mum's gentle questioning of Adrian had hinted at her hidden doubts. She suddenly missed her madly, her Mum who never judged, who had always stood by her, regardless of the mistakes she had made.

A rustle in the trees behind her made her jump. She turned her head to see a little brown face watching her, ears pointed forward, nose twitching, its whole body poised to run. An elegant roe deer. She felt Rory stir and looked down to see him fixated on the little creature. Then it disappeared back into the trees.

She shivered and realized she'd gotten cold sitting still on the bench. It was time to go.

Rory slept again on the drive home and as she

opened the front door, Adrian came into the hall-way, surprising her.

"Left the set?" she asked, a little concerned.

"Liz is there. She, er . . . it was important for me to come home."

Carrie squirmed with embarrassment. She didn't like other people knowing her business, but it was likely that most of the crew and cast would know by now that her husband had slept with both producers and she'd be the topic of much discussion in the endless waiting around between shots.

She hung up her coat and started to make her way down to the kitchen, carrying Rory in his car seat.

"Don't go," said Adrian. "I . . ."

She turned.

"I was hoping we could talk."

She looked at him, his tufty hair sticking up at odd angles, something she'd always found endearing. He was staring at her earnestly, desperate for her to say yes.

"It's four o'clock," she said, tightly. "Time for Rory to be fed. As per his routine. Surely you know this by now?"

"Course," he said, quickly, eyes shifting to the floor, and she momentarily felt bad for putting him in his place. But she knew he had no idea of anything to do with looking after Rory, and it suddenly made her feel incredibly sad and lonely.

After she'd seen to Rory and taken him upstairs

for a nap, she reluctantly left the sanctuary of the bedroom. The living room was empty and part of her wanted to close the door and curl up in front of the TV, but she knew this . . . thing . . . had to be faced.

In the kitchen, Adrian was pounding a pestle and mortar. "Just making a marinade for the chicken. Kebabs, that okay?" he prompted.

He was looking for reassurance their conversation would be civil. It was nearly five. Was that too early for a drink? She considered the rows of white wine in the rack in the fridge—stuff she hadn't touched for months, although she knew Adrian kept them circulating. She suddenly knew she couldn't face any sort of a hangover, not with a young baby to look after.

She poured two glasses of water, pushed one his way.

He watched her as he took a sip. "Thank you." Then he pushed aside the pestle and mortar. "I realize you probably hate me right now. . . ."

She felt a flash of irritation. Why did he say it like that? Like it was so simple, so trivial. As if she wasn't so speared with pain, it hurt to look at him.

"I need you to know that I regret what I did from the bottom of my heart."

"So why did you do it?"

"I don't know. Flattery?"

"You're saying she came on to you?"

"I know it sounds like a cop-out, but . . . yes."

"And you couldn't resist."

"I . . . I'm not going to say it's been a long time since . . ." He looked awkward mentioning their sex life.

"You just did."

"What?"

"You've just said we haven't had sex in ages, which is why I'm assuming you felt the need to go elsewhere."

"No!" He was exasperated, as if she'd mis-construed his words. "No," he said more calmly, "it wasn't like that. It was . . ." She saw him searching for the right phrase. "A mistake. A one-off, stupid, pointless mistake."

"Did you want me to find out?"

"No!" he exclaimed hotly for the second time. "Of course not."

"So when she blackmailed you, why did you pay her out of the joint account?"

"I don't know. I wasn't thinking."

She recalled the scarf he'd bought her as a gift—paid for out of his personal account so she wouldn't know the cost. If he could remember to buy his wife a scarf and not use the joint account, he could certainly remember not to pay his floozy. He just wouldn't have made that sort of mistake.

"*Really?* Someone's blackmailing you who you've had an affair with and it's not uppermost in your mind to keep it a secret from your wife?"

"I just . . . forget which account is which."

Carrie didn't believe a word of it. A painful thought kept nagging at her—had he deliberately let her find out because he was too cowardly to tell her to her face that their marriage was over? She was too scared to ask.

"Why was she blackmailing you?"

"I told you—she threatened to tell you about us—unless I paid her money."

"How much?"

"You saw . . . five grand."

"That's not very much considering she's sabotaged her career."

Adrian had picked up the pestle again, was smashing into the bowl, and Carrie got a strong smell of garlic. "No . . . well . . . maybe she was planning to ask for more later."

"But she must have known these things come out. I would've thought she'd have done anything to keep it secret."

Adrian shrugged. Didn't meet her eye.

"Especially after all the effort she put into making the job work. My God, she couldn't do enough to show everyone how brilliant she was, how qualified she was to have my job, kick me out and take over."

He looked up at her strangely.

"What?" she said, suspiciously.

"Nothing."

His dismissal was more than she could bear.

Carrie was suddenly spitting with rage. "Has she been whispering in your ear while you were lying in our bed together, about how she's wanted to oust me from my work and you . . . you've been *listening?* What did you do, encourage her? Give her tips?"

"No, Carrie, no, nothing like that." He looked mortified. "If anything, she looked up to you. She didn't want your job. She wanted to work with you."

Carrie realized she was shaking, was on the verge of tears. Sod it. She went to the fridge and got out a bottle of wine, then poured herself a large glass and downed half of it.

"Where do we go from here?" asked Adrian, quietly.

She shook her head. "I don't know."

"Can we fix this?"

She didn't know if he was asking her permission, or actually, if he was asking whether it was possible. Maybe they were too broken to be fixed?

A cry went up from the monitor. Both of them stiffened.

As she got up, she caught a glimpse of something that frightened her, a tiny moment. Before Adrian looked away, she saw his eyes cloud over with defeat.

47

Emma swilled the last remaining coffee around the takeaway cardboard cup to try to get some warmth into her glove-clad hands. There was barely any heat left; it had gradually petered out as if its very life was slipping away. It was the third morning in a row she'd walked out of the house with her bag and a pleasant goodbye to her parents, who were both under the impression she was headed for work, as she had done the last few months.

Instead she'd gotten a coffee from the café on the main street and, not wanting to be sitting in the window when her parents made their own way to work, had walked into Wandsworth Common. She'd stroll briskly amongst the few dog walkers who braved the extreme cold, until she could safely go home again.

She only needed to do this for another couple of weeks and then they would move to Italy, and she'd be in her new flat. Anxiety gripped her, as it always did when she thought about her new home. She had some money now, but it wouldn't last forever and she didn't have a job. She'd gone back to the pub where she'd worked the previous spring, but they had no vacancies; neither did the other half dozen in the area.

She shivered; the cold was always more penetrating when thick clouds hung low in the sky, trapping the freezing air near the ground. Seeing a bin, she dumped the cold coffee and, checking her watch, decided enough time had passed for her to go back home.

Warmth, she thought with relief as she turned the key in the lock and opened the door.

"Emma, is that you?" called her mother's voice and then Alice was there, standing at the top of the stairs, a figurine in each hand. "What are you doing here?" she called down in surprise.

Emma quickly covered her shock. She turned her back so her mother wouldn't see her face as she lied, bending over and pulling off her boots. "Adrian's not on set. He's asked me to do a bit of research on the computer—send it over to him. He just called me on my way in, said it made more sense to work from home."

"Right," said Alice, brightly. She trotted down the stairs. "I'll make us both a drink."

"What are you doing here, anyway?" asked Emma.

Alice held up the figurines. "Packing. I've got a few days' leave to use up so I thought I'd make a start."

That means she's here all day, thought Emma.

"Tea or coffee?" called Alice from the kitchen.

"Tea, please," replied Emma, following her in.

Alice looked around, waved her away. "I'll bring this up. You get on."

Emma had no choice but to keep up the pretense. Up in her room, she switched on her laptop and sat at the desk. What she really needed to do was research for a new job—but she'd have to wait until after her mother had brought up the tea so she didn't see anything on the screen. She also needed to get back to her writing, her true love. She needed a spec script that she could send out to agents to try to secure herself representation. Maybe Liz would help introduce her to a couple of people, she thought suddenly. She'd detected an element of sympathy from her for how things had played out; maybe there was a favor she could cash in.

She opened the script she'd been working on for the last several months now, started to read it through. Her mind was only half on the words on the page; the other half pictured Adrian as he'd brazenly insisted he'd done nothing wrong, that he'd in fact created both his shows single-handedly, and the old anger flared up again.

Breathe, she instructed and took a deep inhale, then let it out. Tried to find her place on the screen. Cheered herself with a thought that she'd make this script so brilliant, she'd become a success, elevated to the upper echelons of television, perhaps even surpassing Adrian himself.

CUT TO:

INT. BAFTA—NIGHT

EMMA is at the BAFTA after-awards dinner, dressed in a fine gown. She is being wooed by the HEAD OF DRAMA FOR NETFLIX; behind him the HEAD OF DRAMA FOR AMAZON is vying for her attention.

> HEAD OF DRAMA FOR NETFLIX
> I'm so thrilled for you. What a win! Best Drama, Best Screenplay, and you scooped up nearly all the craft and acting awards. You're our star writer, Emma.

Out of the corner of her eye, Emma can see her former colleague ADRIAN, thief and adulterer. He looks disheveled, drunk.

> EMMA
> Excuse me a moment, I must just catch up with an old acquaintance.

Emma approaches Adrian, who is slugging back a glass of champagne.

290

EMMA

Sorry you weren't nominated for anything this year, Adrian.

ADRIAN

(puzzled, slurring)

Do I know you?

EMMA

You thought you did, once. Funny how things turn out, isn't it?

They are interrupted by a commotion at the entrance. A group of POLICEMEN swarm in and head straight for Adrian. One puts him in cuffs.

ADRIAN

Hey!

POLICEMAN

Adrian Hill, I am arresting you for the theft of a television program idea. You do not have to say anything, but it may harm your defense if you do not mention when questioned something which you later rely on in court.

CUT TO:

Amusing as it was, it wasn't helping her to write. Emma realized she'd lost her thread and hadn't taken the last few pages in. Frustrated, she scrolled back to a familiar place and started again.

The door opened. "One tea," said Alice as she came in.

Emma tensed, but hid her reaction and turned around, a smile on her face. "Thanks, Mum."

She expected Alice to go, but her mother took herself over to Emma's bed and sat down. Looked around the room.

"Not started packing yet?"

"No."

"When is it you move into your flat?"

"Two weeks."

Alice nodded. "What are you going to do when your contract ends on this job?"

I've slept with my boss and have already been fired, ran through Emma's head, and she envisaged her mother's response—it was almost laughable. No, her mother was not the type of person she could confide in, especially not when she'd voiced so much disapproval of her daughter's career choice.

"I've already been offered something else," lied Emma.

"Same company?"

"No, somewhere else. A development executive role."

Alice was looking at her with something like resignation. "Well, if you're determined, I suppose there's nothing we can do to stop you. I still think you're making a mistake."

"I'm not like you, Mum. Or Dad. I just can't get passionate about medicine."

"It doesn't have to be medicine. There are plenty of other stable careers out there."

"But I want to write. Make TV shows. Can't you understand that?" Emma privately wondered if she'd ever get the chance again.

"I wouldn't mind being an astronaut, but no one's going to pay me to do it." Alice sighed. "I'm not going to try and persuade you anymore—you've obviously made up your mind." She stood, gently touched Emma's cheek. "I never felt I understood you. I'm sorry for that, Emma."

A lump formed in Emma's throat. She didn't know what to say.

"Will you come and see us in Italy?" asked Alice.

"Course," said Emma quickly, knowing it would be perhaps just once, to see the renovations, take in the novelty of the move, and then what? How much time would pass before she went back?

Alice nodded. "Good." She straightened, smiled brightly. "I'll let you get on."

As she left, Emma listened to her footsteps go back down the stairs until they disappeared completely. She swallowed and made herself sit up. Refocused on the screen. *Right,* she thought, with a determination she didn't feel. Stared at her script. Nothing. She inwardly screamed with frustration, stabbed her fingers aggressively at the keys, stopping just short of actually touching them, for fear of her mother hearing. She held her head in her hands, despair cascading over her.

After a while, she sat up, wiped away the silent tears, and smoothed back her hair. She opened a new document and slowly began to type.

48

It had been sleeting for an hour now and a lumpy, wet mess covered the cars parked outside the window. Carrie gazed out dolefully, in half a mind to stay indoors and not go to the baby Rhyme Time session at the library. Although if she didn't, she'd more than likely be stuck in the house all day, a thought that made her shudder, so she continued to pack the baby bag with the large amount of items she'd need for an hour's venture away from home. She put Rory in his fleecy all-in-one and was about to tuck him into the stroller when the doorbell rang.

Her arm locked tight when she opened the door and saw who it was.

"Hello, Carrie," said Emma.

A blast of freezing air invaded the house and Carrie instinctively glanced down at Rory in her arms, to make sure he wasn't cold or upset, but he was smiling and burbling at Emma, pumping his arms up and down in delight.

Carrie drew him closer to her and started to close the door.

"Wait!" cried Emma. "Please, let me speak."

Carrie looked at her hard. The sleet was

splattering the hood on her coat, which was pulled forward over her eyes. Emma suddenly pushed it off, looked desperately at her.

"I'm truly sorry for what I did, but . . . I didn't want to . . . It was a mistake."

Anger suddenly ignited her. "How dare you," said Carrie, her voice loaded with emotion. "How dare you come to my home like this? You have no right to be here. You take over my job, you . . . you are *obsessed* with my husband."

"Obsessed?" said Emma, taken aback. "I'm not obsessed."

Carrie pointed a finger, lividly. "I catch you in here, in my home, playing with his BAFTA mask, you snoop around to find out how much he's paid, and then you . . ." *You sleep with him,* she was supposed to say, but it stuck in her throat.

"No, I—"

"Get away from my house," Carrie demanded. To her irritation, Rory was still cooing at Emma.

"No, you've got it all wrong. I want to *protect* you from Adrian."

Carrie let out a strangled laugh. "You're a fruitcake. Now you listen to me and listen good. You are going to go away from here and I am never going to see or hear from you again. You got that?" She went to close the door, but Emma put her hands on it to stop her.

"Please," she begged, her hair now plastered to her face. "Let me explain."

Carrie pushed against the door. "I'm calling the police."

Emma started to cry, something that surprised and annoyed Carrie. She eyed her with distaste—all this because she'd lost her job? She should be behaving with dignity, not snivelling on her boss's doorstep like a child. "Get off!" she snapped, pushing harder against the door. Then suddenly the resistance went and it slammed shut. Carrie waited a moment, expecting a knock. When the letterbox opened and an envelope fell to the floor, she jumped. She waited some more and eventually heaved a large, tension-relieving sigh. Saw Rory was looking at her.

"You need to know which side your bread's buttered on," she muttered to him. "I am your mother, yes me, Mummy. Mum . . . my," she said, pointing to herself. "That girl out there is nothing to you. To any of us."

Rory smiled at her and despite still feeling shaken, Carrie smiled back. "We've got to work on that parental respect," she said, then went to put him in the stroller. She almost changed her mind about going again but pulled herself together. She wasn't going to let Emma ruin her plans, have any more of a negative effect on her life. She quickly checked out the living room window to make sure she'd gone and then came back into the hall.

The envelope was still on the floor, her name

handwritten on the front. She picked it up and stuffed it in the middle of a pile of flyers ready for recycling. Then she braced herself and left the house.

49

Friday, January 12

Half an hour of singing bloodthirsty nursery rhymes (whoever thought a song about cutting off the tails of mice was suitable for young children?) and still Carrie couldn't shake the uncomfortable feeling she'd had since Emma's visit. She'd gone to the baby-friendly café afterward with the other mums, where they'd let their offspring crawl over one another in the mini soft play area, occasionally rescuing one from a wallop on the head with a sponge brick. Now they were at home, Rory was asleep, worn out with the exertion and delight of noticing his feet for the first time.

The afternoon was turning dark. Carrie tried to get through some household chores while Rory slept, but she still felt restless. Questions went round and round in her head as if they were on a spinning game-show wheel, questions she wasn't entirely sure she wanted to know the answers to. What had Emma meant, protect her from Adrian? It was nonsense—*wasn't it?*

Adrian came in around seven and poured himself a large glass of red wine. They were being coolly polite to each other, unsure of where their relationship was going. He soon escaped to watch TV, something Carrie would've ordinarily found a relief, except that tonight she wanted to speak to him.

She followed him to the living room, sat on the arm of the sofa across the room from him. "Emma came to the house today."

He started. "What for?"

"To apologize."

He gave a wary nod.

"And explain."

"What did she say?" he asked carefully.

"I wouldn't let her speak. Sent her away."

She was watching him carefully. Was that a glimmer of relief?

"She did mention one thing, though," continued Carrie. "She said she wanted to protect me from you." She waited a moment to see what effect this would have on him, but he was blank.

"What did she mean?" pressed Carrie.

"I've no idea."

There was a loud burst of laughter from the panel show on the TV and Adrian was distracted, eyes pulled to the screen.

Carrie glanced at him, tried to read his face. *Do you really have no idea?* she thought.

She gathered an empty mug from the coffee table and took it from the room. Downstairs in the kitchen, she placed it in the dishwasher.

She looked across at the recycling bin. Turned

away and put the kettle on. Dropped a mint tea bag into a fresh mug. The kettle seemed to be taking a while. She listened and heard Adrian laugh at one of the jokes on the TV. She used to think she could read him so well but lately cracks had appeared, things that were chipping away at her sanity. His insistence over the confusion with the accounts, *those texts.* So many unanswered questions, half the time she didn't know whether to trust him or not.

Carrie went over to the recycling bin and plucked out the letter. She held it between her fingers for a moment. So much harm this girl had done to her family, really she should just tear it up. But . . . a small part of her couldn't settle. She wanted to know. The kettle still wasn't ready and so she ripped open the envelope.

Carrie,
If you're reading this then we haven't been able to speak and I therefore haven't been able to convince you of how sorry I am.

Here is something, though, that I'd like you to know, which may go some way to explain my recent failures.

When I was in my second year at University, I already knew I wanted to work in television. I wanted to be a writer and came up with an idea that I planned to send to you, as someone I admire greatly, in some fantastical hope that you might see merit in it and advise me—perhaps even help me take a step further in my dream career. I was incredibly nervous about contacting you for all sorts of reasons, but mostly for fear of you not liking the idea and that I would ruin any future chance of working with you. So instead, seeing that you were married to a screenwriter, someone I saw as an ally, I decided to write to Adrian. I sent him my proposal and outline about a mutiny in a secondary school, along with a note asking for advice on contacting agents.

I never heard back from him. Instead, a couple of years later, I discovered he'd taken my idea and sold it to the BBC, under his own name.

A few weeks ago, Adrian caught me searching his office at your beach house for my original letter—which I have now retrieved. I enclose a copy here. I was so panicked, I did a very foolish thing so that he wouldn't realize what I was doing there. Something that I now regret with all my heart.

You may wonder why I'm writing this. Part of me wants to explain my actions.

Another part of me hopes that one day you might be able to forgive me.

Yours,
Emma

Carrie heard footsteps come down the stairs and quickly stuffed Emma's letter back in the envelope and into her pocket.

"Everything okay?" asked Adrian.

She gave a quick nod and realized the kettle had boiled some time ago. "Just making tea," she said, pouring water into the mug.

He got himself some more wine and then turned to go back upstairs.

"Are you coming?" he said.

"In a minute." She watched him go, deeply disturbed by what she'd read.

50

Carrie claimed exhaustion again, an easy enough pass to get out of Adrian's company and be by herself, as she'd done it countless nights before. She lay on the bed they'd chosen together several years ago, staring up at the shadowy ceiling, conscious of Rory snuffling beside her in his Moses basket.

Carrie tried to think back to when Adrian was developing *Generation Rebel*, tried to remember what he'd been like when he'd gotten the idea. It had been quite sudden, she thought, and she remembered the frisson of excitement she'd felt when he'd told her. It had been different from anything he'd come up with before, and she had been immensely proud and had known with her gut producer's instinct that it was fresh and brilliant and that Elaine would likely get a commission. She remembered also being relieved; he'd been trying with several ideas over the years, all good, but not quite good enough.

The subject matter had been a surprise to her. Adrian had had an uneventful schooling, had never really shown an interest in those years. In all their time together, he'd never once spoken to her about wanting to write such a passionate piece. And the characters; they'd been so much of their time, people who were youthful, contemporary. None of it had seemed like a natural fit.

But that doesn't mean he couldn't have made it up.

Carrie turned over on her side, unable to sleep. There was, of course, the very strong possibility Emma had fabricated this whole story. Some kind of revenge for losing her job. But . . . she didn't believe it somehow. Carrie was suddenly reminded of something Emma had said. It seemed a lifetime ago now. Something about Adrian not being as good as he thought he was. It had infuriated her at the time, but now she wasn't so sure. Goose bumps rose up on her skin under the duvet. She stiffened, remembering something else. The texts. She tried to remember exactly how they were worded—"tell her it was my idea"—was that it? Maybe it hadn't been about Emma launching a new show with Adrian, but to reclaim what was rightfully hers.

Nothing was what it seemed, and Carrie felt as if she was losing a grip on the very fabric of her life. Facts that she had taken for granted were crumbling without warning.

She suddenly had a thought. There was one person who might know more about this: Elaine. She was the one who'd worked closely with

Adrian all those months on *Generation Rebel*. Carrie resolved to go and see Elaine first thing on Monday morning. It was a conversation that needed to be had face-to-face.

51

Sunday, January 14

It was a relief to Emma to be alone in the house. Alice and Brian were in Milan for their last weekend of checking over the villa renovations before they moved out there. As soon as they'd left for the train to take them to the airport, Emma had inwardly collapsed. She'd gotten very drunk on Friday night on a bottle of wine from her father's cellar and had woken up with such a hangover on Saturday, she'd barely left her bed. Instead she'd looked around the room, thinking that soon it would be someone else sleeping there, hanging their clothes in the fitted wardrobe, fixing their pictures on the walls.

Emma still had to pack. Her new flatmate, Lucy, was expecting her in less than two weeks, and under any other circumstances, Emma would have been excited to be moving in. But Lucy knew nothing of her current unemployed status, and a condition of the lease was that she had a job. The thought of getting up every day and pretending to go to work, as she had done for her parents, was utterly exhausting.

Her stomach churned with anxiety and she curled up in a ball to try to squeeze it away, but couldn't relax. It was a fear that plagued her, day in day out. It entered her dreams and woke her at night, leaving her writhing with trepidation. She had a sense she was moving steadily toward the edge of a very tall cliff and was unable to stop herself going over.

She glanced at the clock. Her parents would be home in ten hours; then the whole farce would start all over again. She momentarily contemplated telling them the truth, coming clean about losing her job, but she knew she wouldn't be able to bear their looks of disappointment.

Emma had sent e-mails to several TV companies to ask if they were currently hiring, but no one had gotten back to her. She was beginning to think word had gotten out already, that the long arm of Adrian's dismissal had tainted her. Employment seemed like an impossible goal.

To add to her woes, Emma hadn't heard from Carrie. The letter she'd left for her had been mostly truthful, but she couldn't bring herself to say how Adrian had threatened her. She was too ashamed.

Emma had tentatively hoped that what she had written would have made some difference. Adjusted the way Carrie thought about her. But it was a lost cause. Either Carrie had read it and it had had no effect, or she'd just thrown the letter away without opening it.

Unable to stand the sound of her own thoughts

any longer, she jumped out of bed. By the time she'd showered and had something to eat, the winter sun was making a brave attempt at breaking through the gray clouds. She decided to get out, walk on the common, even though she was beginning to despise the place, so often had it been her prison when she was exiled from her own house in her pretense of going to work.

As she crossed into the common, the sun was claiming victory over the sky and Emma saw the year's first snowdrops clustered around some of the trees. With the sun, so came more people. Their company cheered Emma to begin with, but then she became aware of how everyone was wrapped up in their own business. Families with children, groups of teens listening to music, and countless couples, arms entwined, gloved hands clasped together. No one took any notice of her.

She forced herself onward. She'd go down to the lake and then turn around and head home, although she didn't want to consider what she'd do once she got back to the quiet, empty house.

She could see a family with two small children feeding the ducks, but they finished as she approached; then she was the only one there. She looked out at the lake; at the ducks swimming through icy patches in the blackish water, then walked alongside the edge, feeling lonely and a bit foolish, until a little dog suddenly ran up and fell in beside her, its tail wagging happily.

311

Surprised, she stopped, and the dog stopped too. She smiled and bent down to pet it, laughing as it put its paws on her knee. Then she stood and carried on walking. The dog followed.

"No, little dog, you need to go back to your owner," she said.

The dog looked up at her and seemed to want to stay with her. Its friendliness lifted her spirits. She scratched it behind the ears and had a vague notion she might have seen it before. She looked up to see if she could spot whom it belonged to and then from behind some trees she saw a face she recognized, dragging on a cigarette and looking her way.

Emma stared at her: the woman who'd gotten her sacked, who'd told Carrie about her stupid, nauseous mistake with Adrian.

"Go on, little dog," she said softly. "You need to go back now."

The dog lay down at her feet.

Emma watched as Elaine started to head her way. She should turn and go, but she felt rooted to the spot, watching, as Elaine grew ever closer.

And then suddenly she was right in front of her.

"I hope Monty hasn't been bothering you," said Elaine.

Emma glanced down at the dog lying contentedly beside her. "Not at all."

"We only came out for a bit, thought the fresh air would do us both good. I haven't been feeling too well, been stuck indoors all day catching up on work."

Emma nodded at Elaine's forced small talk, grains of resentment building in her throat.

"Right," Elaine said brightly, clearly eager to get away. "Those scripts aren't going to read themselves." She whistled for Monty, who stood, and they started to walk off. Emma watched, anger building as she saw Elaine head back to her life, one with work and purpose and scripts to read.

She stepped forward and put her hand on Elaine's shoulder. Elaine turned in surprise, nearly losing her balance.

"Why did you tell Carrie about Adrian and me?" asked Emma.

"What?"

"Don't pretend you didn't," snapped Emma.

"I have no idea what—"

Emma was suddenly overwhelmed by a bright explosive fury, like a star, full of hot, dangerous energy.

"You are lying to me. You couldn't keep your bloody mouth shut, could you? Did you enjoy it? Talking about me behind my back, gossiping? Have you any idea of the damage you've done? You're nothing but a mean, poisonous old woman—"

She stopped abruptly as Elaine clutched the top of her chest and seemed to sway. Then, dramatically, she fell to the ground.

Emma's mouth opened wide. *What . . . ?* She suddenly realized that Elaine appeared to be in great pain, and uncertainly knelt down on the ground next to her.

"Are you okay?" she asked.

Elaine couldn't answer, but it was the look on her face that scared Emma, a look of terror and raw fear. It galvanized Emma into action and she was suddenly at her side, with no idea what to do, clutching Elaine's wrist in an attempt to check for a pulse, the only thing she could think of.

The dog was barking madly now, distraught at seeing its owner in distress, and Emma started to scream for help. She grabbed Elaine's hand and shook it, but there was no response. Her eyes were unfocused. Frantic, Emma placed her mouth over Elaine's and blew in panicked breaths. Suddenly there were people beside her, a man who pushed her aside and began to administer regular chest compressions and mouth to mouth, then a woman taking her own coat off and laying it over Elaine's still body.

Emma could only watch in horror. The crowd had grown quite big by now and then the sound of sirens, green uniforms running across the grass with a stretcher. They dropped it beside Elaine and took over from the man giving first aid. More air was blown into Elaine's lungs. A defibrillator was pressed against her chest and jumped her off the ground, once, twice, three times.

Emma was suddenly aware she was chanting under her breath, her hands clutched to her head: "Please, please, please, please, please. Please, God, please . . ."

After an indeterminable amount of time, the paramedics sat back on their haunches, exhausted.

A few faces in the crowd turned away. Some had tears running down their face. Emma saw a policeman approach her.

"Did you find her?" he asked.

She looked at him, too shocked to answer.

"She did," said a voice, and she recognized the man who came to the scene first. "She was screaming for help, trying to resuscitate her."

"Do you know this lady?" asked the policeman, subtly indicating Elaine on the ground.

Terrified, Emma gave a barely perceptible nod.

He lowered his head respectfully. "I'm very sorry, but your friend is dead," he said gently. He wrapped her shoulders in a blanket that had been handed to him by one of the paramedics.

Still stunned, Emma looked across at Elaine's body, stretched out on the ground. Everyone was shocked into a hushed state, except for a woman who let out a soft sob every now and then, and Monty, who was howling beside his mistress.

52

Carrie had debated whether to call first, but in
the end had decided against it. She wasn't in the
mood to be given the run-around again. This was
too important, too serious. Of course, by just
turning up, she ran the risk of Elaine's not being
in the office, but it was first thing, only nine-
thirty, so chances were good.

She buzzed the entrance pad on the Soho
street and heard the door click open. Carrie
walked along the hallway and suddenly heard
the sound of crying. Perturbed, she continued to
the small green reception room and was taken
aback to see Leanne, Elaine's assistant, in tears.
A policewoman stood by her side, a comforting
arm around her shoulders. A young girl, whom
Carrie recognized as the runner, stood awkwardly nearby, and two other staff members were
sitting at desks, silenced, with stunned expressions on their faces. All looked up as she came
in.

"What's happened?" asked Carrie, an ominous
sensation beginning to stir in her stomach. She
looked around the room, but it seemed normal.
"Have you been burgled?" she ventured. Then it

suddenly struck her that one person was missing.
"Where's Elaine?"

"That's all I know," said Carrie, looking at Adrian's and Liz's dumbstruck faces. "She collapsed at Wandsworth Common sometime yesterday afternoon and died of a heart attack. There, at the scene apparently."

Adrian was looking at her, appalled. "I can't believe it." He shook his head.

A knock came on the office door. It was the third assistant director. "Script query on set," he said uncertainly when he realized he'd interrupted something.

Liz stood. "I'll go. You give yourselves a few minutes. I'll call if I need you." She left with the assistant director, closing the door behind her.

Carrie was suddenly hit by an incredible sadness. She looked out of the window down to the lot, which was as busy as ever, boasting the highest concentration of walkie-talkies for miles as people walked with purpose, full of the importance of their productions. A plane flew overhead, on its way somewhere with its hundreds of passengers, each with a different story, a different place to be. Life everywhere was still carrying on. Except for Elaine. Elaine was dead.

"What were you doing there?"

She looked up, had almost forgotten Adrian was in the room. "Sorry?"

"What were you doing at Elaine's office? This morning."

She stared at him blankly. Knew she didn't want to explain, not yet. "She had some résumés for me."

He frowned. "Crew?"

She murmured something indistinguishable. Could have been a yes.

"Why didn't she e-mail them?"

"DVDs as well. Show reels."

He looked at her. She didn't like his scrutiny, broke his gaze and looked out of the window again.

"A friend of hers was there," she said quietly. "Saw her die."

"Oh my God," said Adrian. "Who?"

"Don't know. Policewoman didn't know," she explained. "Imagine that. Watching someone you care about die in front of you." She shuddered. "I feel for them, whoever it was."

53

"So you saw her collapse?" Detective Sergeant Bryant was looking at her across the coffee table with his unusually pale blue eyes. Emma forced herself not to break his gaze, although she could feel the terror bubbling away inside her, threatening to burst through and if it did, she knew she'd become hysterical.

"Yes, I was out for a walk. We were just chatting . . ." She suddenly had an image of Elaine's stricken face and felt as if she couldn't breathe. She dropped her gaze and, looking at her lap, inhaled deeply, again and again, and managed to get the panic under control.

"Take your time," said DS Bryant, and the younger male police officer who sat beside her on her mother's pale-gray sofa nodded in agreement. This was just a formality, they'd said. They always took a statement after a tragic event like this, but Emma couldn't help feeling as though she were under suspicion. It was the guilt; it invaded her on every level. She felt pickled by it.

"Out of the blue, she fell to the ground. I tried to resuscitate her," continued Emma, "but it didn't seem to have any effect. I was screaming for help and someone came. A man. He took over."

DS Bryant was still watching her, but nothing she'd said was untrue. She was also pretty confident the man would say exactly the same thing—as he had yesterday—she'd been trying to save Elaine when he'd heard her cry out and came to help.

"How did you happen to be with Ms. Marsh in the first place?" asked DS Bryant.

Emma frowned. "It wasn't planned. I've seen her before, when she's been walking her dog. We both live near the common. I assume she uses . . . used it regularly."

"So you just bumped into each other."

"Yes, she said she hadn't been feeling well and thought fresh air would help."

"Did anything frighten her? Shock her?"

Emma slowly shook her head. "Not that I noticed."

"It's just that we had a report of raised voices. Perhaps there was an argument?"

Emma did her best to look bemused. "No . . . we were talking about Monty. Her dog. I mean, I did shout." The detective raised an eyebrow. "To get help," explained Emma. "Maybe that was what they heard."

She could feel DS Bryant scrutinizing her face and then after a few seconds, he nodded. "How well did you know Ms. Marsh?"

might be. She would still be crippled by guilt. She'd hated Elaine for telling Carrie about her horrible night with Adrian, but she'd never meant for this to happen.

DS Bryant was putting on his coat. "Thank you, Miss Fox, for taking the time to talk to us."

"No problem," Emma said, quietly, not quite believing it was over. The two police officers stood and she did the same. She half raised her hand as if she wanted to speak.

"Was there something else?" asked DS Bryant, eyes once again alert.

"I was just wondering what happened to Monty. The dog," said Emma.

"Battersea Dog's Home . . ." said DS Bryant. "That's where they usually go when there's no one to take them."

Emma thought of the friendly little dog that had lifted her from her black mood, and felt such a pang of sorrow; she was in danger of drawing attention to herself. She swallowed hard. Nodded at the police officers and then saw them out.

Afterward she went to join her parents in the kitchen.

"How was it?" asked Alice, kindly.

Emma shrugged. "Okay. They just wanted to take a statement." She realized her hands were shaking and quickly busied them so her mother wouldn't notice. "Anyone want a coffee?" she asked, filling the kettle.

Emma shrugged. "Not that well. As I said, I saw her in the park every now and then." She paused, knew she had to say it. They almost certainly already knew and if they didn't but found out, it would only paint her in a bad light. "I used to work for her as well. For a very short time."

DS Bryant looked surprised and Emma was unsure as to whether or not it was genuine. It unnerved her. She had to hold it together.

"Well, it was more for some of her staff. I was an intern. Too junior to really interact with her."

"Good job?"

"It was all right," she said nonchalantly.

"So why did you leave?"

Emma stared at him. Was thankful that she'd managed to persuade her parents to wait in the kitchen while she spoke to the police officers. "I got fired," she said, "for looking through confidential papers. It was a mistake. And a long time ago now."

"So you left on bad terms?"

"No, not really."

"But you got fired . . . ?"

Emma spread her fingers on the seat next to her thighs. "I deserved to be. I was unprofessional." She looked up at DS Bryant, her heart racing in her chest, and suddenly knew he could pin nothing on her. If she could only hold it together for long enough, they'd go and leave her alone. This thought actually wasn't as comforting as it

They both accepted and Emma got the sense it was so they could spend a bit of time with her after her ordeal of the last two days. They'd been horrified when she'd told them the night before, on their return from Italy, and had offered to delay their move date, but she'd quickly insisted they stick to the original plan.

Her father came over to her at the sink, rested a hand on her shoulder. "I know it's hard, Emma, but you have to take comfort from knowing you did a wonderful thing. A very brave thing. You did your best to save that poor woman, and that's the most anyone can ask of you."

Tears pricked at Emma's eyes. She could hear the pride in his voice and couldn't remember the last time she'd done something that made her father speak to her like that. Words she'd been longing for most of her life. She closed the kettle lid and her tears dripped into the sink. If only he knew the truth.

54

Friday, February 2

"So are you going to the studios today?" Emma looked up as Lucy took her bowl of cereal and sat across from her at the tiny table in the tiny kitchen. She could hear the hope in Lucy's voice. Ever since the interview when she'd said she worked in television, and Lucy's face had lit up, Emma suspected this might have been what swung it so she, Emma, got the small single room in this flat, instead of any of the other people also looking for somewhere decent and (just) affordable to live.

She shook her head and played around with the toast on her plate. She really should eat something. "No," she said. "I'm working from home this morning, then popping out for a meeting."

When Emma had moved in the previous weekend, she'd been clear to Lucy that she worked from home quite a bit so she was at least able to avoid pretending to go out each morning. Lucy had given a badly hidden look of disapproval, but Emma assured her she wouldn't be running up a big heating bill. "I have a small plug-in heater," she said. "I'll just be in my room and I can pay a bit extra."

Placated, Lucy had resumed her enthusiasm

for Emma's job, plying her with questions and hugging the answers to herself as Emma explained the intricacies of her so-called glamorous job in television. Emma could see what was coming and so was prepared.

"Do you think . . ." asked Lucy, coyly, "what are the chances of being able to visit the set?"

Emma smiled in a positive way and said she'd have to see. It wasn't just up to her and it might not be "until further on in the shoot, when everything has settled down properly," but it was definitely a possibility. She needed to keep Lucy on her side. She looked across at her, with her swept-back hairdo and strong lipstick, her dark suit pulling just a little over her plump frame, all part of her self-styled "successful" look for her job in the city.

Emma wondered what Lucy would think if she knew what was really going on in her life. There was no meeting this afternoon. Instead she was going to Elaine's funeral. She was petrified but knew she couldn't avoid it. She planned to arrive at the last minute and sit at the very back. She would be alone with her thoughts. She wanted to make peace with Elaine.

The organ was playing something melancholy as Emma slipped into the small church, which was surprisingly warm. Weekly chapel at boarding school was held in a drafty stone building that chilled the girls right to the bone.

She took a seat in the very last pew, which was thankfully empty, and was relieved to see that there was no one in the three pews in front of her either. She huddled up near the imposing stone pillar, her face half-concealed by it, and instinctively pulled her black scarf up over her chin.

She looked at the dark-clad bodies in front of her, several rows of people who had known Elaine and come to say goodbye. She recognized a couple of the actors from *Generation Rebel*, sitting together. One woman was wearing an elaborate black hat, with netting over her eyes. Emma suddenly realized she had no idea who Elaine's family was and with a sense of dread, forced herself to look toward the front, to see who might be there. Their faces were all turned forward and she couldn't make anyone out. It was still, silent, with only the odd rustle of a Bible or hymn sheet turning.

Emma made herself look toward the altar, where just in front, there was a long, narrow table. On the top of the table was a lacquered wooden coffin. On its lid lay an arrangement of orange lilies. Feeling herself start to tremble, Emma looked away, glanced down at the shadows under the pew where the kneelers lay, waiting for her to get on her knees and seek repentance. She suddenly had a desperate urge to leave and was about to get up when the organ started a new tune, loud and thundering, and the vicar began his saintly glide up the aisle. She could still slip out, she thought, once he'd passed her, but she glanced over her shoulder and saw another church figure, a steward or something, close the doors. He stayed standing there, like a sentry.

They were being asked to find the first hymn. It was something she recognized from school and she began to mouth the words, while the congregation sang along, the actors' voices louder than anyone else's.

Emma was suddenly engulfed by a sense of remorse and shame so strong she felt as if she were falling. She grabbed the pew in front and slowly, her balance returned. When she looked up, a face was turned back to look at her, a face on which was an intense look of dislike. Emma held her breath for what seemed like an age; then Carrie turned away and continued to sing. Emma could tell by the backs of their heads that Carrie was next to Adrian and Liz, but there were no nudges, no nods to the rear of the church, and Emma's presence remained something between only her and Carrie.

A hand was outstretched at the door and Emma's heart sank, but she knew it would be rude to ignore the condolences of the clergy. She was desperate to step out into the air, get away from the church, which had given her no reprieve, but she allowed the elderly man in his white robe to take her hand in his and look kindly upon her. She glanced backward; people were just leaving their pews, so she needed to be away. A few platitudes later and she escaped, almost running into the cold winter afternoon. It was only half past four, but dusk was already settling and a fog was lingering near the ground. A small glow of red flickered by a gravestone and Emma saw Liz throw a depleted cigarette on the ground, grinding it out and depositing the butt in a drain.

"Hello, Emma. I didn't know you were coming."

She didn't answer.

"How have you been?"

"Fine."

"Working?"

Emma quickly shook her head and Liz's resigned smile told her it wasn't surprising. It was a tough business and news traveled fast.

"I heard Bread and Butter Productions is looking. Script Editor," said Liz.

The kindness wounded her. Small scraps handed out as an acknowledgment she'd been made a sacrificial lamb. Liz clearly felt sorry for her, not enough to do the right thing but still, maybe she wanted to assuage some guilt.

"I've already approached them. Anyway, I want to write," Emma said defiantly.

To Liz's credit, she didn't smile in amusement or dismiss this as a lofty ambition. "Do you now? You know you need a spec script."

Emma nodded, heavy hearted, as she was reminded again of how hard she was finding it to break her writer's block.

"Well, when you have one, let me know. I might be able to introduce you to an agent friend of mine. In the meantime, try again at Bread and Butter. But maybe next time don't sleep with the boss, or at least make sure he doesn't tell his wife," said Liz, wryly.

Emma's head snapped up. "What?"

"Well, I think it's obvious," said Liz, bemused. She took out another cigarette, tried to get the lighter flame to hold. "What's that expression, don't doo doo on your own doorstep?"

"No, no," said Emma, impatiently. "About Adrian telling his wife. You mean he was the one to tell Carrie?"

Liz's cigarette was still clamped between her lips and then finally, the lighter's flame managed to catch the end. She took a long drag. "That's right. Confessed on the first day of filming. His timing was *shitty . . .*"

Liz continued talking, but Emma had tuned out. A boiling noise was throbbing in her ears, deafening her. *Adrian* had told Carrie. Not Elaine at all.

"Are you okay?"

Emma looked up, realized Liz had a hand on her arm, and was looking at her, concerned.

"You looked like you were about to faint," said Liz, by way of explanation for her hand. She gingerly let go and Emma straightened. She needed to get out of there.

"I'm fine. I just need a hot drink or something. It's cold," she added, unnecessarily, pulling her coat closer. She started to walk toward the road.

"Not coming to the wake?" Liz called after her, but Emma didn't answer. She couldn't believe what she'd just learned. Adrian had lied to her. Made her think Elaine was the one who'd blown their secret. When all along the bastard had done it himself.

55

The lime-green submarine surfaced about two yards from the rocky Nova Scotia shore-line. Large boulders guarded the snowy beach beyond which dramatically vertical cliffs soared up into the sky. On the cliff top grew countless tall pines, those at the very edge with their roots exposed where the cliff had crumbled away. Their dark green branches were laden with snow, which every now and then, when the wind blew, would tumble to the ground in a powdery thump.

"I need a coyote," said Kenny, the director, as he stared up into the trees. "Three, in fact. At least three."

Carrie caught Liz's eye. "I think that might be a bit of a challenge," she said to Kenny. "We're filming these scenes tomorrow."

"Leon's gone on a survival weekend," said Kenny. "He's taken his sub to the wild coasts of Canada to get back to nature. I need nature."

"There are trees and snow and not a Starbucks in sight," pointed out Liz.

Kenny smiled indulgently. "It's where his agent calls him and breaks the news he's lost the movie deal. I think it would work better if he was up against the elements."

Adrian cocked his head. "It does add to the tension of the scene. If his life is under threat at the same time as his livelihood."

Carrie refrained from gritting her teeth. She needed to rein this one in quickly. "The scene is set in the day. Coyotes are nocturnal."

"Are they?" said Kenny, not entirely convinced.

"Absolutely."

Liz held up her phone, having rapidly Googled. "Mr. Attenborough confirms it. Not the movie star, the wildlife one."

Kenny was looking disgruntled. Carrie indicated the giant green screen behind the fir trees. "We can always add some in. If it's crucial."

"Won't be in close up."

"Cutaways?"

Kenny frowned. "Close up with *Michael,*" he said sulkily.

"No, the coyote won't be in the same shot as Michael," replied Carrie patiently. "But I think it's going to be hard to find a trained coyote—three trained coyotes for tomorrow. And anyway, wouldn't it be better to keep the budget for the extra crane? I'm sure we can stretch to both of those you asked for if we save in other areas."

Kenny was weighing it up. Shrugged. "Okay."

A runner came hurrying up to them. "Are you

free to block the next scene?" she asked Kenny. "Lighting's complete."

Carrie let out a silent sigh as Kenny followed the runner back into the studio.

"*Coyote?*" said Liz, under her breath.

"I liked the idea," said Adrian.

"You would," said Liz, lightly.

"Looks good, though, don't you think?" said Carrie, gazing up at the set. The art department had done a phenomenal job—it looked exactly like a rugged beach on the wild Atlantic coast of Canada.

"Amazing," agreed Adrian.

"You planning on taking us around the world in your next show?" asked Liz.

It was said lightly enough, but Carrie's antennae prickled. She knew what Liz was getting at. Liz wanted to know how Adrian's next idea was coming along. The one he'd been contracted to write.

"Not sure yet," said Adrian. "Haven't written it." He laughed, but it was slightly forced.

"Got any thoughts?"

"Yeah."

Liz smiled. "Care to share them?"

"Not yet," he said, with a hint of irritation.

"Honestly, Adrian, I'm not pressuring you."

"Really?"

"Promise."

Adrian indicated the Nova Scotia beach.

337

"There's been another show to get on the road. Not to mention a whole load of personal stuff to deal with."

Carrie glanced away, embarrassed.

"I'm talking about Elaine," said Adrian. "We only buried her on Friday."

"Elaine would have had you storylining at her wake," said Liz. "You know once she called a writer at the hospital as his wife was giving birth. Gave him his notes over the phone while his wife was screaming through her contractions."

"Idiot should have turned his phone off," grumbled Adrian.

"I'm not saying you need to deliver all six scripts of a new series by tomorrow, but it would be good to get a sense of what you want to write."

Adrian went silent and Carrie wondered if he had any ideas he was mulling over. They hadn't spoken about work for weeks, beyond what was immediately necessary on *Leon*. Other events had taken over. Was he dreaming up new ideas?

An uncomfortable feeling settled over Carrie as she was reminded of the letter Emma had delivered, the one in which she claimed Adrian's first success was actually her idea. She still didn't know whether to believe it or not, but it wouldn't go away. Thoughts of Emma plagued her constantly. Emma, who'd been a thorn in her side ever since she'd walked through the door to interview for her maternity cover. Carrie couldn't seem to shake her; the woman had infiltrated every part of her life. It had jolted Carrie to see Emma at the funeral when she hadn't expected her to be there. Emma had worked for Elaine for only a few months and had been unceremoniously fired from the job. Why would you attend the funeral of someone who fired you over a year ago? Someone you hardly knew?

"I'll get you some thoughts in the next few days," said Adrian.

"That would be great," said Liz, smiling. "I'm seeing Luke soon and it would be good to have something to talk over with him. Now it's freezing out here. Anyone for a coffee?"

She headed off toward the studios and Adrian glowered at her back as she went. The malevolent look on his face took Carrie by surprise. She saw him quickly readjust his expression when he saw her; then she watched as he followed Liz.

She shivered. It wasn't just anger she'd seen in Adrian's eyes; it was fear too.

56

The mobile started to turn, the farmyard of tiny stuffed animals gently dancing to Brahms's "Lullaby" above Rory's enraptured face. Carrie switched off the lamp and softly closed the door, crossing her fingers. It was her nightly superstitious ritual, complete with a plea to the gods that he would drop off. If she was honest with herself, it had become easier of late—Rory did seem to have learned how to fall asleep.

She crept down the two flights of stairs and stood in the empty kitchen. She could see a crack of light under the door of the office. Adrian must be in there working. She wondered if he was concentrating on ideas for the next show. *The next show.* Even if everything went according to plan (unheard of in the obstacle-strewn world of television development), the absolute earliest they'd be filming was two years' time. Where would they all be in two years?

Carrie wondered about making something for dinner but wasn't particularly hungry. She looked in the fridge; there was a bag of carrots nestled in the salad drawer and a bunch of only slightly wilted coriander. Maybe she could rustle up some soup.

She went over to the office door and raised her hand. Gently tapped on the wood. It was a moment before Adrian answered, and in that moment she imagined his frustration at being disturbed.

"Yep?" he called.

She opened the door. He was sitting at his desk, computer switched on. As the door swung open, the draft stirred the noose rope, as it always did, and as she always did, she wished he'd move it. She didn't like it swinging macabrely on the wall like that.

"I was thinking of making some carrot soup," she said.

He looked around. "Sounds great. Thanks."

Carrie glanced at the computer screen. She couldn't read it from where she was standing, but she saw some dark lines of text. "Working on some new ideas?"

He threw his arms up in a faux nonchalant flourish. "Yeah, just jotting a few things down, you know."

She did know. It meant he was stuck—that the ideas weren't flowing. Ordinarily, this would be her cue to park herself on the sofa, bounce some ideas around with him. But she wasn't sure anymore. *Two years* . . . Would they still be together in two years?

"You want to chat?" she asked, cautiously.

She could see he knew what she was getting at. Their professional and personal lives were so intrinsically entwined and there was a gaping hole in one of them. Although Adrian's night with Emma had hurt her badly—and still did—deep down Carrie knew this wasn't the problem. Emma had just been a symptom of the problem. She looked at the man in front of her, whom she still loved in so many ways, and felt as if she was looking at her past. Before Rory.

He looked at her. "I don't know," he said, gently. "Do you?"

Tears threatened to overwhelm her, something she couldn't deal with right now. She plumped up the cushions and sat down on the sofa. "Why don't we talk about the ideas instead," she said with a forced brightness, indicating his computer.

He glanced back at the screen. "Er . . . well, I'm still at the very early stage. Trying to nail the concept . . . I've been looking at politicians . . . after all that stuff in the news recently—what's his face's fall from grace. Having to move out of the family pile and sell the heirlooms . . ." He trailed off and she suddenly felt embarrassed for him. It was essentially the same idea as *Leon*, just in a different setting. Certainly nowhere near innovative enough to get a commissioner excited.

It was now or never, she suddenly thought. She had to know. "Adrian, there's something I wanted to talk to you about."

He looked wary. "Oh yeah?"

Her nerves were making her stomach flip over,

but she carried on. "I had a letter. From Emma."
She saw him flinch. "She claims that she sent you
a TV project several years ago asking for some
advice, and that you took that project and made it
yours. She said it was called *Generation Rebel.*"

He said nothing; his jaw was locked in anger,
his hands linked across his chest as he stared out
of the window.

Carrie waited but still he said nothing. "Is it
true?" she asked, tentatively.

He swung his chair around then to face her.
"What do you think?" he snapped.

"Well, I don't know—"

"You'd really believe some fantasist over your
own husband?"

A husband who's already lied to you, said the
devil in her ear. "I just wanted to hear what you
had to say."

"She's looking for revenge. She wants to dis-
credit me—blacken my name, because she got
fired."

Carrie nodded. "I can see that, but . . ."

"But what?" he challenged.

"You still haven't answered the question."

Briefly, she saw a flicker of fear in his eyes.
And suddenly she knew what he was frightened
of. Not that he'd been caught, but that he wasn't
the writer the world believed him to be. He was
afraid he couldn't deliver. She was closer to his
screen now and he saw her glance up at it. There

was nothing really on there. A few half-finished sentences.

Her eyes went back to his and she saw he knew she understood. She knew his weakness, his secret: without Emma, or Elaine, or herself, he was unable to function.

"Why?" she implored him, not just for the act of the theft itself, but for everything it had brought with it. Emma's determination to work with him, to find the proof, everything that had upended their lives.

"Don't you start acting as if you're an innocent party here," he lashed out.

She recoiled, not understanding. "What?"

"You sit there and dare to judge me for getting the job done, for getting work, but you forget you've benefitted just as much as me."

"I haven't . . ." she began to protest.

"You enjoy the beach house, don't you?"

"But—"

"And what about *Leon*? Do you really think that would've been commissioned without the success of *Generation Rebel*? Your career has done very well, thank you; now you're hanging on to my coattails, so don't start judging me when you've been very happy to go along for the ride when it suited you."

Carrie's mouth was open with hurt and bewilderment. Unable to speak, she closed it, forced herself to stand, despite feeling as though she'd been punched in the gut. She caught a glimpse of regret on Adrian's face, but needed to get out of there. As she left the room, pulling the door shut, she heard the draft send the noose swaying back and forth across the wall.

Later, in the solitary early hours of the morning, just after she'd fed Rory and put him down again, Carrie lay in bed with a strange sensation that took her a while to put her finger on. When she did, it heralded a small glow, a chink of light that was brighter for the long time it had been in coming.

Relief. That was what she felt. The lightness of relief. She had been wrong all along. Emma hadn't wanted her career, or the kudos of working with her husband. She hadn't even wanted to steal him from her. She'd just wanted to get at the truth and she, Carrie, had been collateral damage. Emma wasn't some monster who wanted to take over her life. She had no *interest* in her life! Carrie almost laughed then, at how completely she'd got it wrong, at the ordinariness of it all. Carrie was no one to Emma, nothing. She stretched out with a sense of pure joy. It was such a wonderful sensation. She was free. She was free!

57

Despite its being the hardest thing to do, every morning Emma made sure she was out of bed and down in the kitchen fully dressed, making breakfast. She'd always put the kettle on and poured the water on two tea bags in two mugs so there was one for Lucy. Two slices of toast popped out of the toaster and she automatically buttered them and knew she would eat them or at least one in this whole pretense that everything was normal. Behind her, Lucy wittered on as she made some quinoa thing in Tupperware for her lunch, quinoa and kale being the latest nutritional combination that she was convinced would help her shed the extra few pounds she was carrying.

Lucy suddenly held her phone up in front of Emma's face. "Oh my God, look, it's your actress, you know, the one playing the Hollywood ex-girlfriend. She's coming out of some nightclub." Lucy peered closer. "God, she looks amazing considering it's three in the morning and she's no doubt drunk several gallons of wine." She sounded peeved, as if the actress had no right to be so beautiful *and* have a good time.

"Champagne," said Emma.

347

"What?"

"Anna-Maria." She pointed at Lucy's phone. "She likes champagne. Taittinger."

"Seriously? That's all she drinks on a night out?"

Emma shrugged. "So she says."

Lucy stared enviously at the phone. "Nice life. Hey, she's tweeted a message: Loving working with the guys on Leon—awesome show. Was in a hot air balloon today!!!!! She looked up. "She was in a hot air balloon? Flying over London?"

"In the studios probably," corrected Emma.

"What do you mean, probably? Don't you know?"

Emma inwardly cursed her slipup. "Yeah, course. It was shot against a green screen. The background will go in after—special effects."

Lucy's eyes were agog with wonder. "Wow. Did you . . . I mean, is there any chance . . . ? I'd still love to visit the set. I wouldn't get in the way. Just, you know, blend invisibly into the background. Only talk to the actors at lunch."

Emma looked up sharply.

"Joke," said Lucy, wounded, although Emma knew she would seize the chance to speak to them or ask for an autograph, if the opportunity arose. Which of course it never would, as she didn't work there anymore.

"So what do you think?" prompted Lucy.

Emma swallowed her mouthful of toast, which

seemed to refuse to go down. "I'll check in again. See what the schedule's like over the next couple of weeks."

Lucy brightened. "Thanks. Today?"

"Today what?"

"Can you check today?"

"No," said Emma, a little too quickly. "I'm working from home," she explained.

Lucy sniffed. "Again?"

"Is that a problem?"

"No, just seems you're hardly ever there. At the studios . . ."

Lucy had trailed off, waiting for an explanation, but Emma was damned if she would give her one. She was fed up with her constant needling about visiting the set. She could do without it. There was enough on her plate already—she was barely sleeping and had lost weight, something that Lucy had also made the odd remark about. "You don't want to get too skinny or you'll fade away," she'd said while pointedly staring at her waistline the other day, when Emma, unable to stomach her dinner, had scraped most of it in the bin. She hadn't replied as she didn't want to get into any sort of debate but instead had gone to her room, where she'd done what she always seemed to do now: think about Elaine.

She'd wrongly accused her. Screamed at her. She had blood on her hands because of Adrian and his false accusation. There wasn't a day when the nightmare image didn't come to the forefront of her mind again and again; Elaine's terrified face as she realized she was dying.

Emma looked at the rest of her toast, her appetite nonexistent.

"Rent's due tomorrow," said Lucy, and Emma looked up. "Just saying," shrugged Lucy.

"I know the rent is due," said Emma, sharply. "You don't need to remind me." In fact it was another thing adding to her misery. There was still no promise of work on the horizon. She suddenly felt as if she were suffocating. She threw the remaining toast in the bin and grabbed her coat and bag.

"Where are you going?" asked Lucy, taken aback.

"Think I will go to the studios after all," said Emma, pointedly. "I could do with a change of scene."

Lucy looked put out and a little sheepish— no doubt regretting her words in case they'd jeopardized her set visit, but Emma was already through the front door.

The cold, biting air nipped at her cheeks as she strode furiously down the road. Who did Lucy think she was, nagging at her, constantly going on with her little jibes and comments? Emma couldn't stand it. This new place wasn't home; it was somewhere to rest her head, and she felt as if she never wanted to go back. Everything was lost and the world was conspiring against her. And Lucy wouldn't shut up. Emma marched angrily on, feeling in a dangerous mood.

Christ, it was cold. In her hurry to get out of the house she'd left her gloves behind and her hands were numb. She stuffed them in her coat pockets and marched on further, fueled by a burning desperation. Flakes of snow started to drift down from the sky, little pieces of floating softness, soundless, but filling the air like some sort of alien invasion. Emma stopped, looked around in dismay. She stretched out her arm and watched as the white flakes landed on her coat, staying there for a few seconds before disappearing. The snow was getting heavier. She hunched her shoulders and headed toward a parade of shops nearby, which she knew included a café.

Once inside, she ordered herself a coffee and took it to the till to pay. Digging around in her handbag, she was mortified when she couldn't find her purse. *Oh God,* she thought, *don't tell me I've gone and left it at the flat.* Throwing an apologetic look to the European guy at the register, she took her bag off her shoulder and searched frenetically, plucking things out and shoving them on the counter. Then just as she thought she was going to have to hand the coffee back, to her relief she saw her purse had fallen into a small pocket inside the lining of her bag.

She pulled it out and was about to pay when something else caught her eye.

A single Yale key, glinting at her from the creases in the pocket seams. She fished it out. It was cold in her fingers.

"Are you ready to pay, miss?" said the man at the register.

She quickly handed over the cash and then went to a table. She placed the key down in front of her and an idea began to form.

58

Carrie pushed the pram along the streets, buoyant after her session at Baby Swimming with Rory. She loved seeing him in the water, reaching out for her with his fat little arms. In fact, everything seemed more enjoyable. It was as if a weight had lifted, now she knew she wasn't in Emma's firing line.

It was cold and she picked up her speed as she was running late for Rory's lunch. If he wasn't fed at bang on noon, he'd start wailing, and it was too cold to sit on a bench and pull out a bottle of milk.

As she turned into her road, snow started to fall and she stopped, full of delight. Then she glanced down at the pram and weighed it up. If she was quick . . . She got Rory out and held him in her arms.

"Look, Rory, snow!" she said, pointing. He gazed at the falling white flakes, puzzled, and she laughed. Then he waved an arm about, trying to touch some. She caught a flake on the fingertip of her glove and showed it to him, and his soft, downy eyebrows dimpled and rose as it disappeared. She smiled. Another first. So many and she wished she had someone to share them with. *Mum would've loved this moment,* she thought, and looked up at the sky. Instead of a celestial being she saw billions of tiny flakes cascading down. They got in her eyes and she blinked; then Rory started to fuss. She pushed her thick coat sleeve back with her clumsy glove-clad hand—it was three minutes to twelve!

Quickly, she tucked him back in and hurried home. The house was empty when she walked in, something she already knew; Adrian had gone to the Soho office to work on the new idea. She had a suspicion it wasn't going too well but following their argument about his stealing Emma's idea, they had stopped talking to each other about anything meaningful. It was funny, she thought, as she heated up a bottle of milk, those fraud police she'd always been afraid of: ironic how she was the one who'd had the least to fear.

Carrie got the milk into Rory's hungry mouth just before the all-out meltdown and sat back in the chair with him on her lap.

She'd thought a lot about Emma's letter since Adrian had admitted what he'd done, and actually felt a little sorry for her. It was stupid, naïve of her to have written to him in the first place—you never sent your ideas out to anyone, especially not a total stranger, unless you went through an agent. Emma had put herself in a vulnerable position, but still, Carrie didn't like the notion her husband had taken advantage. She wondered if Emma was planning on doing anything else to make the truth public—but knew deep down that even if Emma cried foul play, no one would genuinely challenge Adrian, the successful writer, for fear of losing a chance to work with him.

She'd seen it again and again, A-list writers who'd created shows the nation adored, bringing riches and kudos to themselves and the channel. When there were hints they'd lost their mojo and relied on drink or drugs or both to keep them functioning, or when they'd become egotistical monsters to work with, nobody dared criticize them or point out their failings. There might be a whisper or a raised eyebrow between friends, but nothing public. Ever. They were safe as long as they were still riding the crest of their last success and didn't fail with anything new, exposing their weakness. It was an industry that favored the powerful, and anyone who tried to disrupt that order got chewed up and laughed out of town. If Emma were to speak up, it would do nothing but embarrass her and ruin any chance she had of getting a foot on the slippery ladder. Nobody liked trouble in this business; they steered clear of it like a bad smell.

So Adrian had won. He'd done the dirty and gotten away with it.

Carrie had considered whether she should say anything—morally, now she knew, perhaps it was her duty. But whom would she tell? Elaine, who had made the show with her husband? But Elaine was dead. Maybe she'd already known, or suspected, but had taken the secret to the grave.

It had been just over a month since she'd died, thought Carrie. Time went by so fast, marching on with no regard to who had been left behind. She wondered about Elaine's poor friend, the one who'd tried to save her. Elaine's relatives, who were left to grieve. Carrie knew she had an ex-husband, whom she'd divorced in her thirties, but there were no children, as far as she was aware. Just that dog she took everywhere. Her company would most likely be wound up, those who worked for her forced to look for something else. The show that Elaine was in the middle of developing with the A-list screenwriter would likely find a home elsewhere. In fact, producers would be lining up to take over, like vultures, except pretending to be acting in her memory, to take her last show to the screen, an homage to the great Elaine Marsh.

Carrie balanced Rory's bottle in her left hand and stretched over to the table to pull her laptop toward her. She idly Googled Elaine Marsh and the screenwriter's name. The show came up in an old ITV press release, announcing it had been green-lit and was due to be shot the following year. She scrolled farther down the search page, but there was nothing about who would be making it now. Too soon, perhaps. She was about to close the laptop down, when suddenly she jerked it forward, causing Rory to fret. She soothed him, one eye still on the screen: there was a local newspaper article about Elaine's death and in the introductory text was Emma's name. Puzzled, she tapped on the link.

Her eyes widened as she read, unable to believe the words in front of her.

A friend of the victim who had valiantly tried to save her was a local woman by the name of Emma Fox.

Emma. Carrie looked up from the screen, tried to take it in. *Emma* was the one who'd been there, the friend who'd witnessed Elaine's death?

A sudden chill ran down the back of her neck.

59

Friday, February 23

When the train pulled into the station, Emma's sense of rebellion hadn't waned. Energy surged through her, pushing her onward. She didn't care that what she was about to do wasn't right, not legally. But morally, well the cards were stacked in her favor. She had absolutely nothing left to lose.

Once she reached the High Street, she stopped at the supermarket for some essentials. She pushed the small cart down the aisles, stocking up on food, also throwing in some toothpaste, a tooth brush, and some underwear.

Carrying two full bags, she decided to take the road along the cliff top that followed the sea, and walked another half a mile until she came to the North Foreland Estate. Pulling up her hood and keeping her head down as she passed the CCTV, she took the pedestrian path alongside the barriers. The estate was quiet and she met no one as she followed the private road down toward the cliff edge and then past The Thirty-Nine Steps. At the house, she checked through the bars of the gates. There were no cars, and a look at the house told her it was empty. She considered the gates. There was nothing for it but to climb over. She checked up and down the road at the other grand houses that stood some distance away, but no one was around. Emma dropped each of the shopping bags over the gateposts as carefully as she could, thankful there was nothing glass in them, and then went over herself.

At the front door, she took out the Yale key she'd been holding in the coffee shop in London that morning and let herself in. Remembering the code from her previous visits, she made only a few pushes to the keypad and the alarm was disabled.

Emma stood there for a moment, listening to the silent house. Realizing how cold it was, she looked for the boiler, finding it in a cupboard in the kitchen. It didn't take long to work out how to switch on the central heating and as she heard the boiler fire up, she took a relaxing breath. She then placed her perishable food items in the fridge and found a cupboard for the rest. She shivered, then decided to make herself a hot drink while the heating kicked in properly. In her search for the cutlery drawer, she came across a small gray plastic box. It took a second for her to recognize it, then she plucked it out of the drawer with elation—a spare remote control for the gate! She'd no longer have to climb over the gatepost to get in—good for her clothes but also good for keeping any suspicious neighbors at bay.

Carrying her hot tea upstairs, she avoided what was clearly Adrian and Carrie's room and chose a large spare with a dual aspect that overlooked the sea and the side garden. She hummed to herself as she made up the king-sized bed with the clean sheets and coastal striped duvet cover she found in the wardrobe. The chest of drawers was empty and she opened up the packet of underwear she'd bought earlier. Individually unfolding them, she placed them carefully inside. Tomorrow she'd have to buy a bit more. Bras, socks, tights. In the en suite she placed the toothbrush and toothpaste, lining them up just so on the shelf. She then went back into the bedroom and, lying on the bed, texted Lucy to say she was staying with a friend at the coast for a few days, as her friend's mother was unwell. She didn't elaborate where she was or how long she'd be away.

Her stomach started to rumble. Time to make dinner. She thought about the groceries she'd just unpacked. Should she cook the chicken or make some pasta? Emma decided she was in the mood for Italian, so she went downstairs and started to chop an onion for a tomato sauce. She suddenly stopped midway, knife poised in midair.

Something was wrong. She cocked her head, listened. Music! She needed music. She switched on the radio and shook her hips as she continued

60

Neither Carrie nor Adrian had thought much about where they should go for their "talk," and so they'd fallen back on their favorite local restaurant run by couple Dominic and John. As soon as Dominic held open the door of The Fig Tree for her, a smile stretched across his face, Carrie realized it had been a mistake—there would be no anonymity for the difficult conversation ahead. But she returned the smile and allowed him to take her coat.

"It's been so long!" said Dominic, pulling out their chairs.

"Six months," said Adrian.

Dominic clutched his chest in horror. "No!"

Carrie noticed he wasn't actually hamming it up. "That's what happens when you have a baby," she said, lightly, which was met with a look of sympathy from Dominic, while Adrian pretended not to hear, his face buried in the menu.

"John will be out to say hello in a bit," said Dominic, "when he gets a moment away from the kitchen. You're in luck; he's still got two of the venison loin left. Can I get you both a glass of something? We have a new pilsner in from the Czech Republic, golden yellow in color with a taste of orange."

They both agreed to try Dominic's recommendations, Carrie relaxing her rule on not drinking when she knew she'd have to be up in the night. She felt as if she needed it to get through the evening, anyway.

She placed her phone on the table alongside her drink and noticed Adrian's frown. "What?"

"Do we have to?" he said, eyes on the phone.

"It's a new babysitter. The *only* babysitter we've ever had," she corrected, feeling the anxious pang again at leaving her baby for the first time. With no family or available friends nearby, they'd had to use an agency and Carrie had been aghast at the expense: twelve pounds an hour. Still, what price to save a relationship, she'd thought.

She saw he still looked disgruntled. "I'm not going to be taking any other calls," she said. "It's only if Marnie rings." Her tone was final and he backed down. Inwardly, she took a breath. This was already proving hard and they hadn't even opened up discussions yet.

"How are the ideas coming along?" asked Carrie without thinking, then immediately regretted her words.

Adrian tensed. "Can we not talk about work tonight?"

"Course," agreed Carrie, readily. She tried to think of something else to say and it suddenly struck her she'd forgotten how to speak to her husband. A few more seconds ticked by and each was aware of the awkward silence. They smiled at each other with sad, desperate eyes.

"What shall we talk about?" Carrie said, trying to make a joke out of it.

"I don't know . . . Us?" said Adrian, and she instinctively stiffened, while knowing they had to face up to it.

"I'm unhappy," Adrian suddenly blurted out. He slumped down in his chair as if the admission had taken all the air out of him, air that had been building and building until it just needed to be released.

"Okay . . ." started Carrie slowly, taken aback by his frankness.

"I'm sorry to say it like that, so bluntly, but it's been preying on my mind. For weeks . . . months now."

Clearly, thought Carrie, before chastising herself. Sarcasm was not helpful to either of them at a time like this. She knew why she'd thought it; she was unhappy, too—he was the one who'd had the affair.

"And I know a lot of that unhappiness has been my own fault," continued Adrian. "I've failed you . . . wow, so many times." He shook his head with the breathless realization of it all. "Not just the affair but as a husband. Now our lives have changed."

"You mean Rory," said Carrie.

He nodded and she saw it was difficult for him to admit.

"I feel guilty," he said, quietly. "I . . . I don't want to be a parent. And I know that's a taboo thing to say, something that society doesn't like, but I can't help it. I miss my old life. We have so much less sleep, less sex, less fun. *Less joy.* I'm sad, too, sad for us and for our relationship. And the *guilt,*" he repeated. "I'm not the parent Rory deserves." He suddenly stopped and took a gulp of his beer. Then inhaled deeply and looked at her. "I've been afraid to be honest with you," he said.

Carrie watched him, feeling her world crumbling away. Actually, she realized, it had already disintegrated; she'd just been clinging to the remaining few bricks that had once made up Adrian and Carrie, Carrie and Adrian. Sixteen years of a life that had been so different from where they were now that it felt like it was a figment of her imagination.

"Please say something," said Adrian.

"I don't know what to say."

"Do you understand?" he asked desperately. "I know it's probably different for you, but I don't want you to think I'm some sort of monster. It's important that you don't think that," he said hollowly.

It was the most honest he'd been with her for months—more than a year. Ever since he'd said he was "happy" to go along with the pregnancy, something she now knew, perhaps had known back then, that he was just hoping would be all right.

"I don't think you're a monster," she said.

A glimmer of deep-felt relief appeared in his eyes, only for a second, and then the sadness took over again.

"Sorry," he said.

A single word that brimmed with regret and finality. It was the sound of the death knell to their relationship.

Tears started to gather behind her eyes and he quickly placed a hand on hers, his own eyes glistening. "I want him to have a good life," he said. "I'll provide, of course."

She was unable to speak and blew her nose into a tissue. Out of the corner of her eye she saw John approach from the kitchen, proudly carrying aloft two plates of food. She quickly composed herself and smiled, and she and Adrian both engaged in pleasantries and catch-up conversation, the most united they'd been in months. Ironic it should be as they were breaking up.

It was a quick dinner, neither much in the mood to drag it out, and they returned home early. Carrie paid Marnie, the young babysitter, who was piqued that she'd received less than she'd been expecting; then Carrie and Adrian each went to their own bedrooms.

Carrie silently undressed and got into bed. She could hear Adrian on the other side of the wall, the faint rise and fall of a TV show he was watching quietly on his tablet. Part of her longed to go in, to snuggle up to him and engage in some of the silly banter that used to come so naturally to them both. But those people they'd once been had long gone, changed irrevocably, now ghosts of another life.

The Decision had been hers. She'd known all along that she was the one who'd driven the pregnancy, who'd convinced Adrian—superficially at least—to have a child. He had protested, she remembered, but she'd glossed over it, so determined had she been to seize this last chance in her life. She was the one who had set their relationship on a new path that had led to a dead end.

Next to her, Rory stirred, flinging an arm up above his head in his sleep. She looked over at him, his soft blond hair still barely visible, his fat cheeks flushed pink. Her baby—their baby—who had caused such a seismic change in their lives. The most demanding, most exhausting thing she'd ever had to cope with.

She suddenly remembered how she'd been frightened of him at the start, when he'd first arrived and she'd had no idea what to do with him. At what point had that feeling gone away? When had the transition taken place? Now she couldn't bear the idea of being parted from him.

She had no regrets. Given the choice, she'd do it all again.

PART THREE

Adrian

61

Saturday, February 24

Emma woke naturally the next morning, the late-winter sun filtering through the cracks in her curtains. She lay in bed and stretched, enjoying the pleasant sensation in her muscles, then looked around the room, taking in her surroundings. It was a lovely house, full of light and space. As long as she kept out of Adrian's study, she knew she'd feel at home here, and the reason for that was because it had been bought with the proceeds of what was her TV project. Her project had earned these walls, these large, airy rooms. She got out of bed and looked out of the window. Her idea had procured that amazing view of the sea, the sun glittering on its aqua-gray waves. So really she had no qualms about staying there at all. In fact, if you thought about it, the beach house was rightfully hers.

After a shower, Emma slipped on some of her new underwear and contemplated her clothes. The jeans would be okay, but she could do with a fresh top. She wandered out onto the landing and then into Carrie and Adrian's bedroom, where she opened the wardrobe. She was in luck. Carrie had several items of clothing hanging there, and there were more in the chest of drawers. Emma looked through them, holding garments up in front of the mirror. It wasn't ideal, but she could hardly return to the flat and get her own. Arms full, she carried the clothes back to her room, where she carefully started hanging them in her own wardrobe. She caught a glimpse of herself in the mirror as she did so, a snapshot of herself in one of Carrie's tops and she smiled.

Breakfast was a simple affair of toast and honey; then Emma headed out for a walk. The day was cold and windy but bright, and she decided to go down to the beach. The tide was out and she walked along the vast swaths of sand, glancing behind at her footprints defiling the otherwise smooth beach. Funny how in another five hours her marks would be washed clean again, no traces left of them.

As she continued along the beach, Emma looked up at the cliffs to her right, holding her hair back so it didn't blow in her face. They towered above her, imposing blocks of white chalk, and she was again struck by the lack of railing or fence at the edge. She liked this section of the beach; it was deserted and still belonged to nature. As you headed closer to the town center and Bleak House it became more populated, and there were shops and amenities designed to serve the summer tourists.

She walked among them, up toward the High

Street, where she stopped and got herself some more milk, a phone charger, some socks, and a plastic bucket. She thought of her possessions back in the flat with Lucy. Lucy wouldn't throw them out just yet, even when it became clear in a few days that Emma hadn't paid the rent. They were safe for a couple of weeks at least, which was just enough time to put her plan into place.

62

It was officially the day after her marriage had broken up. The first day of not being Adrian's wife anymore, at least not spiritually. The divorce—as that's what they'd presumably agree to—had still to be arranged. Carrie had heard Adrian get up, shower, and then knock on her bedroom door. He'd said that he was going to go to the office, which would be quiet as it was the weekend, and he'd work on the new idea. She knew by the sounds coming up through the floor that he had opened the front door and so was about to leave. She lay there, waiting for the clunk of the door closing; when it came, she involuntarily slumped back against the pillows. Lay there and reflected on her feelings.

How was she now her marriage was over? Carrie was surprised to find that in among the deep sadness, something she dared not dwell on for too long for fear of its ambushing her, there was a curious release. She considered the sensation for a moment, mentally tossing it around. There was still pain, but also the relief of not needing to try to avoid the inevitable anymore. The metaphorical tooth had been pulled. Despite all her hopes that things would change, if she'd actually been honest with herself the last few months, she'd known their marriage was never going to work out once Rory had arrived. At one point she'd hoped Adrian might adapt, come around to the massive change in their lives, but that was like asking a polar bear to live on an African plain. Sooner or later it was going to die—inside if not literally.

Carrie got out of bed and pulled back the curtains, letting the room fill with sunlight. The snow had all gone—it was as if it had never happened. She dressed Rory and took him downstairs, where he played happily under his baby gym while she made coffee and checked her e-mails. She fired off a few replies and was about to close the laptop when she saw the tab she'd been reading the day before: the article on Elaine's premature death.

She clicked on it and Elaine's smiling face stared out at her from the screen, a publicity shot from some professional event. Carrie read the article again. A man called Nick Aston was identified first—he was the passerby who'd been trying to resuscitate Elaine when the paramedics arrived. She slowed down when she came to the mention of Emma, but there was nothing she'd missed. Nothing to explain why Emma had been there. It was weird, thought Carrie, and she shut the laptop. She finished her coffee and looked at Rory, who was batting the monkey with a bell in its ear that was hanging above his face.

"Shall we go out for a walk?" she said, and he looked over at her and gurgled happily. She took that as a yes.

Carrie managed to find a parking space right next to the common, outside a parade of shops. After the usual five-minute delay of extracting the stroller from the trunk, assembling it, and transferring Rory from his car seat, they were ready to go. She wheeled him across the road into Wandsworth Common and strolled down the path in the sunshine. She headed for the lake and could see the spot before she got there; a small shrine had been laid on the bank.

Carrie stopped and bent down to see. People had left flowers, now dead, and a small teddy bear, which was more than a little bedraggled. There were also messages of condolence. Most were simple—*"Rest in peace"* or *"God bless"*—but one card caught her eye because it had more written on it than the rest. It was tucked inside a cellophane-wrapped bunch of decaying, small yellow roses and so had mostly survived the weather battering, and only a few words had run.

I am so sorry I couldn't help. May you rest in peace. Nick Aston.

Carrie looked up, thoughts whirling in her head. This was the man who'd tried to save Elaine; she recognized his name from the newspaper article. He'd been here when Emma was here. She stood up and, taking off her gloves, got her phone from her bag. It would probably come to nothing, but she typed his name and "Wandsworth" into Google. Almost instantly, the search revealed its findings. Second down on the list was a link to a vinyl record store, and in the blurb underneath, a name was highlighted: the owner Nick Aston. Carrie clicked and the site opened up. The shop was right next to where she'd parked.

She put her gloves back on and, giving a respectful nod to the shrine, turned and pushed Rory across the common.

The door had an old-fashioned tinkling bell that jingled incessantly as she manhandled Rory's stroller into the shop. A man looked up and came hurrying over to help her, holding the door so she could get the stroller in. Once the obstacle course was completed, Carrie looked up, seeing a pleasant-faced thirty-something with a goatee, dressed in a hip T-shirt and jeans.

He had an expectant, helpful look on his face; he was waiting for her to say something and it suddenly struck her she didn't really know what she was doing there.

"Are you looking for anything in particular?"

he asked, and she gazed absently around the store at the shelves and upended pigeonholes of records, feeling totally fraudulent.

"Um . . ."

He waited patiently, the helpful smile never leaving his face.

"Are you Nick Aston?" she asked.

He nodded.

"Actually, I wanted to ask you about the incident on the common. Last month. The lady who collapsed and died by the lake."

The smile faltered and Carrie felt the welcome cool a little.

"I'm a friend of hers," she explained, quickly. "We know each other from work. I went to her funeral, but . . . well, I just had to come here too. To see the place where . . ." She took a deep breath and became misty-eyed, not all fabricated. "It makes it easier to say goodbye," she said, while thinking, *Dear God, Elaine, do not strike me down.*

"I'm sorry," said Nick. "It must be terrible for you."

Carrie nodded. "I saw your name in the paper," she said, "and the flowers by the lake. Thank you," she added, "for everything you tried to do."

His face clouded over. "I wish I could've done more. But I only heard her friend's shouts some moments after she'd collapsed."

381

"That must've been so awful for her. Not being able to help Elaine like that."

"Do you know her?" asked Nick.

"No," lied Carrie. "I guess she was struggling . . . with giving Elaine mouth to mouth? When you arrived?"

"She was so upset . . . you know, I don't think she quite knew what to do."

Carrie nodded. "Was she alone?"

Nick looked at her strangely. "Of course. Or she would've had help sooner."

Carrie nodded, realizing she was coming across as a little odd. It was making Nick suspicious.

"What was she like? At the time? Her manner?"

For a moment she thought he wouldn't answer. His voice was cold. "She was distraught. As you might imagine. Were you looking for help with any records? Otherwise, I really need to get on."

Carrie nodded and wheeled the stroller out through the door and took Rory back to the car. As she started the engine she glanced over to the shop and saw him watching her through the window.

He was deeply unimpressed by her nosiness. She wasn't sure what she'd been expecting by coming here, but something was bothering her. Maybe Elaine and Emma had bumped into each other in the same place at exactly the same time. It was a bit of a coincidence, but they were both local so it was possible. But she couldn't get rid of the niggle that it wasn't the whole story and she allowed herself a deeply unsettling thought: What would Nick Aston have seen if he'd been at the lake five or ten minutes earlier?

She put the car in gear and drove off, feeling his eyes on her until she disappeared from view.

63

Saturday, February 24

He was a free man. he could do whatever he wanted. go away whenever he wanted, take up cycling as he'd promised himself he'd do and had resented not being able to, thanks to feeling guilty once Rory had arrived. He was free to lie in bed until whenever he liked (actually, he did that anyway, but conveniently glossed over this fact). As of this morning, this first day of his new life, he had nothing tying him down. So why did he feel as though a thick cast-iron chain was hanging around his neck and his shoulders and pinning him to this goddamn chair so he could barely breathe, let alone move? He suddenly sprang up, the wheeled chair flying across the room behind him. He ran his hands through his hair. Christ, he missed Carrie. The old Carrie, not the new one who'd been taken over by a small baby. Carrie would know what to do.

He stared at the computer screen, its reciprocating white glare mocking him. An idea, he needed an idea. He wasn't greedy, only one, but it had to be good, brilliant in fact. It had to reflect his current standing in the television industry, make his contemporaries widen their eyes and grin ruefully as they realized—yet again—just what a genius he was. He could feel himself breaking out in a cold sweat. He'd spent days waiting for a bolt of inspiration and nothing came. Christ, at times like this, he was even willing to admit he missed Emma.

Calm, he thought. *You have to keep calm.* He slowly retrieved the chair and sat back at his desk in the tiny room at the Soho office. He didn't much like it there, tucked away, lonely, with no one around to tell him how brilliant he was and briefly wondered if he was addicted to praise.

He lifted his hands over the keys. *Come on, come on,* he urged his brain, waiting for divine inspiration, even while knowing it was fruitless. Ideas didn't come like that; at least they never had for him. He sensed the returning specter of his past creeping up over his shoulder. Sixteen years of toiling away on a soap or working as a writer for hire on other people's shows, waiting for his big break, secretly wondering if he was good enough.

He'd had ideas, of course he had; he'd had ambition, too, and had spent years working on his free days, through his unemployed stints, developing new TV shows. Occasionally he'd managed to get those shows funded by a production company, which led to draft after draft written and rewritten while Adrian had watched two years of his life drift by, until finally the producers professed themselves happy enough to submit to a commissioner, only for it to sit on the commissioner's desk for another six months while they decided whether it was worth taking further.

The rejections would come by e-mail; Adrian never even met the individual in the ivory tower who had so much power over his career and his life. They were brutal in their politeness or their vagueness. "Not quite for us," or "So sorry, but now with the success of XYZ show, there really isn't room for this on the channel as well, as *brilliant* as it is." Well, XYZ show wasn't even conceived when he bloody thought up his idea! He'd fume internally, while of course remaining politely disappointed. The industry was too small to spit and rage.

Adrian had been in the game so long, he'd watched what seemed like the same writers get commission after commission, building their status into something untouchable while he languished at the bottom of the ladder, sometimes even staring into the chasm of defeat. *Should I give up?* had raised its ugly head on more than one occasion. Maybe he just couldn't do it. And then Emma's letter had arrived and he'd instantly seen something special in her project, its rawness, its visceral power, and he'd done what any talented writer would have done, made it into a living, breathing show, at the same time proving to all the doubters that he *is* the brilliant writer he'd always known he was deep down. Not for the first time, he kicked himself for his utter foolishness at not destroying her letter and documents. He thought he had, but the heady sensation of victory must have distracted him. It was extremely busy being successful—so many demands on his time by so many people—and it had been hard to keep track of everything.

He looked at the blank screen again, silently pleading with it, but nothing happened. A deep, strangled sound of frustration and fear came from his throat and he stabbed his fingers into the keyboard. What the fuck was he going to deliver to Liz? He'd already gone way past the time when he should have gotten her something, and he was afraid she could smell the whiff of failure. And if that got out . . . his blood ran cold. He couldn't bear the thought of everyone whispering behind his back, gleefully relishing his inability to do anything else, perhaps even picking up on the fact that Carrie had brought *Leon* to him— and Christ, what if Emma started spreading rumors about *Generation Rebel*? His industry was an unforgiving one and if he couldn't keep up with his success, it wouldn't be long before he was shunted to the writers' graveyard.

He rested his head in his hands, as the full weight of expectation seemed to crush him. Time ticked on and he knew he should move but didn't want to look reality in the face again.

A pinging sound came from his computer. He looked up—an e-mail. His stomach jolted as he saw the sender: Emma. He looked at it suspiciously. Should he? His hand moved of its own accord and he clicked:

Hi Adrian:

I know we haven't always seen eye to eye, but no one can deny how well we work together. I don't think we should throw that away. I have an idea that I could share with you. Conditions attached, of course. A librarian who becomes a corrupt kingpin in her community. Might sound insane, but I think it has legs. Perhaps we could have a coffee together, confidentially, at least at first, given everything that's gone on.

Emma

Adrian stared, his heart racing. Of course, he should turn her down. It was madness, especially after everything that had happened. In fact, he should just ignore the e-mail, delete it, and pretend it had never arrived. He moved the cursor over to the trash can symbol, poised to click. *A librarian who becomes a corrupt kingpin . . .* It *was* bonkers—but also intriguing. . . .

He shook his head. *No.* He reduced the e-mail so it went to the bottom of the screen and behind it, his blank page popped out at him again. Bright white screen. Liz was expecting a pitch. His breathing quickened as he thought about the conversation they'd have, the excuses he'd blunder through, the humiliation. He couldn't do it. He brought the e-mail back up and started to draft a reply.

64

Emma sat back at the kitchen table and contemplated the effect her e-mail might be having in London. It was difficult to predict, and she didn't want to get her hopes up. Needing to distract herself, she put on her coat and went out into the garden. Some early daffodils had opened up their sunny heads in the flower bed alongside the covered swimming pool, and she breathed in the sea air and watched as they bobbed in the wind. She liked their cheerful optimism and decided to pick a few. Emma continued to walk around the garden, uplifted by the tiny shoots and buds on the bushes and trees. It was large—about a hundred feet long—and along the back and the sides of the plot were tall conifers, much like those at the front of the house. Their dense green branches rose nearly twenty feet up, obscuring the view from the neighboring houses. Behind the trees stood a fence. The garden was secured and private in the strongest way possible. No one could get in. No one could see in.

Going back into the house, she couldn't help but glance at her laptop screen; there were no new messages. The daffodils went into a vase, which she placed in the middle of the kitchen table, smelling their green unripe scent.

Emma decided to make herself a hot drink and then go out for a proper walk to take her mind off the wait. The kettle boiled and she was just pouring the water on the coffee granules when a beep came from her laptop. She abandoned the coffee and went over to the table. It was a reply! On tenterhooks, she clicked, eyes scanning the response. It was a yes! Her heart did a little victory dance. Then she composed herself. She went back to finishing the coffee, allowed a few minutes to slip past. Then she sat down and typed.

Glad we can be grown up about this. I would suggest we meet away from London. I'm having a small break down at the coast in Kent, not far from Broadstairs. Am happy to travel down to your house, but it has to be this afternoon as I'm leaving this evening.

Emma

She hit send. Almost immediately, a response came back—he was in agreement and would meet her at his house at two p.m.

Emma looked up at the clock. She didn't have much time. She quickly searched her laptop and found a large anonymous chain hotel in Margate, just a few miles away. Phoning them, she booked herself a room for seven nights. Then she took her laptop upstairs and hid it under her bed. Hurrying back down to the dining room, she assessed the space. She heaved the large, glossy wooden table across the floor so it was up against the window and then placed all the chairs on top. The room looked out onto the garden, which she knew was like a fortress. She then took all the tools away from the fireplace and made sure there was nothing that wasn't fixed to the wall or floor within three yards of the marble hearth. The bucket she'd bought earlier she placed on the floor. Then she surveyed the room again and was hit by a wave of sadness. All this was no less than Adrian deserved, but she couldn't help thinking of Carrie too. They'd been a team once, albeit a very long time ago, and now her relationship with Carrie was so damaged, she couldn't see any way of repairing it. Adrian really had a lot to answer for.

Emma went back into the kitchen, washed and dried her mug, and put it away. She took the daffodils and regretfully threw them out of the window then tidied away the vase. Everything was back to how she'd found it when she'd first arrived. She grabbed her coat and bag, and closed the front door behind her.

Emma walked into the town center and got a

65

Saturday, February 24

Adrian turned into the North Foreland Estate, tapping his fingers on the steering wheel in time to a song he admired on the radio. He was intrigued by Emma's proposition. It wasn't as unusual as one might think at first. Plenty of artists who worked together couldn't bear the sight of each other for at least part of their working relationship. Simon and Garfunkel, Lennon and McCartney, Noel and Liam Gallagher. He realized as he thought this that these were all musicians, but hey, surely the same principles applied.

He'd dropped a text to Carrie before leaving, just to let her know he was working on something. He knew she felt sorry for him and he hated it. Well, his message would give her food for thought: Going to the beach house for the rest of the day. Got the seed of an idea: Local librarian becomes corrupt kingpin in her community. Think it's got something!

He'd received a simple acknowledgment in return and he'd smiled to himself, knowing she wouldn't have expected him to have come up with an idea.

Up ahead someone was waving him down and he suppressed a groan. He pulled up to the curb and pushed the electronic window button. Into the car came freezing air and Geraldine Kidd's beaming face as she bent down to talk to him. He could smell her perfume, the overpowering reek of Chanel No. 5, something she'd once told him she'd worn since her twenties.

"Hello, stranger," she said. "How's our local superstar?"

He smiled. "Been busy, you know. Working."

"You work too hard," she admonished. "Writing all these TV shows. Anyone famous in your latest one?" she pressed.

"One or two," he said.

"Well, you know my hero. Sean Connery," she said. "Did I tell you, I once nearly got a part as his Bond girl. *Diamonds Are Forever*. Missed out by a whisker."

"Their loss," said Adrian, thinking, *How many more times will I hear this story before I die,* and then uncharitably, *Actually, she'll probably die first; she's at least two decades older.*

"You on your own?" asked Geraldine, somewhat pointlessly as there was no one else in the car.

"Carrie's in London with Rory."

"Well, in that case, I'm bringing round a casserole. Tonight—"

"Thank you, but there's no need," he instantly protested.

"Nonsense. Can't let you starve. I bet you never leave your desk."

"Honestly, Geraldine. I'm only here for the afternoon."

"Oh, right. Well, okay, then." She looked put out, as if his plans had no right not to fit in with hers.

"But it really is very kind of you. I'll never forget your lamb and rosemary. Best I've ever tasted."

She thawed a little then. "You're not the first to say so," she said, pleased. "Maybe I'll keep an eye out, in case you find yourself staying the night. I always go past your place on my evening stroll with Poppy." She indicated the pug, attached to the end of a leash. "If there's a light on, I'll knock!"

He forced a smile and said how lovely that would be and then managed to extricate himself so he could continue to his house. As the electric gates shut behind him, he breathed a sigh of relief, then parked the car and walked up to the front door.

He let himself in and removing his coat, he saw he still had half an hour before Emma turned up. He decided to fix himself a drink: a large rum and coke; very large. He bloody deserved it after the week he'd had.

He made his way to the kitchen and reached for the door handle when he suddenly staggered sideways and clutched the back of his head in agony. He cried out and instinctively raised his hands to protect himself, while simultaneously trying to turn and face his assailant. His eyes widened in bewilderment as he saw Emma holding something metallic and heavy above her head. Before he could work out what was going on, she brought it down again and he crashed to the floor like a sack of potatoes.

66

Saturday, February 24

Emma stood there for a moment, breathing heavily. she'd been horrified when Adrian had turned, dazed, to face her. In a panic she'd lifted the juicing machine and brought it down again, before he could properly steady himself.

She waited to see if he'd get up, but he didn't move. Emma put the juicer on the floor and tentatively went up to him. Not so close he could grab her, but near enough so she could see he was still breathing. *Thank God.* It had been a risk, knocking him out, but she could see no other way to get him where she needed him.

She braved it and quickly nudged him with her foot. He didn't stir. There was no time to lose so she took off his shoes and threw them aside, then emptied his pockets. Taking hold of his hands, she dragged him into the dining room. Despite his slight build, he was a dead weight, and it took more effort than she'd thought. Finally she got him in front of the open fireplace, where she took the handcuffs she'd hidden in the coal bucket, attaching one end to his right wrist and the other to the fixed heavy iron ring that was screwed into the brick fire surround for the tongs. Only then did she feel a sense of relief.

Now all she had to do was wait for him to wake up.

67

Adrian's eyes started to flicker around mid-afternoon and Emma's first reaction was nervousness. She watched warily from the dining room chair she'd placed a good distance from him as he opened his eyes, clearly bewildered by his position on the floor. Wincing, he tried to sit up, but his arm pulled tight on the handcuff, which jolted a sense of urgency in him. He lifted his head and that's when he saw her and she could tell everything came flooding back.

"Emma . . . ?"

He tried again to get up off the floor and she waited while he looked at his hand and saw the handcuff.

"What the . . ." He turned back to her, flummoxed. "What are you doing?" Then a pain gripped his head and he groaned and held it with his free hand. "What did you hit me with?"

"The deluxe nutri extractor."

"My freakin' *juicer?*"

"There's some tablets," she said, pointing beside him to where she'd placed a plastic cup of water and a blister pack of aspirin that she'd found in the bathroom cabinet. "And an icepack," she added, which was a packet of frozen peas wrapped in a tea towel.

He stared at her. "I don't understand. Why am I tied up?"

"Because we need to have a serious talk."

"You don't need to handcuff me to the fireplace so we can have a talk." He pulled at the cuffs again, more strenuously this time, and Emma watched anxiously, but they held.

"Okay, joke over," he said. "I think it's time you let me go."

She didn't move.

"Emma, stop dicking about," he said tersely. "Unlock these things. Where did you get them, anyway?" He stopped as he recognized them. "Seriously? These are from my office? They're *props?*" He tugged at them again, yanking furiously.

"They won't break off," said Emma. "They're the real thing, remember? You told me. Now listen," she continued. "This is what I want. You need to transfer half a million pounds straight into my bank account. We'll call this my share of *Generation Rebel.* This is extremely generous on my part, as I know for a fact you will have got a huge amount more than that. I also want you to write a letter of apology saying what you did, how you stole my entire TV series and how sorry you are, and I want this to be a full-page advertisement in *Broadcast* magazine. Then we can talk about the new idea we'll work on together."

She saw he was staring openmouthed at her. Then he started laughing. Hearty, mocking guffaws. So be it. If that was the way he wanted to play it, he could sweat it out for a while. She got up and headed for the door. Instantly, the laughing subsided.

"Where are you going?"

"You need to think about what I've just said."

"Emma? Emma! Fucking let me go!"

She closed the door behind her as the shouts got louder and angrier and thought that actually it would do him good to realize she was prepared to leave him to rot in the house. She slammed the front door shut and headed down to the beach.

It was dusk by the time Emma returned. She walked back through the estate, hood pulled right over her head as always. She glanced up at the houses as she went, mentally trying to measure their distance from one another. Were they far apart enough that the neighbors were unaware of what went on in one another's homes? She knew Geraldine had seen a light on in Adrian's house once when she'd been out walking her dog, Emma's own flashlight, and that had made her alert Adrian to burglars, but what about sound? As she rounded the bend toward Adrian's house, she suddenly stopped dead. There was someone up ahead. Speak of the devil; it was

Geraldine herself, ringing the buzzer on the wall persistently. *Shit.*

She fixed on a smile and threw back her hood so as not to look intimidating as she hurried up. Geraldine was dressed for the cold in a woollen coat with brass buttons and a hat. Between her gloved hands she held what looked like a steaming casserole dish.

"Hello," said Emma.

Geraldine looked at her but didn't register who she was. Emma was under no illusion that she would recognize her; Geraldine came across as the type of person who only made a point of remembering those who might be useful or important to her. She tucked the casserole dish under one arm and pressed the buzzer on the wall again. Emma inwardly flinched. She strained her ears, listening for Adrian's shouts but, thank God, could hear nothing.

"Can I help you?" she asked. "I work for Adrian."

Geraldine looked at her a little more closely this time. "Is he in? The lights are on. He said if the lights were on, I should pop round."

"He's working," said Emma.

Geraldine buzzed again, which irritated Emma. She wanted to swipe her hand away. She looked up at the thick pines that encased the house on either side of the drive gates. "I don't think he'll come to the door. If he's working."

"But it's me. We spoke this afternoon."

Adrian must have bumped into her on his way to the house, thought Emma. "You know what he's like. Gets so engrossed."

"Can still hear the door, though," said Geraldine, peeved.

Why wouldn't this woman take a hint, thought Emma, and know when she wasn't welcome?

"Is that for him?" she asked, nodding at the casserole dish.

"Well, it was," said Geraldine.

"I'll take it in. He'll be delighted."

Geraldine looked over at the house again. "I was rather hoping to do it myself."

Emma sniffed. "Is that lamb? Adrian's favorite. It's Geraldine, isn't it? Adrian's mentioned you many times."

The woman had been about to ring the buzzer again but paused. "Has he?"

"Oh yes. In fact, and I shouldn't really be saying this, but between you, me, and the gatepost, he finds you something of an inspiration."

"He does not," said Geraldine, but Emma could see she was pleased.

"Seriously. The idea he's working on at the moment. I do believe . . . oh, I'm not supposed to say . . ." She left it hanging and sure enough, after a moment Geraldine took the bait.

"What?"

Emma pretended to wrestle internally with herself. "Oh, I can't, can I? Would you promise not to say I told you?" Geraldine smiled. "He's based the main character on you," Emma stage whispered. She shook her head, chiding herself. "There, look, now I'm in trouble." But she was smiling.

"Has he really?" asked Geraldine, surprised, but this news was stoking the fire of her ego faster than a match to a pile of dry leaves. Her eyes shone. "Well, I never."

"You do have the look of an actress about you, actually," said Emma. "Have I seen you in anything before?"

Geraldine's eyes grew wistful and Emma could see a story coming. She put out her hands and quickly spoke: "Shall I take that in for you? He usually breaks late, around seven or eight, and I know this'll be a godsend. I'll make sure it's left warming in the oven for him." She held out her hands farther and Geraldine reluctantly passed over the casserole dish. Emma smiled. Waited. After another moment, Geraldine took her cue.

"Right, well, who am I to interrupt the maestro at work?" She went to walk off, but then turned back. "There are three bay leaves in there," she said. "You might want to let him know. They'll need to come out before—"

"Don't worry. I'll make sure it's done," called Emma, and waited until Geraldine was far enough away that she could slip safely through the automatic gate without being followed.

As she walked up the drive, getting closer to the house, she started to hear him. The sound was still muffled from where she was, but he was shouting, yelling for help, telling anyone who cared to listen that he'd been tied up. She opened the front door, slipped in, and slammed it shut behind her. He fell silent at the sound.

Emma put the casserole dish in the kitchen and lifted the lid, sniffing approvingly at the contents. Then she went to take off her coat. She took her time.

When she was ready, she went into the dining room. Adrian was exactly as she'd left him, except perhaps angrier. He shot her a venomous look from across the room.

"There was someone at the gate," he said.

"There was," agreed Emma. "Geraldine, with what looks like a very tasty casserole. And FYI no one can hear you from the road. It's the long driveway," she explained, indicating with a flourish of her arm, "and the tall pines. The combination of distance and sound barrier means you are rendered silent." Actually, this was something of a relief. Emma had been a little concerned that any noise from the house might be overheard, but now, with Geraldine stopping by, her fears had been put to the test. She had nothing to worry about. No one could hear him.

He glowered at her but as the news of his isolation sank in, she thought she detected a flash of fear too. "You cannot do this," he spat. "I demand that you let me go."

"Not gonna happen, Adrian. Not until you do as I asked. Give me the log-in details to your bank account; let me transfer the money. Honestly, this could all be over so quickly."

"You're deranged."

"Nope, just getting what I deserve. You need to understand, Adrian, that you have screwed up my life. You took my project. You got me sacked. You threatened me if I didn't have sex with you. You've ruined any future I have with Carrie."

"She wouldn't work with you again, anyway."

This made her so incredibly sad she didn't like to dwell on it. But it wasn't the limit of the awful things he'd done to her. There was Elaine, too, thought Emma, as the guilty demons spread their dark wings up inside her again. He'd made her think Elaine had told Carrie they'd slept together. He'd directly had a hand in Elaine's death, but she knew she couldn't say anything, as he'd know she'd been there, shouting at Elaine when she'd had her heart attack.

"Do you really think this is going to work?" he said angrily, pointing at his tethered wrist. "You really believe this is a sane, reasonable plan?"

"It's not that far-fetched. Happens on TV all the time."

"TV's made up!"

"It's a reflection of true life."

He exploded then, incredulous fireworks erupting out of him. "You're living in some sort of fantasy world, Emma!"

She decided it was time to give each other some space. She closed the door on his shouting and expostulating, and went into the kitchen. She ate a portion of the casserole, carefully removing the bay leaves first. It was as delicious as it had promised to be. Afterward, she saw it was getting late and Emma yawned and stretched in her seat. It had been a long and busy day, and seeing as Adrian clearly wasn't going to give in to her demands just yet, she might as well go to bed.

She went upstairs and got a pillow and a blanket from his room. She took these and a fresh cup of water into the dining room, throwing the bedding on him, and then while he was distracted, she placed the cup on the floor within reaching distance.

He was agog. "What? This goes on?"

She sighed, a little irritably. She'd surely made it clear enough. "Do I really have to spell it out again?"

"Where are you sleeping? *Upstairs?* In my *house?*"

"Technically speaking, you could argue it's mine," she said. Then, fed up with his over-dramatic, incredulous scoffing, she left the room.

She lay in bed for a while, reading a book she'd borrowed from the bookcase on the landing. It was hard to concentrate, though, as Adrian was so noisy. She found herself questioning her moral conscience. Was she right to do this? But then she kept coming back to what he had done. He had screwed her over again and again. She had to salvage what was left of her life.

She turned off the light but could still hear him shouting downstairs. Mostly profanities, calling her a "fucking bitch" and suchlike. Half an hour later it was still keeping her awake. For Christ's sake, she was *tired!* She threw back the covers with annoyance and went downstairs in the dark, stopping in the kitchen first.

Then she opened the door to the dining room and from behind her back lifted the wooden pizza peel and brought it down on his body. Not hard enough to really hurt; this was more a lesson in who was in charge.

"Ow!" he yelled in indignant outrage.

"Please be quiet," she said. He instantly opened his mouth to protest and so she raised the pizza peel again. All of a sudden he hesitated and then eyed the pizza peel warily.

"I am going back upstairs and you are going to stay quiet," said Emma.

His mouth opened again and she lifted the peel. This time it had the desired effect—he shrank back and she felt a satisfaction at that, at his humiliation, lying on the floor at her mercy.

Then she went back to bed, and thankfully, Adrian stayed silent.

68

Emma had hit him with the wooden pizza peel. The one he'd gotten from the specialist kitchen shop in town two summers ago and had insisted on using at a party they'd had to celebrate his birthday. They'd invited down their London friends, able to put them up in this new beach house with all its spare bedrooms. He remembered being so proud, feeling so generous and sharing the love: "There's loads of room!" "Just bring yourselves!" and secretly reveling in the fact he could accommodate eight extra people in his new house and not have to pull out one sofa bed. They'd all oohed and aahed enviously, and he'd basked in the security of knowing he'd made it. His success had secured this second home and all its aspirational extras: the view, the private gated position, the culinary gadgets that made him feel that cooking—and life in general—could only be easier, better. He'd be healthier now he had a deluxe nutri extractor. The built-in thousand-pound pizza oven and accompanying peel meant he'd get crispy-based pizzas every time—no need to order delivery anymore, so ultimately it would pay for itself.

411

Adrian remembered it had been hot that Saturday in August and they'd all sat outside on the new patio set. The wine had flowed and everyone had wanted to talk to him about *Generation Rebel*, the hit show that had taken the nation by storm. How brilliantly it was written, how he had captured a moment, how he was dealing with the new-found fame. He'd been happy to let the conversation revolve around him and answer the questions of how he spent a writing day, what inspired him, how he came up with his dialogue. It reinforced in him the confidence that he had actually done it. Him, Adrian Hill, who had floundered near the bottom of the pond for so long. Being able to answer his friends' questions with such flair and knowledge *proved* his abilities.

He'd had to extricate himself from the flurry of questions every now and then to go back into the kitchen, where he'd smiled modestly to himself, contented as he'd pulled out the latest pepperoni from the pizza oven, sliding it onto the peel, the base making contact with the wooden implement with a temptingly light, crispy sound that he knew meant another delicious creation to marvel his friends.

And now, she had hit him with that peel. To shut him up. He'd been so shocked, it had worked.

There had been a series of stunning moments that day. The first being one of great joy, like a gift from the heavens: Emma's offer of an idea. Something that he now knew to be a trap, set to lure him to this house—*his* house—which she was treating as her own. This thought alone was enough to enrage him, but he was beginning to realize that he needed to keep his cool, to start thinking a little more, as Emma had got the better of him ever since he'd walked in the door.

Adrian was still unsure whether this thing—this tying him up—was all a great prank. A stupid way of Emma making her point. He knew she was feeling a great sense of injustice, and he could see why. But half a million! It was truly laughable. Emma was utterly deluded. As for the public apology, who the hell did she think she was? She watched too much TV—that was clear. He ruefully looked at his position on the drafty floor, his head having to lie on a pillow on the marble hearth so his arm wasn't stretched out in agony. The soft feathers were no match for the hard stone that dug into his skull. He plumped it up again with his free hand and tried to sleep. He needed to keep his wits about him so he could get out of this ridiculous situation as soon as possible.

He reflected back to another time when he'd been with Emma in this house—just a couple of months ago they'd been screwing on the sofa up in the office. An amusing thought popped into his mind: if only she'd been into tying him up then!

413

It was inevitable this would come to an embarrassing end, with Emma going off with her tail between her legs. Stupid girl. He'd bet she hadn't thought beyond the initial sweet taste of revenge. Well, he would have the last laugh. Probably get her for Actual Bodily Harm. The police would be totally on his side. But he wouldn't threaten her, no. Not because he thought she was in any way dangerous and he was worried what reaction he might provoke— she was just a stupid, young kid with a chip on her shoulder—but he didn't want to delay his release any longer. He'd save the retaliation for after she'd set him free. Then she'd see just whom she'd been fucking with.

No more shouting, no more outrage. From now on he was going to play it smart.

69

When Emma woke, her head still full of her dream, she had a warm, safe glow inside her that she didn't want to let go of. She'd been at Carrie and Adrian's London house; he was nowhere to be seen and she'd known in her dream that he'd gone; he didn't exist anymore and there was a lightness and happiness to the atmosphere in the house. Rory was tucked away asleep upstairs and it had been just her and Carrie, in the kitchen. The doors to the garden were wide open and it was warm and sunny. Carrie was baking, Emma was sitting at the kitchen table reading through a script she'd written, which she knew Carrie was going to produce, and all through this she had the sensation she came here a lot; she and Carrie were relaxed in each other's company.

Carrie pulled a tray of fairy cakes out of the oven and put them to cool on the counter, which was already piled high with them. There were so many it felt like there were hundreds stacked up on one another, little bites of soft vanilla sponge, and even in her dream, Emma could smell their buttery warmth.

They'd looked in amazement at how many

there were and laughed, both knowing there were still more to come; then Carrie had begun to fill some more paper cake cases. Emma knew they needed more; the more cakes they had, the safer they'd be somehow, and she felt an overwhelming happiness as she'd watched Carrie spoon in the mixture. Then she'd woken and that happiness was a physical feeling in her chest, which was now dissipating rapidly.

When it had finally gone, it left a hole that Emma couldn't stand so she got up. While she ate breakfast, Adrian's phone buzzed on the counter and she saw it was a message from Carrie. She desperately wanted to read it so she thought for a moment, then typed in Adrian's birthday in the hope it would be the PIN code, August 12th: 0812. The screen unlocked and she shook her head at how easy it was. She composed a reply while she put on some more toast for Adrian, and then tucking the phone in her jeans pocket, she picked up the toast and some water and went into the dining room.

Adrian was sitting up, his hair and clothes disheveled, though he looked surprisingly calm considering he'd spent the night shackled to the fireplace. There was a faint whiff of urine from the plastic bucket and she wrinkled her nose.

"Sorry," said Adrian, "but needs must. You could always set me free. Then I'd be a lot more civilized."

"Have you composed your letter?" asked Emma. "Are you ready to give me your bank details?"

"They'll call to check," said Adrian. "Such a large amount, they'll want to know it's not fraud. You answer my phone, it'll be obvious there's something up."

"That's why the money's coming out of your joint account," said Emma. "And we'll make sure the number registered for Carrie is here, the house phone."

She saw his pleasant mask slip. "They'll notify her, by e-mail. Check it was she who changed the number."

"By then it'll be too late. The money will have gone across. Anyway, I personally think that she'll agree it's only fair I get something. She knows it was my project."

By the look on his face, Emma realized then that Carrie had read her letter and knew the truth. It gave her a surge of hope.

"You're not going to get away with this, Emma. Why don't you just let me go and we can talk like two grown adults? I'm not going to freak out or hurt you or anything. And I'm sure we can come to some sort of agreement."

She looked at him and his badly hidden attempt to withhold his anger and didn't believe a word of it.

"Do you really think I'm that naïve?"

"No one's saying that," he quickly reassured

her. "It's just, all this"—he gestured at himself—"because of some silly misunderstanding that I'm sure we can sort out."

Emma bristled. *Silly?* Was it silly that he'd taken something of hers, used it to further his own success, and then refused to acknowledge the fact or share the spoils? Was it silly that he'd used her a second time, taking her ideas and relying on her to shape his next show and then getting her fired the minute she was no longer useful to him? Was it silly that he'd deliberately planted the idea in her head that Elaine had been the one to blame for opening her mouth, causing her to lose her temper, and then poor Elaine had died of a heart attack? Was any of this *silly?*

"I don't think you're taking this seriously enough."

"Carrie's going to wonder where I am," he snapped.

Emma took his phone out of her pocket, held it up. "No, she won't. You've texted her to say you need space to work, a week at least, maybe more."

His face darkened. "You've no right to do that."

"Have you two broken up?" asked Emma, suddenly. "There was something about her reply." She opened his phone and read aloud. "That's fine. In fact, stay as long as you like. It might do us good to have a little break and it'll probably end up being your place anyway. I would prefer to keep the London house."

"It's none of your business," he growled.

Her heart sang then, lifted up off its perch and soared around her chest. A smile blossomed across her face.

"Why are you so obsessed with her?"

She looked at him. "Not obsessed. Just knew she deserved better than you. So back to our arrangement. I have a very good idea, even if I do say so myself. An idea that I think you'll love. Pay me my money, write the letter, and there's no reason we can't go on writing brilliant shows together. I'm prepared to forgive everything you've done, but we need to hit the reset button first. It needs to be fair."

"You don't have an idea. That line about a librarian—that's bullshit."

She smiled at him. "I think it's quite brilliant." In actual fact this wasn't true. Not fully. She did have a new idea and thought it had potential, but it wasn't complete. She was struggling to make it work, but he didn't have to know that.

She looked across at the toast and water she'd placed on the sideboard. "Perhaps we need to speed up your decision making," she said, and picking them up, she took them from the room.

"Hey, Emma—" he shouted, but she was out the door and back in the kitchen. She cocked her head, but he'd gone quiet. Time to leave him for a bit. She had some errands to run.

At the Margate hotel, Emma went up to her

room, noting the DO NOT DISTURB sign was still hanging on the doorknob. She carefully checked the room for anyone's presence. The bed was as she'd left it, the creases in the duvet the same as she'd made them. A glass was in exactly the same position as she'd placed it. Good. That meant she might even be able to leave it a couple of days or so before coming back.

On the way out she made sure she spoke to the girl on the reception desk, asking about the opening times of the Turner Contemporary art gallery, which was down on the seafront; then she went to enjoy a day out.

70

It had upset Carrie that Adrian hadn't come home the previous night. Actually, that wasn't true. It had upset her that he hadn't bothered to tell her and she'd had to prompt him this morning, sending a text asking where he was. It had felt strange doing so: what were the new rules for recently separated couples? They were no longer together, but did that mean they switched off all those thoughts and actions that had been so much a part of their lives? Did they no longer tell each other where they were going and when? Did they still eat together, cook for each other? It seemed odd to do so, but at the same time, it was ludicrous to both be in the kitchen, each cooking a separate, solitary meal. And there was Rory— Adrian was still his father and yet had made no reference to any future plans other than monetary.

She sighed. In truth, it was probably easier he'd chosen to be away for a while. The breakup, although on the cards for some time, was still new and painful. And the memories, the good ones, would stalk her around the house, stopping her in her tracks. It didn't help that there were so many photographs of the two of them around.

She would have to put them away, something she'd maybe do later today.

She had to get used to the idea of being single, of being alone in the house, just her and Rory. It had felt strange the previous night, not knowing if or when Adrian would come back. The more she'd wondered, the more she'd felt alone and her anxiety had grown as the hours ticked by. She'd locked the front door, double-checking it, and she knew why she was feeling so anxious. Ever since she'd discovered that Emma had been present at Elaine's death, she couldn't settle. Emma knew where she lived and had been inside her house. Emma had been looking through their things. It had seemed merely invasive at the time, but now everything had a darker slant to it.

Why had she been at the lake? Was there something about Emma that she, Carrie, didn't know? Something she *should* know? She looked at Rory and felt a wave of vulnerability.

"What shall we do today?" she asked him as she fed him his baby rice.

He looked at her askance, food covering his hands, mouth, and chin, and much of the baby bouncer.

"I know," said Carrie. "I can't decide either. It's weird, isn't it? How she was there. I can't stop thinking about it."

She cleaned him up and then sat with him on the floor, playing with him, but couldn't relax.

422

Was this how it was going to be now? She tried turning some music on, but her mind kept going back to Emma. She didn't know why, but she had an unnerving feeling that Emma wasn't done with her yet after all.

"I think we need to go out," she said to Rory. She couldn't stay in the house any longer, wondering, waiting—for what? She thought ahead to the day coming to a close and having to lock up and be alone in the house.

Carrie jumped up and, looking through her work files on the kitchen table, copied down an address. It was Sunday. There was a good chance Emma's parents would be home.

Carrie looked through the car windscreen at the smart Victorian terrace. It was on a 4×4-clogged street, not far from Wandsworth Common. The front door glistened in the sunshine, not least because a man in overalls was covering it with a layer of fresh black paint.

She got out of the car and the man looked up and gave her a friendly smile before refocusing on his brushwork.

"Excuse me?" called Carrie.

He looked up again, just as she noticed through a ground-floor window that the room on the other side of the glass was completely empty. She frowned.

"Is this the Foxes' house?" she asked, unsure.

423

"That's right."

"Are they . . . no longer here?"

"Gone to Italy. Renting this place out." The painter held his brush and tin of paint aloft. "I'm on a deadline to get it finished."

"Italy?"

"Got a place on one of the lakes. All right for some," he said, lightly.

"What about their daughter? Emma?"

"Don't know of any Emma," said the man. "That who you're trying to get hold of?"

Carrie was trying to think. Had Emma ever mentioned her parents going away? That she'd had to move?

"When did they move out?" she asked.

"Um . . . let me think. A few weeks ago? I've got their number. Brian and Alice. If it's of any help?"

Carrie said yes, it would be a great deal of help and found a piece of paper on which she could copy the number that he read out from his phone. Then she got back in the car and with a wave to the helpful painter, she drove back home.

After she'd put Rory down for a nap, she sat on the sofa, the slip of paper with Emma's parents' phone number in her hands. She didn't know what to say to them. It was one of those things you couldn't overthink, she suddenly decided and started dialing. She listened to the long, foreign ringtone and then a woman's voice answered.

424

"Is that Alice?" asked Carrie.

"Speaking. Who's this?"

"It's . . . I'm Emma's boss. From the TV show. *Leon*."

"Oh, hello." Alice sounded surprised, and Carrie couldn't quite make out if she knew that Emma no longer worked there. "Is she okay?" Alice suddenly asked.

"Oh yes, fine. Emma's fine," said Carrie. "At least, I assume so. She finished working with us a short while ago."

"Oh yes, she mentioned. She had a new job to go to."

Did she, thought Carrie? Since when? "I . . . um we have some pay slips to send on to Emma and I know she recently moved, but we don't seem to have her new address. And for some reason I can't get through on her phone. I had this number down on her contact details as a backup. I'm sorry to bother you, but I wonder if you might have her address? Just so I can get these in the post."

"Hang on," said Alice in her ear, and Carrie could hear the shuffling of papers. "We're still getting sorted here, boxes everywhere. Oh, here we are!" Carrie copied down the address as Alice read it to her over the phone.

"Thank you," said Carrie. "I'll make sure these get to her safely."

"I'll let Emma know you called," said Alice. "What did you say your name was?"

There was no real reason not to give her name, thought Carrie. It might even flush Emma out more quickly.

"Carrie Kennedy," she said.

A long silence filled the airwaves and Carrie wondered if she'd been cut off.

"Hello? Are you still there? Alice?"

More silence. "Hello—?" said Carrie again.

"Yes, yes, I'm still here," said Alice, quickly. Carrie couldn't be sure, but she thought it sounded as if Alice's voice had become tense, strained.

"Right, well, I'd better get on," garbled Alice. "Goodbye." And she'd hung up before Carrie could reply.

She looked at the now-silent phone in her hand. *Strange.* Outside it had started to rain. Miserable slashes of wet splattered the glass. Carrie checked her watch. Rory was still asleep and would be for at least a couple of hours.

Her visit to Emma could wait until later.

71

The wander around the gallery didn't take long and afterward Emma caught the train back to Broadstairs. She stood on the pavement outside the station and wondered what to do. The days stretched out when you had nothing to fill them. She could go back to the beach house, but she didn't feel in the mood to be anywhere near Adrian, and actually, the longer she left him, the quicker he might toe the line. She shivered. It was too cold to stand around being indecisive so she headed toward the town, her scarf pulled up over her chin.

As she neared the bustle of the high street she felt less isolated and found herself slowing down. Maybe there was something she needed, a shop she had to pop into; then a door opened onto the pavement next to her and a waft of warm, scented air briefly enveloped her. She turned her head and saw she was outside a hair salon. It would kill at least an hour and she could totally relax, hand her life over to someone else for a short while.

"Do you have availability for a cut and blow-dry?" she asked the black-clad girl at the reception desk.

A few clicks on the computer and she was allocated a stylist and then found herself in a high, deep chair having warm water and shampoo gently massaged into her head. She closed her eyes, enjoying the sensation of feeling temporarily trouble free. Once it was done, she sat back in the stylist's chair, her hair being combed through.

"So, just the ends, yes?" asked the stylist, confirming what they'd discussed when she first came in.

"That's right," said Emma, taking a sip of the complimentary orange juice, an escapist magazine on her knee. She watched as he started to trim the ends of her hair, tiny half-inch blonde pieces falling onto her protective gown. It would be the same. The same hair, the same Emma, the same life. Nothing would change. She would go back to the beach house and Adrian would still be handcuffed to the fireplace. She suddenly felt an urge to derail everything, to take back some control of a situation she wasn't sure she knew how to handle.

"Actually, I've changed my mind," she said to the stylist. "I want something completely different."

72

Sunday, February 25

She had to ask her outright. that was the only way she was going to be able to gauge what had happened—by watching Emma's reactions.

And then what?

It wasn't as if Emma was going to invite her in for a coffee and confession. Carrie needed to know *something,* though, a greater sense of what had happened, an understanding of Emma and Elaine's relationship, anything to give herself some insight into whether or not this feeling of foreboding was warranted or a sleep-deprived new mother's paranoia.

She rested a protective hand on the top of Rory's squirrel-hatted head as she walked along this neat road opposite a large cemetery. It was fairly ordinary with irregular trees planted in the pavement, their branches trimmed to bare nubs. Carrie always hated the way the trees were shorn in winter; they reminded her of something out of a horror movie, hands severed from arms. She glanced down at Rory. He was enclosed in a pouch close to her chest; she'd wanted him cocooned next to her when she went to this flat. It would be easy to flee should she need to.

Carrie shook her head: *flee?* What did she think was going to happen?

She was nearing the flat now and went up the narrow concrete path that led to the front door, the paint chipped and worn.

Carrie rang the bell and waited. Rory, sensing they'd stopped, was looking quizzical. She bent down and kissed the top of his head.

Then the door opened. A plump girl with dark hair pulled back in a ponytail was staring at her— rather irritably, thought Carrie. She was wearing a onesie made of fake leopard skin fabric, and Carrie had obviously interrupted a lazy Sunday. As she glanced through the window to her right she saw the TV was on, an overseas property show. On the coffee table in the middle of the room was an open packet of chocolate biscuits.

"Can I help you?" said the girl.

"I'm looking for Emma Fox," replied Carrie.

The girl's irritation deepened. "She's not here."

"Do you know when she'll be back?"

"No."

Carrie deduced that Emma had done something to offend this girl, judging by her curt responses. "Will it be later today, do you think?"

"Your guess is as good as mine. I haven't seen her since Friday morning."

Carrie stood up straighter, surprised. "Oh?"

"Went to work and never came back."

"Did you not . . . ?" prompted Carrie.

430

"What?"

"Worry?"

The girl snorted. "No, she sent a text. Staying with some friend now apparently. God knows how she gets away with it at her work. She's never there. Either working from home or on some jaunt. And I thought filming TV shows was meant to be some all-encompassing, grueling marathon."

"It can be," said Carrie. The girl raised an eyebrow. "I'm one of the producers," Carrie explained. "Of the show Emma's been working on."

"Oh, right." The girl suddenly warmed, then seemed to remember her manners. She thrust out a hand. "I'm Lucy Quinn. Emma's flatmate."

"Carrie Kennedy." She paused. "I don't suppose there's any chance I could come in for a bit? Save chatting out here in the cold?"

Lucy seemed to weigh up abandoning her private date with the packet of biscuits and talking to a proper TV producer, then held the door wider. "Course!"

As Carrie walked past her into the flat, Lucy leaned in, too close. "Is that little Rory?" she cooed. "Emma talked about him a lot."

The hairs went up on the back of Carrie's neck. She looked down and saw Rory had fallen asleep on her chest.

She was directed to the living room and offered a drink, which she declined. The room was simply and inexpensively furnished, almost everything had that cheap minimalist style that was indicative of somewhere like Ikea.

"So is it going well? The filming?" asked Lucy as she quickly muted the TV and tucked the biscuits onto a lacquered black shelving unit behind a photo frame. The photo inside was of Lucy, Carrie saw, on a night out of some sort, dressed up with shiny clothes and skin, the flash giving her a bit of red eye. In fact, *every* photo was of Lucy: her graduation, with friends, with a very self-assured male who draped an arm around her shoulders while he grinned into the camera, his bow tie hanging loosely around a naked neck as his shirt buttons were open down to his mid-chest. There were no photos of Emma at all.

"Extremely well. Thanks for asking."

"Emma's been telling me about some of the stuff you've been filming. The hot air balloon."

"That was a fun scene. It's nice she enjoys her work. Has she ever told you about any of her other jobs?"

Lucy looked puzzled. "Like what?"

"Oh, I don't know. Other shows she's been involved in, other people she's worked with."

Lucy's eyes lit up. "Oh, you mean like famous people? No, she has not! Why? Who else has she worked with?"

"That isn't quite—"

"Come on, you can tell me. Emma and I are best friends."

That is a barefaced lie, thought Carrie. Anyone can see you can't stand her. "I was thinking more of directors . . . producers . . . that sort of thing."

"Not that I know of. Hey, I'm *so* excited about *Leon* coming on the TV. It sounds like such an awesome show. I've been following all the PR stuff, you know, finding out about how it's come together."

"Great. She ever mention anyone called Elaine?"

Lucy frowned. "Elaine . . ." she repeated, pondering. "I don't think so. Do you still have lots to film?"

A loud warning bell was ringing in Carrie's ear. She ignored Lucy's question. "Elaine was her old boss," she persisted. "She died recently."

"Oh my God," said Lucy. "Sorry to hear that."

But the news had barely impacted her at all. Instead she was sitting upright, her legs tucked under her leopard-clad backside and her eyes shining with hope.

"Do you know," she ventured, boldly, "Emma kindly asked if I would like to go to the set. To visit," she added, pointedly.

Carrie somehow doubted the absolute truth of this statement and she resented this girl forcing herself on her, putting her in a position where she was required to substantiate Emma's alleged invitation. She smiled. "That was very nice of Emma. But I'm afraid she no longer works with us."

It was as if she'd poured a bucket of cold water on Lucy. Her mouth had dropped open in shock.

"What?"

"She's left."

Just as Lucy was processing this, another realization popped. "So where does she work now, then?" she asked suspiciously.

"I believe she's what they call 'between jobs.' "

Lucy's face grew thunderous. The legs came out from their relaxed position and landed on the floor.

"Is there something wrong?" asked Carrie.

"She owes me rent—that's what's wrong," Lucy blurted out. "And it turns out she's been lying about her job. When did you say she left?"

"I didn't."

Lucy looked at her mutinously and Carrie relented. "Beginning of January."

"January!" Lucy exploded. "That was weeks ago!" Then it dawned. "Working from home, my arse! She didn't have a bloody job to go to! She signed a bloody rent contract knowing she had no job," she fumed.

Carrie could tell Lucy's longed-for set visit had just sprouted a pair of wings and flown out of the window.

"I want my rent," said Lucy, darkly. "Who is this person she's staying with, anyway?"

"What makes you think I know?"

"You two know each other quite well, don't

you? I mean . . . she's kept everything. I assumed you go way back."

Carrie looked at her, puzzled. "What do you mean?"

Lucy lifted her head defiantly. "I was just putting some of her stuff away in her room. Happened to see."

A nervous ripple ran down Carrie's back. She stood. "Would you show me?"

Lucy reluctantly got up and led Carrie to Emma's room, which was obviously the smaller of the two in this flat. Carrie watched as Lucy stepped inside and opened the bottom drawer of a tall chest. She pointed.

Holding Rory carefully, Carrie bent down to see. She saw her own face smiling back at her. It was a printout of the press release announcing the *Leon* green light. She flicked through other papers. There were industry magazine clippings and online printouts that charted her entire career, going back a decade or more. Her move to Hawk Pictures. Her BAFTA nomination. Interviews she'd done for various newspapers' art sections— *The Guardian*, *The Times*, *The Observer*—on her factual programs. Her blood ran cold—what did Emma have these for? What did she want with her?

She saw Lucy watching.

"So are you two mates, or what?" asked Lucy, mulishly.

Carrie stiffened with anger. This insufferable girl was nothing but a malicious, self-serving gossip. "Funny how you just happened to see these. When you were placing stuff in her room."

Lucy flushed with embarrassment and indignation. "I'm actually expecting someone," she said, glancing deliberately at her watch. "Any minute now."

"Don't worry, I'm leaving," said Carrie, already walking toward the door.

"Hey, the next time you speak to her, tell her I want my rent," said Lucy to her back, "or all her stuff, including her precious papers, is going in the bin."

Carrie suddenly remembered something. She swung back. "Where did you say her friend was? The one she's staying with?"

"Dunno. The coast somewhere."

Her heart was suddenly racing. Surely not . . .

73

Emma was looking at herself in the mirror while the stylist waited anxiously for her verdict.

Her long hair lay in disheveled clumps on the floor. She touched her hairstyle, getting used to its new shortness, and smiled. "I like it," she said, and the stylist beamed with relief.

"It suits you, a bob," he said, patting the ends admiringly.

He was right, it did, thought Emma. She should've known, really.

Her haircut gave her a new energy and a sense of optimism as she walked back to the beach house. As she headed into the estate she heard a car pull up beside her.

"Hello," called Geraldine from the window. "How did the casserole go down?"

Emma leaned down to speak to her, ignoring the growls from the pug on the front seat. "Very well. In fact, I think it fueled him for hours. He was still going when I'd left for the day and all I could hear was a continuous clicking of the keyboard."

Geraldine gave a self-satisfied smile. No doubt, thought Emma, pleased with her contribution to Adrian's genius.

"He's such a wonderful writer," said Geraldine. "I loved *Generation Rebel*. Such a powerful show. Those kids! They were utterly nightmare-ish. I suppose he wrote a reflection on what kids are like today, and very clever, too, but I found myself wanting to murder every one of the little so-and-sos. And it was the poor headmaster who got it!"

"You don't think that they had been unnecessarily pressured by the teaching establishment and that after the suicide of one of their friends as a result of the unattainable goals they were subject to, they were justified in making a stand against the education department? That however much their teachers were 'just following the curriculum,' they were just as responsible, and the whole series was a comment on the way we educate our children today?"

Geraldine looked at her strangely. "No."

Emma smiled but said nothing, ignoring the slightly awkward pause that now existed between them.

"How's Carrie?" asked Geraldine.

"Fine."

"I haven't seen her down here for a while."

"She's been very busy, you know, juggling work and the new baby."

"Of course. Oh, I hope she comes down soon. I'd love to meet little . . . Rory, isn't it?"

"That's right."

Geraldine nodded, clearly finished with small

talk. "I'd better get on. I'll pop by for the casserole dish at some point."

"It's okay, I'll drop it off," said Emma.

"Not at all. I wouldn't dream of putting you out," said Geraldine firmly. She held Emma's gaze. "Have you had your hair cut, by the way?"

Emma nodded as Geraldine openly appraised her. "Nice," she said approvingly, then drove off even as the window was going back up.

Emma watched as she disappeared down the road. Interfering old busybody, she thought, but wasn't overly threatened by Geraldine's determination to come to the house. She could see on the camera who was buzzing at the gate and would simply ignore her.

As she let herself into the house, Adrian started up from the dining room.

"Emma! Emma! You cannot fucking do this. This is against my human rights!"

She sighed and opened the dining room door; his rant stopped mid-sentence.

He was staring at her. "Jeez . . . you've had your hair cut."

"Yes," she said, impatiently.

"You look . . ."

"Different?"

"Like Carrie," he said. "Carrie has hair like that." His eyes roved over her, a new realization dawning. "And you're wearing her clothes . . ."

"I've been wearing her clothes ever since I got

here," said Emma with another sigh. Was he really that unobservant? No wonder he struggled with his writing. "I didn't bring any of my own and yours didn't fit me."

"You're nuts," he said, warily. "Totally cuckoo." He was looking at her strangely. "How long are you going to keep me here?"

"We've already discussed this."

He jerked his arm, angrily. "You are just some jumped-up little kid with ideas above her station. How dare you do this to me? You were my *assistant*."

"No, Adrian, I was more than that. A junior to you, yes, you're right about that, perhaps even a pupil, but you need to watch us downtrodden pupils. We can fight back against our 'mentors.' " She looked at his arm. "You're tied up in handcuffs, just like the headmaster. Just remember, Adrian, what happened to him."

He paled. "Jesus Christ . . . you're not going to . . . those kids hanged that man!"

"Forced his head into a noose and pushed his body out of the window so he broke his neck," agreed Emma. "Perhaps that noose should also be here, where you can see it. A little reminder."

He was staring at her incredulously, but she couldn't be bothered with it. She shut the door and went into the kitchen to get herself something to eat. As she cooked a simple pasta dish, she considered how long it had been since she'd given anything to Adrian. Twenty-four hours had passed since she'd provided him with any food or water and she wondered how much longer he could go on, what it would take for him to realize she wasn't going to just come in the room and let him go.

She knew he thought she wasn't serious, not deep down. That he saw her actions as a child's tantrum, and it irritated her that he was so dismissive of her. She suddenly had an image of him lying there, sometime in the future.

CUT TO:

INT. ADRIAN AND CARRIE'S BEACH HOUSE—DAY

It's the year 2025. ADRIAN is still handcuffed to the fireplace, but now he exists as a skeleton clad in some dirty, faded rags. The skeleton's jaw starts to chatter.

ADRIAN
Let me go, you deluded child. I'm telling you, this isn't funny anymore!

CUT TO:

Emma smiled, amused by her own fantasy. She ate her dinner in solitude and then tidied

441

away the dishes. Afterward she thought she'd go and watch some TV, so she switched on the oversized screen in the living room. A new drama was about to start, something that had been heavily trailed and was a big show for the channel in every way—cast, budget, scheduled slot. The industry had been talking about it for months, dining out on tidbits of gossip about how the original lead actor had been fired just a week into the shoot after a sexual harassment story broke (thank goodness it wasn't any longer and they didn't have to reshoot the whole thing), and how halfway through, the director had broken her wrist on set but had continued filming for another two days before being persuaded to go to the emergency department—then was back on set again at dawn the next morning, directing with a plaster cast.

The opening titles started: monotone and moody, declaring that the spy show about to start was coolly stylish. Then as the show began, a set piece kicked in almost immediately: a car explosion. It certainly grabbed her attention but as the drama continued to unfold her interest started to wane. The actors were good, the production stylistic, but the story felt like something she'd seen before. The same familiar tropes of numerous spy shows kept cropping up; the same twists in the story that she'd seen dozens of times before.

She fidgeted in her seat, deeply disappointed. Such an opportunity! Why waste it by writing something derivative? She sat forward, chin on her hands; there they go again—she would bet a tenner that a rival in the spy's department would report him to the boss as a maverick, a loose cannon and unworthy of the mission, and his career would hang in the balance unless he could rapidly prove himself. A few seconds later that was exactly what happened.

Frustrated, Emma jumped up and left the room.

74

Sunday, February 25

Adrian watched Emma cautiously as she charged into the room and turned on the TV: what was this all about?

"Have you seen this?" said Emma, pointing at the screen.

He looked up. It was the new primetime spy show that had been lauded for months. By the tone of Emma's voice, she wasn't that impressed.

"It's just a rehash of every spy show you've seen before," she said. "Oh my goodness, did you hear that?"

Adrian had heard it and he had to admit, as dialogue went, it wasn't that impressive. "Where did *she* come from?" he asked suddenly, as a female character appeared on screen.

"I thought she was supposed to be in mourning?" said Emma, dryly. "I guess he's too hot for her to resist."

"No, no, no," protested Adrian, as the female character led the spy to her bedroom. "It's mad!"

"Bonkers," agreed Emma, and they both laughed.

"So you reckon you could do better?" said Adrian. He kept on watching the screen in an attempt to sound casual.

She turned and looked at him. "Yes," she said, although he could tell she was hesitant, nervous almost.

"What's your idea?" he asked, as nonchalantly as he could.

Her gaze turned skeptical, but she didn't shoot him down in flames.

"As I said, it's about a librarian, a timid, unassuming woman. Her local library is threatened with closure and she has to prove there are two hundred visitors a week in order to persuade the council to keep it open. So she starts to offer the things in the community that austerity budgeting has cut."

He immediately felt a frisson of intrigue. "Go on."

"As the library grows in popularity, the community gets stronger and she gets more powerful. She ultimately goes from this timorous lady to a local kingpin. Kind of like a female Mafioso. And then someone crosses her so she has a vengeance to play out."

"And?"

"What?"

He waved his hand. "What's the vengeance?"

She was looking at him hard. "Are you having a laugh?"

He feigned innocence. "Don't know what you mean."

"You think I'm so dumb I'm going to tell you the whole thing?"

"I didn't say that—"

"You are unbelievable." She suddenly went to the built-in shelving behind the television, rummaged around, flinging DVDs off the shelf until she found what she was looking for. Then she angrily popped a case open and stuffed a DVD into the machine. He flinched at her rough handling and had half a mind to tell her to be careful but sensing her mood, decided to keep quiet. The TV screen came alive and as soon as he looked up, he knew what she'd put on. Emma pressed the remote control so that the screen jumped forward a couple of scenes. The midway point of *Generation Rebel*'s first episode blasted into the room.

"You see that?" said Emma, jabbing her finger at the screen. "That scene there where that girl is being told she has to drop her football club and stay after school for extra lessons in math for the foreseeable in order not to let the school's overall grades drop? That girl was in my class." She fast forwarded a bit further. Pointed at the screen again. "That girl who's e-mailing her teacher to say she's unable to go to school because of anxiety attacks, that character is a version of several girls in my school." She kept on pressing buttons, fast forwarding the picture, then playing it again. " 'Pep talk' assembly!" she said, her eyes blazing at him, then going back to the screen. "Teacher's marriage on the rocks because he can't cope! Twenty-second test and they're still in the *first term!*" Then she pressed a few buttons and played a new episode. "That girl there, crying in the bath, holding a knife to her wrists, that girl is a version of my best friend's little sister."

Emma stopped, breathless, and Adrian watched her. She was visibly upset. Okay, so she obviously went to a very high-pressure school. They couldn't all be like that, although actually, he'd heard that most were, the continued pressure to get good exams results to keep the Ofsted vultures at bay was putting the mental health of the kids today at risk. He recognized the passion in her, the way a writer draws on personal experience to write something powerful and send a message. He'd had moments like that himself.

His conscience stabbed at him. Maybe he had overstepped the mark. Perhaps he'd robbed her of more than just her project, perhaps he'd stolen part of her makeup, stripped her soul. She was watching him, waiting for him to say something. Now would be the time to admit to what he'd done and apologize.

The seconds ticked on and he wrestled with himself. He looked at her and in her eyes was a mixture of things: expectation, hope, pleading. He took a deep breath.

"Could've happened to anyone."

Her face fell and then grew thunderous. Adrian braced himself, but then, unexpectedly, her eyes went wide, throwing him. She stared at him, a beatific smile on her face. And then suddenly, she left the room.

He heard her run upstairs and he was alone.

Goddamn it, what was going on now? She was so frustrating. But that idea . . . the Mafioso librarian . . . Adrian could tell there was something good about it, something fresh.

And all of a sudden he wanted it. It suited him perfectly. It wasn't quite there yet but between them, they'd build on it. He'd write it *brilliantly*, he just knew. He imagined Liz's face when he told her; saw her eyes light up the way he knew his had just done. He felt the thrill of the big-name cast signing up to act in it. Saw the army of crew working to make it, to bring his scripts to life, and he saw the gushing reviews, the impressive audience figures, and the BAFTA nomination. He saw his peers making a point of crossing a room to speak to him, to congratulate him.

Adrian considered Emma. She was good. *Really* good. Better than she knew. Maybe he should rethink this situation he was in. Be a little more generous. He could stand to benefit quite a lot. She could be his ticket out of the hellhole he'd found himself in, and he wasn't just thinking about his position on the marble hearth. This idea could propel him to a new level of fame.

But she wanted half a million pounds! And the

most humiliating piece of writing he'd ever have to do. An apology! In public! Having to admit *Generation Rebel* wasn't all his. He cringed angrily at the thought. No way, not while there was breath still in his body. He seethed, wishing he was free so he could just get up and fly upstairs to where she was hiding out. Put his hands around her neck and let her know she couldn't do this to him.

Generation Rebel was still blaring on the TV on the wall in front of him. He waited, but she didn't come back. He shouted her name, several times, but he was ignored. For Christ's sake, he was hungry! He was thirsty! And he was stuck to this goddamn fireplace with a total nut for a jailer!

Adrian suddenly jolted, sleep snatched from him again in an endless torturous circle of agony. Every time he dropped off, *Generation Rebel* would lurch him awake. He closed his eyes and groaned in pain, his nerve endings shredded. The TV erupted again.

He opened a bloodshot eye: it was still there. The remote control. A piece of small black plastic that was the key to his peace. It was on the sideboard, out of reach. One push, one tiny push of a button and he could be put out of his misery.

Generation Rebel's relentless attack continued.

How he craved silence. He put his free hand over his head, trying to block out the racket, but it just battered at his arms, finding a way into his ears, his brain. Adrian yelled out, an angry, frustrated, animalistic roar, then lay there, half whimpering.

Right in his line of sight was the plastic cup Emma had left for him the first night she'd cuffed him. He quieted, hope blooming. If he was careful, he might be able to do it.

Adrian stretched out his fingers and grabbed the cup. He weighed it in his hand, turning it this way and that. It was heavy as plastic cups go—he'd insisted Carrie get the expensive ones. If they were going to have patio "glassware" he'd wanted his gin and tonic to be in something solid. He sat himself up as best he could, half-propped up on his elbow. He closed one eye, squinting at the TV. Raised up the hand holding the cup. *You've only got one chance,* he reminded himself grimly. *Don't mess it up.* Then he pulled his arm back and threw the cup in the direction of the TV as hard as he could. It crashed into the screen and in an instant the screen cracked and blacked out.

Adrian whooped, pumping his arm in the air. *What a shot!* He fell back down, exhausted but euphoric. Ah, the blissful silence. It caressed his ears. His body began to relax, muscles growing heavy with relief. The lights he could do less about, but he could pull the duvet over his head to block out most of it.

He lay there for a while floating on an enchanted cloud. Sleep crept its tendrils nearer and he felt himself begin to drift. As his brain started to scurry around, locking doors and turning off lights, he suddenly had a thought of Carrie and he wondered how she was doing, alone in their house. Was she missing him? How long would it take before she realized something might be wrong and tried to get hold of him? Heart sinking, he knew it would be several more days, perhaps even weeks as Emma had effectively told her to back off.

The lights in his head suddenly switched back on. There must be *someone* who'd be missing him. Someone who'd become concerned, raise an alarm? There was an entire film crew shooting his work, but he knew they were deeply wrapped up in the demanding task of filming. Yes, the director might notice he hadn't been around for a while, but his concern would last for a few minutes at most. He wasn't part of the machinery; no one actually needed him. He was wallpaper, really.

What about Liz? He owed her an idea. Something that he knew she was getting deeply skeptical about his ever delivering. He'd brushed her off with so many excuses, her prompts had diminished of late. And anyway, she'd probably check in with Carrie, who would just repeat what she'd been told: he was at the beach house working—doing what he was supposed to be doing and if they left him alone he'd come up with the goods.

Maybe his friends. He'd lost touch with many as they all seemed to be acquiring babies, who grew into demanding young children, and he just didn't have any interest in spending his spare time having his conversations interrupted several times a minute, nor getting on his hands and knees to play a mind-numbingly dull game.

No. Adrian began to realize there was nobody who would miss him for quite some time. He was very much alone.

75

The words came to her slowly, a gradual trickle like the tiny stream she'd seen suddenly appear in the middle of the African dust bowl on those nature programs on TV. As if out of nowhere, the water carved a much-needed darkening streak through the parched landscape. She was afraid the words would dry up, no match for the long, barren drought she'd endured. What if it wasn't real? A false start? But she banished those thoughts as soon as they appeared and just concentrated on the script that was beginning to emerge on her laptop screen. A mere embryo at the moment but still . . .

Something had happened when she'd been in the dining room with Adrian earlier. The half idea that she'd struggled with for so long had suddenly grown a new branch, had flourished. She'd felt something that hadn't happened to her in absolutely ages. A tiny flicker of excitement, a miniscule flame, which she was nursing right now, tending it carefully so that it would stay alight.

I'm writing again! came the internal whisper, hardly daring to make itself heard. She came

455

to the end of a scene and paused. What would happen next? The answer didn't come immediately and in order to dodge the looming panic, she plumped up the pillows behind her. Sat back on the bed for a moment and thought. *Power corrupts,* she reminded herself. *Power corrupts.* And then it came to her; the trickle continued. She leaned forward with a new energy and continued to type.

76

He was so terribly thirsty.

Adrian listened to Emma move around upstairs. She was sleeping in the front spare bedroom; he could tell by where her footsteps fell. It had an en suite and he heard the toilet flush. A short time afterward he followed her footsteps as she came downstairs and went into the kitchen. He heard her open a cupboard, then help herself to his water, cascading from his tap. Christ, he was so thirsty.

He rolled onto his back, his shackled arm twisting at an uncomfortable angle, and looked across at the window. It was pitch-black outside, so he could see nothing but the room reflected back at him. Somewhere out there were the dense pine trees that surrounded his house. Behind these trees was Geraldine's place. He remembered the day he'd looked around his soon-to-be house, delighted with the privacy and distance from the neighbors. He'd stood in the back garden, gazing up in appreciation, thinking he and Carrie could maybe get a hot tub installed. He imagined sultry summer nights, the two of them naked in the frothing water, cold champagne on ice.

What he'd give to take a chain saw and fell every single one of those trees now.

A blustery wind blew rain against the window pane. Everywhere, the sensation of water being close and yet so out of reach. It was torture.

He rolled back onto his right side so he was facing the door. He longed, ached to get up. Sitting was awkward because the cuffs kept his arm so low, and of course standing was out of the question. He had to piss kneeling, his cock held over the goddamn bucket, which stank. Thank God he'd not had to do anything else. At least that was one good outcome of not being given any food.

The marble hearth was digging into his shoulder again and in a flare of anger and frustration he punched it. His knuckles cracked against the stone and he yelped and held them to his mouth. *Stupid idea.* It didn't matter which way he turned his body, it dug into him. His shoulder, his neck, his head. He deeply regretted using up the rest of the blister pack of aspirin so quickly to abate what now seemed to have been a trifling headache. Some of it would have helped numb his pain.

He tried propping himself up and the hearth's cold hardness grated on his elbow. How he wished he hadn't insisted on a fireplace. There had been nothing there when they'd moved in; the fireplaces had been covered up to make way for something more modern. But he'd wanted to renovate. Take the house back to its original glory! He'd paid an eye-popping amount for a professional to remove the plasterboard, and he remembered feeling as if he'd struck gold when behind it was revealed the original 1930s cast-iron surround and tiles. The builder had suggested replacing the whole lot, including the iron rings he was now shackled to, but he'd refused in some nostalgic wave of preservation. *Big mistake.* There was no hearth, of course, and he'd gone to a specialty shop and insisted on a slab of black marble that gleamed. The same black marble that was now trying to slice his arm in two by some slow, torturous method, like a blunt knife trying to amputate a limb.

Why hadn't he got a hearth made of thick foam or a finely sprung mattress? He groaned yearningly at the idea, almost feeling a soft, supportive cradle beneath him, and then snapped his eyes wide open. No. He mustn't think like that because that meant he was accepting where he was, what he was doing on the floor. He had to get free, get out. He yanked the cuffs again, even while knowing it was futile, and yelped as they cut into his wrist. *Where is the key?* Emma must have taken it out of the picture frame that had been hanging on the office wall. Over the long hours lying there he'd scanned the room as best he could from his low vantage point, but the small piece of metal wasn't at ankle or knee level. Any surface that was hip height or above he had no view of. She wouldn't leave it in here anyway; she'd have it hidden away somewhere—perhaps in the room she was sleeping in.

His mood darkened at thoughts of Emma. That crazy, loopy girl. How long was she going to keep him here? More worryingly, how long was she going to deprive him of food and drink? He could smell something divine. It was her toast from the kitchen: thick, warm slices spread with melted dripping butter. *The bitch.* It was sending him into madness. All he could think about was water, long, cool gulps of the stuff, and cramming his face full of toast, an entire loaf of it.

He hated her so much. Hated her for tethering him like an animal. For making him feel so angry and helpless and for blackmailing him. It was laughable that she wanted an apology—so she could resurrect her career presumably. Well, when he was done with her, any career she might have had would be ripped to shreds until it was completely unsalvageable.

But then she does have good ideas. That idea she'd been talking about earlier had the makings of something bloody brilliant. For a short moment he envisaged a scenario in which they teamed up, her coming up with something rough, perhaps hesitantly voicing her thoughts, then him sitting at his desk, screen in front of him, shaping

460

and molding it, the sculptor of the two, the true artist.

He was suddenly startled by the sound of her going upstairs again. *Is she not even going to come in? Water, I need water.*

"Emma!" he shouted, or at least that had been the intention, but his vocal chords seemed to have dried up. "Emma!" he shouted, again and again, bellowing as loudly as he could.

In response he heard the door of the spare room close.

Fuck's sake!

77

It had stopped raining sometime around three in the morning and a short time afterward, Adrian had been alerted to the fact there was some sort of blockage in the gutter outside his bedroom window. He knew this because the bedroom was right above the dining room and the leaves, or whatever had caused the obstruction, had built up with water that dripped down, past the bedroom window, down, down to outside the dining room window, through his line of vision to the leaves of the patio rose below. Drip! Drip! A torturous rhythmic sound that ended with a splash as the rose leaf bent under the weight of the drop, which then exploded in some sort of aqueous firework, sending a tiny spray against the window.

He was so thirsty.

Splash!

Don't look. Don't look.

He turned his head away, closing his eyes as he did so, but with the rest of the house so silent, the drips had the stage.

Splash!

Splash!

He grit his teeth, his eyes flashed open. And rested on something.

Really?

He looked at the purple plastic bucket. That was what you did in extremis, wasn't it? Drink your own urine? Oh, for Christ's sake, where was Emma? She couldn't *do* this to him. She had no *right*. She— He abruptly stopped this line of mental raging; it had achieved nothing so far and would only send him into madness. As would shouting out for her. Not once had she acknowledged, let alone answered, his roars of frustration. No, what he had to do was make a decision.

How long was he prepared to dig his heels in for? At the beginning of this farce, he'd had no belief that she would keep him here like this, but now . . . well, he wasn't so sure. The logical part of his brain that was still functioning (not much to be honest, as it was in near collapse with dehydration) told him she couldn't possibly keep him here until he *died*. How would she explain such a thing?

But the other part of his brain, the one that said, *wake up and smell the roses. Look what the mental bitch has done thus far,* that part was standing over him, arms folded, eyes rolling, impatiently tapping its foot.

And right now, that part of his brain was the loudest.

78

Monday, February 26

All Carrie wanted was a message: a call, a text.
something to reassure her that Adrian was alone
in the house in Broadstairs. She briefly considered the alternative, but couldn't picture it.
He'd told her the fling with Emma was a one-
off that he bitterly regretted, but what if she'd
been too gullible, too stupid, and had fallen for a
bucket load of lies?

It didn't really matter, her common sense told
her, as she knew her own relationship with Adrian
was over anyway, but actually, she thought
angrily, it *did*. It mattered to her if her husband
had fallen for someone else; it mattered because
at one point she'd cared about their marriage
deeply. Not once had he mentioned wanting to be
with Emma and she needed to know if this was
the real reason for their breakup.

Why didn't he text her? Just check how she was
doing? Check how his *son* was doing?

She felt Rory falling asleep on her shoulder,
sated from his three a.m. feeding, and so she
gently laid him down in his Moses basket. Once
he was settled, she rested her head back onto the
pillows and the other unsettling problem niggled

away at her. Those pictures and articles. What was Emma doing with them? Why was she so interested in her? There had been nothing about Adrian in her little collection.

It frightened her. She imagined them together, entwined in bed. Emma already had an unexplained presence at one premature death. What if she was planning another? Was she, Carrie, in the way?

She suddenly reached over to the bedside table and picked up her phone. If he wasn't going to get in touch with her, she'd text him. She held the phone aloft, thumbs poised. What to say? It would come out as an accusation, especially if she texted now, in the dead of night. *So what?*

She was being ridiculous. Of course they weren't shacked up together in the beach house, Emma planning her demise.

Shaking her head, she put down the phone and pulled the duvet over herself, looking for sleep.

79

Count them again, count them! Well, no need to count them, just look at the number at the bottom of the screen—thirty-one pages of beautiful script. Thirty-one! That meant thirty-one minutes of heart-stopping, spine-tingling television. More than half a BBC episode! Two thirds of a commercial hour! This revelation was so powerful, Emma had to fall back against the pillows and catch her breath. But it didn't last long. The excitement propelled her back up again and she stared in wonder at the screen.

Something was working, something was definitely working. She'd never written like this before, as if the words themselves were fighting to get out of her, landing in glorious Technicolor on the screen. Characters shouting to be heard, waving at her to get her attention, telling her their stories, and insisting she put down what they said. She could hardly type quickly enough and then when she finished a scene, believing that was it, that the whole thing was a mirage and she was back in the desert, the ideas would once again come thick and fast, and she'd scribble them down in her notebook: twists to the story; character embellishments; *further episodes.*

She looked up at the clock and was startled to see it was just after three in the morning. She'd spent the whole night writing and hadn't thought of Adrian once. She popped out her earphones and that's when she heard it. He was calling her, shouting her name.

She considered. Maybe it was time to go and see him.

80

He could hear her coming downstairs and he ceased his shouting. She would be here in a minute. He'd made his decision, but it didn't mean he would be offering it to her on a plate. He didn't want to feel as though he'd lost.

You're in control here, he reminded himself. *You'll be free and you can start on your next big show.* Adrian had been thinking a lot about Emma's idea and the more he rolled it around his head, the more convinced he was it had the makings of a winner. So what if it cost him half a million pounds to get his hands on it? It wasn't like he didn't have at least ten times that in the bank.

He heard Emma go into the kitchen. He waited. She would come to him. And then she did. The door swung open and she stood in the frame holding a glass of water and a plate of crackers.

Adrian watched as she placed them on the floor a small distance from him, pushing them closer with the pizza peel, as if he were an animal that might attack at any moment. His first instinct was to drink and he quickly shuffled over to the water and started to take great gulps of it. It was

469

so cool and pure, he felt dizzy with ecstasy as it cascaded down his throat.

"Not too fast," said Emma. "Isn't that supposed to make you sick?"

He'd heard that also, but it was too late. He'd emptied the glass and in fact wanted more. Instead he took one of the crackers and devoured it, then heeding her advice, ate the second a little more slowly, while he watched her, watching him.

"You broke the TV," she said, glancing at the wall.

What? Oh yes. That felt like weeks ago now. "You left it on. Loud."

He sat up, somewhat lopsided, because of the handcuff, but he wanted to be as close to her eye level as possible when he delivered his news. He could already feel the effects of the peasant-style meal, clarity and strength returning to his body that felt almost euphoric.

"I've decided to pay you," he said. "Not because you deserve it—you don't. There was only ever one creator of *Generation Rebel* and that was me. But nonetheless, despite your irritating insistence and your stinking method of blackmail, I'm prepared to give you the sum you've asked for. Here are my conditions: When we work on the librarian show, and there's no beating about the bush here with this, I see myself as the lead writer. I'm clearly the more experienced and a name on the commissioner lists. Oh, and I'm not writing any letter of apology—you can forget that. Consider this my final offer."

He sat there, head held high. She was just looking at him. Surprised, perhaps, that she'd gotten her own way. Well, it would sink in in a minute. He took another cracker off the plastic plate and placed it in his mouth. Just as his jaw was about to come down, a realization struck him. She'd brought him this food and water when she'd come into the room. *Before* he'd made his offer. *Before* she'd gotten what she wanted.

Why?

He took the cracker out of his mouth, suspicions gathering fast.

"You brought me food," he said.

"Yes, I'd left it too long. Sorry about that."

"But you deliberately left it a long time. 'Perhaps we need to speed up your decision making,' " he repeated in a mocking tone.

"I know. But now there's a change of plan."

Rage built at a ferocious rate from the pit of his stomach, up through his chest, and exploded out of his mouth. "You fucking *what*? You're not getting any more money. How *dare you?*"

She held her hand up and he stopped talking, his breath ragged as he seethed.

"I don't want it anymore," said Emma.

What the . . . ? What was she playing at? "Well, pardon me for not following, Sweet Cheeks, but it was my understanding that was why you've

471

kept me shackled here like a goddamn animal for the last thirty-six hours."

"I know. And it was. But things have . . . changed."

His eyes narrowed. "Changed how?"

She looked awkward then, evasive. But in the depths of her shifty eyes there was something else he saw, something he would've noticed more clearly when she first came in the room if he hadn't been dying of thirst.

She looked happy.

What had happened since he'd last seen her? Nothing miraculous; it wasn't possible. She'd been upstairs all night. He suddenly realized something. She was fully dressed. It was the middle of the night and she was still fully dressed. She also looked wide awake, not like someone who'd been disturbed from sleep by his shouting. Which meant she hadn't gone to bed. *So what had she been doing up there?*

"What's going on?" he asked.

"What do you mean?"

"What are you doing upstairs?"

"Oh." She paused. "Writing."

His mouth dropped. "Writing what?" But he knew.

"My idea," she said. "The librarian."

He felt a physical blow to his stomach as the realization hit home. She was writing without him. She'd taken the idea she'd dangled like a carrot in front of his nose and kept it for herself, the selfish, *selfish* bitch.

With a deep sense of fear, Adrian knew in his gut that it was good. Whatever she was creating upstairs, it was something that would make people sit up and take notice. It would take her places.

She didn't need him anymore.

"It's only for another day, max," she said.

Still stunned, he didn't understand what she meant.

She pointed. "The handcuffs."

As she left the room he let out a terrible roar of rage and betrayal.

81

Monday, February 26

INT. BEACH HOUSE, DINING ROOM—NIGHT

ADRIAN stares at EMMA with an intense hatred and then something strange starts to happen. His features begin to warp, become grotesque. The black of his pupils begins to spread, like an inky pool filling his entire eyes; his skin coarsens and grays; the very humanness of him ebbs away and in its place is something indescribably evil. The evil thing smiles. Poised.

In an instant the room snaps as cold as the Arctic. EMMA trembles.

The only sound is their breath, across a terrifying stillness. The tension is unbearable as we wait for the inevitable attack.

CUT TO:

Emma flung the image from her head. She couldn't let him distract her now; he'd already taken so much from her. Don't let him put you off your stride, she told herself sternly, banishing the fear, and when she opened up her laptop and looked again at the screen, the light from the page seemed to draw her in and she felt herself falling into the world that was calling her. Distantly, she could still hear Adrian shouting, but she put her earphones in and he faded away, as her hands began to dance up and down the keyboard.

82

He'd kill her. He'd fucking kill her.

He was raging like a pierced bull, incensed by the powerlessness that oozed through him. The depravity of being tethered, the humiliation of having his offer thrown back in his face, trampled on. He was sickened by the knowledge that if he'd only changed his mind sooner, if he hadn't stubbornly held on, he'd be the one writing now, in the office upstairs, Emma feeding him ideas as he sat upon the throne of judgment at the desk, the ruler.

Actually, no, none of this was his fault. She had no right to do this to him. She'd played with his feelings, toyed with him. Hey, she probably had never intended to share the idea with him in the first place, it was all just some sick punishment she was getting off on. At this, he let out another bellow of rage, yanking his cuffed hand again and again, even while knowing it was futile. And it hurt, God, it hurt so much. After a few seconds, he stopped, exhausted, and saw blood in the weal on his wrist. His reward for his outburst.

Adrian shifted himself closer to the fireplace to ease the tension and pulled himself into a

477

crouching position so he could prop his elbow on his knee to try to stop the metal cuff from touching his wound.

He stared into the grate, feeling miserable and helpless. After a while, his quads could stand it no more and he began to move his stiff body back down to the floor. Of course his arm moved, too, exacerbating the pain in the wound on his wrist and he winced, but then something happened that took a moment or two to register.

When he'd moved his arm, a tiny smattering of brick dust had fallen from the iron ring, or more accurately, from the spot where the iron ring was fixed onto the fireplace.

He jiggled the handcuff a second time, yelping as he did so, but there it was again. Brick dust coming from the screw that held the iron ring to the fireplace wall. Which meant only one thing.

It was loose.

Excited, he sat up. Looked at it closely. With his uncuffed hand he pulled directly on the ring itself. A tiny bit more dust came away from the fixing. Holy moly . . . Adrian stared. He yanked again at the ring. More dust. So it wasn't exactly loose, but it wasn't as tight as it had once been, and if he could get something between the screw and the brick, if he could chisel away, he might just be able to free himself.

Quickly, he looked around. In his tantrum, he'd kicked out of reach the plate and cup Emma had brought earlier and he cursed himself for his stupidity. He could've smashed the plate on the marble hearth and taken a sharp shard and scraped away at the brick. *Damn!* He scoured his reachable surroundings again for something—anything—that might work, but there was nothing.

Except maybe . . . A small piece of wood was tucked at the back of the fireplace, missed during the last sweep out. He reached and grabbed it. It was about four inches long and thicker in the middle, flattening to a point at one end. With his free hand, he jabbed the pointed end into the miniscule space at the side of the screw. A puff of brick dust. His heart began to race. *This could work.* If he could keep chipping away, it would be just a matter of time before the screw got loose enough that he could pull it out of the wall.

The adrenaline from this revelation kicked in with the food and water Emma had brought him earlier and he could feel it feeding his nerve endings, his muscles, bringing him back to life.

Shit, why did I shout so much? He got himself into a hunched position and began to work away at the brick, jabbing and scraping and watching the tiny clouds of dust fall away.

83

The sun crept up over the sea; dawn breaking on this cold February morning. The sky filled with a faint pink hue and the few clouds became hot embers, ringed with fire.

In the bedroom, Emma was oblivious. She was still working, as she had done the whole night, earphones in, the sounds of the outside world blocked out. A great sense of exhausted fulfilment was building in her as she was nearly finished. The marathon had almost been run. And then the last few lines were written and she was done.

She stopped. Couldn't quite believe it was over. She popped out the earphones and the spell was broken; she was back in the real world. The sound of a blackbird could be faintly heard through the window and she looked up, surprised. It was morning! She got off the bed, stretching out her back, and looked outside at the sunrise. It felt like a personal welcome. A celebratory display to mark her achievement, for not only was she finished—*she was finished!*—but she'd done something that had been impossible for the last two years.

She'd broken away from the anger that had

caused her writer's block. She let this sink in a moment and the enormity of it made her feel almost tearful. No, it was not a time to cry, even if they were tears of happiness. She stood tall as a tingling lightness swept over her and she grinned at the sunrise, feeling strong and evangelical. She was a new person. She was reborn.

Emma laughed delightedly and stretched out her arms. She glanced at her watch; it was only just past six-thirty—and today she was going to call Liz. Take up her offer of the agent introduction. There was no reason to wait. But cashing in favors at dawn might not procure the right results and so she could afford some sleep. Just a couple of hours and then she'd ring. Emma made doubly sure she'd saved her script on her laptop and then got under the covers.

84

Monday, February 26

There was a hole now. a very definite hole against the side of the screw. When he moved the iron ring, it wobbled tauntingly, but it still wouldn't come out. The screw must be long, buried deep into the brick.

Adrian had worked at it all night, except for the moments he'd been so exhausted he'd had to lay his head down to rest and had found himself sleeping for snatches of time. After these moments he'd woken with a new urgency and had jabbed the piece of wood into the growing gap in the brick again and again. The pain in his cuffed arm was almost unbearable in this position, but the sweet taste of freedom kept him going.

He was worried, though, as the piece of wood had broken several times over the night, small chunks bruising and softening before breaking away. What had once been a reasonable makeshift chisel was now a blunted stump. He had to keep going, though. There really couldn't be much more of the brick to wear away.

85

Monday, February 26

The alarm on Emma's phone woke her at nine. she hadn't wanted to waste any more time sleeping. She quickly showered and dressed and then found the number for Liz in her phone's contact list. As it rang, she crossed her fingers. Please answer.

"Hello?"

"Hi, Liz. It's Emma Fox."

A surprised silence and then: "Emma. How have you been?"

"Fine. Better than fine, actually. I've been really busy. Writing."

"Congratulations."

"And I was wondering . . . you said to me once that you'd introduce me to your agent friend."

"Harriet Seward?"

Emma's heart started racing. She hadn't realized Liz was referring to Harriet Seward, who represented some of the greatest writers in television. She composed herself. "Yes."

"She's one of the best in the business."

"I know." Emma spoke confidently. There was a brief silence on the other end of the phone; then Emma heard the amused approval in Liz's voice.

"Okay. I'll drop her a line. Tell her to expect a script from you."

"Thank you."

"You'll have to send her a hard copy. They don't accept e-mails."

"No problem."

"Well, good luck."

"There's just one thing," said Emma.

"Yes?"

"Can you send the e-mail today?" She'd never been so demanding before. "Please," she added.

"It must be good," said Liz, with a challenging note to her voice, "if you're in such a hurry."

Was it? Emma thought so but was too close to it to really know.

"I'm sure Harriet will tell me," she said.

"Indeed she will," said Liz. "I'm intrigued. Will you send it to me as well?"

Emma's heart spiked with nerves. "Okay."

"E-mail is just fine."

"Thank you, Liz. How's the show, by the way?"

"Going well. Almost at the halfway point."

She wanted to know if Adrian had been missed. "And everyone okay? Carrie and Adrian?"

"Both fine," Liz said brusquely. "Adrian's writing."

Emma breathed a silent sigh of relief. They'd not noticed anything untoward.

After the call, Emma e-mailed her script to Liz and a local print shop she found online. She tucked her laptop back under the bed and went downstairs, quickly throwing some fruit and crackers on a plate and pouring a glass of water. When she took them in to Adrian, he was already sitting up. She'd been expecting him to rage at her, but he was strangely well behaved.

"Going out?" he asked, looking at her coat.

"Yes."

"Taking a break from the *writing?*"

She looked at him. "I've finished actually."

"What? The whole script?" His eyes were agog.

"That's right. Just going to get it printed."

She didn't wait to hear any more. Impatient to get her script sent, she put down the food and water, and left the house.

86

"It's gonna be after lunch."

Emma looked at the man who ran Print and Paper with dismay. "Seriously?"

"Monday morning. Always busy," he said. "You want to go ahead or not?"

There were no other printing shops in town and so she nodded. It didn't matter that the printing would take a few hours. It wasn't as if the postman would get the script to Harriet any sooner—it would still arrive tomorrow morning as long as she posted it by five p.m.

She left the print shop and headed down to the beach. It was too cold to sit on the sand and so she kept on walking until she reached St. Mary's Bay. The wind blew her along the promenade, occasionally taking her by surprise as it sped her up, pushing her into the path of the waves that came crashing up and over the wall, spraying her with cold gray water. She laughed but still moved back toward the cliff base, away from the sea. The tide was high and the waves were huge, great monstrous surges of water. Gulls screamed overhead, wheeling and diving. They almost seemed excited by the sea's display of power and arrogantly declared their lack of fear for it. Out in the distance the turbines turned, their great blades constant and reassuring in their movement, and Emma thought of her script as it emerged from the printer's rhythm.

Tomorrow it would land on the desk of Harriet Seward, one of the industry's most respected agents. Oh God, what if Liz didn't send the introductory e-mail as she'd promised? She could be called away on set and forget. Or what if Harriet took an age to read it? Or didn't read it at all? She might automatically pass the script to a reader, an inexperienced freelancer employed to wade through the dozens of submissions they received every week. The reader, likely a new graduate, might be resentful of the tiny fee they were paid, when all they wanted was a full-time position in a TV company. They would type up a brief report with the damning summary word all but killing her only real chance to change her future: *PASS*.

Emma shivered. Mustn't think like that. She had to hope.

87

Monday, February 26

The screw was tantalizingly loose now. When Adrian yanked on it he could feel that only the very tip was held tight. The makeshift wood chisel lay discarded on the hearth, long since rendered ineffectual, and he now just pulled on the screw, back and forth, back and forth.

He was aware Emma had been gone some time and deep down he knew why. Now she'd finished her script, she was sending it out to someone. An agent or a producer. If it were any good, then she would be noticed. Her idea would be nurtured. She would be handled with sensitivity and care, with an underlying excitement from whoever was championing her. She'd be supported with whatever she needed to allow her to create. Ties and relationships would form, allowing confidences to be shared. Questions might be asked, dressed up as an interest in another show's creation, but in reality questions about what it was like to work with him. How he came up with his ideas; what his early drafts were like; his temperament. These questions would be difficult for her to answer. She might be too professional to disclose the truth at first, but people's antennae were highly tuned. It wouldn't take much for conclusions to be drawn: an involuntary look of embarrassment from Emma, or perhaps a diplomatic laugh. And even if they were suspicions rather than certainty, the virus would have taken.

A wave of fear and nausea rampaged through Adrian. He would not be humiliated, his career picked over by the vultures in television. He would not have people feel sorry for him, consider him a has-been. He yanked again at the screw and a satisfying crumble of dust fell out.

No, he wasn't going to let Emma get away with it.

88

Monday, February 26

It was hard to concentrate. Carrie said a silent prayer of thanks that the day's filming was—so far, touch wood—going without incident and she was left to herself in the office. She still hadn't heard from Adrian and was wondering how much longer he was going to wait before he bothered to contact her. Once again, the image of Emma and him flashed through her mind and she felt uneasy.

Emma was hiding something; she was convinced of it. Things weren't adding up. Emma had written that letter about *Generation Rebel*, accusing Adrian of stealing her project—something that Carrie believed to be true. But all those photos and articles . . . it was as if Carrie was being *targeted*. What did Emma want with her? She'd held on to Rory a little longer this morning, not wanting to leave him, but then his key caregiver had cheerfully plucked him out of her arms and she had no reason to stay at the nursery any longer.

A knock on the office door made her jump. It was the first assistant director letting her know they were ahead of schedule and so were going to pick up another scene before the crew broke for lunch. She nodded her thanks; then he left.

Carrie tried to focus on her work. She had to review the post production schedule, but the highly complex chart full of dates and blocks of color representing everything from music to additional dialogue recording swam in front of her eyes. Irritated, she started again, looking to see where she could buy herself another couple of days to accommodate the delivery dates.

She was just beginning to see a solution when she was interrupted again by her phone ringing. Frustrated, she glanced across at the screen. It was a number from Italy—the same one she'd called Emma's mother on. She tensed and abandoned the chart. Answered the phone, bracing herself for something, though she didn't know what.

"Is that Carrie Kennedy?"

"Hello, Alice."

"Hello. I'm glad I've caught you."

There was a pause and Carrie waited. She'd heard the solemnity in Alice's voice. Then Alice began to speak and Carrie listened, blood draining from her face. She said very little. When the call was over, she quietly picked up her things and went to Liz's office.

"I need to go out for a bit."

Liz was distracted by something and it took her a moment to look up. "What? Yes, sure. Everything okay? You look a bit pale."

"Everything's fine. Well, hopefully. Rory has a temperature," lied Carrie.

"Poor thing. Don't worry, all's good here. You get away."

Liz was grinning, not because of what Carrie was telling her, but because of what was on her desk. Her eyes kept glancing down to whatever she was reading.

Something made Carrie stop and ask.

"What is it?" she said, her hand on the door.

"Huh? Oh, this?" Liz held up a sheaf of paper, looked a little awkward. "It's a script. Written by Emma."

Carrie's chest tightened. "Oh?"

"It's . . . well, it's okay," said Liz, deliberately offhand, but she was still grinning.

"You've heard from her? Recently?" asked Carrie.

"This morning."

"Where is she?"

"At home. She's been writing."

Except she hadn't, Carrie knew. She hadn't been home for days. She was about to go when a sudden thought hit her. "What's it about?"

"Sorry?"

"Emma's script. What's it about?"

"Oh! Well, it sounds kinda strange, but it's quite brilliant, actually. There's this librarian and she . . ."

The room began to spin as Liz continued

speaking and Carrie gripped the door handle tighter. *The same idea that Adrian had texted her about.* "I need to go," she mumbled, and left the office.

Please don't let her be there, she begged as she half stumbled down the stairs to her car.

89

Emma clutched her still-warm printed script to her chest as she selected a suitably sized envelope from the post office shop. She wrote a succinct cover note and then allowed herself one last look at the printed pages. Beautiful in their freshness, paper unthumbed and gleaming, the crisp contrast of black on white. Her words, all her own words. She slipped them into the envelope with the letter and went to the counter. It was weighed and branded with a next day delivery sticker. And then the post office clerk picked it up and put it in a sack behind him. Emma watched it disappear and quietly crossed her fingers. She'd done all she could.

Outside on the street she felt a sense of completion and suddenly the exhaustion of the last few days hit home. It was tempting to go and buy a coffee, and daydream about what the next few days might bring as the envelope she'd just posted was transported across the country, the words captured inside ready to dance in front of someone's eyes, hopefully captivating their reader as soon as they were released. She glanced at her watch. What would another hour hurt? She was starving and feeling faint from lack of sleep. Just a coffee and a sandwich; then she would go back and sort out the problem that was Adrian.

She sat in the warm café overlooking the beach, devouring a ham and cheese toastie, and wondered how to solve her dilemma. There was no need to keep Adrian tied up any longer, but it would be impossible for her to let him go free. Despite his outwardly calm demeanor earlier, he was probably furious with her, and she had no desire to release him and bear the brunt as he retaliated like an angry wasp that had been kept captive in a jar. On the other hand, she could hardly leave him there to die. Right now, she didn't know what would be best.

Emma finished and paid, then walked back to the beach house in the fading light. She was looking forward to leaving and realized it was the last time she'd ever come back to this house. She opened the electronic gates, then waited to make sure they closed again. She didn't see Geraldine walk past on the other side of the road. The mechanism stopped whirring as they clanged shut and Emma went up to the house.

She got the keys from her bag and put them into the lock. Entering the shadowy hallway made her suddenly want to be away as soon as possible. It wouldn't take long to stuff her few possessions in her bag, she thought; then she could be at the station and on a train within the hour. She still hadn't decided what to do about Adrian but would figure something out.

There was no sound from the dining room as she closed the front door behind her. She flicked the switch for the hall light, but it didn't come on. Puzzled, she tried it again, back and forth. Nothing. She stopped for a moment, listening intently for a rustle, a movement, but all was quiet and in her eagerness to get away she headed straight for the stairs. She flicked the stair light but again, the bulb didn't come on. *Odd.* She looked about her, still puzzled, and then started to climb the stairs.

She'd only got to the second step when she turned and looked back. Something was wrong. The dining room door, although still ajar, was slightly wider than she'd left it.

She knew this because she could see farther into the room. She could see part of the fireplace. And Adrian was most definitely not tied to it.

90

Emma suddenly felt very, very cold. She stood there, hand gripping the bannister, knuckles white. Her breath felt heavy and loud, and she tried to still it so she could listen to every creak of the house.

Nothing.

Slowly, silently, she placed one foot in front of the other and went back through the hallway. She cocked her head at the dining room door. Heard nothing. She tried to peer through the crack along the hinged side of the doorframe. A haze of fading light where the window was but nothing else.

Emma stalled. Should she find a weapon? The idea seemed so ludicrous she almost laughed out loud, but her mirth died in her throat. Truth was, she didn't know. A quick glance around the shadowy hall revealed a few coats and an umbrella stand, which would be too heavy to lift. She stood there for a few more seconds, then slowly pushed open the door. Waited. Nothing happened. She glanced into the room.

On the hearth, placed upright in the center of the marble block, was a long screw. The metal shank was dusty, but the hardness of it, the sharp tip, the horror-movie thread with its never-ending curves made her shudder. It was a message, a defiant retaliation. She whipped her head over her shoulder but saw nothing. The screw pulled her gaze back down and behind it, right in the fireplace, was a hole in the place where Adrian had been tethered, the bright redness of the fresh brick where he'd torn himself free like a raw wound.

Slowly, she stepped into the room. There was no one there. She looked for bulges in the curtains, concealed bodies behind furniture, anyplace Adrian could hide, but it was empty.

Get out! Get out! her inner survivalist screamed. Her skin prickled with fear and every instinct told her to run for the front door, but she couldn't. Her laptop was upstairs with her script saved on the hard drive. Briefly, she thought that maybe Adrian had left the house. But his car had still been in the driveway, she remembered.

She turned and left the room as quietly as she could. Crossed the hall, listening for sounds in the kitchen, the living room, but all was quiet. She looked up the stairs, trying to remember if any of them creaked. The house was dim in the dying light and she couldn't see into the shadows up on the landing.

Emma took the stairs as gently as she could, one by one, but still it was almost impossible to make no sound. The slowness of her journey was agonizing; all she wanted to do was get her laptop and run.

She reached the landing and glanced at all the doors to the rooms to see if any were different from how she'd left them, but she couldn't remember. Adrian could be behind any of them, she thought, and the hairs went up on the back of her neck. She silently made her way to the bedroom she'd been using and stopped at the door. There was no sound from inside so she slowly pushed it open. No one jumped out at her. She peered in, then entered the room.

Lying on the bed were the handcuffs and next to them, the key she'd kept in her bedside cabinet. *He's been in here.* She thought frantically, her brain feverish with activity. She started gathering her things, stuffing them into her bag, making sure she took the handcuffs and key too.

She felt under her bed for her laptop and at first her hands landed on empty carpet. Heart racing, she stopped still. *What if he's under the bed?*

Slowly, slowly, she bent down until she was on her knees. She peered under the bed. No Adrian.

No laptop either. Her heart plummeted. Where was it? Had she put it away somewhere else? No, she distinctly remembered putting it back there.

It felt colder down on the floor and Emma looked behind her toward the en suite bathroom. There was a draft coming from inside the room.

She tentatively made her way across and looked inside. The window was wide open, the wind blowing the top of the raised venetian blind against the glass. She stepped over and looked out. Down on the patio, smashed into a thousand tiny pieces, was her laptop. She gasped. Stunned by the revelation, she suddenly realized she'd been standing there in the bathroom too long. She pulled herself together, grabbed her toothbrush and gel, and peering back out onto the darkening landing, saw it was empty. Softly, she made her way to the top of the stairs. Below her, in the shadowy hall, she could see the front door. Only a few steps, then she was free. But first she needed to go back into the dining room, get rid of the bucket, the screw. She cursed herself for not doing so earlier.

Carefully, she placed her foot on the top stair, and that was when she heard the noise. A muffled sound, barely audible, coming from below.

Adrian was somewhere downstairs.

91

Emma considered making a run for it. she'd race down the stairs, fling open the front door, and bolt across the driveway. But the electronic gate would take too long to open and the alternative, to climb over . . . well, Adrian would be on her in seconds. She gazed longingly at the short distance between her and freedom but knew it was impossible to cross.

Her mind quickly began to run through the alternative options, but there were no other stairs and jumping from a second-floor window would likely end in a broken ankle or worse. She was trapped.

A faint light outside suddenly caught her eye, startling her; the lighthouse had started its nocturnal vigilance. She stood rooted to the floor as it went through its five-second cycle. One second of light and then darkness. Then, to her horror, in the fleeting glow cast into the house, she saw the kitchen door open the tiniest amount.

The house suddenly went dark again as the lighthouse came to its rest period. She could no longer see the door and imagined it opening wider, Adrian coming out and catching her on the stairs. She backed away, terrified. *Hide, I have to hide.* She quickly dived into the closest room to her and found herself in Adrian's office. There she waited, heart pounding. The noise in her ears was deafening and she strained to listen—had he heard her? She started to look for somewhere to hide.

92

Carrie pulled into the North Foreland Estate, with Rory asleep in the back of the car. It had been a long drive, made longer by the fact she'd had to stop and feed him. As she drove along the estate's genteel roads, she saw Geraldine up ahead waving her down. She slowed the car, and Geraldine, who was out walking her dog, looked delightedly into the back. Carrie lowered the window.

"Oh, but he's a *darling!*" exclaimed Geraldine in a loud whisper. "*Look* at him! Is he good? Keeping you up at night? Have you got him into a routine? Oh, look at those tiny hands!"

Carrie smiled. "He's not too bad. Allows me a few hours every now and then."

"I'm so glad you're here," said Geraldine. "I've been dying to clap my eyes on this little man. And you, of course. Are you staying a few days? Perhaps I could come over and see you both?"

"Um . . . sure," said Carrie. She wasn't certain whether she would drive back that night but didn't want to get into a discussion on it with Geraldine.

"I've hardly seen Adrian the whole time he's

507

been here. Holed up, writing by all accounts."

Carrie nodded vaguely. She wanted to get away, go to the house. "I really ought to get on . . ." she started, apologetically.

"Of course. Need to get this little one in the warm, eh?"

Carrie smiled. "That's right."

She was just about to raise the window when Geraldine put her hand on the glass.

"It's funny, I thought I saw you earlier," said Geraldine. "Same blond bob. But it must have been that assistant person. Funny how alike you two look."

A piercing, ringing sound was screeching in Carrie's ears. Her worst fears were realized; Emma was here. She was vaguely aware of Geraldine still jabbering on, but her brain had tuned it out. She needed to go now.

"I must get on," she interrupted. "Before Rory wakes."

"Oh, does he need feeding?" asked Geraldine, looking at the sleeping Rory in puzzlement.

"That's right," said Carrie, taking her cue. She said a very rapid goodbye and drove off. As she turned into her street, she knew she wouldn't park in the driveway. She wouldn't give Adrian the benefit of any warning. She'd leave the car in the street and walk up to the house from there.

93

Emma frantically glanced around the room. the only place to hide was behind the sofa and she scrabbled around the back of it as quickly as she could. There she crouched, vulnerable, kicking herself for not picking something up—even the glass paperweight from Adrian's desk. There was no time to get it now as she could hear him climbing the stairs. Creeping footsteps, those of a predator stalking its prey. Then at the top of the landing he stopped. She curled herself up as small as possible, tried to still her breathing. Adrian walked across the landing and paused outside the office door.

Emma tensed, *please no, please no,* but then miraculously she heard him move on, toward what she estimated to be the bedroom she'd been sleeping in. Blood was pumping in her ears, thunderous, and she knew it was only a matter of minutes before he came back. Maybe not to the office first, but he'd methodically work his way through each room, one by one, until he found her.

She had to get out. Petrified, she started to back away from behind the sofa until she was visible again. She stood in the corner of the dark room and listened, trying to work out where Adrian was, but she couldn't hear a thing other than her heart thudding. She forced herself to step toward the door, slowly, silently, one foot, then the next. Suddenly she froze. She'd heard a sound, but it had come from downstairs, in the hallway. Confused, she stood stock-still, straining her ears. *What is going on?*

94

Carrie closed the front door softly behind her, careful not to wake Rory, who was still sleeping in his car seat over her arm. She looked around at the dark house, puzzled as to why no lights were on. She turned on the hall light, but it didn't work. She frowned—had there been a power cut? Geraldine hadn't mentioned anything.

She went into the living room, but the lights weren't working there either. There were tea lights in the dining room she knew, in the sideboard. She placed the sleeping Rory in his car seat on the living room rug and with a last look to make sure all the movement hadn't woken him, left the room.

95

Emma could hear another sound, this one much closer. Adrian was creeping back along the landing, heading toward the office. She could sense he was a yard, maybe two from the door. Sweat broke out under her armpits and she was rigid with fear. Then his footsteps continued and she heard him begin to descend the stairs. She realized she'd stopped breathing and gulped silent lungfuls of air. He must have heard the sound, too, and she realized he probably thought she had gone downstairs.

Very, very quietly she crept to the door and opened it the tiniest fraction, then peered out. Through the gloom she thought she saw him enter the dining room. Two near misses were enough. She knew it was dangerous, but she had to get out of there. Her bag still clutched to her side, she started to creep down the stairs, praying he wouldn't come out and ambush her.

One more step. And another. Soon she was halfway down. The lighthouse cast its momentary glow and she cowered against the wall. But on she went; then miraculously she was at the bottom. She could see the dining room door was open and knew as she crossed the hall to get to the front door she'd be in the line of vision of anyone who was inside—but only if they were looking her way. It was risky, but she had to chance it.

Her legs were shaking. *Just go, just go,* and she began to walk toward the front door when suddenly a piercing scream came from the dining room. A female scream. Startled, she was thrown off course. Everything then began to run at great speed as if it were on fast forward. A baby began to cry. She looked around in confusion. *Rory?* But if he were here then . . . She automatically glanced toward the dining room and saw two figures—a larger one with his back to her who seemed to be wrapping something around the neck of someone else. *Carrie.* Instinctively, Emma ran into the room and launched herself at Adrian, climbing onto his back like an animal. With a roar he reared up and the last thing she saw was the fury in his eyes turn to confusion before she felt herself fall backward and everything went black.

96

Carrie held her throat, still choking, trying to breathe. She needed to get to Rory, to save him. She'd fight to the death before he was hurt, and she turned to face her attacker—

Adrian.

Stunned, Carrie couldn't take her eyes off him. She didn't understand. She clasped her throat again in fear and utter bewilderment.

"I'm . . . it wasn't supposed . . ." stuttered Adrian. "I thought you were Emma. I wasn't trying to hurt you—it was Emma."

Carrie backed away, frightened. She glanced at the floor where Emma lay, prostrate on the ground.

"What?" she whispered, hoarsely.

Adrian began to step toward her, arms outstretched.

"Get away from me," she snapped.

"No, you don't understand."

She looked at this man who was once her husband and barely recognized him. Unkempt, dangerous. The skin on her throat burned. *He tried to kill me.* She could hear Rory screaming for her now and every sinew in her body strained to get to him.

Adrian took another step toward her and in fear she shoved him away with all the force she could muster.

He stumbled backward, crashing into the side of a chair. Losing his balance, he continued to fall, arms windmilling, trying to regain his footing, but his body had gone past the tipping point and he plunged toward the fireplace, his bewildered eyes on hers, as the back of his head landed on the marble hearth.

His eyes, fixed forever wide in shock, suddenly and instantaneously became lifeless. A small pool of liquid that looked black in the shadows began to trickle from under his head and ran ominously along the hearth.

PART FOUR

Rory

97

Emma stared at the pale olive hospital walls, watching the pattern of light as the sun shone through the venetian blinds. She still had no idea how she'd gotten out of that house—how she was still alive. She had a flash memory of Adrian throwing her, a nightmarish vision that came to her again and again when she slept, waking her with a start, heart racing, head pounding. It did nothing to help mend her severe concussion, and she'd lain in bed in the dark for hours, aching from a grinding headache, which never seemed to diminish, despite the copious amounts of painkillers she'd been administered.

She'd asked the nurses, but they'd been unable, or unwilling, to say anything, brushing her off with claims of ignorance as they bustled from her to the next person. Whatever had happened, she didn't want to talk to the police. She didn't want to talk to anyone. However, the police were here. One of the nurses had asked if they could come in, and she knew she'd have to speak to them sooner or later and so reluctantly agreed.

She saw them approach, two detectives in plain clothes, a woman and a younger man. They introduced themselves as the woman sat down beside her. She was Detective Sergeant French. There was only one chair so Detective Constable Baker stood awkwardly as the nurse pulled a curtain around them all, enclosing them in a fabric bubble.

"Thank you for seeing us," said DS French. The smile she gave was designed to put Emma at ease, but it was so over-practiced, it didn't reach the detective's eyes. Emma stiffened. She had been told they only wanted a statement but from the look of DS French, she was planning on being here a while.

"We'd like to talk to you about the events of last night," continued the detective.

Emma looked down at the bed sheet, inspected her hands.

"We believe that a man, Adrian Hill, attacked you and that you fell and hit your head."

Well, that's true. "Yes," she said.

"Can you tell us why?"

No. It's too long, too complicated, too sad. She turned her head toward the window. Sensed DS French glance at DC Baker, exchange a look.

"Were you trying to stop him from hurting his wife?"

She didn't answer.

"Had he mistakenly identified her as you? Was he in fact trying to hurt you?"

Please go away.

"You know he's dead?"

Emma froze. Her heart started to pound. She looked back at them, eyes wide.

"How?"

"He had a fall, in the dining room of his house, and a loose screw that had been left on the ground unfortunately entered his skull. I'm very sorry."

"It was one of those things no one could predict," said DC Baker, on seeing Emma's eyes widen in horror. "Just the wrong combination of timing and luck."

Goose bumps erupted on Emma's skin. She turned her face away. *One of those freak, unlucky accidents,* she thought, twisting the line Adrian had once used to taunt her.

"What about Carrie?" she asked. "And Rory? Are they okay?"

"Both fine," said DS French, but she didn't elaborate. "So perhaps you'd like to tell us your version of events?"

She seemed impatient to get on, to hear what Emma had to say. She was hiding something, Emma thought. Not telling her the full picture. *And Adrian is dead.*

"There are a few unexplained things we'd like to clear up. We think you might be able to help us."

She tensed.

"You went to the house daily, is that right? To help Adrian with his work?"

Geraldine would confirm this, thought Emma. "Yes."

"And where would you work with him?"

"Mostly in the office. Sometimes the kitchen."

"What about the dining room?"

"Not really."

DS French nodded. "So you didn't ever spend any time with Adrian in the dining room?"

"Well, I might have gone in there at one point, he might have been there, too, but it wasn't where we worked."

"Okay." DS French paused. "Adrian had weals on his right wrist, consistent with being tied up for a significant period of time. Can you tell us anything about this?"

Frightened, Emma shook her head.

DS French watched her. Then continued. "There was an iron ring on the hearth in the dining room, and we believe that the screw that went into the back of Adrian's head was at one point used to hold the iron ring in a brick in the fireplace. There is a hole there, and brick dust, as if the ring had recently been removed."

Her mouth was dry and she had to force herself to stay calm. "I don't know anything about that."

"A bucket was found in the room, partly filled with urine. We believe this to be Adrian's urine. It's as if he was tied to the fireplace for so long, a bucket was deliberately left there for him to relieve himself."

Emma kept her expression blank.

The look on DS French's face was indecipherable. Emma held her gaze for as long as she could, knowing all she had to do was not crack. If she denied everything, then she had a chance. The only person who might know what had happened was Carrie. Had Adrian told her before he'd fallen and died? She thought not by the way these detectives were questioning her. If Carrie didn't know, no one did. No one would know what had happened.

Emma was suddenly exhausted, frightened. Tears inexplicably began to run down her face. The stress of the last few days crashed over her like a tsunami and she refused to say anything more, asked them to leave. When she kicked up a fuss and called the nurses, they did.

98

Miraculously, Emma had managed to sleep. She woke groggily to the sounds of the hospital at visiting time and on checking her watch, was amazed to see she'd been out for an hour. She pulled herself upright and blinked at the room. A scattering of visitors with flowers and foil balloons. People dressed in coats bringing the outside world in.

Emma wanted no part of the outside world. She had no one she wanted to see, no place to go back to. Her mother had called, alerted by the hospital that she'd been admitted, but Emma had played her injuries down. She'd insisted Alice and Brian shouldn't rush over and had managed to persuade them to wait until the following week before visiting from Italy.

She leaned over to the cabinet at the side of her bed to pour some water from the jug. As she sat back, she nearly spilled the entire glass over herself.

Carrie was standing there, beside her bed. Emma watched as she sat in the chair next to her.

"Hello, Emma."

Emma found her hands were shaking and she

525

replaced the glass, then tucked them under the sheet. "Hello."

"How are you? The nurses said you'd hit your head but should be discharged soon." It was warm in the room and Carrie took off her coat and draped it on the back of the chair. "I wanted to have a chat with you. You see, there are a few things that have happened that I can't quite make sense of. The first thing I'd like to know is what you were doing at our beach house. I didn't get a chance to ask Adrian and . . ."

Emma could hear her voice cracking and saw the gargantuan effort she took to get herself back on track. Carrie looked her square in the face. "Were you two having an affair?"

Emma's mouth opened in horror. "No! God, no, never. I mean, there was . . . but that was one time. A mistake. A terrible, awful mistake. No . . . please, we . . . we didn't even like each other."

She could see by Carrie's face that she believed her.

"So why were you at the beach house?" asked Carrie.

Emma thought of Geraldine. "I was . . ."

What? Working for him? She'd never believe that. It was nonsense and an insult to Carrie to say such a thing.

"I wanted Adrian to pay for everything he'd taken from me. I told him I'd meet him there to talk about a program idea, one that I'd share with him if he paid me some money." She saw the look of distaste on Carrie's face. "Oh, come on, he got me *fired*. He stole my first idea and passed it off as his own," she snapped, and a flicker of shame crossed Carrie's face.

"Okay," Carrie relented, her voice going tight. "He did take your idea, but he didn't exactly get you fired. That was down to you—to both of you for sleeping together."

Emma swallowed hard. "You don't understand. . . ."

"What is it I don't understand, Emma?"

It was suddenly too much to keep in. "He begged me to keep it quiet, but then told you about it himself. And worse . . . he pretended to me that you'd found out through someone else."

Carrie was frowning. "Who?"

"It doesn't matter."

"It does. Who did he say had told me?"

Emma turned away.

"Was it Elaine?" Carrie suddenly asked, trepidation in her voice.

Emma's throat grew thick with the dammed-up tears and the petrifying truth.

"Is that why you were with Elaine at the lake? Were you confronting her?"

Emma turned back, eyes blazing.

"Oh, my God . . ." said Carrie, her hand at her mouth.

"You've got it wrong," said Emma, defiantly.

527

"It was a chance meeting. We'd bumped into each other there before. But when I saw her, I did ask her about it. I was angry. I . . . I shouted at her." It was as good as a confession but somehow she didn't care anymore. "Adrian set me up. He deliberately let me think Elaine had told you. I never wanted to hurt you, never." She began to cry silent tears while Carrie stayed silent, just watching her. Ashamed, Emma blew her nose.

"Are you going to tell the police?" she asked.

"I've been arrested," said Carrie. "On suspicion of murder."

"What?"

"Adrian was trying to kill me, thinking it was you. You've changed your hair," Carrie said accusingly, looking at her bob. "I pushed him away. The police took me to the station last night and interviewed me under caution. They took Rory away from me for a few hours. Placed him with a foster family. Strangers. If I go to prison, that's where he will end up."

The terror and anger in Carrie's voice made Emma shake. "But . . . but it was self-defense," she stammered. "He was trying to kill you."

"He's *dead,*" snapped Carrie. "You started all this. With your lies."

"No, I—"

Carrie cut across her. "I know who you are."

The words were a guilty hook in her heart, wrenching it out. Emma looked at Carrie in badly

528

disguised alarm. Her gasping heart started to beat faster. *Thump, thump.*

"I spoke to your mother. Alice."

Thump, thump, thump.

"She called me to tell me something. You see, I spoke to her a few days ago and as part of that conversation, naturally I told her my name."

Thump, thump, thump, thumpthumpthumpthump.

"You're the baby I had when I was seventeen, the one I gave up."

Emma closed her eyes, unable to take in the blinding lights, the screaming truth. And yet, this was what she'd wanted, wasn't it? She took a few deep breaths and then slowly reopened her eyes. Carrie still sat at the side of her bed, watching her.

"Why didn't you say anything?"

Emma knew there was a logical answer to this but couldn't form the words.

"Why did you write to Adrian all those years ago? You knew we were married. You knew who I was the whole time."

"Yes," started Emma, tentatively. "Yes, I did. I originally wanted to write to you, to ask for *your* advice. I admired you so much. It seemed so . . . serendipitous when I found your name in my parents' documents and on a curious whim decided to look you up. It only took a couple of searches . . . I couldn't believe it. It was as if you'd been listening all along. As if you'd been there the whole time. Waiting. You worked in television, you had interests like my interests. But in the end I didn't write to you, because I was afraid. I couldn't take it if you didn't reply. If you . . . rejected me. And so it was safer if I wrote to Adrian. It wouldn't hurt so much if he didn't write back."

Heart in mouth, Emma forced herself to meet Carrie's eyes.

FADE IN:

INT. HOSPITAL ROOM—DAY

EMMA is terrified. She feels like a little girl again, all her hopes pinned on the one person. On her mother.

CARRIE begins to stand and raises her arms. Hope blooms in Emma's heart. She moves toward Carrie, tentatively raises her own arms for an embrace. But then Emma realizes something is wrong. Warmth does not emanate from Carrie's eyes. Carrie's arms go to encase themselves in her coat sleeves.

CUT TO:

Emma watched as Carrie walked out of the ward.

99

Emma cast her eyes around the ward, but no one was paying her any attention. She surreptitiously opened her bag and rummaged inside. All her stuff was still there from her frantic packing the night at the beach house. Buried at the bottom, hidden underneath her clothes, were the handcuffs. Putting the bag on her shoulder, she quietly left the ward. Her wrist bracelet still identified her as a patient but if anyone asked, she was going for some fresh air. She followed the overhead signs out of the building until she was in the cold, bright February morning. It felt good to breathe in the cool air, and she took a few breaths before beginning to circumnavigate the building. It wasn't long before she found a walled area that contained waste bins and checking no one was around, she took the handcuffs from her bag, wrapped them in a plastic bag she'd gotten from the hospital shop, and dropped them in the industrial bin. Then she quickly walked away.

She found a bench overlooking a tiny patio garden and getting out her phone, started to type an e-mail.

Dear Carrie,

I wanted to let you know that I'm going to speak to the police, tell them everything. It's important that you know what it is I am going to say, so that you can prepare yourself.

As she went on to detail her confession, she decided she'd call the police that afternoon. It was best this was wrapped up as soon as possible.

100

Detective Sergeant French had bought her a weak tea from the hospital café and they were sitting in a quiet corner, DC Baker flanking Emma on her other side. She was struck again by their names. French and Baker? What would happen if they got together? Would they have a croissant? This stupid joke made her want to guffaw with laughter—she must be more nervous than she thought. Stop it. DS French was looking at her expectantly.

"I was upset," said Emma. "My head was pounding and the news of Adrian . . . it was hard."

"That's understandable," said DS French. "Are you sure you're happy to make a statement now?"

Emma nodded. "Fine. I had been working there, helping Adrian to develop his new series. As I've done in the past. I stayed in a hotel in Margate and would come over to the house every day and we'd go through his ideas." She looked at the detectives, who were both listening intently. "On that night, a couple of days ago, Carrie had come to the house. Adrian and Carrie are—were—estranged." She lowered her eyes,

533

looked penitent. "He and I . . . we'd had an affair and it had come between them. You see, it wasn't *me* he thought he was attacking, it was actually Carrie. He *wanted* to hurt Carrie."

She looked at them again; saw the surprise in their eyes.

"How can you be so certain?" asked DS French.

"Because just before she came in, he was upstairs with me. We were in the office, working together."

"In the dark?" asked DC Baker.

"The lights had just tripped. Adrian was going down to the fuse box when he heard Carrie come in."

She took a deep breath. "It's because we are mother and daughter."

The younger detective's mouth dropped ever so slightly. Emma continued. "Carrie put me up for adoption at birth. Adrian had only just found out, and he was furious that she'd kept it a secret from him. It was what made me feel a relationship with him was difficult, perhaps impossible. He hated that it stopped us from being together."

It was her story and she was sticking to it. She'd deny knowing anything about him being tied up for the rest of her life. No one could prove any different. The police would be unsatisfied but as the binding had no bearing on his actual death, she was pretty sure they'd eventually drop it.

She felt a tear well up and let it roll down her cheek. Let them think she was crying over him. It was worth it if it meant Rory got to stay with his mother.

101

Carrie watched Rory as he lay on the floor, a rattle in his chubby hand which he alternated between chewing and haphazardly waving above his head. He was, of course, oblivious to his father's death and the events of the previous week. His innocent determination that they get on with the day to day helped Carrie not to dwell.

When he slept and she was alone, she'd often be overcome by a black, paralyzing fear that these moments with her baby would be taken away from her if she were sent to prison. She'd asked her solicitor what would happen if she were found guilty and knew she could apply for a place for Rory to be with her if she were sentenced. This was little comfort, however, as it would only last until he was eighteen months old. After that he would be sent to a foster family.

Since Emma had made her statement to the police, insisting that she and Adrian had been having an affair, things had shifted. All Carrie had needed to do was admit she'd got her own statement wrong. She told the police that Adrian must have lied to her when he'd said he was trying to hurt Emma, not his wife. She admitted

537

that she'd let herself believe him because deep down, a part of her still loved him.

That part, the bit about still loving him, or loving what they'd once had, that part was true. The rest was lies, but this way she had a chance of staying out of prison; her solicitor had said as much. The actions, which had led to Adrian's death, had come firmly out of self-defense and the charges had already been reduced from murder to manslaughter. Her solicitor was optimistic that the evidence provided wouldn't be enough for the Crown Prosecution Service to warrant taking the case to court, and they'd know for sure in a few months. By the summer, her solicitor had said.

The first tendrils leading to that season were already beginning to show out in the garden. The daffodils were out in force, and red and orange tulips were just showing their heads, their rich colors catching the sunlight.

It was warm in the kitchen with the sun streaming through the glass. On a whim, Carrie got up and opened the patio doors and the soft, fresh spring air embraced her. Sensing the change, Rory dropped his rattle and held out his arms to be picked up.

Carrie carried him into their small garden and walked around, showing him the buds on the trees and the new tulips. His eyes roved over everything, fascinated, and Carrie couldn't help smiling at his wonder and occasional puzzlement.

Yet more firsts, each week presented them, and she delighted in every single one. This morning he'd put his fat, little arms around her neck, his first hug and she'd felt such an overwhelming sense of love, she'd wanted to hold him forever. She'd wanted to tell someone of this tiny, yet momentous milestone, but there was no one to call, no one who'd recognize just how special it was.

A ladybird suddenly landed on Rory's hand. His eyes opened wide as he stared at the bright red insect and then raising his arm, he promptly tried to put it in his mouth.

Carrie laughed. "No, no," she said, gently, holding his hand. *Maybe Mum isn't missing everything after all,* she suddenly thought, and almost immediately shook her head, amused by her fanciful thoughts.

They watched the ladybird together as it crawled from Rory's hand onto hers.

Could it be?

The ladybird journeyed across her hand, seemingly unhurried and unafraid. Then stopped, settled and content.

There they stayed: the three of them, peaceful, caught in the sunshine.

102

Eyes blinking, head spinning, Emma stepped out of the office door into the Soho sunshine. She was unable to fully take in what had just happened.

The real world hurtled around her: black cabs speeding down the narrow streets, cycle couriers dodging the crossing pedestrians, and she looked at it all, almost in surprise, as if she'd forgotten such things existed. For the last hour she felt as if she'd been in a parallel universe.

It had all started with the phone call. She'd been discharged from the hospital the week before and with nowhere else to go had thrown herself at the mercy of her old university friend, Amy, who had a one-bedroom flat in St. Albans. There, she spent her days walking around Clarence Park while Amy went to work in her marketing job, already a deputy manager having joined her firm as a graduate trainee. In the evenings they drank wine and cooked dinners together, and Emma had told her a little of what had happened. Amy would ask what she was going to do next and all Emma could say was that she wanted to continue writing. She knew she had to find somewhere to live, another flatshare, and she had to retrieve her possessions from Lucy. But she was somehow unable to get the focus and the energy together. Her life felt as if it were on hold.

Emma was anxious not to overstay her welcome on Amy's sofa and so when her phone had rung three days into her stay, a call from Harriet Seward's assistant asking if she would like to come into the office to discuss her script submission, her heart had leapt with nervous optimism.

The meeting had had a surreal quality to it. Harriet loved her script and wanted to sign her. That, in itself, was an extraordinary thing, but Harriet had gone on to talk about several well-known producers who would want to meet her and felt there was a good chance her script would sell quickly. Emma's euphoria was held in check by a sense of impending loss. She looked at her watch. It was almost time to see Carrie. That was the other unexpected contact she'd had. A text asking if they could meet up.

Emma was anticipating bad news. Carrie was going to say how she wanted nothing to do with her after everything that had happened. She knew this with a sense of fatalistic gloom. It seemed more brutal that Carrie had arranged to do this in person. It would have been much less painful if she'd just sent her a message, instead of expressing her disillusionment to her face.

The coffee shop where they'd arranged to meet was only a couple of streets away and she made her way there, stopping outside when she saw Carrie sitting in the window, Rory in a buggy beside her. Carrie looked up and they held each other's gaze for a moment before Emma took a deep breath and went inside.

She took a seat opposite Carrie and ordered a drink from the barista. Then he left and it was just them. Emma was stiff with nerves and couldn't think of anything to say.

"How is your head?" asked Carrie.

"Better, thanks."

Carrie nodded. "Good."

There was an awkward pause.

"And you?" asked Emma.

Carrie looked confused.

"Are you well?"

"Yes, fine."

The barista brought over her latte, signaling the end of their agonizing small talk, and Emma knew she had to ask. She needed to know, to be put out of her misery. Her hands shook, so she wrapped them around her cup, looked at the milky coffee with the white frothy heart that the barista had fashioned on the surface.

"You didn't need to see me, you know. To tell me to stay away. You could have just e-mailed."

She saw Carrie start. "Is that what you thought?" Carrie shook her head. "That's not why I asked you here."

Emma's hands trembled even more then and

unable to speak, she took a mouthful of coffee. It scalded her tongue and she winced.

"How was your meeting?" asked Carrie.

Emma was startled and Carrie gave a small smile. "Liz told me," she said.

"Oh. Right. It went well, actually. Really well. Harriet wants to sign me."

It was the first time she'd said it out loud, shared the news with anyone, and it felt good.

"She seems to think my script will sell."

"It will," said Carrie.

Emma looked up in surprise.

"You didn't hear it from me, but Liz has already put an offer in. But don't rush. There'll be others."

A small tingle danced over Emma's skin. The sensation of possibility.

"I hear it's quite something," said Carrie.

Emma blushed.

Rory, who'd been sucking on a fabric book, suddenly got bored and started to grumble. Carrie leaned over and got him out of the buggy, put him on her lap.

"The reason I asked to meet you is that I wanted to thank you," said Carrie, her voice wavering, "for what you did. My solicitor thinks it will make all the difference."

The news took her breath away. Emma gazed at Carrie, her eyes lit up, her heart flooding with an emotion she didn't really know how to deal with.

"So you'll get to stay with Rory?" she asked.

"It looks like it."

Emma saw something flicker across Carrie's face as she looked down at her baby, a tightness full of pain and love. A tear escaped and rolled down Carrie's cheek. She brushed it away quickly, but not before Emma felt her own eyes fill up. Self-conscious, they both looked at Rory as he happily banged the palms of his hands on the table.

Suddenly realizing he was the center of attention, he beamed and they both laughed, catching each other's eye.

Epilogue

Sunday, May 10
Two years later

Carrie glanced across at Emma, who was sitting in the seat beside her, staring up at the screens showing clips of the shows nominated for Best Drama Series. There was something about the way Emma held her chin, a certain tilt that she recognized: it was the same as Rory's. She got that strange feeling again, a mixture of protectiveness and great vulnerability. She sometimes imagined she saw glimpses of what Emma would have been like when she was small, but she'd never know for sure. There had been various points in her life, mostly when she'd least been expecting it, when she'd been ambushed by thoughts of the baby she'd given up. Curious wonderings underwritten by an unfamiliar pain that she reasoned away with a stern talking to about how her life could never have been as it was if she'd taken the "wrong" road by keeping her, when she was no more than a child herself. Carrie looked again at Emma, who was trying to keep an impassive expression on her face, and smiled. These moments, her children, you had to appreciate each and every one.

547

Rory had been told his sister might get a prize tonight, and his eyes had lit up at the idea there could be a "trophy" coming home. He'd been less receptive to the idea he had to go to bed, even though the prize-giving was going to be on television. Carrie had half-worried he might act up for the friend who was babysitting, but she'd had a text saying he was snoring away happily, clutching his cuddly dog. He'd only had it a few weeks. Emma had taken him to a toy shop in the Lanes in Brighton, when they'd had enough of paddling in the sea. Much debate had been had on the dog's name, with both Carrie and Emma coming up with various meaningful suggestions, but Rory had rejected every bit of his mother's and sister's creativity and insisted on "Doggie." Which, actually, was perfect.

Emma had won her trophy. Her show about the Mafioso librarian had been awarded the BAFTA for Best Screenplay, beating off some hefty competition. When Carrie had watched her go up onstage, she'd been surprised at how emotional she'd felt. She knew this was partly because the last time she'd been here, watching a writer claim his award, it had been Adrian, and the memory stirred deep inside, a time now long gone.

Watching Emma, her *daughter,* she thought again, still finding this word pause on her tongue in its extraordinariness, go up and receive a BAFTA was one of the proudest moments of her life. Her heart had swelled and she'd felt so incredibly happy for her. She'd gazed at the young woman onstage, knowing she was a part of her, yet being in awe of what she had independently become.

Now, with Emma back in her seat, Liz on her one side and she, Carrie, on the other, they were waiting to hear if the luck would continue, if the show that they had all worked on together as producers and writer would win.

Emma watched the clips on the large screen, knowing the cameras would be cutting to her, Liz, and Carrie at some point during the sequence. Try as she might, she couldn't get used to the exposure and in doing her best not to look self-conscious, was aware that was probably exactly how she was appearing. Her first thought was what Brian and Alice would think, before reminding herself it didn't matter. She inwardly sighed; old habits die hard.

She knew her adoptive parents were watching the show from their hotel in central London. They'd flown over from Italy especially and would take her out for a celebratory meal later in the week. They were also coming to see her first flat. She'd finally been able to afford a smart two-bedroom and after discussion with Carrie, had decided on Blackheath. That way she could see more of Rory, the little brother she adored.

Alice would take a full tour, admire (or critique) her décor and comment on the choice of artefacts and pictures. Everything would be on display . . . well, not quite everything.

When Carrie had cleared out Adrian's office, she had asked Emma if she wanted any of the memorabilia from *Generation Rebel*, seeing as it had been her idea in the first place. Anything personal to Adrian, Emma had rejected. The signed cast photo, the BAFTA. Then she'd taken the noose out of the cardboard box and holding it up, Carrie had stopped still, no doubt remembering how Adrian used to have it hanging on his office wall, how it had swung every time anyone had gone in the door. It was strange to think now that the thing Adrian had loved so much had also symbolized his undoing.

Emma wasn't sure why she'd wanted to keep it, but it had seemed fitting somehow, as a mark of order restored, or perhaps a warning.

The screens cut back to the BAFTA logo and the actor presenting the award stepped up to the mike, an envelope held up to the audience.

A hush fell over the Royal Albert Hall as he opened the flap and pulled out the card.

Nerves gripped Emma and she tensed in her seat. Suddenly, a soft hand held her fingers. She squeezed Carrie back and they waited to see what life would bring them next.

Center Point Large Print
600 Brooks Road / PO Box 1
Thorndike, ME 04986-0001 USA

(207) 568-3717

US & Canada:
1 800 929-9108
www.centerpointlargeprint.com